THE GOLD COLLECTION

SUSAN

Stephens

TAMING THE ARGENTINIAN

D1440371

THE GOLD COLLECTION

June 2016

July 2016

August 2016

September 2016

THE GOLD COLLECTION

SUSAN
Stephens

TAMING THE ARGENTINIAN

MILLS & BOON

First Published in Great Britain 2016
By Mills & Boon, an imprint of HarperCollins*Publishers*
1 London Bridge Street, London, SE1 9GF

TAMING THE ARGENTINIAN © 2016 Harlequin Books S.A.

A Taste of the Untamed © 2012 Susan Stephens
The Untamed Argentinian © 2011 Susan Stephens
Taming the Last Acosta © 2013 Susan Stephens

ISBN: 978-0-263-92213-4

24-0716

Our policy is to use papers that are natural, renewable and recyclable products and made from wood grown in sustainable forests.
The logging and manufacturing processes conform to the legal environmental regulations of the country of origin.

Printed and bound in Spain
by CPI, Barcelona

A TASTE OF
THE UNTAMED

For Penny

Susan Stephens was a professional singer before meeting her husband on the Mediterranean island of Malta. In true Mills & Boon style they met on Monday, became engaged on Friday and married three months later. Susan enjoys entertaining, travel and going to the theatre. To relax she reads, cooks and plays the piano, and when she's had enough of relaxing she throws herself off mountains on skis, or gallops through the countryside singing loudly.

CHAPTER ONE

'Nacho Acosta is back in circulation!'

Screwing up her eyes as she stared at the screen, Grace blinked and tried to clear her vision. The virus she had contracted must be affecting her eyesight, she concluded, reading on: *'Romily Winner, our Up-Town sleuth, reports on the trail of who's hot and who's not.'*

Oh, damn...

Now there were white spots dancing in front of her eyes and the monitor screen was flashing. Pushing her chair back, Grace stood to stretch her aching limbs and inhale a lungful of stale basement air. She squeezed her eyes shut again and then blinked several times.

Better.

Relieved to find the problem had cleared, she checked the PC connections.

All good.

Tiredness, Grace concluded. It *was* almost one a.m. Working as a cocktail waitress in the half-light of a nightclub in Cornwall and then sitting in the club's office working on accounts for half the night was hardly going to make for happy eyes.

Tired or not, Grace made one last trawl over the countless images of aggressively handsome men featured on the society pages of *ROCK!* magazine, finding it hard to believe that she had met the infamous Nacho Acosta in the hard, tanned flesh. They could hardly be said to inhabit the same world, but fate played funny tricks sometimes.

Finally managing to drag her gaze away from the photographs of Nacho, she got on with devouring every word the journalist had written about him...

With the wild Acostas all grown up and fully fledged, this reporter doubts that Nacho—at thirty-two the oldest of the notorious polo-playing Acosta brothers—will be in much hurry to quit the London scene, where he seems to be finding plenty to keep him entertained!

Grace felt a pulse of arousal even as her stomach clenched with jealousy at the thought of all the other women *entertaining* Nacho, as the reporter so suggestively put it. Which was ridiculous, bearing in mind she'd only met him twice, and on each occasion had felt so clumsy and awkward in comparison to Nacho's effortless style she hardly had any right to feel so much as a twinge of envy.

But she did.

The first time they had met had been at a polo match on the beach in Cornwall, which Grace's best friend and Nacho's sister, Lucia, had arranged. Nacho had done little more on that occasion than lean out of the window of his monster Jeep to give Grace a quick once-over, but no man had ever looked at her that way before, and she could still remember the effect on her body of so much heat. She'd spent the rest of the day watching Nacho playing polo from the sidelines like some lovesick teenager.

They had met for a second time at Lucia's wedding,

held at the Acosta family's main *estancia* in Argentina. This trip had been the greatest thrill of Grace's life—until she'd seen Nacho in the giant marquee and his keen black stare had found her. He'd been tied up for most of the evening, hosting the event, but she had felt the effect of his powerful charisma wherever she went, so that by the time he'd found a chance to speak to her she had only been able to stare at him like a fool, wide-eyed and stumped for words.

Growing up with parents who had extolled her virtues to anyone who would listen had left Grace with crippling shyness, for the simple reason that she knew she could never be as beautiful or as gifted as they made her out to be. A lot of that shyness had been knocked out of her at the club, where the patrons appreciated her efficiency, but it had all come flooding back that night at the wedding in front of Nacho, transforming what could have been a flirty, fun encounter into a tongue-tied mess.

Shifting her mind from that embarrassing occasion, Grace studied another shot of the man who'd once rocked her world. There was yet another beautiful woman at his side, and Grace had to admit they made a striking couple. And the girl's expression seemed to warn every other woman off.

'You can have him,' Grace muttered, dragging her gaze away. Nacho Acosta might be gorgeous, but that night at the wedding had proved he was well out of her league.

The sound of the nightclub pianist running through his repertoire provided a welcome distraction for Grace, who had always found company in music and books. Her parents had once had high hopes that Grace would become a concert pianist, but those dreams had ended when her father had died and there had been no more money to pay her fees at the *conservatoire*. Grace hadn't realised how cosseted she had been until that moment, or what loss really meant. Losing her place at college had been devastating, but losing her father had been far, far worse.

Leaving music college had forced Grace to find a job, and she had been grateful to find a position in a nightclub where one of the top jazz musicians of the day performed. Being close to music at that level had been a small comfort to Grace, who had still been suffering greatly from the death of her father.

Turning back to the computer screen again, Grace studied the picture at the end of the article showing Lucia and her brothers. Lucia was smiling, while each of her brothers either appeared dangerous, brooding or stern. Nacho was at the dangerous end of the spectrum.

It must have been hard for Lucia, Grace reflected. The only girl in a family of four men, how had Lucia ever made herself heard, or seen, or taken account of at all? Lucia had once mentioned that being alone in the Acosta family had never been an option. It was little wonder that she had made a bid for freedom, Grace mused, leaving the family home to work in the club where the two girls had met. Nacho had raised his siblings when their parents had been killed in a flood, and though Lucia was always upbeat by nature she referred to that time as like being under the heel of the tyrant.

Grace shivered involuntarily as she studied Nacho's face. Everyone knew Nacho Acosta to be a forceful man, who got everything he wanted.

'Piano-time, Grace?'

She turned at the sound of Clark Mayhew's voice as he poked his head around the door. Clark was the club pianist she so loved to hear.

'Come on, Grace,' Clark prompted. 'Shut that computer down and get out here. You've got a real talent.'

'Not like you,' she said, smiling.

Clark shrugged. 'The only difference between you and me is that I have more confidence.'

'I wish!' Grace exclaimed, laughing as she walked across the club, sat down and adjusted the piano stool. 'I can't even play without music like you. I only wish I could.'

'But you can,' Clark insisted. 'Close your eyes and let the melody flow through your fingers...'

A bolt of panic hit her as Grace realised she had no option but to close her eyes. The moment she tried to focus her eyes on the music notes and lines began to wheel and collide on the page.

'Close your eyes, Grace,' Clark encouraged, oblivious to what was happening. 'Didn't I tell you?' he said when she managed a few bars.

She would definitely have to cut down her screentime, Grace realised when she opened her eyes again. The flashing lights plaguing her vision hadn't gone away. If anything, they were getting worse.

Two years later

The girl had been eyeing him up since he'd entered the ballroom. It was a magnificent room, currently set out for a formal dinner with small tables laid for eight. An armada of glass and silverware glittered beneath huge Venetian chandeliers, which proved the perfect spotlight for the girl trying to attract his attention. Her figure alone was enough to scramble any man's head, and the heated invitation in her eyes promised only one conclusion—if he were interested.

He'd pass. He was restless tonight, and bored by the round of engagements his PA had set up for him in London.

Tonight was a so-called power dinner, for movers and shakers in the wine industry. Nacho was better known for playing polo at an international level and running an *estancia* in Argentina the size of a small country, but his decision to restore the family vineyards was something he had been forced to do in order to protect his siblings' inheritance. Nothing else would have persuaded him to return to that particular family home in Argentina...

'Nacho.'

He turned to see the dapper figure of Don Fernando Gonzales, the chairman of the event, approaching. 'Don Fernando.' He inclined his head politely, noting the sultry beauty was now standing at the chairman's side.

'Nacho Acosta—I would like to present my daughter, Annalisa Gonzales...'

As Don Fernando stepped back an all too familiar sensation came over him as he briefly clasped the woman's carefully manicured hand. He'd heard Don Fernando was in financial trouble, and the portly chairman wouldn't be the first father to parade his pretty daughter in front of Nacho. Everyone knew Nacho held the reins to the family fortune, though they seemed unaware that Nacho was wise to schemes born out of desperation, or that he could do more damage to those he cared about than those misguided parents could possibly imagine.

It was almost a relief when he was distracted by the glimpse of a shining blonde head. He stared across the room, trying to work out if he had met the blonde before. His sixth sense said yes, but with only the back of her head to go on it was hard to be sure...

'Am I keeping you, Señor Acosta?' Annalisa Gonzales asked him with a knowing look.

Her father had peeled away, Nacho noticed, giving them the chance to get to know each other better. 'Forgive me,' he said, forcing himself to concentrate on what was undeniably a beautifully designed face.

'Are you really as bad as they say you are?' Annalisa asked, as if she hoped it were true.

'Worse,' he assured her.

They were both distracted by the sound of a dog barking, and Annalisa laughed as she turned to look for the culprit. 'If I had known dogs were permitted at this dinner I would have brought Monkey, my Chihuahua—'

'Who would have provided a tasty snack for Cormac, my Irish Wolfhound,' he countered. 'If you will excuse me, Señorita Gonzales, I believe the MC is about to call us to our tables...'

Grace sat down, relieved to have the woman sitting next to her introduce herself right away. Elias, Grace's elderly employer and mentor, was sitting on Grace's other side, but he had been immediately swept into greeting old friends and colleagues, and Grace was keen to prove that she could do this by herself. This annual event in celebration of the wine industry was Grace's first major outing since becoming blind. It was also the first big outing for her guide dog, Buddy, and Grace was as nervous for Buddy as she was for herself. She hoped they would both get through the evening without making too many blunders.

While Grace was chatting easily to the lady at her side she took the chance to discreetly map the tablecloth and all the various hazards confronting her. A battalion of glasses was waiting to be knocked over—and then there was the cutlery she had to get right. And the napkin she had to unfold without knocking anything over. There were a lot of different-sized plates, along with groups of condiments and sugar bowls. The potential for sugar in her soup and salt in her coffee loomed large.

'Here's the pepper, if you want it,' the lady next to her remarked, flagging up the arrival of the soup. 'I like pepper on everything,' she added, 'though you may want to taste first. It might need salt—'

Grace felt a rush of emotion as the woman placed a second container close to her hand, where Grace could feel it. Small kindnesses counted for a lot now she was blind. They meant she could leave the house and do things like this. Elias was right. All she had to do was buckle on her courage each morning along with Buddy's harness. It was harder doing that sometimes than talking about it, but it helped to know there were some really nice people in the world—and thank goodness for them.

'You work for one of the great men in our industry,' the older woman commented, obviously impressed when Grace explained that Elias had trained her to be a sommelier.

'I guess Elias is the closest thing I've got to a father figure,' Grace admitted. It wasn't enough to describe Elias as her employer when he'd done so much for her.

'You lost your father?' the elderly lady prompted gently.

'Yes,' Grace murmured, growing sombre as she thought back.

'I lost my father when I was very young. You're lucky to have Elias on your side. He's a kind man and a good man, and there aren't many of those around—though I'm sure you'll meet a good man of your own one day and get married.'

'Oh, no!' Grace exclaimed. 'I could never do that.'

'Why ever not?' Grace's companion demanded as Buddy barked at the change in Grace's voice.

'I wouldn't want to be a burden,' Grace explained.

'A burden?' her new friend exclaimed. 'Whatever gave you that idea?'

Grace would run a mile rather than be a burden to anyone. She'd felt the same way when her mother had found happiness again after her father's death and had wanted to marry a man with children of his own. Grace hadn't wanted to get in the way of her mother's happiness, and had taken the marriage as her cue to leave home for good. Then, when her sight had deteriorated, she had become doubly determined not to be a trouble to anyone.

But she wasn't about to spoil this evening with dark thoughts. 'I've still got a lot to learn and a lot to get used to,' Grace said lightly, 'so I think perhaps I'd better get myself sorted out before I go looking for love,' She laughed, realizing what she'd said. 'Perhaps it would be better if I let love come looking for me.' She stilled, feeling a warm, papery hand covering hers.

'You're a brave girl, Grace. You deserve the best,' Grace's new friend insisted. 'And don't you dare settle for anything less.'

Nacho was growing increasingly impatient—although as Annalisa shrugged her slender shoulders and walked away he was forced to ask himself when the chance to accept a free gift in such attractive packaging had become so meaningless.

The past had made him hard and cynical, Nacho concluded. Most of the women he encountered seemed so obvious and shallow, and they all wanted the same thing:

someone—anyone—to take care of them, financially and emotionally. And, having spent his teens and twenties caring for his siblings, he found his emotional bank was drained.

His married brothers often talked of how lucky they were to have found a soul mate. He always laughed and asked what chance they thought he stood. If they answered him he never listened. He didn't believe in fate or luck. Hard work brought results, and he didn't have time to waste searching for a woman. The only woman who could possibly stir his interest now would have to be strong and independent.

He cast one last look around the room, searching for the blonde again, but she seemed to have gone. He could be doing better things with his time, and as soon as politeness allowed he made his excuses and left.

On the drive back to the family penthouse in London he couldn't shake the feeling that something of significance had happened at the dinner, though what that might have been eluded him.

Working in a vast wine warehouse was easy for Grace now she had Buddy to guide her. The big Golden Retriever could happily steer Grace across London, and navigating the now familiar maze of passages at the warehouse was a breeze for him, so Grace was curious when he started to growl.

'What's the matter, boy?' she said, bending low to give him a pat. The strange thing was she could feel something too. It was the same sense of foreboding she got when there was thunder in the air.

Since her sight had failed Grace had come to rely on her other senses, and they had quickly become more developed. But apart from the thundering of her heart she could hear nothing now. 'We've only got one more section to check,' she reassured her guide dog. 'Take me to Argentina, Buddy...'

Hearing one of his command words, Buddy led Grace unerringly to the section in the warehouse where wines from Argentina were stored. If Grace had said Spain, or France, or New World, the highly trained guide dog would have known exactly where to take her. To make doubly sure there could never be a mistake each section was labelled in Braille as well as in script.

Grace had had to learn a lot of new things since losing her sight to a rare virus. At first numbness and denial at the bleakness of her prognosis had swept over her, keeping her chained to the bed, to the house, but then anger and frustration had taken over, and they had demanded action. She'd decided that didn't want to spend the rest of her life blundering around and falling over things, and had finally determined she would learn to trust the hated stick.

'The Stick' had sat in a corner of Grace's bedroom since her return from hospital, where a therapist had assured her in no uncertain terms that if she didn't use it to get out of the house she would spend her life in darkness.

'But I *am* in darkness!' Grace had yelled in angry desperation.

There had been a lot of screaming and yelling as well as quiet sobbing through those dark, difficult times. It had changed nothing. Having Elias in the background, nagging her constantly to get on with her life, had worked, and finally picking up 'The Stick' had changed her life. It had been her first step towards independence.

But just when she had gathered enough courage to walk down the road she'd realized everything above waist-height slapped her in the face. On one outing she

had crept home, feeling her way an inch at a time...
like a blind woman. And another week had been wasted
grieving for what couldn't be changed. It was only when
Lucia had turned up with a representative from the Guide
Dogs' Association that Grace had been persuaded to try
something new.

At first she had protested that she couldn't look after
herself, never mind a dog, but to her shock Lucia had
snapped angrily, 'For goodness' sake, pull yourself together, Grace. Buddy needs feeding—and he needs regular walks. This isn't all about *you,* Grace.'

Grace had slowly realized that she had been behaving incredibly selfishly and had immersed herself in a
lonely world of her own making. She had given Lucia
every cause to be worried about her progressively withdrawn friend.

When Buddy had arrived everything had changed.
From the moment the big dog snuggled up to Grace it
was a done deal. Buddy alerted her to every hazard, and
by doing so opened up Grace's world. Lucia, as usual,
had gone overboard, enthusing and saying that as Buddy
was already chipped and inoculated, and had his very
own doggy passport, there was no excuse for Grace not
to go travelling.

As if! Grace had thought at the time. Though now,
thanks to Buddy, her confidence was building daily.

'What *is* your problem?' Grace demanded fondly as
Buddy continued to growl. She relaxed when she heard
the voice of her mentor, Elias Silver. Elias had used to
supply the club with wine, which was how they'd met,
and he'd offered her a job when no one else would, encouraging Grace to retrain as sommelier. 'Elias must be
meeting someone,' she commented, stroking Buddy's

silky ears. 'You'll have to get used to people you don't know now we're both working full-time.'

Grace had barely returned to her office when Elias came in, full of suppressed excitement.

'The new wines I've just been tasting are exceptional.'

'And?' Grace prompted, sensing there was more to come.

She grew increasingly uneasy as the silence lengthened.

'I've known about this vineyard for years,' Elias started telling her, in a tone that suggested he was choosing his words carefully. 'I was planning for us to go to Argentina together, Grace—'

She did a mental double-take. This was the first she'd heard of it.

Argentina—so far away. And impossible for her to visit now she was blind.

Argentina—the home of the Acostas and Nacho—

'Don't look so shocked,' Elias insisted. 'You know I've been slowing down recently...'

Grace's thoughts whirled. Elias being less than fit was a terrifying prospect. He was a dear friend.

'You'll have to go to Argentina without me,' he said.

'Sorry?' she breathed in a shocked voice.

'If there was any alternative, believe me, I would suggest it, Grace, but my doctor has insisted I must rest.'

'Then you *must* rest, and I'll look after you,' Grace insisted.

'The business can't afford for both of us to be away at the same time, and I'm not going to risk losing out on top-quality wine to a competitor. You have to go, Grace. Who else can I ask? Who else can I trust?'

'But what if I let you down?'

'You won't,' Elias assured her. 'I believe in you,

Grace. I always have. You must go to Argentina to check this vineyard and its wine production for me.'

She was filled with concern for Elias and fear at the thought of failing him. 'I want to help, but—'

'Don't say *But I'm blind,*' Elias warned her. 'Don't ever say that, Grace, or everything you have achieved since losing your sight will be lost.'

'And you've been there for me from the start.'

'Yes, I have,' he said pointedly.

When he had first heard about her illness Elias had sought her out with an unconditional offer of help, saying it was his way of repaying Grace for all her small kindnesses over the years.

'You know how short we are on Argentinian wine,' he said. 'Would you have me turn customers away?'

'No, of course not. But do I really need to go to Argentina? Can't we find someone else to go?'

'No,' Elias said flatly. 'Apart from the little matter of trust, I think you need to go to Argentina to prove you can do it, Grace. It's the next step for you. And if you won't do it for yourself, then do it for me. I'm trying to make a businesswoman out of you, as well as a connoisseur of wine, and you must always satisfy yourself that things are what they seem to be before you place an order. It won't be so bad,' he encouraged. 'You'll only be there a month or so—'

'A *month!*' Grace exclaimed, horrorstruck. Just when she'd been about ready to say maybe, Elias had moved the goalposts.

'And you must leave right away, to catch the harvest at its best,' he continued. 'I'll need a full report from you, Grace.'

One of the things she loved about Elias was that he never made any allowances for her being blind. But this was too much. This wasn't the 'next step'—it was a huge leap across an unknowable chasm.

'But you know I can't travel—'

'I know nothing of the sort,' Elias argued. 'You can get about London, can't you?'

'Only because I have Buddy to help me—'

'Exactly,' Elias interrupted. 'Grace, I can't trust anyone else to do this. Are you saying I wasted my money training you?'

'Of course not. I can't imagine what I'd be doing now if you hadn't helped me. You know how grateful I am.'

'I don't want your gratitude. I want you out there doing the job you've been trained to do.'

'But I haven't left the country since—'

'Since your sight was reduced to looking at the world as if through the wrong end of a telescope? Yes, I know that. But I thought you liked a challenge, Grace?'

'I do,' Grace insisted, remembering the staff at the rehabilitation centre telling her she must keep pushing the boundaries—but not as far as Argentina, surely?

'I can't travel,' Elias said flatly, 'and taking on a new supplier is a huge risk for the business. We have to be sure these wines are as good as they promise to be.'

'Surely sending me in your place is an even bigger risk?'

'Grace, my father taught me, his father taught him, and now I've trained *you,* with many patient tasting sessions—'

'Patient?' Grace interrupted, starting to smile.

'I love to hear you happy, Grace. Don't let life frighten you. Please promise me that.'

'But do I know enough?' she said, still fretting.

'I know sommeliers who have been judging wine for forty years and don't have your natural ability,' Elias insisted. 'There's only one amateur I can think of who comes close to matching your palate and he just left the building.'

Grace felt the same tremble of awareness she had felt at that dinner, when Buddy had started barking, but she didn't believe in coincidence, and there had to be more than one family in Argentina that owned vineyards. And hadn't Lucia said the Acosta vineyards had been languishing for years?

'You don't have to worry about Buddy,' Elias was saying. 'He won't be a problem as you'll both be travelling in style on the Acosta family jet.'

'The Acosta family?' Grace's throat closed up as her worst fears were confirmed. 'Who exactly is it I'm meeting in Argentina?' she managed hoarsely.

Elias laughed, as if to confirm his thoughts that she was overreacting. 'Don't worry, you don't have to face the whole tribe at once—just the kingpin, Nacho.'

'Nacho?' A sound that was half a laugh and half a hysterical sob squeezed out of her throat. 'You *have* warned Señor Acosta that I will be travelling to Argentina in your place?'

Elias took too long to answer.

'You haven't?' she said.

'I won't lose out to a competitor,' Elias said stubbornly. 'And I can't see why you're making such a fuss. You know the Acosta family, don't you?'

'You know I do. Lucia is my best friend. You must remember we worked together at the club. And, yes, I've met her brothers, too,' she said, making sure to keep all expression out of her voice.

'Well, there you are!' Elias exclaimed. 'You'll be flying to the far west of their property, where I'm told it's very beautiful. You'll see the snow-capped Andes, and all those glorious rivers that feed the vines. It's perfect wine-growing country—' Elias stopped. 'Oh, Grace, I'm so sorry...'

'Please don't be,' she said. 'What I can't see I can't tell you about, but I'll make up for it in other ways, I promise. I'm sure the air will be different—and I can still smell. I can still feel the sun on my face. And the rain,' she added wryly as the latest in a series of angry winter storms rattled the windows. 'There will be so many new experiences—' She stopped, remembering the one experience ahead that really frightened her: meeting the most formidable of the Acosta brothers again. 'Was Nacho Acosta here today, by any chance?'

'Yes. Nacho's taken charge of the family vineyards,' Elias confirmed breezily. 'I've got every confidence in you,' he stressed. 'I know I couldn't have a better representative. This trip is going to be a piece of cake for you, Grace.'

It was to be hoped the cake didn't choke her.

CHAPTER TWO

GRACE'S decision to go to Argentina had been made by the time Elias left the room. She wouldn't let her elderly mentor down. She'd always been thankful Elias didn't treat her any differently because she was blind, and now she had to rise to the challenge. It was just a little harder because Nacho was involved...

Okay, it was a whole lot harder. Nacho wasn't exactly noted for his tolerance, and this would be her first big job. Was she trying to run before she could walk? Would Nacho even listen to her views on his wine and the way he ran the family vineyard? Apart from the extensive training Elias had given her she had no real experience in this area, and certainly no money or lofty lineage like the Acosta family.

She must stop with the negatives and concentrate on the positives, Grace concluded. But her thoughts were all over the place at the thought of meeting Nacho again. Their first meeting had been a disaster, and her body had reeled at the sight of him, but this next meeting would be very different. It was business, and she didn't have the option to be a shrinking violet. Now she was blind she had to get out there and make her presence felt.

She thought back to the wedding again, and how

painfully shy she had been. She had felt out of place amongst so many glamorous, confident people, and had been horrified when Nacho had come to her rescue. She hadn't been able to think of anything interesting to say to him, and had stood transfixed like a rabbit trapped in a car's headlights when he had brushed a gentle kiss against her lips. First chance she'd got, she'd bolted. 'Like Cinderella,' as Lucia had later chided her, adding the unsettling news that her brother had been less than pleased.

Grace couldn't begin to imagine what Nacho would think of her now she was blind and also in a position to put a curb on his business objectives.

This wasn't the first time since her sight had failed that she had felt like beating her head against the wall and screaming, *Why me?* Unfortunately, she always came up with the same answer: why *not* me?

Later that night Grace packed a case with an assortment of clothes taken from her carefully organised wardrobe. Lucia, who had always been strong on the organisational front, had come up with a foolproof plan that enabled Grace to find colour-co-ordinated outfits. By tagging the various suit bags and drawers with Braille labels, Lucia had made finding her clothes and accessories easy.

If only handling inner turmoil could be managed as easily, Grace fretted.

She was excited and yet terrified at the prospect of seeing Nacho again. But she couldn't actually *see* him, so it couldn't be that bad.

Even she didn't believe that.

Not wanting to spoil Grace's chances of making the trip, Elias had e-mailed Nacho immediately to say that at the last minute another expert would be taking his place.

'Well, it's true,' Elias had protested when Grace had pulled him up on it.

Grace might not approve of Elias's methods, but he had her loyalty—and if she stopped to think how Nacho was going to react when he saw who it was taking Elias's place she would never get on that plane.

A blind sommelier? Wouldn't *that* be a thrill for Nacho? He was expecting Elias Silver, master vintner and emperor of a European wine distribution network, and he would get Grace and her guide dog instead.

The journey to Argentina was so much easier than Grace had imagined. A chauffeur-driven car picked her up at home, and her transit through the airport was seamless. Maybe that was something all private plane passengers experienced but, blind or not, she thought it was quite something to be escorted and fussed over.

The moment she stepped out of the plane she noticed how warm it was, and how good it felt to have the sun on her face instead of the prickly chill of a damp English winter. The smell of jet fuel still caught in her throat, but there was spice in the air too, and the foreign language sounded musical and intriguing.

There were interpreters on hand to lead Grace to yet another chauffeur-driven car, and the driver was chatty, spoke perfect English, and took a very obvious pride in his country—which led to an illuminating travelogue for Grace. Apparently there were billboards of the Acosta brothers all the way down the main road, and as they travelled across the flat expanses of the pampas he told her about the jagged mountains there, with eagles soaring on the updrafts around their snowy peaks.

The driver showed no surprise that Grace was blind.

Nacho's PA had made all the arrangements with Elias, he explained, when Grace made a casual comment. It was just the great man himself who didn't realise he had a beautiful woman coming to taste his wine, as Nacho had been away on a business trip, the driver joked.

Ha-ha, Grace thought weakly, but the driver went on to tell her about the broad river that flowed like a sinuous silver snake through emerald-green farmland until it passed the *hacienda*, where it roared down to a treacherous weir. Even if she could have seen everything the driver was describing to her, Grace began to think that she might have rested back after the long journey anyway, and allowed him to colour in the scenes outside the window for her.

It was a long drive to the vineyard, and she fell asleep after a while. When she woke she felt rested in mind and body, knowing the first hurdle—travel—was behind her. This was the first time she'd been abroad since losing her sight and she'd travelled halfway across the world! That should give her *some* confidence.

Remembering Elias's enthusiastic description of the vineyards, Grace realized she was looking forward to discovering them for herself. She might not be able to see all those wonderful sights, but she would hear the river the driver had told her about, and she would smell those lush emerald-green farmlands. She smiled, convinced that in spite of all the Nacho-sized problems ahead of her she was going to like it here.

His schedule had been ridiculous recently—one business trip on top of another—but when he visited this particular stretch of the river he began to relax.

It was like visiting a grave and speaking to his long-dead parents, Nacho reflected darkly.

When he had first returned to the vineyards every inch of the estate had taunted him with one painfully familiar scene after another, but he had continued to ride the paths until he had conquered the demons and made some sort of peace—enough, at least, to revive the vineyards. Perhaps he gained a sense of perspective in the shadow of the Andes, and all the small irritations in his life could be swept away in the broad silver river as it flowed to the sea.

Murmuring reassurances to his newly broken horse, he slapped the proud, arched neck with approval. When his stallion stilled to listen to his voice he wondered, not for the first time, if he didn't prefer animals to people. As the stallion struck the ground aggressively he was reminded they were both experiencing great change. The horse had lost his freedom, while Nacho had gained his after years of caring for his siblings. But the shallow life of a playboy had not been for him, and his freedom had soon proved disappointing. So Nacho had returned to Argentina full of renewed determination to turn the failing vineyards into a valuable asset for his family.

'We both need something to distract us,' he murmured as the stallion's muscles balled beneath him.

Keen to inspect the vines, he urged the horse forward. Under his rule order had been restored and another considerable asset added to the Acosta family fortune.

The sun on his back after the chill of London was an almost sensual pleasure, and he couldn't have been in a better mood. Until he saw the dog. Unleashed and unattended, a big yellow mutt was relieving himself on his vines. And then a flash of movement drew his attention to the riverbank. Filled with fury at this unauthorised intrusion, he kicked the horse into a gallop, closing the distance at brutal speed.

'This is private land!' he roared, drawing the stallion to a skidding halt.

Grace hugged herself in terror. That voice, the raging hooves—this was everything she had been dreading and more.

And everything she had hoped for, Grace's inner voice insisted.

Had *dreaded*, Grace argued firmly. She had planned to have a businesslike first meeting with Nacho, in the calm surroundings of his office—not the furious drum of steel-shod hooves crashing to a halt only inches away. His horse's hot breath was on her face, and she could feel Nacho glaring down at her. Being this close to him slammed into her senses and memories flooded back, colouring in the void behind her eyes. Nacho was bigger, stronger, darker—more intimidating than any man she had ever known before.

So had she wilfully courted danger? Hadn't Nacho's housekeeper warned her that the master might be back home soon? Hadn't she mentioned that he always liked to ride along the riverbank when he came home?

Nacho wheeled his snorting stallion to a halt within a few inches of the girl's back. She didn't flinch, as he had expected. She didn't move at all. She kept her back to him and ignored him. Her dog showed more sense, sinking to its belly and baring its teeth.

'This is a private land,' he repeated harshly, 'And you are trespassing.'

'I heard you, Nacho.'

Dios! Dear God! No!

As the girl turned around, shocked curses without number or form flooded his head. When he saw who it was…when he saw her unfocused eyes…*he knew her.*

Of course he knew her. But not like this.

'Grace?' he demanded.

'Of course it's Grace,' she said—with false bravado, he suspected, noticing how she quivered with apprehension like a doe at bay. 'Didn't Elias e-mail ahead to warn you I was coming?'

'My PA said something about his replacement.' His brain was racing to find the right words to say. There were none, he concluded. He was angry at this obvious deception by Elias, but he was shattered at seeing Grace like this.

'And you can't believe I'm that replacement?' she said. 'Is that it?'

'How can you be,' he demanded, 'when Elias is the best in his field?'

She fell silent and he took a better look at her. It felt strange to be staring at someone who couldn't see—as if he were taking advantage of her, almost. But apart from the vague, unfocused eyes Grace hadn't changed that much at all.

He didn't need this sort of distraction in his life. He had marked Grace out as interesting at Lucia's wedding, only to find her disappointingly immature and naïve.

'I'm sorry to disappoint you,' she said, crashing into his thoughts. 'I felt sure that Elias would have mentioned that I work for him when you came to see him in London.'

'The subject never came up,' he said brusquely. 'Why would it?'

'Well, please don't be angry with Elias. He trained me well, and he has every reason to trust my judgement.'

'And you expect *me* to?' Nacho cut in with scorn.

His horse had started stamping its hooves on the ground, as if the big beast had had enough of her too. She could smell it and feel its hot breath. She could hear the creak of leather and the chink of its bridle as it danced impatiently within inches of her toes.

'I can't believe Elias would send a young girl in his place when I was expecting a master vintner,' Nacho said from somewhere way above her.

'And you're wondering what I can possibly know about fine wine?' she said, determined to keep her voice steady.

'I'm wondering what you're doing here at all. Did you learn about wine at the club?' he suggested scornfully.

The wine they had served there, by Elias's own admission, had been his cheapest brand, Grace remembered.

'There's definitely been some mistake,' Nacho insisted.

'There's no mistake,' Grace insisted, growing angry. 'I can assure you I've been very well trained.'

Nacho laughed. 'So has my horse.'

She looked as if she'd like to unseat him, her jaw fixed and her hands balled into fists. She was angry. So what? But what should have been a simple solution—send Grace home on the next flight—was immeasurably changed by the fact that she was blind. And she was his sister's best friend. How could he rage against a girl scrabbling around on the ground searching for her dog's harness?

'It's over there—to your left,' he said impatiently.

Dios! What had he said now? Grace couldn't see anything to her left *or* her right.

'Thank you, but Buddy will find it for me,' she snapped, still angry with him.

Sure enough, the big dog put the harness in her hand.

The last time Nacho had seen Grace had been at Lucia's wedding, where he'd felt a connection between them he couldn't explain. Wanting to pursue it, he'd found her as nervous as a fawn. Perhaps she had sensed something of the darkness about him? he'd thought at the time. She had certainly changed since then—because she'd had to, he realised. There was a resolve about Grace now that piqued his interest all over again.

'I realise that my coming here must be a shock for you, Nacho,' she said. She deftly fastened the harness while the big dog stood obediently still.

'Somewhat,' he conceded, with massive understatement. 'What happened to you, Grace?'

'A virus,' she said with a shrug.

However casually she might treat it, he felt angry for her. 'How long do you plan to stay?' Before she had a chance to answer he gave his own reading of the situation. 'I expect you'll take a few notes, have a look around, and then report back to Elias. Shouldn't take long—say, a day?'

'A *day*?' she exclaimed. 'I'll need to do more than take a few notes!'

In spite of his outrage at the trick Elias had played on him, his overriding feeling was of dismay when Grace turned her head and her lovely eyes homed in on the *approximate* direction of his voice.

'I've brought a Braille keyboard and a screen with

me,' she explained matter-of-factly. 'I expect to be here for around a month.'

'A month?' he exploded.

'Possibly a couple of days more,' she said, thinking about it. 'Please don't be concerned,' she said briskly. 'I am a trained sommelier, with a diploma in viticulture—'

'And how much experience?' he demanded sharply. What the hell was Elias playing at? He would just have to send someone else to evaluate his wine.

Sensing his growing anger, the stallion skittered nervously beneath him. Grace had started walking up the path ahead of him, with her dog at her heels.

'Aren't you going to put your sandals on?' he called after her

'I'm not a child, Nacho.' Without turning she dangled her sandals from one finger and waggled them at him in defiance.

She couldn't let Nacho see that she was as tense as a board, and that she couldn't stand his scrutiny a moment longer. She just had to get back to the guest cottage where she was staying and regroup. She hadn't anticipated feeling that same stab of excitement when was she near him, but nothing had changed. Nacho couldn't have made it plainer that she was not only the last person he wanted to see but an unwelcome intruder on his land—and a fraud. At the wedding she had allowed her head to fill with immature fairytale notions and had had her bluff well and truly called when he had sought her out. But she was here now, and she was staying until she got this job done.

They walked on in silence. She felt as if Nacho were tracking her like a hunter with his prey. She could feel his gaze boring into her back, flooding every part of her with awareness and arousal. It made her recall his touch on her arm at the wedding and the brush of his lips on her mouth. She remembered the terrifying way her body had responded—violently, longingly. Common sense had kicked in just in time, reminding her that she was inexperienced and Nacho Acosta was not, and that any more kisses would only lead to heartbreak in the end. As far as Grace was concerned, love and lovemaking were inextricably entwined, while Nacho, according to the popular press, was a notorious playboy who drank his fill at every trough around the world.

But he was right about one thing. *If only she could see.*

The path was stony. She stopped to put her sandals on.

'Please don't,' she said, hearing Nacho move as if he might dismount to help her. 'Buddy will stop me falling,' she insisted—which should have been true. But for the first time in ages she was stumbling around *like a blind woman*. She hadn't felt so unsure of herself since the shadows had closed in, Grace realised, beginning to panic. She even missed when she went to grasp Buddy's harness.

'Here—let me,' Nacho said brusquely.

It was too late to say no. He had already sprung to the ground.

'Thank you, but you'll only confuse Buddy,' she said tensely, feeling quivers of awareness all over her body as Nacho closed in.

'My apologies,' he said in a cold voice. 'I realise your dog can do many things, but can he catch you if you fall?'

'Buddy prevents me falling,' she pointed out. 'And we're fine from here. Buddy? The cottage.'

She was walking faster and faster now, practically running from one kind of darkness to another, with no landmarks in between. She was frightened of the strange territory, and she was frightened of Nacho. She heard him mount up again and now he was right behind her, his horse almost on top of her.

'We know our way,' she insisted, fighting off the terrifying sense of being hunted in the dark. She wished he'd speak, so she could tell exactly where he was. She wished she could see his face and know exactly what he was thinking. As long as there wasn't any pity on it. She couldn't have borne that. She'd had enough of people treating her as if her brain was faulty along with her sight. 'Really, we're fine from here,' she called out, hating the fact that her voice was shaking.

'Can't I show you some basic civility?' he said, giving her some indication that he was keeping his horse a safe distance away. 'While you're here in Argentina you're my guest.'

While she was there? That sounded ominous, as if she wouldn't be here very long—which was bad news for Elias. 'Look, I must apologise,' she said, drawing to a halt. 'I realise we haven't got off to the best of starts. I want you to know that I'm really looking forward to tasting your wines…' She stood and listened. It had gone very quiet again. 'Elias spoke so highly of them…'

She breathed a sigh of relief as she heard Nacho's horse move and its harness chink.

'I'm sorry if my being here instead of Elias has been a disappointment for you,' she said.

Not half as sorry as he was.

'And I realise you must be wondering—'

'Wondering *what*, Grace?' he interrupted. Shortening the reins, he brought the stallion under control. 'Elias has kept me completely in the dark. I feel let down. What am I supposed to think when Elias sends a young girl with little or no experience in his place? If you're asking me to be blunt, I can't imagine how you can possibly do the job.'

She flinched, and he felt wretched, but people's livelihoods were at stake. And now she was about to fall down a bank.

'Grace, watch out!' he yelled.

'I'm not going anywhere,' she said as the dog led her safely back onto the path.

'You nearly did.'

'Buddy wouldn't let me fall.'

He admired her confidence and hoped it wasn't misplaced. This was not the naïve young girl he remembered from Lucia's wedding. This was a woman with steel in her spine and she intrigued him—which complicated matters.

'How did you find your way to the river in the first place?' he said, trying to imagine himself blindfolded, with only a dog to lead him.

'Buddy heard the water—smelled it too, I expect. He started barking, and after the long journey I thought we both needed some fresh air.'

'I can't understand why my sister didn't mention your illness.'

'Because I asked her not to.'

'Why keep it a secret?' he said suspiciously.

'Because I'm handling it,' she said, marching on. 'Because I don't want to be treated any differently just because I can't see. I don't want to be defined by being blind. I don't want it to influence what people think about me.'

'I think you're being overly optimistic, Grace.'

'Well, maybe I am, but I don't want smothering,' she snapped. 'I'm quite capable of looking after myself.'

'Don't you think it would be more considerate if you warned people in advance, so that they can make the necessary provision for you?'

'What provision?' she flashed. 'That's exactly what I *don't* want. Why should I—?'

'Compromise?' he suggested as he battled to keep the stallion in check.

The horse was bored with inactivity, and it didn't like the turn this conversation was taking. Animals could sense tempers rising faster than humans, and Nacho was determined that passions of any kind would not be roused between him and Grace.

Passion could kill, as he knew only too well, and he never made the same mistake twice.

CHAPTER THREE

'SURELY compromise is all part of adapting to your new situation?' Nacho insisted as he continued to follow Grace along the riverbank. He caught a glimpse of her face as she strode along. Her jaw was firm and the set of her face was still angry. He could almost see her thinking, *What would you know about it?* And the answer to that, for once in his life, was absolutely nothing.

'Why should I compromise?' she said, confirming those thoughts. 'That sounds too much like defeat to me.'

'Grace! Watch that branch—'

'I'm okay,' she fired back, and the big dog adjusted direction seamlessly to lead Grace safely round the fallen branch.

But she still couldn't know she was so very close to the edge of a steep bank, or that from there it was just a short fall into the fast-flowing river. Nacho's head reeled with sudden dread as he thought back to another time and a tragedy he should have been there to prevent.

'I might not be able to see the river,' Grace said, as if she could read his thoughts as well. 'But I can hear it. And with Buddy to guide me and keep me safe—'

'There's absolutely no danger of you falling in?' he demanded sarcastically as the ugly memories continued to play out in his head. 'And if such a thing were to happen, your dog would, of course, leap in and save you.'

'Yes, he would,' she said, ignoring his sarcasm. 'Buddy has more ability than you can possibly imagine.'

His imagination was all too active, unfortunately, and while Grace was staying here she was *his* responsibility. 'Next time you feel like putting your life at risk, call me first.'

He ground his jaw when she laughed. It would be better if Grace left immediately.

'I'm sorry if I shock you with my independence,' she said. 'Would you have preferred me to remain cowering in the guest cottage until you arrived?'

'If you expect to do any sort of business with me you should think firstly about being more polite, and secondly about being more compliant.'

'More compliant? What do you think I *am*? And if you speak like that to everyone you meet, no wonder they're not polite to you. My job, as I understand it, is to independently judge your wine—so I would have thought that for your sake, and for the success of your business, my *compliance* would be the last thing you should want.'

She had an answer for everything. His practised gaze roved over Grace's slender frame. She had changed completely in all ways but one—physically she was every bit as attractive as he remembered.

'Elias has been very good to you,' he observed, curious about this new Grace.

'Yes,' she said, relaxing for the first time. 'He took me on when no one else would even give me a job. And he paid for my training.'

It was interesting to see her open up, though the training must have been recent, which was hardly what he hoped for in an expert. 'I'm surprised Elias was less than frank with me. He only had to pick up the phone to explain what he intended to do.'

'And would you have allowed me to come if he had done that?'

He had no answer to that.

'And please don't blame your PA,' Grace insisted. 'You must have been in the air when Elias e-mailed. Your housekeepers have made me very welcome, so it would seem she has done her job to perfection.'

His PA *had* called him, but he'd hardly been listening. One of the old-timers at the business meeting he'd been attending had been telling him that Nacho's visit to London had reminded them all of the old days—when his father had gone tomcatting around Europe, he presumed. Nacho had wanted to defend himself, to protest that that might have been his father's way but it wasn't his, but he wouldn't betray his father. The conversation had taken him back to being a boy, standing tall and proud in front of his parent, and being told that Nacho would be in charge of the family while his father was away.

It was only at school that he had learned the truth. His parents weren't the only ones who had been good at keeping secrets. Nacho had kept secrets most of his life.

'You *won't* blame your PA for this, will you?' Grace pressed him.

'No, of course not,' he said, frowning as his thoughts snapped back to the present and Grace.

She nodded her thanks as she continued to walk confidently behind the dog.

She might have been on a footpath in London rather than a remote trail in the shadow of the Andes.

How could she know the difference?

Whatever he thought of Grace arriving in Elias's place, it was impossible not to rage against her fate.

'The air's so good here,' she enthused, oblivious to his thoughts as she sucked in a deep, appreciative breath. 'It's like the finest wine: crisp and ripe, laced with the scent of young fruit and fresh blossom.'

His expression changed. Perfect. A romantic. Wasn't that all he needed in a business associate? Not that Grace would be around long enough to do business with him. As soon as he could politely get rid of her he would.

But as the wind kicked up, lifting her glossy blonde hair from her shoulders, he felt exactly the same punch in the gut attraction he'd felt at the wedding.

Turning towards the mountains, he searched for distraction. The Andes were always a glorious sight—a towering reminder of the majesty of the land entrusted to him. It was a trust that even the most bitter of memories couldn't alter. The rugged peaks sheltered his vines from the worst of the weather, while the glacier-melt flowing down the slopes of those peaks sweetened the glistening purple grapes.

And Grace could see none of it...

Meeting a beautiful young woman in the first flush of her beauty and wanting her, and then barely two years later seeing her like this, was a stinging reminder that nothing in life remained the same.

'Your housekeeper mentioned you had business in South Africa?' Grace said, obviously in an attempt to get the conversation going again.

'I was there on business,' he said curtly.

No wonder Nacho had a reputation for being the most difficult of the Acosta brothers. But Grace thought she could see a reason for it. As the oldest child, responsible for his siblings, Nacho hadn't had much time for himself. Even on the polo field he was the leader of the pack, with all the responsibility that involved.

She tried again. 'I hope my using your family jet didn't leave you slumming it on a scheduled flight?'

'I'm not that precious, Grace.'

As she laughed Grace turned her head in the direction of his voice. Another solid blow to the gut hit him when he saw that gaze, so lovely, yet so misty and unfocused, miss his face. He stamped on the feeling it gave him. Grace was his responsibility only while she was here. Once she was gone that was an end of it—and she wouldn't thank him for his pity.

'Are you still there?' she called out.

'Battling to keep up,' he mocked, riding with the reins hanging loose. He had kicked his feet out of the stirrups some way back.

'You're very quiet,' she said, marching on.

'You'll know when I've got something to say.' He stared at her back—the upright stance, the pitch of her head, chin lifted. He couldn't get over how confident she had become.

Because she'd had to.

'Just let me know if I'm going too fast for you,' she mocked.

She made it hard for him to remain angry for long. In fact she reminded him in some ways of his sister, Lucia. Lucia was always pushing the boundaries, always testing him, and he could see now why the two girls were such good friends.

'I can see you have picked up some very bad habits from Lucia. And as you're not my sister, and merely work for me—'

'*With* you,' she flashed.

'As you're not my sister,' he repeated patiently, 'your privileges do not extend to goading me while you're here.'

'So you *have* accepted that I am going to be here for a while?'

'I didn't say that.'

'You didn't have to.'

This time when she turned her head in his direction he saw the smile hovering round her mouth. His gaze remained on her lips for quite some time.

'Can I ask you something, Nacho?' she said, turning back again.

'Of course,' he said, feeling the loss now he had to content himself with a view of the back of her head.

'Will you give me a list of all the places that are out of bounds so I don't make any more mistakes? In Braille, of course,' she added, tongue in cheek.

A muscle worked in his jaw. He wasn't used to this sort of insubordination. Most people obeyed him gladly. 'I'll tell you what I'll do,' he said, realising that he was going to have to play Grace's game for the short time she was here. 'I'll get a translator for you. Or you could learn my rules by rote, if you prefer.'

'Are you smiling?' she said. 'I can't tell.'

No. He was learning fast and had kept his voice carefully neutral.

'If this visit is going to be a success,' she said, bearing out his theory, 'we'll both have to make adjustments— won't we, Nacho?'

'Will we?' he said.

The breeze was on Grace's side. Catching hold of the hem of her flimsy summer dress, it flicked it, giving him a grandstand view of her smooth, tanned legs. Arousal fired inside him, but he instantly damped it down.

'Do you remember when we first met in Cornwall?' she said, pulling his attention back to her hips as she strode along. 'You had just arrived for that polo match on the beach. You rolled down the window of that monster Jeep, and—'

'And what, Grace?' he pressed, seeing her cheeks had flushed bright red. A very masculine hunger filled him at the thought that she had wanted him back then.

'I was just wondering if you remembered, that's all,' she said casually, closing the topic with a flick of her wrist.

He remembered.

When Grace fell silent it gave them both a chance to think back. She broke the silence first. 'I could see you properly then.'

Very cleverly, she gave him no clue as to whether that had been good or bad. 'You'll be pleased to know I haven't changed—'

'Hard luck,' she flashed.

How was it possible to ignore a woman like this? Or ignore the way she made him feel? No woman had made him laugh in what seemed like forever. He was glad the so-called appeal of the Acosta brothers was lost on Grace, and he would be happy if he never had to hear again in his life that he looked like his father. His gaze returned to Grace's slender hips, swaying to a rhythm that was all her own. One thing was certain: if this banter between them was a ruse to keep his interest, she had succeeded where many had failed.

'I was over-awed by you,' she admitted.

'Why?'

'Because you were so famous and seemed so aloof. And even compared to the other polo players you were huge—and so confident.'

'And at the wedding?'

'You frightened me half to death,' she admitted bluntly.

He laughed for the second time in who knew how many years. 'So how do you feel about meeting me again, Grace?'

'Well, at least I can't see you this time,' she said.

Laughter was becoming a habit he would have to break if he was to retain his title as the hard man of the Acostas. 'And does that help?'

'It certainly does,' she said.

It was a good, brave answer, but he was suspicious and couldn't resist asking, 'So, are you here to pick up where we left off?'

'As I recall,' she countered, 'when we met at the wedding I was the one to leave.'

Correct. '*Touché*, Señorita Lundström.'

A blast of white-hot lust ripped through him when she angled her head as if to cast him a flirtatious glance—though of course she could do no such thing. He liked this verbal jousting. He liked the way Grace stood up for herself. And he liked Grace. A lot.

'Is something wrong?' she called back to him. 'You've gone very quiet...'

'I'm enjoying the day,' he said, thinking it wise to confine himself, as the British so often did, to talk of the weather.

'It *is* beautiful,' she agreed, stretching out her arms.

Her arms were beautiful—slender and lightly tanned. *Grace* was beautiful. He only wished she could see how beautiful the day was—but that was a ridiculous investment of concern on his part. As was his growing admiration for Grace. Far better he got this conversation back to business, where Grace was sure to fall short and disappoint him. Then he could send her packing, and that would be the end of a fantasy where he changed from a hard, unfeeling man into the sort of hero Grace might admire.

'Buddy's certainly enjoying the weather,' she said.

'Oh, good,' he said without enthusiasm.

He stared at the dog. The dog stared back at him. He loved animals, and they normally gravitated towards him—but not this one. The big dog's loyalty was firmly fixed in stone. Nacho's attention switched back to Grace. From the back you wouldn't know anything had changed about her. Life could be very cruel sometimes, but that didn't change the facts. What the hell had Elias been thinking? What use was a blind sommelier?

'So, tell me about your job, Grace,' he said, starting to seethe as he thought about how he'd been duped by the wily old wine importer. 'How does that work?'

'What do you mean, how does it work?' she said without breaking stride. 'I might be blind, but I can still taste and smell.'

'And what about the clarity of the wine?' he pressed with increasing impatience. 'What about the sediment—the colour, the viscosity?'

'The colour I have to take on trust, when people describe it to me, but like most people I can detect sediment on my tongue. And I wouldn't expect to be offered thin or cloudy wine by anyone who took their wine seriously.'

Was that a dig at *him*? 'You seem very confident.'

'That's for you to judge when we hold the tastings.'

'We haven't got that far yet,' he reminded her, wondering if he had ever encountered this much resistance from a woman.

His gaze swept over her again. Subduing Grace would give him the greatest pleasure. And was something he would most certainly resist. He knew all about the long-term consequences resulting from impulsive actions, and he had no intention of travelling down that road again.

'Why else would I be here if not to taste your wine?' she said. 'Elias can't wait to get my verdict—and not just on your wines but on the way you produce them too.'

He heard the dip in her voice. Was she holding him to ransom so she could stay and do her job? The thought of being judged by Grace was anathema to him, but her employer, Elias, was not only one of the most respected voices in the wine industry, he was the biggest distributor in Europe. Nacho needed him. Bottom line? He couldn't risk offending Elias. But Grace had neither the experience nor the wisdom for this work. How could she match a man like Elias, who had a lifetime devoted to the development of top-quality wine?

'I know what you're thinking,' she called back. 'And I understand the reasons why you want to send me home. I apologise again if I don't fit the mould of expert you were expecting, but you should know I take my work extremely seriously and I'm very good at it—which is why Elias trusts me to do this job. Why don't you wait until you've seen me in action before you act as judge and jury and send me home?'

Was he that obvious? And as for seeing Grace in action—

Kill those thoughts. Being much younger than he was, *and* his sister's best friend, meant Grace occupied a very privileged position—not that she would ever know that.

Her dog had slowed as they approached the white picket fence marking the boundary of the guest cottage, and as Grace reached out at fence height in answer to some unseen tension on the guide dog's harness she said, 'Thank you for escorting us home, but we can take it from here...'

She was dismissing him? His gaze hardened. What if he wasn't ready to go?

Those thoughts were turned on their head by the sight of Grace tracing each blunt tip of the fence with her fingertips as she made her way to the gate. Her independence and her vulnerability touched him somewhere deep.

Having reached the gate, she was feeling for the latch. A shiver coursed down his spine at the thought of the darkness surrounding her. His instinct was always to protect and defend, so he dismounted—only to be dismissed with a blithe, 'See you later, Nacho...'

'I'll see you in,' he argued firmly. Grace was on foreign soil, and the little he knew about blindness said familiarity was everything where confidence and safety were concerned.

Opening the gate, he walked ahead of her to the front door. They'd talked the whole way, he realised, and yet his head was still full of questions: *How long were you ill? Did your sight fade quickly or slowly? How long did it take you to regain your confidence? How long have you had the dog? How much can you see—if anything?*

'It's very chivalrous of you, Nacho,' she said, pressing back against the door as if to keep him out, 'but it's really not necessary. I can manage perfectly well on my own from here.'

'Please allow me to decide what is and isn't necessary,' he said, and reaching past her opened the front door. He didn't play second in command to anyone. He'd taken the lead all his life and that was how it would stay.

'Goodbye, Nacho.'

Before he knew what was happening Grace had felt the gap between him and the door and had slipped through it with the dog at her heels.

The door closed.

So she had no more need of him? Good. He should be pleased.

He wasn't pleased.

Springing back onto his horse, he wheeled it round and galloped off.

CHAPTER FOUR

HE WAS still overheated from his exchange with Grace when he got back to the *hacienda*. The call he made to Elias would be straightforward. All he had to do was explain that Grace would be on the next flight home, and that if Elias couldn't provide an acceptable replacement Nacho would have no alternative but to look elsewhere for an expert to evaluate his wine. His hope was that it might be possible to keep Elias on board as a distributor and find an expert in whom they could both place their trust.

He should have known life was never that simple...

A coward? He had never been called a coward before by anyone—let alone by an elderly wine merchant.

A misogynist? Okay. Maybe he'd been called that a few times.

Safe to say, the conversation with Elias didn't go well.

Was Nacho referring to his Grace? Elias asked. Did Nacho dare to condemn Grace before even giving her a chance to prove herself?

All this was said on a rising cadence of wrath.

Was Nacho bigoted? Was he prejudiced against visually challenged individuals? Or was he frightened to put his wines to the test by a true expert, perhaps? Should

Elias be seriously concerned? Did Elias even have time for this nonsense?

And Nacho's answer…?

He subscribed to none of the above. He was the least prejudiced individual he knew.

He handled Elias coolly, remembering that the last time he had given free rein to his feelings the day had ended in tragedy.

'Give Grace a chance,' Elias insisted. 'You won't be disappointed.'

What did he have to lose? He could be looking for another expert while Grace did as much as she could do, he reasoned.

Having allowed Elias sufficient time to vent his anger, he ended the call with a reassurance that for Elias's sake he would give Grace another few days.

'That's too kind of you, I'm sure,' Elias snapped, and he cut the line—but not before Nacho heard the want and need in the other man's voice. They both needed something from the other, so for now Grace was staying.

And so the games begin, he thought as he stowed the phone. But, however intriguing he found Grace, he would send her home before intrigue turned to something more. If he had learned anything from the past it was that women could appear strong and then disappoint in ways that led to disaster.

Dismounting his horse at the gate of the cottage where Grace was staying, Nacho lashed the reins to the fence. Striding up the path, he rapped firmly on the door. The dog answered with a bark. Steadying his breathing, Nacho heard Grace's murmured thanks to Buddy in a voice that was gentle and affectionate, and then he heard her footsteps crossing the room to open the door.

'Nacho,' she said, in a very different tone from the one she'd used for the dog as she swung the door wide.

'You knew it was me?'

Coming straight from his call to Elias, Nacho was strung tight as a drum.

Sensing this, Grace lifted her chin. 'I will always know when it's you. Your horse has a distinctive stride. And the way you knock on the door is quite unique. I'm surprised it's still standing. And I could feel your tension a mile away—'

'My *what*?' he said.

'Exactly,' she said. 'So, what can I do for you, Nacho?'

No other woman spoke to him like this—with the possible exception of his sister, Lucia. Was this aloof attitude some defence mechanism Grace had perfected since going blind? Did she push everyone away now?

'You should move into the main house,' he said brusquely.

He had already turned and was on his way, having anticipated Grace's immediate compliance—her gratitude, even.

'Is that your acceptance speech?' she said, calling him back. 'Have you been speaking to Elias, by any chance?'

'You've spoken to him too?' he said.

'I might have done,' she fudged. 'So, am I to stay, Nacho? Is this your invitation?'

'I suppose you could call it one,' he conceded brusquely.

'But why would you want me to move into the main house?'

'Because you'll get the assistance you need there, obviously.'

'I beg your pardon?' she said.

'You'll be more comfortable,' he explained impatiently, knowing he should try to be more diplomatic.

'I'm very comfortable where I am, thank you,' she said coolly. 'And I wouldn't dream of inconveniencing you.'

'Don't be so ridiculous, Grace. How would you be inconveniencing me?'

'By making you more angry than you are now? By having you walk on eggshells during my stay? By making you feel duty-bound to watch over me?' She finished the tirade with an angry gesture. 'How much more time must I waste convincing you that I don't need any special treatment, Nacho?'

'How much time would *you* waste?' he fired back incredulously.

'Haven't you got it yet?' she said. 'I'm completely independent.'

'Don't tell me what to think, Grace,' he warned. 'If you're going to work for me, I'll show you the same consideration I show all my staff and not one iota more. Unless, of course, you're looking for pity?'

'Well, thanks for the heads-up,' she flashed, 'but I'm not working for *you*. I'm working for Elias. And if I were looking for pity—which I'm not—you would be the last person I'd turn to.'

He took a step back as she slammed the door in his face. Raking his hair with angry fingers, he was forced to admit that she'd got one thing right—he was the last person she *should* turn to. But that didn't change anything. His mind was made up.

Balling his fist, he hammered on the door.

'What now?' Grace demanded, flinging it wide.

'Do you mind if I come in for a moment?'

'It's your guest cottage,' she reminded him with a shrug. She stood well clear as Nacho walked in, and was glad

of Buddy's warm presence nestling protectively against
her legs. Closing the door after him, she heard Nacho
start to pace. The room seemed smaller suddenly, and
the air swirled around him as if it were in turmoil too.

No one had ever affected her like this. No one had
ever frightened her quite so much, or made her want
things so much she couldn't think straight. She'd been a
fool to imagine she could ever do business with Nacho as
if they had never met—as if she had never felt his hands
on her arms or his lips on her mouth.

'I can see you're coping really well, Grace.'

Not right now she wasn't.

'Please don't patronise me,' she flashed. 'And please
don't feel you must make a speech. There are people far
worse off than me who pick up their lives and get on with
things. I don't need your sympathy, Nacho. I'm here to do
a job. All I ask is that you treat me like anyone else and
make no allowances. You don't even have to be around
while I'm working. I'm quite happy to liaise with your
people and with Elias back home. I can draw up a report
and send it to you as soon as we're finished. You don't
even have to know I'm here.'

'Grace, please sit down.'

'I prefer to stand, if you don't mind,' she said, keeping the back of the chair between them like a shield.

'As you wish. You're right. I have spoken to Elias and
we have agreed that you may taste the wine.'

'Really?' For the sake of her old friend she somehow
managed to hide her affront.

'And when you've finished the tasting,' Nacho went
on, 'I'll arrange for your flight home.'

'There's more to this job than tasting wine.' She was
in turmoil, and her promise to Elias hung by a thread.

Her body was pulled one way by Nacho's sheer magnetism, while her mind was being pulled another. She wanted to stay, to experience more of Nacho, and yet she wanted to tell him to go to hell. She forced her thoughts back to business. 'Elias needs a lot more information before he's in a position to place an order.'

'Enough,' Nacho said firmly. 'That is all.'

'Are you firing me?' Before he had chance to answer, she demanded, 'On what grounds?' Her resolve to remain calm and concentrate on business had completely vanished as her anger increased. 'You haven't even given me a chance to prove myself.'

'I don't have time to waste on a novice. And I won't take chances with family money. I need an expert *now*, Grace.'

'So let me get this straight. You're prepared to allow me to taste the wine, but any comment I make will be classified as one amateur chatting informally to another?'

'I'm sorry, Grace. I realise how disappointed you must be.'

'You have no idea,' she said bitterly.

'Please don't worry about your homeward journey,' Nacho went on, as if she hadn't spoken. 'You will be flown home in my jet, and I'll smooth your path at the other end—'

'I don't need you or anyone else to *smooth my path,*' she interrupted angrily. 'Believe it or not, Nacho, I've been doing very well on my own without your help. I'm quite capable of booking a scheduled flight and having a cab take me to the airport!'

'And your dog?'

Grace went still. Hadn't they warned her at the rehabilitation centre to always give herself time to think? Couldn't she see why now? 'I'm sure I can arrange something,' she insisted, her stomach churning as she hoped that was true.

'There's no need,' Nacho assured her calmly. 'It's all in hand. And you don't have to worry about Elias, either. I'll explain that you didn't feel ready for an assignment of this size.'

'And he'll laugh in your face,' she said, realising time was running out as she heard Nacho's hand on the door handle. Against all that was sensible she wanted— needed—him to stay.

'My decision on this is final, Grace.'

'You're making a big mistake.' Following the sound of his voice she put her hand on his arm—only to draw it back again as if she had been burned.

'It's a job that's too big for you, Grace,' Nacho argued. 'Elias expects too much of you. And the outcome is far too vital for me to take a chance—'

'On a blind woman?' she flashed.

Silence greeted this, even as shame scorched her cheeks. That had been a low blow, and one she had promised herself she would never resort to.

'You disappoint me, Grace,' Nacho said quietly. 'I was about to say for me to take a chance on a novice like you. Restoring the family vineyards is a multi-million-dollar venture and I won't risk failure.'

'Which is why you consulted Elias, presumably?' she said, playing her last card. The thought of leaving this job unfinished, of leaving with her tail between her legs—the thought of leaving Nacho and maybe never seeing him again—was devastating to her. 'Don't you trust Elias's judgement?'

'Up to the point where we met in London—and then Elias conveniently forgot to tell me that he wouldn't be coming to view the vineyards himself.'

'He hasn't been well recently.'

Silence told her that Nacho had had no idea about this.

'I only saw him recently,' he said in a puzzled tone.

'He hides it well,' she admitted.

Shifting position, Nacho exhaled heavily. 'I'm sorry to hear that.'

But not sorry enough to change his mind, Grace concluded, hearing the door open. Nacho was happy to accept the judgement of a master vintner like Elias, but he was not prepared to listen to a girl he associated with nightclubs, silly costumes and trays of drinks.

With nothing left to lose, she said, 'As my time here is short, shall we get the wine-tasting done tonight?' The only way to convince Nacho she had anything to offer was to prove herself to him.

The door squeaked, as if he were pulling it to again, which she took to be a good sign.

'How about a blind tasting?' she suggested without a trace of irony. 'Elias warned you have a very fine palate...for an amateur.'

'Are you insulting me? Or is that meant to be a compliment?'

Was that a touch of humour in Nacho's voice at last? Her body heated at the thought while her mind told her to remain focused on her job. 'I thought it might appeal to your competitive spirit,' she said innocently, dragging greedily on the scent of warm, clean Nacho.

'Go on,' he prompted.

She heard the door click shut. 'I'm inviting you to share a sensory evaluation of your wine with me.' Why did that sound so suggestive and risky? She pressed on. 'You'll have the advantage of sight, while I can only use my other senses.'

'How many advantages do you think I need, Grace?'

Nacho's voice was carefully neutral, but she suspected he had decided to accept her challenge. 'This will be your chance to discover if I'm as good as Elias says I am.'

'Okay,' he said. But just when she was silently rejoicing he added, 'Pack your case and if you fail you'll be ready to leave.'

'I won't fail,' she said, firming her jaw.

'I guess we'll find out tonight, Grace,' Nacho murmured, sounding utterly confident that the result would go in his favour.

She felt the cool night air on her face as he opened the door.

'I'll be back to collect you at six,' he said.

'And I'll be ready for you,' she promised as she moved towards the door.

With a gasp she stumbled over a chair leg, and would have fallen to the floor if Nacho hadn't caught her.

'Grace—'

She was in his arms, which felt so good, so safe, so right. But it wasn't supposed to be like this. Nacho wasn't supposed to be rescuing her because she couldn't see where she was going. The only time she wanted him to hold her like this was under very different circumstances. And that clearly wasn't going to happen...

She pulled herself upright.

'Sit down, Grace. Catch your breath,' he said, stepping back.

The cold tone in Nacho's voice told her everything she needed to know. He had been as far from being about to kiss her as it was possible to get. Why would he want a blind woman when he could have any woman?

'Goodbye, Grace.'

He closed the door carefully behind him—and then hit the wall backhanded with his fist. He barely felt the blow. All he felt was Grace—in every part of him. However hard he tried to fight off the feeling, Grace fought back with her indomitable spirit, her unique qualities, and her sheer unadulterated sex appeal.

Saving Grace when she'd stumbled had only reminded him how attractive she was—and how emotionally inconvenient spending time with her this evening would be for him. The thought of kissing Grace had lost none of its appeal, and if he hadn't seen first hand how one rash decision could spread disaster like ripples on a pond he would have done more than kiss her. But he had enough on his conscience already without yielding to his every whim.

Her world seemed darker than ever now Nacho had gone. She curled up in a chair with her thoughts in pieces. Mostly they were centred on her arms, where he'd held her, and on her mouth, where he *hadn't* kissed her.

Why would he? Why would anyone want to kiss a blind woman? She could prove herself to as many people in as many ways as she wanted, but she could never get past the fact that she was blind. That was how people saw her—how they would always see her—how Nacho would always see her. The joke of it was she had forgotten she was blind while she had been with him. She'd smiled and laughed and parried his comments, even got angry with him—all of which had felt perfectly normal and exciting. He'd made her forget what she might be missing out on and had filled her world with so much more besides.

But now he'd left it was as if that light had gone out and now there was nothing but darkness around her again. And fear was back, fierce and strong, and fear said no one would ever see past her blindness.

CHAPTER FIVE

It was no use. Feeling sorry for herself would get her absolutely nowhere. She held the record for proof of that. She had to get on with things.

The room was becoming increasingly chilly, which meant the sun was close to setting—which in turn meant Nacho would soon be back to take her to the wine-tasting. Whatever had happened between them—now or at the wedding—her job came first, and she was going to look the part by the time he knocked on the door.

Getting ready for a night out wasn't so different these days from the way it used to be—other than the thought of spending a whole evening in close proximity to Nacho, which put her on edge. She would just have to get over it, Grace reasoned.

Having showered and rubbed her hair dry on a towel in the bathroom she had mapped out carefully when she had first arrived, she dressed in what—thanks to Lucia's system—she knew was a pair of white capris, flesh-coloured sandals and a pale blue, short-sleeved cotton top. She smoothed her hair and tied it back. Make-up was easy. She'd been lucky in that she'd had some warning her sight was going, so she'd had a chance to practise her technique.

It was so easy for her now that she could actually do

her make-up without even thinking about it, Grace reflected wryly as she slicked some gloss on her bottom
lip and pressed her lips together. Her cheeks felt hot
enough from the thought of seeing Nacho again not to
need any rouge, and she was lucky to have been born
with black eyelashes. But she still liked her eyeshadow.
Two sweeps of the small brush across the pot, blow on
brush, apply, repeat. In the early days Lucia had used
to stand ready with wet wipes to correct any errors, but
then one day Lucia had done nothing, and they had both
shrieked in triumph as they threw their arms around each
other and hugged.

A sharp bark from Buddy warned Grace that her visitor had arrived. Carefully feeling her way downstairs,
she paused to draw in a steadying breath before opening the door. That bolt of excitement—the way her heart
reacted when Nacho was close by—had nothing to do
with being blind and everything to do with Nacho. Just
the thought of being close to him again made her world
tilt on its axis. She didn't want his pity for being blind,
but even more than that she didn't want him thinking
she was an impressionable female incapable of function-
ing normally and doing her job while he was around.

'Well, this is it, Buddy,' she said, firming her jaw.
'We're all set.'

She opened the door and the breath left her lungs in
a rush. So much for her good intentions, Grace thought,
taking a moment to get over the Nacho effect.

'Grace…'

No matter how cool Nacho's greeting, the masculinity firing off him was hot, hot, hot. She knew he was
towering over her, staring down, and she knew he was
very close.

'Hi...' She spoke brightly, with a smile, trying to sound as if this were a regular day at the office.

But it didn't work, she realised when he didn't speak. Her cheeks fired red. This was like stepping out into the void without a safety net. She couldn't really tell if she'd managed to dress and put her make up on without making too many goofs. Her hair might be standing on end for all she knew. She smoothed it self-consciously.

'Ready to go, Grace?'

'Yes, of course.'

Her throat felt tight as she reached for her briefcase. That was a small victory. She heard Nacho swoop to get it for her, but she got there first. She rarely lost anything these days, because it was so crucial she knew where everything was, and she had left it ready. Hanging the strap crossways over her body, she called Buddy, found the handle of his harness and reached for the door.

Was the air actually fizzing with electricity as she walked past Nacho or was that all in her head?

He closed the door behind them, and somehow managed to be at the gate in front of them.

'The Jeep's ahead of you, Grace. Would you like me to put Buddy in the back?'

'That's all right. I'll do it.'

She was going to start as she meant to go on. This was business and she was going to do it right. She felt her way round to the back of the vehicle. It was already open, and she did a good job of loading Buddy. It was only when she came round to the passenger door that she hit a snag. She mapped the door time after time, with increasingly sweaty palms, but she still couldn't find the handle. She felt so stupid—so hot and bothered—so frustrated.

'I presume I'm allowed to do *this* much for you?'

She took a step back as the door opened. Did she appear *so* prickly and defensive? Grace wondered as Nacho helped her in.

The answer to that was yes. She wasn't cut out for the role of victim. But there was no reason to overreact to every little comment he made, either.

Feeling for the seat, she settled in and Nacho swung in beside her. When he closed the door she had the sense of being contained in a very small space with him. He was a huge physical presence, but then she had always known that. It was Nacho's physicality and energy rather than the sheer size of him getting to her now, and she was heating up all over just at the thought of his big body closing in on her own small frame. She could smell that he was still damp from the shower and had used some sort of menthol soap…or perhaps that was toothpaste? Anyway, he smelled really good.

Were her nipples erect? she wondered suddenly. Could she risk checking? She decided not, and crossed her arms over her chest instead as he started the engine and they moved off. She could imagine his powerful hands on the wheel, controlling their direction with the lightest of touches. The leather seats were big and comfortable. She explored hers discreetly, and then relaxed. The seats were huge. There was no chance they could rub up against each other accidentally.

'It's just a short drive to our newly refurbished wine facility,' Nacho explained. 'We could have walked there, but I thought you might be tired after the upheaval of the day.'

Now she couldn't tell if he was smiling, frowning, or even laughing at her. He'd cottoned on very quickly to the fact that she could read a lot from a voice and was becoming increasingly clever at masking his opinion.

'That's very thoughtful of you,' she replied, settling for not making anything of his comment. 'I'm looking forward to tasting the wines.'

'Viticulture in this area goes back centuries,' he said, going on to explain something of its history.

She breathed a sigh of relief, realising that Nacho was actually treating her like an intelligent human being. 'So you're the guardian of history around here?'

'That's a nice way to put it,' Nacho agreed, and this time there really was some warmth in his voice.

Her first compliment, Grace registered—not that she was looking for any. Especially as they made her cheeks burn red.

'I'm only sorry you won't be able to see the old buildings we've been restoring,' Nacho commented.

She was taken aback for a moment, but then she realised she appreciated his frankness. 'Don't worry,' she said. 'I process loads of mental images through my other senses. And don't forget I have a whole library of images to draw on from the days when I *could* see. I'm lucky in that respect.'

'Yes, you are,' he agreed.

For the first time she began to relax. Nacho's candour suited her. To be treated normally was exactly what she wanted.

'So, what are your impressions of Argentina so far, Grace?'

'Well, it's certainly lovely weather after a freezing cold British winter, and the people are very kind. And there are all sorts of wonderful new scents and sounds here.'

'Horses?' he suggested dryly.

'Different,' she said. 'And there's a sort of samba rhythm in the air.'

Nacho laughed. 'Still the romantic, Grace?'

Was she?

'Still mining for choice pieces of information to add to our forward promotion for your wines—if Elias places an order,' she said coolly.

They fell silent after that sally, each rebalancing their opinion of the other, she thought.

Cocooned in darkness, she was given a chance to think back to the first time she'd seen Nacho. She'd found him frighteningly attractive, and in particular had seen something incredible about his eyes. He had such a keen stare it had seemed to suck information from her brain, while Nacho's own thoughts remained guarded. She remembered he rode with a bandana to keep his unruly hair from his eyes. When she had first seen him dressed for polo, with that bandana instead of a helmet, she had thought he looked exactly like the king of the brigands as he led his team out. He was clearly the boss and everyone accepted his leadership.

Maybe it was that edge of danger about Nacho, that sense of him having seen things and done things that might shock her if she knew about them, that perversely made him all the more attractive. An inconvenience she would have to get over if she wanted to appear business-like tonight.

'Grace?'

'Sorry.' She rejigged her thoughts. 'I was just thinking—I mean, I was just trying to imagine your wine facility.'

'I'll describe it to you.'

'That would be great,' she said, surprised to find him so amenable. 'Is the river close by?'

'Why do you ask?'

His voice had changed completely. She could have

kicked herself. Of course she knew about the tragedy—
everyone did—but there was something in Nacho's voice
she hadn't heard before. Something that suggested that
although his parents might have drowned in a flood there
years ago the tragedy still affected him. What really surprised her was that Nacho had always appeared to be the
ultimate in grounded men, but there was a strand of defensive anger in his voice, along with what could only
be described as guilt and raw grief.

'So, I gather you like it here?' he said, changing the
subject.

She guessed that was a welcome relief for him, and
needed no encouragement to enthuse about her experience so far.

'Like it here? I *love* it,' she said impulsively. 'What
was it like growing up on the pampas, Nacho?'

She had said something wrong again, Grace realised
when the silence thickened.

'It was all sorts of hectic chaos,' he said at last.

'Go on,' she prompted, eager to keep the faltering
conversation going.

'There was no privacy,' he said, revealing the other
side to Lucia's coin.

It probably hadn't ever occurred to Lucia that her
brothers had been fighting to express their individual-
ity too.

'Not nearly as much freedom as you might expect,'
Nacho went on. 'And nowhere to go. When you're young
all you want is the city and the nightlife, and what you
get here is miles of wilderness, mountains and the stars.'

'And because you were the oldest you always had
to look after your brothers and sister?' Grace guessed.
Grasping the nettle, she dived back into the past, where
she suspected Nacho's ghosts lay. 'Lucia said that after

your parents were killed you worked very hard at looking after them.'

'I did my best,' he said, clearly not willing to be drawn on this point.

'That must have been hard for you,' she probed.

'Not really,' he said, shifting restlessly in his seat. 'Lucia had the worst of it,' he said after a few moments. 'Growing up must have been hell for her, with four brothers looking over her shoulders.'

'God help her if she got a boyfriend, I suppose?' Grace suggested with a grin.

This time she could imagine Nacho's ironic expression as he murmured, 'So she told you?'

As the tension eased a little she decided she would have to be patient. They'd get around to talking about Nacho eventually—she'd make sure of it. 'What about your brothers?'

'Ruiz was the perfect student,' Nacho explained with a shrug in his voice. 'He was also the perfect son and the perfect brother. In fact Ruiz never put a foot wrong. He always knew how to get on with everyone and how to get his own way. Diego was the dark side of that coin— dangerous, some said, though I always thought that was overstated. Diego was just deep.'

'And what about the youngest? Kruz?' she pressed.

She heard Nacho scratch his cheek, the stubble resistant against his fingernail. 'Kruz was a handful...' He sighed. 'Kruz was always in trouble.'

'And you?' she slipped in, sensing that talking about Kruz was opening up a whole can of worms. Nacho would probably prefer talking about himself—as difficult as she knew he found that.

'Me?' he said. 'I spent most of my time getting Kruz out of trouble.'

'That's not what I meant and you know it,' she chided, realising he'd eluded her again.

'I know what you meant,' Nacho assured her. 'And all I'm prepared to say on that subject is that what you see is what you get with me, Grace.'

Right up to that moment she'd had no reason to disbelieve a word Nacho said, but now she did.

'The gates,' Nacho explained as the Jeep dropped a gear and began to slow. He brought it to a halt.

'They must be big gates,' Grace observed, noting the length of time it took for them to open.

Nacho confirmed this, and then the Jeep growled and they drove on.

'We're approaching the old buildings down a long, tree-lined drive,' he explained.

'It's brilliantly lit,' she said. 'One of the things I can still detect is a big change in light.' She felt she had to explain this as she sensed his surprise that she should know anything about the light levels. 'I'm really lucky in that I can still detect light. It has helped me to work out which way round I'm facing on many occasions. When you can't see anything much, you're happy to take what you can get.' She laughed, but Nacho was silent.

They drove in silence. She could imagine Nacho steering with just his thumb on the wheel at this low speed, perhaps sparing her a glance from time to time. She sensed he was totally relaxed and yet thoroughly observant—as he was on horseback, and as he had been at the wedding where they had kissed. Even when he was still she thought he gave off about the same level of threat as a sleeping tiger.

'The building is old—mellow stone,' he explained, breaking the silence as he brought the Jeep to a halt again. 'It's beautifully preserved. Right now the moon-light is making the stone glow a silvery-blue.'

'And the sun will turn it rose-pink in late afternoon,' she guessed. 'There's more light now,' she said with in-terest, sitting up. 'A different light.'

'Wrought-iron lanterns hanging either side of the main doors,' Nacho explained. 'They give off quite a strong glow. It makes the mullioned windows on either side of the door glitter. How am I doing, Grace?' he said with a hint of amusement as he applied the brake.

'Not bad,' she said with a small smile. 'And how about the front door? No, don't tell me. It's huge and arched… stout oak with iron studs?'

'Argentine sandalwood,' he explained. 'But other-wise that's not a bad description, Grace. Welcome to Viña Acosta.'

Where my trial by wine begins, she thought, releas-ing her safety belt.

She climbed down carefully when Nacho opened the door, guessing his hand was there to help her if she needed it. She avoided it in the interests of independence, but she did feel it brush her back, where it lit a series of little fires she couldn't ignore.

Nacho let Buddy out of the back of the Jeep and when the guide dog came to her side she attached the leash to Buddy's harness. 'We're all set,' she confirmed.

Nacho led her into a pleasantly warm entrance hall with a stone floor. It wasn't large. She could tell that by the way their voices bounced off the walls and were very quickly muffled. The smell was distinctive and familiar. It reminded her of the tasting room at the warehouse, but here she guessed the woodwork would be impreg-nated with centuries worth of fruit and must and skins and juice.

'This is the tasting room,' Nacho explained as he opened another door. 'There aren't any steps.'

Grace had already guessed as much from the way Buddy was leading her, but she thanked Nacho for the warning.

'If you'd like to sit down, Grace?'

Recognising this request, Buddy led her across an uneven stone floor to a wooden bench. He stopped when Grace felt it nudge her legs. She reached forward to feel for the table she knew must be there and, gauging the space in between bench and table, she slid into the seat. While she was unhitching Buddy's harness she heard a rug hit the floor.

'He might as well be comfortable while we do this,' Nacho explained.

She smiled, remembering Lucia telling her that where animals were concerned nothing was too much trouble for her brothers. But if you were human…? Basically, forget it.

Now she could hear glasses chinking, and bottles being moved around. 'Are we alone?'

'Absolutely,' Nacho confirmed as he put bottles on the table. 'I had some of these wines opened earlier.'

'Good idea,' she said, and knew that just when she should be at her most professional she was feeling disorientated again. This was a familiar feeling in new surroundings, and one she would have to conquer, but there wasn't time tonight. At least she was sitting down. It wouldn't be the first time she had tripped over something. Even with Buddy's help, she sometimes forgot her restrictions and went flying.

But that wasn't going to happen tonight, Grace reassured herself firmly.

'Buddy?'

Hearing the big dog shift position, she was pleased to note he wasn't too far away. Buddy knew he was still on duty, but he hadn't heard the imperative note in her voice that called him to action. She mapped the table in front of her, feeling for glasses and bottles and other hazards. She always put down mental markers so she could understand her surroundings better. She listened intently as Nacho poured. Even the sound wine made as it glugged from the bottle told a story.

As the sound of her rapid breathing compared to Nacho's steady inhalations told another, Grace realised, consciously steadying herself.

'Right. Are we ready?' he said. 'I've labelled the bottles and glasses on the bottom, so that I can't see them when you swap them round.'

'An even playing field,' she agreed.

She had to concentrate fiercely and not think about that husky voice with its intriguing accent, or those dark eyes watching her every move.

As she tasted the first sample she could only wish Nacho's thoughts were as easy to read as the wine. Elias had described him as a gifted amateur, and when it came to wine no doubt that was true, but where women were concerned Nacho was a master of his craft. It was a thought that made her tremble with awareness.

'Well?' he said. 'What do you think so far, Grace?'

What did she think? Where wine was concerned she was utterly confident. Where Nacho was concerned she was out of her depth.

'Grace?'

She tensed when he came to sit beside her on the bench. She hadn't expected that.

'Spit or swallow?' he said.

She almost laughed. Nacho's blunt question while

his hard thigh brushing hers was just the wake-up call she needed.

'At this initial informal tasting I'm going to drink a mouthful of each wine.' She explained why. 'I like to hold it in my mouth and then feel the wine run through me. My stomach usually has something useful to say. I'll need water and coffee beans—to clean my palate and clear my nose. Every sommelier has their own way of doing things and this is mine. Don't worry, I've brought them with me.' She reached into her bag.

'Whatever it takes,' Nacho agreed.

'Not bad,' she commented after tasting the first couple of wines. 'But not great. And don't even ask me to *touch* this one,' she added when Nacho pressed a third glass in her hand. The smell was enough to put her off. 'Please don't waste my time with cheap tricks or rejects. I thought time was important to both of us.'

She felt his surprise, though he made no comment. He was cool. She'd give him that.

She *wasn't* cool, and breath shot out of her lungs when their fingers touched over the next glass.

'Very good,' she said, recovering fast. Burying her nose, she inhaled deeply. 'This is really very good.' She lifted her chin and wished she could see Nacho to show him her enthusiasm.

'It's a deep cardinal-red with bluish purple tones,' he explained.

'Young,' she added, taking another sniff. 'Full of the scent of ripe black fruit...'

'And?' Nacho prompted.

'And very well balanced,' she said, sensing his face was very close. Swallowing deep, she tried to concentrate. 'This is one of the best young wines I've tasted this year.'

'I have another, older wine I think you're going to like…'

She relaxed as he pulled away, and yet ached with disappointment that he had.

More wine was poured. She heard Nacho take a sip and imagined him savouring the ruby liquid in his mouth. 'I hope you're not cheating.'

'I don't need to cheat, Grace. Here—taste this…'

Somewhere in the room a clock was ticking as the tension mounted between them.

'What do you think?' Nacho prompted, 'Do you like it?'

'Yes…' She straightened up. 'This is an exceptional wine. It's older, richer and more complex than any wine I've tasted in England. I can detect more than one variety of grape.' She named them.

'You have an extremely discerning palate, Grace.'

'Isn't that what you're paying me for?' she said with amusement.

He liked the fact that Grace stood up to him, but as she went on to describe traces of chocolate and cinnamon, with hints of blackcurrant and cherry, he liked her a lot more. Not because of her expertise in wine, but because of the way his thoughts were turning to ruby-red wine moistening beautifully drawn lips, and drinking from those lips before sinking his tongue deep into Grace's mouth to capture the last drop, before moving on to lap more wine from the soft swell of her belly.

With his mind happily employed, he spoke his thoughts out loud. 'Is there anything I can do to speed things up?'

'If you mean can I guarantee an order now?' she said, breaking the spell, 'I'm afraid the answer's no. I need to know a lot more about your production methods before we can reach that stage.'

He was disappointed in Grace's businesslike manner. He was more disappointed in that than in the fact that placing an order for his wine wasn't immediately forthcoming. The Acosta name generally provoked a certain type of response—and delay or refusal was unheard of. But not with Grace, it seemed.

His brooding gaze lingered on her face. She had stood out for him at Lucia's wedding amongst all the flashy birds of paradise and she was lovelier than ever now. He found her bewitching, and he knew there was steel lurking beneath that calm exterior, making the playing field between them more even. So where he might have stood off at one time, bound by respect and restraint, those barriers no longer stood between them.

'I can reassure you that so far everything looks very promising,' she said.

'I couldn't agree more,' he said.

Grace had missed the irony. Or had she? What was hiding behind that composed front? Familiar with secrets, he knew the signs and suspected Grace's brave front hid a world of self-doubt. It occurred to him then that she must have cried at some point about her loss of sight. She must have railed against her fate. Who had held her when she had broken down in tears? Had anyone? She reminded him of a wounded bird that was determined to survive—which made his recent thoughts seem like those of a cold-hearted predator wheeling overhead.

'The flavours of this wine are complex, and the aroma is particularly distinct,' she said, burying her nose and inhaling deeply.

'On that we're agreed,' he said, far more interested in watching Grace now than in tasting the wine.

'Then why are you frowning?' she said.

'Am I?'

'Don't deny it. I can hear it in your voice, Nacho.'

'I'll have to frown less,' he said.

When she laughed her soft blonde hair, which had only been loosely held, escaped the band she had tied it up in and came to drift around her shoulders like a gold net veil.

'Oh, damn!' she exclaimed, impatiently grabbing her hair as if it was one of her most annoying features rather than one of her loveliest. 'Let me tie this back.'

'Leave it loose,' he said.

Ignoring him, she made short work of the repair. 'Smile,' she prompted, hearing the irritation in his voice. 'These wines are really good. You should be celebrating.'

It felt good to be like this with a woman—making some sort of real contact outside of bed and having her stand up to him for once.

'In fact, your wine's so good,' Grace went on, 'I'm going to forgive most of your transgressions.'

'I wasn't aware that I was guilty of any,' he said, warming even more to Grace.

'Well, I'm going to move on to the next part of my evaluation,' she said.

'Which is?' he said suspiciously.

'Drinking your health,' she said, disarming him.

They both reached for the same glass at the same time and their fingers touched. Grace snatched her hand away, as if she'd been burned, while his inner voice warned that he was playing a very dangerous game indeed if he wanted to send Grace home, because he could only wish that touch had lingered.

'This wine would benefit from being in storage a little longer,' she said, purely business—though she couldn't know his interest was now drawn to her lips. 'I can tell you now that we won't be ordering this one just yet. I'd like to taste it again next year.'

'Next year?' he repeated with amusement. 'You're very sure of yourself, Grace.'

'Why shouldn't I be?' she said. 'Do you think I'll have left Elias by then?'

He shrugged. 'I wouldn't know.'

Grace could be enigmatic when it suited her, and at other times be surprisingly frank. He wasn't used to mystery where women were concerned. He wasn't used to them holding out on him, either. But Grace was different. Other women had a straightforward agenda that dovetailed nicely with his. They communicated their messages with a glance—an option that wasn't open to Grace. Would she use that sort of tactic anyway? Grace was so forthright she was more likely to come straight out and tell him exactly what she wanted.

Could be interesting, he mused as he watched her roll the wine around her mouth.

'I need a moment,' she said, feeling for a space on the table to put her glass. 'I'd like to get some preparatory notes down. And while I'm doing that shall I e-mail Elias to warn him I shall be returning home tomorrow?'

No woman had ever presented him with a veiled threat before, and Grace had done so in such a clever way that he would have to think up some equally elegant punishment for her. He knew just the thing, and his senses roared as he thought about it.

'You mentioned seeing the wine in production,' he remarked, easing back from the table. 'So you can't leave tomorrow. I want that order, Grace. And there's an event I think you'd be interested in finding out more about.'

'Well, if you want me to stay…'

Clever girl, he thought, making it seem like his idea.

'I want you to finish the job,' he said. 'And I want a positive outcome.'

'Of course you do,' she agreed.

He wasn't ready to let Grace go yet, he realised, when he saw the corner of her mouth tip up. He wanted to know more about her. He wanted to know everything about her.

'What is this event?' she asked, distracting him.

'One of the wildest celebrations of the year—and extremely relevant,' he added in a serious tone, pulling his mind away from its stroll on the dark side.

'And you're sure it's important for me to know more about it?'

'Positive,' he said.

Teasing Grace was a delight, he decided as she reached for her laptop.

But as she took hold of it somehow she lost her grip, and as the computer slipped from her hands it sent bottles and wine glasses flying, spraying wine across the room.

'No harm done,' he said, snatching at Grace with one hand, to stop her falling, and her laptop with the other before it hit the floor.

'I feel such an idiot!' she exclaimed angrily.

'Nothing's damaged except your pride,' he pointed out, but as he settled everything back in place, including Grace, he noticed that she was close to tears.

Recovering fast, she sniffed noisily. 'Did I get you?' she said.

He ruffled his hair. 'Will it disappoint you too much if I say no?'

When she smiled his heart nearly exploded. He reached forward on impulse—to say something, to reassure her, maybe—but as Grace turned to look at him with a rueful expression on her face, and he knew she couldn't see him, a touch or an explanation of how he felt no longer seemed enough.

He leaned forward and kissed her instead. It was a crazy, impulsive thing to do—and more telling than he could have imagined.

'I'll get a cloth,' he said as she gasped, 'and some soda water,' he added, pulling back.

'Please don't worry,' she said tensely, feeling the extent of the damage with her hands. 'I can always soak my clothes overnight.'

Something inside him snapped. 'Do you always have to be so damned independent?' he exclaimed with frustration.

There was a pause, and then she said softly, 'Yes, I do.'

CHAPTER SIX

SHE'D made such a mess of everything. That was the only conclusion she could draw when she woke the next morning.

For a moment she couldn't move or think for her embarrassment. Her head was full of the wine flying everywhere and Nacho's consoling kiss. It was a gesture he might have made towards Lucia in one of his softer moments, and there had been nothing more said about it when he had brought her home. He'd simply seen her to the door and then left.

Grace's only consolation was that she knew she had done a good job with the wine. Elias was right. The Acosta vineyards were producing wine of exceptional quality now. The only question was, could they sustain it? What condition were the vineyards in, for instance. At least she could take some pleasure in knowing she had the edge over Nacho at the tasting. It could take ten years or more to become a master sommelier, but she had such a passion for the work she was getting there quicker than most. But that could never be uppermost in her mind now, because Nacho occupied *that* spot.

Swinging out of bed, she padded across the warm wooden floor in the direction of the open window, following the breeze. Opening the window a little more, she leaned over the sill to enjoy the sunshine. It was going to be a lovely day. She could smell the grass, its scent intensified by the dew, and the blossom that Nacho's housekeeper had explained twirled in big fat loops around the window. She dipped her fingers into the cool damp petals, enjoying both the feel of them and their scent.

She could smell horses too, Grace realised, raising her head. And hear them—along with a group of men's voices.

Conscious that she was only wearing pyjamas, she pulled back and stood to one side of the window, where she hoped she wouldn't be seen. Those older, gruffer voices must belong to the *gauchos* who worked with the horses. She smiled to think they must be herding ponies right past her bedroom window. What an experience! Wild Criollas from the pampas, she guessed. The noise was growing louder and dust was tickling her nose.

'I'd love to ride one,' she informed Buddy, who had come to snuggle at her legs, no doubt as keen as she was to explore outside.

The horses sounded like a crowd of naughty schoolchildren just set free for the holidays, Grace thought, listening hard for the distinctive prance of Nacho's stallion. But even without him this was kind of exciting, with the *gauchos* whooping and whistling as they rode past. If only she could see them...

The pain of loss almost doubled her over. She had been warned about this at the hospital, and though she knew that grieving for something that couldn't be changed was a pointless exercise it didn't stop it hurting.

She would just have to wait it out, Grace reasoned, biting hard on her lip. She refused to let it spoil her day.

A day without Nacho was already ruined, she reflected, wishing she could go home and forget all about this stupid mission.

But that was the last thing she really wanted to do, Grace realised, calming down. She had earned her right to be here, and she was going to stay until the job was done. She was going to take a shower and get dressed, and then she was going to take Buddy for his walk. She had always known that repairing the damage to her confidence when she'd lost her sight was never going to happen overnight. She just had to get used to these setbacks and accept that in the scheme of things two years was only a blink on her journey to recovery.

'Yes, I'm out riding,' he informed Lucia impatiently. 'I've been out since dawn. Why didn't you tell me about Grace? And don't tell me she asked you not to, because you're my sister and this is family.'

'And Grace is my friend,' Lucia fired back. 'And there is such a thing as loyalty to your friends, Nacho. Didn't *you* teach me that?' his sister added sharply. 'I don't know what all the fuss is about. Grace is making a great recovery, and I hate it when people treat her differently. I never thought *you* would.'

'I never said I had—'

'So what's your problem, Nacho? Why are you calling me in the middle of the night?'

'Is it?' he said, only now realising that with his head full of Grace he hadn't considered the time difference. 'Don't you have a baby to feed? What are you complaining about?'

'You're all heart, Nacho. Thanks to you, said baby is now wide awake and howling.'

'So go feed him,' he said as lusty screams threatened

to deafen them both. 'But before you go tell me more about Grace—'

'What do you want to know?' his sister demanded impatiently. 'That Grace is the bravest woman I know? That she copes with what's happened to her without complaint? I hope you're not being mean to her, Nacho. She needs our love—'

'*Your* love, maybe.'

'Just try and be kind to her, Nacho.'

'What do you take me for? I'm curious about her, that's all, and if I can't ask you—'

'If this is curiosity you've picked a strange time to call. Your interest in Grace sounds more like unfinished business to me.'

'*Dios*, Lucia. I hardly know the girl.'

'And you hardly want to take on more responsibility— which is how you must see it,' his sister said more gently.

'My interest in Grace is purely professional. I need to know if she can do the job or if I must call someone else.'

'Right,' Lucia agreed sarcastically. 'You usually canvas my opinion on a member of your staff in the middle of the night. How could I have forgotten that?'

'All I'm saying is, you could have warned me.'

'What?' Lucia snapped, all fired up now. 'That my *blind* best friend is now a sommelier, working for one of the most respected wine merchants in the world?'

'There's no need for you to be like that.'

'And there's no need for *you* to sound so prejudiced when I know you're not.'

'I didn't call you for a lecture, Lucia. As it happens, Grace did very well with the wine tasting, but how can she be expected to inspect a vineyard when she can't even *see* it?'

'I'm no expert, Nacho, but I think you should give

her a chance.' There was a pause, and then Lucia said, 'Grace has really got to you, hasn't she?'

He huffed an incredulous laugh. 'In twenty-four hours?'

'Is that how long you've been back?' Lucia exclaimed. 'If you hadn't told me I would have thought you and Grace had been together for months.'

'Goodbye, Lucia.'

'You'd better not hurt her, Nacho...'

'Who do you think you're talking to?'

'My uncompromising brother. Just don't ruin things before they have a chance to begin—'

'I can assure you that nothing's starting,' he cut in, and as the infant's wails reached a crescendo he judged it the perfect time to end the call.

Was he prejudiced against Grace?

No. He was a realist, Nacho concluded, loosening the reins to allow his stallion to pick its way downhill.

Could he work with Grace?

Of course not. But the annual grape-treading celebration *was* a valuable sales tool. She should not miss it. There weren't many vineyards left that stuck to the old ways, and in today's competitive market they needed all the differentials they could get. He was confident she'd be impressed. Each year at Viña Acosta a small amount of fruit was held back and processed in the old way. For luck, the old timers always said, and who was he to argue? It was good for morale, and everyone loved a party.

Now they were back on level ground he urged the stallion into a gallop. As he leaned low over the big horse's straining neck he wondered what Grace would make of such a high-octane event being used as an excuse for every type of excess. Would Grace loosen up and join in, or would she hold back and resist getting half-naked and drenched in juice?

He'd hold her back, he concluded as his senses roared. His imagination was enough to tell him that he couldn't possibly expose Grace to the sultry light of evening in the grape-treading vat, where everyone was wild and free. Grace, with her long blonde hair gleaming in the moonlight and her skin damp from her endeavors and sweet grape juice? Never...

Grace, her face flushed with anticipation as she moved into his arms...

She was here, he told himself impatiently, blanking the X-rated images from his mind as he straightened up and reined in, and Grace wanted research. He'd give her research. And, if he was looking for more excuses, escorting Grace to the celebration was the least he could do for Lucia's best friend while she was here.

Okay, she was going to be sensible. Well, most of the time. But when the darkness grew heavy and weighed her down she knew from bitter experience that the only way to rise up and find the light again was to do something different—something that really challenged her and took her mind off things. And she desperately wanted to ride a horse. She always had.

So what was stopping her? When would she get a chance like this again? What was the harm in asking? The head honcho could only say no, Grace reasoned as Buddy led her across the road towards the corral, where the men were talking. She couldn't hear Nacho's voice, so that was good. She wasn't going to make a complete fool of herself in front of him, and the banter between the men sounded good-natured.

'*Buenos Diás,*' she called out with a smile.

'*Buenos Diás, señorita.* How may I help you?'

An older man was speaking, and what her shadowy vision couldn't see her mind supplied. He didn't stand too close, which she liked, and when he shifted positions she heard the chink of spurs. Her keen nose picked up the scent of tobacco and horse, along with leather and the smell of clean clothes dried in the sunshine. She could feel the older man's stare, steady on her face, and sensed it lacked opinion or censure. He was merely interested and friendly, and she thought he seemed kind.

'I'd like to ride a horse,' she said, coming right out with it. Angling her head, she put a wry expression on her face as she braced herself for refusal.

'No problem,' he said. 'Have you ever ridden a horse before?'

'A donkey at the seaside,' she admitted with a grin.

The elderly *gaucho* laughed at this. 'Then it will be my honour to teach you how to ride one of our gentle Criolla ponies, *señorita.*'

'Do you mean you're all right with it?'

'Why shouldn't I be?' he said.

Grace exhaled shakily. 'No reason at all,' she said.

He had just crested the hill when he saw Grace riding in the paddock. His heart took a leap as he quickly evaluated the risk at the scene. Having reassured himself that Alejandro, his head man, was riding shotgun alongside Grace, while Buddy rested patiently in the shade, he realised he hadn't felt so anxious for a long time.

He didn't slow his pace until he was close enough for Grace's pony to smell the stallion, at which point he reined in because he didn't want to spook it. Grace was concentrating, her mouth fixed in a determined line, as Alejandro issued instructions. As she squeezed her

knees, urging the pony from a brisk walk to a bouncing
trot, he grimaced, imagining that at any moment she
might be thrown off.

Dismounting at speed, he lashed his reins to the fence.

'Nacho… Is that you?'

He felt a rush of pleasure, he was forced to admit, at
the fact that Grace knew him immediately. 'You caught
me out,' he said in a neutral tone. Alejandro had it all in
hand, he realised, checking again. Propping one booted
foot against the fence, he leaned his chin on folded arms
and settled in to watch.

'Did you think you could stand there watching without me knowing?' she said, bouncing by.

'I thought I could try,' he admitted wryly.

'With a tread that's so distinctive I could never mistake it, and the snorts of your fire-breathing stallion to
confirm what I already know? Yep, you could do that,'
she teased him as she bounced past again.

The first thing he noticed was that she was smiling,
and that she was radiant. 'You seem to be enjoying yourself,' he said.

'I am,' she enthused. 'Alejandro is such a wonderful teacher!'

He exchanged a look with his elderly friend. Alejandro
shrugged as if to say, I was here—where were you?

'I want to ride *your* horse next,' Grace called out to
him from the far side of the corral.

'In another universe,' he called back. 'My stallion's
far too big for you.'

'No surprise there,' she said with a laugh in her voice.
'You could hardly be seen riding a donkey, now, could
you?'

Alejandro laughed with Grace, and even Nacho's lips
tugged in a smile. The events of last night hadn't damp-

ened Grace's spirits, apparently. He liked her spirit. It was hard not to.

'Any chance we can get some work done today?' he said, removing his bandana to mop the dust from his face.

'The grapes aren't going anywhere, are they?' Grace demanded as he raked at his ungovernable hair. 'And why are you trying to change the subject, Nacho? What about the challenge of me riding your horse? Or are you frightened I might show you how easy it is in front of Alejandro?'

He laughed. 'You wish.'

'You could lead us, if you don't trust me not to gallop off with him. I'd love to try him, Nacho...'

'No,' he said firmly. 'Even my brothers are wary of this horse. He's not a tame pony like the one you're riding. He's still half wild.'

'Alejandro already explained that,' she butted in. 'He said your horse used to be the alpha male in a herd of Criollas until you tamed him.'

'Criollas can never be completely tamed. He still thinks he's the boss.'

'Still,' she said, 'I bet he'd be kind to *me*. Shall we find out?'

'Only I can ride him,' he said—with all the arrogance of which an Acosta brother was capable, Grace realised, keenly tuned in to the nuances in every voice.

'If that's the case,' she said innocently, 'the only way I can ever hope to ride him is with you.'

He laughed again. 'You must be joking—'

'What's your problem, Nacho? I realise the stallion is a mountain of muscle compared to me, while the pony I'm riding now is...' she shrugged and pressed her lips together in a teasing, slanting smile '…also a mountain of muscle compared to me.'

Alejandro shot Nacho a sympathetic look before vaulting the fence and leaving him to it. The wily old stockman had left him with no option but to look after Grace. 'You're not even dressed for riding,' he remarked disapprovingly.

'Oh, come on, Nacho,' she goaded him.

Grace was half his size, and slender as a willow. She was wearing a long, floating dress that couldn't have been more unsuitable for riding if she'd tried, and only now he noticed she was barefoot.

And she was blind.

Grace Lundström was the most aggravating woman he had ever known—so perhaps it was time to show her the consequences of biting off more than she could chew.

'Alejandro,' he yelled, before the old *gaucho* disappeared. 'Can you look after the dog for us?'

'*Sí*, Señor Acosta,' Alejandro replied, in an amused voice that prompted Nacho to narrow his eyes.

He turned back to Grace. 'I'm prepared to take you for a short walk along the riverbank.'

'That's very kind of you,' she said—a little too sweetly for his liking.

'But if you're going to ride with me you do things *my* way,' he warned. 'Stay where you are. I'm going to help you dismount.'

'*Sí*, Señor Acosta,' she said, in a perfect take-off of Alejandro's mocking voice.

CHAPTER SEVEN

SERIOUSLY terrified at the thought of riding Nacho's horse, she was still serious about going ahead with it—if only to prove to herself that she could. Plus this was the ideal opportunity for her to prove to Nacho that being blind didn't put a curb on what she could do.

For once she obeyed him, and remained motionless in the pony's saddle until she felt the brush of his hands as he took hold of her reins. Even that brief contact was enough to send heat ripping up and down her spine in yet another reminder that the one mistake she was making was to think she could remain immune to the stallion's master.

'Don't move until I tell you to move,' Nacho instructed, 'and then you must do exactly as I say.'

'Yes, sir.'

'If you can't take this seriously—'

'But I am taking this very seriously, indeed,' Grace protested.

'I said *wait*,' he ground out as she slipped her feet out of the stirrups. 'I'll lift you clear. And don't kick the horse on your way down.'

'If I could see him—'

'I'll be your eyes. Now, slide into my arms,' Nacho instructed, without a moment wasted on pity or scorn.

Her heart was hammering nineteen to the dozen, which made her think that this was one time when not being able to see was a distinct advantage. Launching herself into the unknown, she found herself in Nacho's arms.

Whatever she'd imagined it might feel like, she'd been wrong. Her imagination was in no way equal to the task. Sliding down such a wealth of muscle was like nothing else on earth, added to which Nacho's handprints were now branded on her body. And, yes, it would be safer to concentrate on more mundane things, like business, but mundane things were a little short on the ground right now, and all she was aware of was Nacho throwing off testosterone like a Catherine wheel threw off sparks.

'Steady,' he murmured.

'Me or the horse?'

She gasped when he caught her round the waist, and the next thing she knew she was airborne.

'I'm lowering you gently into the saddle in front of me,' Nacho explained. 'So we don't give the horse a shock.'

What about *her* shock?

As if her swift rise into thin air hadn't been alarming enough, she now had her buttocks rammed up hard against Nacho. Fighting the urge to arch her back and feel more of that hard body against hers was the least of her worries. Nacho had somehow swept her skirt back as he lifted her, so now she was sitting astride his horse with her dress rucked up to her knickers and her confidence evaporating rapidly.

'I thought you were going to lead me along the river-bank,' she protested.

'You thought wrong,' he said, and with a click of his tongue against the roof of his mouth they were off.

At the stallion's first surge forward she was sure she would crash to the ground. She had never felt that much power beneath her before, and not knowing how far she had to fall made each rolling step the horse took absolutely terrifying.

'Are you okay, Grace?' Nacho demanded, tightening his grip on her.

'I think so...' Her voice sounded small and feeble, and he must have felt her tension, but it wasn't just fear of falling that had turned her into such a coward. It was Nacho's primitive energy that seemed to be throbbing through both of them.

She could feel his heart thudding against her back, slow and strong, and his hard muscles shifting behind her. The warmth of his body against hers was intimate beyond anything she could imagine. She sat forward a little, to put some distance between them. For all his wealth and polish Nacho exuded an earthy, animalistic quality that made her ultra-aware of him. She could understand now why women wanted to go to bed with him and why men feared him.

And no one with any sense got this close to danger without expecting to get burned.

Her inner voice of caution might advise that, but clearly she had no sense, Grace concluded, because she was starting to enjoy the sensation. And, as far as the riding went, she was determined to make a go of it.

'What do you need me to do?'

'As little as possible,' Nacho said. 'Just relax. If you tense up the horse will feel it and become restless. You have to go with me—move with me.'

Really...?

With her back to him she was free to smile, and then, concentrating, she tried again.

'That's better,' Nacho approved when she started to get the hang of it.

Grace's legs were slender as a newborn fawn's, but there was nothing weak or unsteady about her. There was a line between weakness and fragility, and no one would ever mistake Grace for being weak. His mother had been weak. He could see that now. Though nothing excused what he had done. He had never turned his back on anyone before or since the fateful day of the tragedy, and he never would again.

'Is this right?' Grace asked, jolting him back to the present.

'Just about perfect,' he confirmed.

She was riding really well, but then no one could ever accuse Grace of shirking a challenge. He could see now that since her illness she had worked hard to prove herself. She had retrained and learned all sorts of new skills. She had proved herself at the wine tasting, and again with his *gauchos*, and now she had somehow talked him into letting her ride his best horse. Perhaps most surprising of all was the way the big stallion was picking his route with more care than usual, as if he knew he had precious cargo on board.

If his brothers could only see this, Nacho reflected with amusement.

'Riding is even more fun than I thought!' Grace exclaimed.

He felt the now customary bolt of shock and pain when she turned her lovely face his way and her gaze flew somewhere to the right of his face.

'There's so much power beneath us,' she enthused. 'This is just wonderful, Nacho.'

Even as he warmed inside he remembered the harm he could do to those he cared about. 'Sit straight,' he rapped, mentally pulling back to concentrate on the practicalities of teaching Grace to ride. 'You shouldn't be looking at me. You should be looking forward, between the horse's ears.'

'If I could *look* anywhere,' she corrected him humorously.

Vicious curses invaded his head. 'Sorry—'

'Don't be,' she said. 'Riding is too much fun for us to worry about anything. Who cares?'

That Grace had lost her sight? He did. 'Feel for his ears, Grace. Good. Now, that's where you should be pointing your nose.'

She started to laugh. 'Are you saying I've got a big nose?'

She had a perfect nose. 'Line up your body,' he instructed. 'Not stiffly like that,' he complained with an impatient sigh. 'Draw yourself up and relax into his gait. That's better. Allow your hips to move easily back and forth in rhythm with his stride. Good. Well done, Grace.' She was a natural. 'Did anyone else ever take you riding?' he asked, feeling a stab at the thought that there might be someone in her past who had done so.

'A man once,' she mused, leaning back against him as she appeared to think about it.

'What man?' he said angrily, moving away.

'A man at the seaside.'

'The seaside?' he cut in suspiciously, as visions of sun-drenched beaches and handsome polo players on half-wild ponies sprang to mind.

'The man at the seaside who ran a team of donkeys,' she said.

'Are you teasing me?'

'Maybe,' she admitted, and there was a smile in her voice.

He was relieved. There was no getting away from it. He was very much relieved.

Clicking his tongue against the roof of his mouth, he urged the stallion on—which gave him every excuse to hold Grace more firmly. 'Trust me,' he said as she grabbed a hank of mane. 'You're safe with me, Grace.'

Safe with Nacho? Was he mad? Was *she* mad, for that matter? And a ragdoll pegged out in a gale would have more poise than she had right now. She was bumping up and down on the saddle like a sack of potatoes.

'I'm going to help you to move correctly, Grace.'

Thank goodness he couldn't see the expression on her face now, she thought.

'You're not frightened, are you?' he said, feeling her tension.

'No,' she protested. But she was. She was frightened of the way Nacho made her feel…his touch on her body, his breath on her skin; the way she felt so safe, cocooned in the warmth of his arms. She could so easily get used to this—and that would only end in heartbreak.

At Lucia's wedding, when Nacho had singled her out, her head had started spinning with wild, romantic nonsense. In the cool light of day she had realised it was pure nonsense without any of the romance. And now Nacho was only being kind to his sister's blind friend. She shouldn't read anything more into this riding lesson.

'You're doing really well,' he said, loosening his grip. 'You're on your own now, Grace.'

'What?' she exclaimed, a bolt of terror running through her. 'I'm not ready to go it alone.'

Nacho said nothing; he just let her go, which was really scary in her darkness. She just had to trust he wouldn't let her fall.

It was completely unnerving at first, but she was so

determined to do it that gradually she found her balance, and once she'd done that she started enjoying herself. Turning her face to the sun, she sighed with pleasure.

'Buddy's come to join us,' Nacho remarked. 'Shall we give him a run?'

'Oh, please,' she agreed, sitting up straight again. 'Let's go faster.'

The speed, the wind in her hair, cantering across the countryside with Nacho—all of it was exhilarating. And also a pointed reminder that she was a novice where so much in life was concerned, while Nacho was notoriously the master of all things with risk attached. She was sexually inexperienced. He was not. Yes, she'd had a few attempts at relationships, but had never seen what all the fuss was about. And there had been piano practice in her young life, followed by hard work when she was older, leaving barely any time to spare for thoughts of romance.

But she could think about romance now. With the stallion's hooves pounding beneath her it was impossible to think of anything *but* romance. She could be galloping across the desert with a sheikh, or riding into the sunset with a cowboy. Or, better still, Grace concluded, smiling to herself, she could be riding across the pampas with Nacho.

He had nudged the horse into an easy canter, knowing the swaying rhythm would be easier for Grace to handle than a high-stepping trot. And it was. But with Grace pressed up against him and all that power harnessed beneath them there was fever in his blood.

'Work your hips back and forth,' he said, trying to concentrate on teaching Grace to ride. 'You need to loosen up, Grace.'

She took him at his word and leaned her head against

his chest in a gesture that was both intimate and trusting, surprising him again.

'Is Buddy okay?' she said, sitting up just as he was getting used to having her resting against him.

'He's fine.' Reining in, he slowed the stallion to a walking pace. 'Did Alejandro mention the grape-treading to you tonight?'

'He did say something about a party,' she admitted. 'He also said he hoped I'd be there. But I suppose I'd need an invitation for that...'

He laughed. 'Stop fishing, Grace. You know you've got one.'

'I know why,' she said. 'You're hoping I might use the event in our forward publicity if Elias decides to go ahead and place an order.' She laughed. 'But if you think my attendance tonight guarantees that order, think again. I've got a lot more to see.'

'Are you playing hardball with me, Señorita Lundström? Because if you are I shall have to frighten you into submission. Are you ready for more speed?'

'Try me,' she said. 'You don't frighten me, Señor Acosta.'

As she spoke she turned, and as she turned his gaze slipped to her lips. 'At least allow me to try,' he murmured.

He had to admire Grace when the stallion bounded forward and she started whooping with excitement. 'Does nothing frighten you?' he called against the wind blowing in their faces.

'Only the darkness,' she yelled back, making him rage inwardly against the cruel fate that had left her blind.

He reined in at the guest cottage, where he told Grace to wait while he dismounted so he could help her down. But, as he might have known, she didn't wait and somehow managed to slip to the ground without his help, only staggering slightly as she regained her balance.

'Thank you,' she said formally, holding out her hand for him to shake. 'That was wonderful, Nacho. And now I've taken up enough of your time.'

She was dismissing him. 'Alejandro has hung Buddy's harness on the fence,' he said. 'It's over there to your right—'

'No use pointing, Nacho.'

'Grace, I—'

'I know. You're sorry.'

'Hanging from the main post,' he explained patiently.

'What time will you call for me tonight?' she said, finding the harness.

'Same time as last night.'

'Fine by me,' she said. 'Thanks again for the riding lesson.'

'There's just one thing.'

'Which is?'

'Buddy can't come tonight.'

'That's okay,' she said with a shrug. 'I was expecting it.'

'Until tonight, Grace…' He vaulted into the saddle.

'Until tonight,' she said, turning for the door.

Being without Buddy for one night wouldn't be a problem, Grace reflected as she let herself into the house. Even back home there were some places he couldn't go. She kept the hated stick for those occasions. It was collapsible, and fitted in a suitcase, which was about the best that could be said for it…

Nacho hadn't gone yet. She could hear his horse snorting and stamping. Nacho must be watching her. It made her nervous.

As she took the key out of the lock she stepped back

and almost tripped over Buddy. She swore like a trooper and then heard Nacho laugh. 'All right for you,' she called out.

'*Dios,* Grace,' he shot back, 'I thought you were so well behaved, but now I realise it must have been you who led my sister astray.'

She laughed. 'Sussed. Decorum was never my strong point. Talking of which—what do I wear tonight?'

Nothing would be his preference. 'I'll speak to someone,' he said, 'and I'll have some suitable clothes delivered to the cottage for you to wear.'

'Really?' she called excitedly. 'Great.'

The thought of Grace in traditional clothes suitable for the grape-treading gave him quite a buzz as he rode back to the *hacienda.* He reflected on the day's events. How it had made him feel having Grace pressed up close against him on the horse. How it would feel tonight, escorting her to the grape-treading. Had he lost it completely, inviting her? Yes, it was a good research opportunity for Grace, but it would be a lot more than she'd bargained for. The annual wine-fest was hardly a sedate affair. Treading the grapes dated from antiquity—pagan times, before civilisation came along to spoil the fun and dictate restraint. It wasn't unusual for the next working day to start at noon, if at all—and those who arrived alone invariably left in pairs.

And now his big horse had bolted and it was his turn to swear. Sensing his abstraction, the mighty stallion had lost no time heading towards the hills and freedom. Wrestling him back under control was a welcome outlet for his energy, but it did nothing to soothe his thoughts. Grace liked teasing him, but then she drew back. She craved independence. Well, she could have it—with his blessing. She would just have to take her chances with the men at the grape-treading.

Are you seriously advocating open season where Grace is concerned?

He wouldn't let her out of his sight tonight.

It was safe to say that the outfit which had arrived at the cottage didn't conform to Grace's usual take on a party outfit. That would be more likely to consist of a knee-length shift in silk or wool, depending on the weather, and safe, low-heeled shoes. But this wasn't a usual party, Grace reflected as she sorted out the clothes by touch. Though 'grape-treading' was probably an old term, used loosely these days to describe what happened to the fruit at the start of wine production, she decided.

She tried on the skirt first. Masses of fabric brushed her calves, making her feel like a country girl in an oil painting. The blouse was flimsy, and it had lace around the generous neckline—which would slip straight off her sloping shoulders. She held it to her face and inhaled the scent of soap and sunshine. As to colour? White was her best guess. The blouse was also cut low across the bust, and fastened with laces rather than buttons.

What would Nacho think of the transformation? Grace wondered as she slipped on her sandals. She should pin her hair up—though that would leave her shoulders bare...

And now it was too late to change. The clock had just struck six. Time for business. With no way of knowing what she looked like, she smoothed the full skirt anxiously. Should she have worn a bra? It was a bit late to be worrying about that now, she concluded, brushing her nipples lightly with the palm of her hands to see if the cotton fabric was thick enough to conceal them. Probably not...

She jumped as Buddy barked. It was too late to change her clothes *or* her mind. She would just have to brace herself and go through with it. She opened the door.

'Grace—'

Why the sudden silence? Did she look ridiculous? Was she wearing everything the right way round? Had she forgotten to tie the laces on her blouse? She checked discreetly as she invited Nacho to come in. The air swirled as he walked past, and her body responded to the pure zap of Nacho's energy like a teenager on her first date. She drank greedily on the aroma of citrus soap, mint toothpaste and hot, hard man. There was a lot of heat— and quite a bit of it on her cheeks.

'You'd better tell me if I look okay,' she said, closing the door behind him.

There was a long pause, and then he said, 'You look great.'

Great was a major understatement. Grace looked amazing in the revealing top and traditional skirt. Her breasts were magnificent. He would definitely have to watch the other men tonight. He might be duty bound to maintain cordial relations with his sister and keep Elias onside, but tonight Grace belonged to *him*.

'Will I fit in at the wine-treading?' she asked him.

No, you'll stand out because you look so beautiful, he thought. 'You'll do,' he said casually. Her skin was luminous, and flushed from riding in the sun, and her hair was gleaming with good health. If he could find fault it was that she'd put her hair up. But as there was only one pin holding it...

'Describe your outfit,' she said, distracting him. 'I

want to make sure I'm not the only one dressed up like a marionette.'

Some puppet show, he thought. And then, while he was thinking how beautiful she looked, she hit him with a zinger.

'I need to feel you,' she said.

'I beg your pardon?'

'I need to feel you so I know what you're wearing,' she said. 'It's how I see now.'

'Don't you trust me to tell you?'

'What do you think?' she said.

She advanced hands outstretched.

'All right, go ahead,' he said with a shrug, lifting his arms.

She started with his face. 'You haven't shaved.'

'I wasn't planning on kissing anyone tonight.'

Her cheeks flushed red. 'I should think not. I've no intention of being a gooseberry.'

He thought she might have had enough of the game by now, but no.

'You're wearing jeans,' she said, brushing his thighs with the lightest of touches. And then she exclaimed with fright as her hands touched naked skin.

CHAPTER EIGHT

'I CHOPPED my jeans off above the knee,' he explained. 'It's easier than rolling them up.'

'You might have warned me.' Her hands moved deftly on, sadly missing any interesting parts of his anatomy. 'You needn't hold your breath,' she said.

'I don't know what you mean,' he defended wryly.

'I think I just got scorched by your affront,' she remarked. 'I'm sure you've got a six-pack at the very least.'

'At the very least,' he agreed.

She mapped the width of his chest and seemed satisfied as she stood back. 'You're wearing a casual shirt,' she said. 'Describe it.'

'Dark blue—a little frayed, a little faded.'

'And you still have tattoos?'

'Of course.'

'The Band of Brothers—I remember,' she said, returning to her investigations. Her little hand didn't make it halfway round his upper arm. 'And I seem to remember something inked in black on this big muscle here...'

'You saw my tattoos during that polo match on the beach?' Should he be quite so pleased she had remembered? 'How much can you see now, Grace?' he enquired, as curiosity got the better of him.

She laughed. 'Enough to know that you block out the light.'

She must be mad. What was she doing, feeling her way around Nacho? She would never have dreamed of doing anything so intimate when she could see—so why now, when she was blind?

There had to be some advantages to being blind, she reasoned.

'I can see fuzzy shapes,' she revealed, in the interest of much needed distraction. 'If the light's good and I lift my chin I can see…' *The vaguest outline of your sexy mouth*… 'Vague shapes,' she said, keeping as close as possible to the truth.

'Is that it?' he said.

'Not yet. Stand still,' she chided when he moved. She was beginning to enjoy this, though her heart was still thundering off the scale. 'I'm glad you remembered your bandana,' she said as she traced the band across his brow. 'Wild hair must be contained at all times, according to health and safety rules,' she teased.

'Don't forget the earring and the scowl.'

Forget safety, Grace thought, hearing the humour in Nacho's voice. 'You're not scowling,' she said.

Nacho laughed.

This was not going the way he had imagined. He had come to the cottage with a clear plan in his mind. This was not a date. He would be polite to Grace—chivalrous, even. He would escort her to the grape-treading, where he would keep her safe and help her to do her research. And that was it. If he'd known she was going to explore him so thoroughly with her hands he might have made different plans—like taking her to bed and to hell with the grape-treading, along with his guilty past and all his worthy resolutions.

'Are we ready?' Grace asked as she walked to the door.

He didn't know about her, but he was ready enough to be in agony. 'What? No laptop, notebook, or phone to take notes?'

'None of the above,' she said. 'Tonight is strictly for enjoyment—I'll learn more that way,' she insisted.

'So what did Alejandro tell you about tonight?'

'He told me to be careful around you,' she said.

'*Me?*' When she laughed he thought he'd have to have a word with Alejandro.

Swinging the door wide, he realised Grace wasn't with him, and felt a punch in the guts when he turned to see her feeling for a stick. It was so easy to forget there was anything wrong with Grace.

'Locking this thing into place is a real pain,' she complained good-humouredly as she wrestled with the stick's extension lever. 'It collapses, so that's good, because I can pack it in my suitcase, but just try and get the damn thing to stay fixed in place.'

'You won't need it,' he said. Taking the stick away from Grace, he propped it against the wall. 'You've got me tonight,' he reminded her.

The barn where the grape-treading was being held was already full of people. He drew Grace close to protect her from the crowd. She felt tiny against him, but she felt full of energy too. Her curiosity was firing on all cylinders, he realised when he stared down into her face.

'Describe the scene to me,' she said.

As he looked around him he realised that he was noticing so much more. He'd never paid so much attention to his surroundings in his life, but that had been before Grace had come to Argentina and now he absolutely had to.

'Well, the barn is packed,' he began.

'I can feel that—and I can hear it,' she said, laughing. She clung to him as they moved through the crowd. 'You'll have to do better than that, Nacho.'

So he, who never fell short in anything, according to popular belief, was forced to try again. But just for now he wanted to absorb the feeling of being close to Grace—protecting her. He had never been so physically close to a woman outside of bed, and this was far better. Grace was almost a friend. She was certainly a very special business associate. He kept her pressed up hard against him—for reasons of safety only, of course.

'I hope you're not isolating me, Nacho?'

'Isolating you?'

'Only it's quieter here, and I'm not being jostled. I don't want to be regarded as an oddity,' she exclaimed. 'And I don't want you making special allowances for me.'

'What if they're steering a wide berth around *me*?' he said.

'Are you so fearsome?' She huffed with disbelief. 'I don't think so. From talking to Alejandro I get the sense that your staff really like and respect you. And, as you're taking time out from your crazy overloaded schedule to revive their industry, I can only think they must really admire you too.'

'Maybe I am being a little over-protective,' he conceded, loosening his grip. Habit of a lifetime, he reflected.

'That's better,' she said. 'Now we can both relax and enjoy the party. So long as you describe it to me…'

He was keen to do that. He didn't want her to miss out on anything. 'We're in a big all-purpose barn, constructed from old, mellow wood, I guess it's a sort of rich golden-brown—'

'High ceiling?'

'Very high,' he confirmed. 'With a pitched roof. The air is—'

'Warm, noisy, boisterous, and scented with old wine and anticipation,' she said, her face illuminated with the eagerness of a child as she raised her chin. 'Go on—'

'I was about to say the air smells of dry hay and it's full of dust motes.'

'Romantic.'

'Do you want me to describe it to you or not?'

'You dare stop. It gives me a lovely warm feeling inside when you describe things. I just think you could use a few more adjectives.'

'Take it or leave it, Grace.'

'I'll take it, thank you,' she said, grinning up at him.

He smiled too, and dragged her a little closer. There was something so innately good in Grace it made him want to know more about her, and at the same time made him wonder if he would spoil his time with her as he had spoiled so many other things. Would the past haunt him until he had?

'Come on,' she prompted, 'I'm waiting…'

He reordered his mind. 'Most people are dressed in traditional clothes,' he explained, determined that Grace wouldn't miss out on anything. 'The older women are dressed in black, and some of the older men have big hats on—'

'And belts with coins dangling from them?' she said.

'How did you know that?'

'Because they're *gauchos*,' she said, as Lucia might. 'This isn't just a celebration for the people who work at the vineyard, is it? It's for everyone who works for you.'

'And anywhere the Acostas are you'll find a horse,' he confirmed.

She laughed. 'I was about to say that.'

They were guessing each other's sentences now.

'Are we anywhere near the grape-treading yet, Nacho?'

'I'm just getting you out of the way of it so that you don't get trampled in the rush.'

'I don't understand,' she said, sounding concerned.

'Don't worry. When the grape-treading starts we'll have front row seats.'

'Do you mean we won't be taking part? No,' she said emphatically. 'I have to do it. How can I possibly report on the grape-treading if I don't?'

'It will be too rough for you, Grace.'

'Nothing's too rough for me,' she insisted. 'And I don't know how you can even say that when *you're* here.'

'You'll be able to hear everything that's going on. I promise you.'

'That sounds like fun,' she said in a flat tone.

'What do you want me to do?' he said. 'Risk you getting trampled?'

'No,' she said. 'Why don't you take me back and lock me away in the cottage, where I'll be safe.'

'Grace—you can't.'

'Why can't I?' There was a pause, and then she said in a soft, angry voice, 'Don't you *dare*...'

He could come up with a whole raft of reasons why a blind woman couldn't take part in the grape-treading, including the fact that Grace could slip and fall, or could be jostled and hurt herself. But she was right. *He* was the coward, fearing something might happen to her and allowing the past to throw up obstacles—like the fear that he couldn't keep those he cared about safe. Grace was strong. She could do anything she set her mind to.

He shouldn't even think of stopping her when he would be there in the vat to protect her.

'Of course you can do it,' he agreed.

'No surrender?' she said fiercely.

'No surrender,' he agreed wryly.

'Like a sheep?' she said. 'So long as that's the worst I have to do.' She laughed as he led her forward.

He had to ask himself if he had ever felt such pleasure in a woman's company before. With most women everything was simply a prelude to bed, but with Grace there was so much more to learn—just being with her felt like a privilege, a gift.

'What's that sound?' she said, shrinking back in alarm.

'That's the sound of the grapes being tipped into the vat,' he explained. It went on and on, but he could see that now she knew what was invading her darkness Grace wasn't frightened any more. She laughed when he told her she would be up to her thighs in grapes inside the vat.

'Which means they'll probably be round *your* ankles,' she commented.

He asked himself again: was taking Grace into the vat sensible? He had noticed several of the local youths eyeing her up, and once they were inside the vat there would be no quarter given and no attention paid to status or rank. He was the acknowledged leader of the pack, but tonight there would be challenges to his supremacy. He had seen it in the eyes of the other men when they looked at Grace—not because she was blind, but because she was beautiful, and because she was with *him*. Combat was in their blood as much as it was in his. Claiming Grace wasn't so much a rational decision as a primitive compulsion. Those youths would stay away from her if they knew what was good for them.

A young woman showed Grace how to tuck up her skirt. She sounded friendly and kind, and Grace thanked her for her help. She was getting better at that, Grace realised. She wasn't always pushing people away now, as she had done initially, when she had first lost her sight. She'd also eased up a lot since she'd been in Argentina. Being with Nacho had done that. He was so no-nonsense he had unlocked something inside her. It was something that said everyone needed help sometimes and that it had nothing to do with pity. Nice people liked to help their fellow man, whatever their physical status might be. It had nothing to do with being blind.

'Do I look okay?' she asked, smoothing her hands over her naked thighs, feeling a bit self-conscious now.

'You look great,' he said.

The hint of a smile in his voice made her feel womanly and sexy for the first time in ages.

'Stay close to me, Grace.'

As if she had any option—as if she *wanted* one, Grace thought as Nacho put his arm around her shoulders and drew her close. He made her feel so safe.

'I'm going to lift you into the vat,' he said, making her heart race even faster. 'Wait there for me—I'll get in first.'

She listened intently when Nacho left her side and heard him vault over the side of the vat. There was a wet, squelching sound when he landed.

'Reach out—let me guide your hands,' he said.

Before she knew it she was over the side and knee-deep in grapes.

'How does that feel, Grace?'

'Wet!' she said.

Nacho laughed. 'Hold on to me so you don't fall.'

Well, *that* was no problem.

And then the band started to play, and as the tempo increased the crowd all around them began to jump rhythmically in the vat.

'This is seriously crazy,' she yelled, hanging on to Nacho for dear life. 'Don't you dare let me go!'

'Not a chance,' he husked in her ear.

She was soon stamping furiously like everyone else. She had never felt so abandoned and free. Her legs were swimming in warm juice and the sensation was erotic and amazing. Nacho should have warned her—but would she have come if he had?

As Nacho let go of her for a moment, to tug off his juice-drenched shirt, she realised her own blouse was soaked through with juice. She could only imagine how transparent it must be. And now her overly sensitive hands were free to roam Nacho's warm, naked skin. She could feel a wealth of muscle beneath her fingertips, and his heart throbbing strongly in his chest.

'You'll fall if you don't hold on,' he warned when she quickly drew her hands away.

She'd fall if she did, Grace thought.

He'd seen the other men looking at Grace with hunger in their eyes, and he felt his power surge even higher as she clung to *him*. He had left the other men in no doubt that he was the one Grace trusted to keep her safe.

The music stopped as suddenly as it had begun and a hush fell over the crowd. He knew what would happen next—though Grace had no idea why he was suddenly holding her so firmly. A few seconds passed, and then a drum began to beat. The sound was little more than a seductive whisper to begin with, but then it grew louder and faster, until everyone was stamping their feet to the same heated rhythm, and the air was charged with a primal energy that made his own senses sharpen in response.

More and more couples were leaving the vat, Grace noticed. There was a lot more room for manoeuvre, and not half so much yelling and laughter.

'I'll need at least an hour in the shower after this,' she told Nacho, laughing. The evening was coming to an end and she was reluctant to leave. Something had changed between them. Barriers had come down. Though she guessed she looked an incredible mess. She was sticky with juice, and without Buddy or her stick she had no alternative but to rely on Nacho to take her back home. 'But I don't want to spoil the evening for you,' she insisted. 'Why don't you come back to the party after you've walked me home?'

'Why would I do that?' he said. 'Come on, Grace. We're leaving.'

She liked that he made no fuss. Nacho just swung her into his arms and lifted her over the side of the vat. Then somehow he was there to steady her on the other side. She paused to straighten her skirt while Nacho found her sandals, but as he began to lead her away she felt disorientated. 'Where are we going?'

A wooden door creaked open in front of her and cool air hit her face. They were outside and away from everyone, with cobbles beneath their feet. And now they were crossing an open space that had to be big because all sound was lost on the wind.

'Where is this?' she said. 'A hay barn?' she guessed as Nacho opened another door. 'What are we doing here?'

'Even *you* can't be so naïve,' Nacho murmured.

CHAPTER NINE

Lacing his fingers through her hair, Nacho cupped the back of her head in a way that was both possessive and achingly tender. The brush of his lips against hers was a remembered pleasure—though so much better now she was full of suppressed heat and longing.

She could feel his power flooding through her, mixing with her own to create some new, stronger force. When he tightened his grip, pressing insistently and hungrily against her, she kissed him back with an answering hunger that found its voice deep in her throat. Teasing her lips apart, he deepened the kiss and, finding her tongue with his, stroked it in a way that made intimate pulses throb deep between her thighs.

She moved against him, wanting more…more pleasure…more incredible sensation. Her mind blazed with a fever that no amount of reason could wipe out. She wanted him. And, impossibly, it appeared Nacho wanted her too.

'Where are you taking me?' she gasped as he swung her into his arms. She still felt that frisson of uncertainty, and wished beyond anything that she could see.

She had to trust him, Grace realised as Nacho soothed her with husky words in Spanish. She knew something of this man now, and she had to trust him to keep her safe.

Shouldering open another door, he let it bang shut behind them. 'I'm taking you to the *hacienda*.'

'To the *hacienda*?' she said.

'And then to bed.'

'And Buddy?'

'I'll make a call.'

Reassured, and yet terrified, she clung to Nacho as he strode across gravel and cobbles, and finally onto an even path. Another door swung wide, and they were inside again, somewhere quiet and calm and warm, where a clock was ticking reassuringly. She heard marble tiles beneath his feet and then a wide expanse of rug. They were inside the *hacienda* in a big hallway, Grace realised as Nacho turned and bounded up a flight of stairs. A *grand* staircase, she registered as they went up and up.

Trust Nacho to have his eyrie at the top of the house, she mused when they reached a thickly carpeted landing. He strode straight on and another door opened. Greeted by the scent of clean linen and beeswax, she guessed this was his bedroom.

The room was big. It ate up several of his strides before Nacho put her down on the bed. The windows were open, and she could feel the breeze and hear the swish of voile billowing.

She heard him switch a light on and smiled. 'I don't need the light,' she said.

'But I do,' Nacho argued, lying down at her side. 'I want to look at you.'

She remained still on sheets scented with lavender and sunshine, her head resting comfortably on a soft bank of pillows. She was trembling with awareness, Grace realised, waiting for Nacho to touch her or to speak.

Grace was the most beautiful thing he had ever seen. He marvelled that someone so tiny and vulnerable could be so strong. She was all he remembered from the wedding and so much more. He smiled to think she looked even better for being flushed and dishevelled after the grape-treading. Her hair had tumbled down and was wild around her shoulders, while the juice-stained blouse did nothing to conceal the full swell of her breasts. Grape juice streaked her cheek and her neck.

Bringing her into his arms, he kissed it away. She laughed against his mouth, and her laugh was the sexiest thing he had ever heard.

'Don't,' she said.

'Don't what?' He pulled his head back to look at her.

'Don't treat me as if I'm made of cut glass,' she warned him. 'I'm a woman like any other, Nacho.'

Not like any other, he thought. His hungry gaze swept Grace's body to find the cotton skirt had wrapped itself around her legs, exposing her elegant thighs. He thought of them spread wide and her legs locked around him… He wanted them joined deep. Moving over her, he teased her, with the weight of his thigh for the pleasure of hearing her groan. Taking his leg higher, he pressed more firmly, rubbing and teasing until she was gasping for breath.

'Don't—don't stop,' she said. Balling her hands, she pressed angry fists against his chest. 'There's nothing wrong with me. *Nothing.* Do you understand?'

'All I understand is that I want you,' he murmured, staring down. 'But what do *you* want, Grace?'

'You,' she said fiercely. 'I want you. I don't want you to see a blind woman,' she added in a voice that tore at his heart. 'I want you to see *me.* I want you to see Grace—'

'I always have,' he whispered, dragging her close.

And it was the truth. After that first terrible shock

he had come to see past the changes in Grace to everything that remained the same, and so much that had grown stronger.

'There's no rush. We've got all night, Grace.'

'And this could take hours, I hope?'

He felt her smile against his mouth. 'At least…'

Happy with his answer, she laughed, and his hunger spiked higher, driving back the ghosts from the past.

She had dreamed of this moment since she first saw Nacho, but never in her wildest dreams had she imagined they would ever be together like this, or that she could have the freedom of his body as he had hers. Nacho had aroused her beyond the point of reason just with his touch, and with the outrageous suggestions he was murmuring in her ear. He was the master of all things sensual, and he had made her want him with a hunger so fierce it frightened her.

'Enough,' she complained. 'Stop teasing me.' She writhed impatiently beneath him. 'Please don't make me wait.'

But Nacho refused to be hurried, and was content to leave her to imagine what might happen next.

'Please don't do this,' she begged in a shaking voice.

His answer was to tease her with his torso, brushing his warm body against her until her nipples were on fire and she was arcing against him, shamelessly seeking contact. When he finally dipped his head to suckle her nipples through the fine fabric of her blouse she uttered a cry of sheer relief. But it wasn't enough. The pulse between her legs was growing ever more demanding. Every time she inhaled she drew in more of Nacho's intoxicating scent, and the thought of all his power, so effortlessly controlled and so completely at her disposal, was more aphrodisiac than she could handle.

He had to curb Grace or it would all be over for her too soon. He had never anticipated this level of hunger, and wondered if he had ever seen anyone so aroused so quickly or so fiercely. Grace was like a lioness fighting for her mate, and it took all his skill to stroke and soothe and make her hold back. When she was quiet again he kissed her tenderly, but even then she couldn't stay still for long. Holding both her wrists, he pinned her on the bank of pillows. He was going to make this good for her. He was going to make this perfect.

He could never have anticipated that the solution to holding Grace back would come from Grace herself.

'I want to explore you,' she said.

He released her and, resting back on one elbow, stared down, wondering if this was another test Grace had decided she must put herself through. Closing his eyes, he traced the line of her full lips with his thumb pad as a reminder that Grace saw the world through touch now.

'Lie back,' she whispered.

This was the first time he had ever taken instruction in bed, but for Grace he would do pretty much anything right now.

She didn't just *learn* through touch he discovered, closing his eyes. Everything a sighted person could communicate with a glance Grace delivered with her hands. They were extraordinarily sensitive. They were such tiny hands, but so cool and strong. They had been as expressive as her eyes on the day they'd first met. He'd learned as much about himself as he'd learned about Grace in those few minutes.

'Stay still,' she told him.

Great though it was, this was a complete role reversal for him. No wonder it took some getting used to.

Having mapped his chest, she moved on to explore the

muscles of his arm and then his hands and fingers. It was the most sensuous experience he'd ever had. When she moved down the bed he held his breath as she stroked his legs. He needn't have worried. She stopped her investigations a prudent distance up his thighs. But apart from that she was a revelation. Some instinct seemed to inform her where he felt the most pleasure and how she must touch him to increase that pleasure. She could tease and soothe in ways he had never imagined—ways that sent his senses soaring to a point where it was he who was in danger of losing control. Something that had never happened in his life before.

'You're not supposed to do that,' he murmured, dragging her back into his arms.

'Not supposed to do what?' she said.

He kissed her, soothing her again. 'Grace?' he murmured seeing something was wrong.

'Did I do something wrong?' she asked in a small voice.

He laughed softly against her mouth. 'You did nothing wrong. You did everything right—which is why we need to pause.' There were tears in her eyes, he noticed. 'What haven't you told me, Grace?'

'It's the way you make me feel,' she said, biting her lip. 'It frightens me.' Mashing her lips together, she gave him that determined look of hers. 'And I'm crying because you kiss so damn well.'

He laughed. 'Then I'd better kiss you again,' he said.

When Nacho released her she realised how close she'd come to telling him how she really felt about him—that she wasn't even sure she could survive the strength of her feelings for him. But she had to be realistic. After devoting his life to his siblings, how could she burden Nacho with a blind woman? It was selfish of her even to think that way. She should save those wild emotions and channel them into something with a future attached—like her career.

She had promised everyone who had helped her that she would live her life to the full. Had that been just an empty pledge?

'Grace?' Nacho prompted, cupping her chin so he could stare into her face. 'What is it?'

'Nothing,' she lied, burrowing her face in his chest. 'I'm just trying to get something straight in my head.'

'And have you?'

Lifting her chin, she wished that she could see Nacho—so she could read him, so she could know him completely.

Feeling overwhelmed him when Grace reached for him. He was filled with a fierce determination to keep her safe and bring her pleasure.

Could those two things exist side by side?

'You taste of fruit,' she said, smiling as she kissed his shoulder. 'Kiss me,' she demanded fiercely, moving beneath him.

Grace's strength was what attracted him, he realised, that and her matchless femininity. Her face was radiant and her hair was tumbling around her shoulders in a billowing cloud. Moving it out of the way, he kissed her neck, before moving down the bed to rasp his stubble very lightly against the soft swell of her belly. Feeling her tremble, he kissed her again and she groaned, arching her hips as she searched for relief for the ache inside her. She tasted better than he remembered. She tasted of warmth and of woman and of Grace—unique and strong. Stripping her skirt off, he tossed it away. Her top followed. Now there was just a tiny lace thong between them. But he attended to her breasts first, suckling and relishing the taste of Grace and grape juice combined. When he lifted his head he allowed her thighs to part, as if she wanted him to see her arousal.

'How long must I wait?' she demanded, groaning in complaint.

'As long as I decide you must wait,' he said, enjoying the pleasure-pain as her fingers bit into his arms.

But she hadn't finished with him yet, and with an angry sound of frustration went straight for the button on his jeans. They were soon off, but he pinned her to the bed as she panted beneath him.

He had always thought sex should be fun, but this was the first time he had encountered a woman who could remotely match his appetite. 'Okay,' he said with amusement, somehow managing to keep her still. 'You win.'

'I don't want to win,' she said. 'At least not this game.'

This new Grace was free to be as provocative as she liked—free to express her feelings in a way she would never have dared to do before—and that made anything possible. The sensations she was experiencing in the darkness were dazzling.

Instead of moving she remained quite still. She wanted to remember every moment of this—Nacho's thigh brushing her just where she needed him, the intense little pleasure spasms engulfing her. He was a master of the art of seduction and she was a most willing pupil. Nacho knew exactly what he was doing, and was totally switched on to her needs as he prepared her for the ultimate pleasure.

'You're so cruel,' she complained on a shuddering breath as he talked to her in Spanish, no doubt promising all sorts of excess.

She exhaled with excitement, feeling the proof of his arousal rest heavy against her leg. He was massive. She had always known he would be. But when she begged him not to prolong the torture he only laughed.

'I'm being kind,' he assured her in a husky whisper.

He had never known a woman to be so full of desire. When Grace rested in his arms, throwing her head back as she was doing now to drag in air, he wanted nothing more than to pin her to the bed and pound into her until they both fell back exhausted. But when she ran those tiny hands across his chest, when she traced the line of his shoulders with a touch so light, all he wanted to do was to treat her exactly as she had asked him not to—like cut glass. No woman had ever seduced him with touch alone, but Grace could. She had magic in her hands and something equally potent in her lovely, lust-drenched face.

'Nacho?' she whispered, sensing the change in him.

The past had intruded without warning, and it had come between them in the ugliest way. Throwing himself back on the pillows he wondered how he could even *think* of doing this.

'Nacho, what's wrong?'

'What's wrong?' he said. 'You're not afraid of me, are you, Grace?'

'Of course I'm not afraid of you. Why would I be?'

Because I destroy people, he thought. *Because I can never give you what you want.*

Grace frowned with concern—*for him*. Since the tragedy he had always known it was his duty to devote his life to family and to the vast territories they owned, and that he must remain free of personal ties so that he could never hurt anyone again.

'I think you've forgotten me,' Grace murmured.

He turned to look at her distractedly, and then she

touched him—not just with her hands, but with her in-domitable will.

'Have you forgotten why you brought me here?' she said, teasing him with a smile.

'Forgotten you?' The past fell away as he stared at her. 'How could I ever forget you?' he murmured dryly.

'That's what I hoped you'd say,' she said, stroking him in a way that made him forget everything.

'Tell me what you remember about me.'

'I remember you sluicing down in the yard,' she said. 'I remember your arms—so sexy, hard and muscular.'

'My arms are sexy?' he said, his lips pressing down as he considered this information.

'Especially if they pin me down,' she said.

'Is that a hint?'

Grace's slender shoulders eased in a shrug. 'What do you think?'

Kneeling between her legs, he eased the tiny lace thong down over Grace's hips.

'What are you going to do?' she asked.

Surprised by the question, he was silenced for a moment—but then he realised Grace was in darkness, trust-ing him to keep her safe. 'I'm going to feast on you and make you scream,' he said.

She laughed. 'See that you do,' she said.

His hunger was raging out of control, but he had only teased her with the lightest of kisses when she cried out, 'Stop! I can't—'

'Hold on?' he supplied as she bucked beneath him.

'That's *your* fault,' she complained, still lost in plea-sure as she gasped.

'I blame myself entirely,' he agreed dryly. 'More?'

'Of course,' she said.

Nacho was amazing. Shouldn't one tumultuous climax be enough for her? Shouldn't that have quietened the hunger inside her at least for a while? Instead it had grown, and with it her fantasies of what Nacho might do or make her feel next had exploded into endless possibility.

When she quietened he made some suggestions that turned her on beyond belief. 'Like this?' she said.

'Exactly like that,' Nacho confirmed when she drew her knees back.

'You like looking at me?' she guessed.

'I *love* looking at you,' he countered.

Feeling him move over her, she uttered a soft cry of excitement, and then he stroked her with just the tip of his erection, back and forth. Raising her arms above her head, she rested them on the bank of pillows. Reading her wishes, he took her wrists in one big hand while he guided himself inside her with the other.

'Oh, *please*,' she gasped.

'You're so small and I'm so big—'

'Yes,' she agreed, in a tone that suggested that was great news. 'More,' she encouraged as her excitement mounted.

'You're so pale, so soft, and your hands are so tiny.'

'And you're big in every way,' she said, remembering the weight of his erection as it flexed against her. 'And those big hands are the most delicate instruments of pleasure,' she added as he proved this to be true yet again. She groaned as each touch coloured in yet another frame in her imagination. 'And now it's my turn to explore you,' she insisted, freeing her hands to reach down— only to discover that, as she had suspected, Nacho was built perfectly to scale. One hand wasn't nearly enough to encompass his girth.

'Stop!' he ground out hoarsely.

Bracing her hands against his chest, she waited. And then cried out with shock as he moved. Had she thought she was ready for this? She could *never* be prepared for this, Grace realised, though Nacho was infinitely careful as he moved steadily deeper. When he inhabited her completely she gripped him fiercely with her muscles, triumphantly claiming him for her own.

'Good?' he murmured, brushing her lips with his.

'Can't speak,' she admitted on a shivering breath, wishing she could see the smile she knew would be curving his lips. But when he moved again she couldn't think, could only feel as she began to move instinctively in time with him.

'Don't hold back,' Nacho advised. 'Take as much time as you want. Take as much as you want.'

And with his promise in her head she fell with relief into mind-stripping release. Her fingers clawed at his back as she thanked him in words she had never used before.

'Again?' Nacho suggested with amusement, when she finally found some sort of holding area.

'Yes,' she breathed.

He made it no easier to hold on this time, and she fell the moment he entered her. He had made her greedy. He had made her want him more than ever. He had made her realise that her life from this moment on would be incomplete without Nacho in it.

'You *are* a witch,' he said when she used her muscles to keep him close.

Rocking into her, he drove the breath from her lungs in a muffled cry, and drove on until they both fell violently and gratefully into the darkness, tangled in each other's arms.

'Sleep?' Nacho suggested some time later, when she sucked in a shuddering breath.

A slow, sexy smile curved her lips. 'Not yet,' she whispered.

'Then ride me?' he suggested.

'All right. But don't help me.'

'I think we're a long way past that—don't you, Grace?'

Straddling him, she was turned on all over again by the way her legs were pressed wide by the size of Nacho's body. But being in control was the best. It felt great. Having his hands on her buttocks helping her to ride him to greater effect felt better still. She threw her head back, basking in sensation. Even now Nacho gave her little more to do than enjoy him. He understood exactly how to increase her pleasure with the subtlest encouragement from the pad of his forefinger as he rocked her back and forth. And thankfully he ignored her when she warned him that she couldn't hold out for long.

A wail of anticipation left her lips when she realised this was going to be fiercer and stronger than anything she had known so far. When she fell she must have blacked out for a moment, because she came round to find Nacho moving over her to an irresistible beat.

'Again,' he growled, and this time it wasn't a question.

He lost it right there. Sensation compacted into a nuclear force that shot from his core, engulfing him.

'Are you okay?' she said, when finally they were quiet again.

'I'm good,' he confirmed. 'You?'

He turned his head on the pillow to stare at Grace. The longing for her to see him had never been greater. He longed for her to know how she made him feel. He longed for her to see. But she couldn't see.

Cupping her face, he stroked her cheek and kissed her

mouth tenderly. 'You're a very special woman, Grace. Very special to me.'

'Unique, I hope,' she said, smiling in that way she had when she wanted to make light of things so they couldn't hurt her.

'You *are* unique,' he said fiercely, wanting her to feel his passion. Making love to Grace defied classification. There had to be some new word for it. Sex didn't even come close. 'I didn't hurt you, did I?' he said, his concern bringing tears in her eyes

'Only here,' she said, clutching her chest over her heart. 'Otherwise I'm fine.'

She said this wryly, with a small smile, and that smile tore at his heart, because he knew Grace would always say she was fine. She didn't want to be a trouble to anyone. She had probably reassured the doctors on the day they had told her she was going blind. But he guessed Grace bottled up her feelings and brought them out when she was alone to examine, and that thought stabbed him in the heart like a knife.

'How can you be fine if you're crying?' he said gruffly, blotting her tears with his thumb-pad.

'Because I'm not crying the way you think I am,' she said.

'And how is that?' he said as she turned her head on the pillow so they were facing each other. 'How many ways are there to cry?' As he spoke he traced the line of her jaw.

'You can cry from happiness,' she said. 'You can cry from feelings so big you can't express them in words. You can cry with amazement that anything can be so good.'

'Are you giving me a compliment?' he asked with amusement.

'Maybe,' she admitted wryly, still defensive, still frightened to commit herself entirely to anything that could bring her hurt. 'You're so gentle and caring…' Her face changed again. 'And so damn good in bed.'

He laughed as he dragged her close for more kisses.

'I didn't think I was capable of making love like that, or even feeling like that,' she admitted when he let her go.

'If there's one thing I've learned about you, Señorita Lundström,' he said, cupping Grace's chin and tilting her face so he could stare into her misty eyes, 'it's that you're capable of anything you set your mind to. Perhaps this isn't the right time to say it, but—'

'But you're going to say it anyway?' she guessed.

'Yes, I am. You've changed since we first met, Grace. You're stronger. You're more capable and more determined. Because you've had to be. I know that.'

'And because I was completely over-awed by you at the wedding—by everyone there,' she admitted. 'I felt so out of my depth. No wonder you thought I was naïve and awkward.'

'I thought you were beautiful.'

'Well, I felt like a fool. It was one thing being Lucia's friend, but being thrown into the type of society you Acostas inhabit—royalty, celebrities…'

'Who have exactly the same problems the rest of us do,' he pointed out.

'Not quite,' she argued wryly.

'So that accounts for your Cinderella flight?'

She laughed as she snuggled closer. 'I didn't feel safe with you then.'

'And now?'

She would never feel safe *without* Nacho again, Grace realised with concern. So much for standing on her own two feet. One night with Nacho and she was back to square one.

'What's wrong?' he said, feeling her tension.

She braced herself, and then told him the truth. 'I always think I've got this sight thing kicked, and then something happens and all the progress I've made counts for nothing.'

'Has that happened tonight, here with me?'

She shifted in his arms, knowing it was too soon to reveal her true feelings for Nacho, or how vulnerable she was. She'd just about convinced him she was strong. What would he think if he realised the truth? That where he was concerned she was utterly exposed, utterly defenceless?

'Hey,' he murmured in complaint when she turned away from him. 'Stop worrying about the future, Grace, enjoy *now*.'

He was right, she reasoned. 'Is that an order?' she said, turning back.

'Yes, it is.' He felt his heart squeeze tight as Grace reached out a hand to find his lips.

'You're smiling,' she said, tracing them.

It was one of those smiles Grace had talked about—the type of smile that could very easily have tears attached. 'I was just thinking we should get some sleep,' he said with no emotion in his voice. 'Tomorrow's a working day for both of us.'

'Liar,' she said. Her lips curved in a smile. 'You're thinking about making love again.'

Capturing her hand, he pressed a passionate kiss to her palm. 'You know me too well, Grace.'

'I wish,' she said quietly.

CHAPTER TEN

SHE woke in Nacho's big bed at the *hacienda* to find she was alone, and in those first waking moments she felt panic. It was like the early days, when she hadn't been able to get out of bed without falling over something—even in her own house. When she had first known she was losing her sight she had practised moving around the house wearing an eye mask, but she had always cheated. Peeping had become part of the routine. One day peeping hadn't been an option for her, and it wasn't an option now.

Nacho must be at the stables, she reasoned, trying to calm down. Lucia had said the stable yard was where her brothers lived, and that the houses they owned were for civilised people to inhabit. She felt for the nightstand, hoping there might be a phone there so she could maybe make an internal call, but there was nothing. And—

Oh, damn! Now she had succeeded in knocking her water over.

She wanted the bathroom, but didn't have a clue where it was, or how she'd make her way there.

She had to calm down. Sucking in some deep breaths, she concentrated on counting the Acosta residences. There was the *palazzo* on Fire Island, the penthouse in

London, and the main *estancia* Grace had visited for Lucia's wedding—and here…

No good—heart still thundering.

Next she counted pianos. Four residences. Four pianos. There was a piano in every home because Nacho's mother had used to play. Perhaps Grace could play one of the pianos while she was here.

Still hammering—hammering so hard now she could hardly breathe.

So now she thought through her favourite waltz, page by page, bar by bar, note by note.

She really couldn't wait any longer. She would have to find the bathroom—crawling if she had to. She'd done it before. She knew that if she crawled around the perimeter of a room she would find doors and hopefully, eventually, the room she needed. Then a noise caught her ear.

'Buddy?'

Grace exclaimed with excitement. She had never been so relieved to hear the scratch of claws on wood before. Nacho must have brought him up before he left so she wouldn't be stranded. She'd been wrong to imagine Nacho would simply get out of bed and leave her to it. She was right about him. He was caring. And sexy as hell.

Feeling confident now, she turned her face into the pillow to drag in Nacho's warm, clean scent. She smiled, absorbing the contented ache of a body that had been very well used. What a night! Nacho had revealed himself to Grace in ways she could never have imagined. Who would guess there was such a tender, humorous individual beneath that autocratic manner? Or that he could be such an amazing lover…?

The hardest of the Acosta brothers?

She didn't think so. Nacho was wonderfully warm.

And she had relaxed properly for the first time in a long time, Grace realised as she stretched contentedly. She had learned a lot about herself too—like her insatiable capacity for passion. She felt womanly and appreciated, thanks to Nacho.

'Go find your harness, Bud,' she called, sitting up and swinging her legs over the side of the bed so she could test the floor with her feet. 'I bet he's brought it up…'

He had, and once she had Buddy to lead her around Grace moved swiftly to get ready for the day. She found her clothes neatly arranged on a leather sofa, and her toiletries waiting in the bathroom. Even her stick was propped against the sink, where she couldn't miss it.

'Someone has guessed that you don't go everywhere with me,' she told Buddy with amusement.

The shower had been left on an appropriate setting, and there was a stack of towels waiting for her on the side. She showered and dressed quickly, trusting her guardian angel had also matched up her clothes: jeans, sneakers, underwear and a tee, obviously brought over from the guest cottage. And then with Buddy's help she found her way down to a warm kitchen, fragrant with the smell of freshly baked bread. The room was alive with the chatter of at least two women.

Nacho's housekeepers, Grace presumed, greeting them brightly. *'Buenos días…'*

'Buenos días, Señorita,' the women chorused gaily, ushering Grace into the room.

If the women wondered at Grace's sudden appearance in the main house they certainly didn't show it. Their welcome couldn't have been warmer. She heard the scrape of chair legs on a stone floor and felt Buddy's tug as he prepared to take her towards the seat that was being offered to her. Releasing him, she sat down.

The two women vied with each other to offer Grace every type of food and drink imaginable. Grace tried to find an appetite, so she didn't offend them, but all she could think about was when Nacho would be back. He would be out riding, she guessed, and one housekeeper, Maria, confirmed this. Señor Acosta was planning to meet Grace later that afternoon, Maria explained.

So long to wait! Grace hid her disappointment. She did have work to do, but first, if there was a piano in the house, maybe she could play it…

She asked the question and was surprised at the long pause. She wondered if it meant the two older women were exchanging glances. 'I understand if no one is allowed to play it,' she said, remembering the tragedy that had killed Nacho's parents, and the fact that Lucia had mentioned it had something to do with a piano. She couldn't imagine what—how could a piano and a flood be connected?—but Grace had never liked to probe around such a sensitive issue.

Maria had obviously come to a decision, as the housekeeper exclaimed, 'It would be *maravillosa*…wonderful to have music in the house again, *señorita*. The piano is in the hallway. Please, allow me to show it to you. But first I must find the key.'

Grace's excitement mounted. It had been so long since she had played a piano—since before she had lost her sight. So she wasn't even sure she still could. And she didn't really know why she had this sudden urge to play again, but she *felt* something here and knew she had to answer the longing. If she could only play for Nacho…

Her heart pounded with excitement at the thought as Buddy led her out of the kitchen and into the hall.

The hallway was big and fresh and filled with light. Grace always rejoiced that she still had a sense of light—

it made everything feel so much better. There was a flower display somewhere…she could smell the blossom. And beeswax. And floor polish. She smiled to think she would never have noticed things like that before. And that she would have found her rubber-soled sneakers annoying as they squeaked across the marble tiles, she realised, smiling wryly. She had so much to be grateful for.

Buddy brought her to a halt next to Maria, who was unlocking the piano. It was tucked beneath the grand staircase. No wonder she hadn't known it was there. Buddy had never had to make a detour round it. She felt for the piano stool, and then remembered that Nacho's mother would have been the last person to sit on it. It felt like a real privilege to be taking her place, hopefully playing the music that had once brought her and her children so much pleasure.

'I'm afraid the piano hasn't been played for years, *señorita*,' Maria murmured as Grace's hands hovered above the keys.

'That's what I thought,' Grace said quietly, thinking about the woman who had sat here before her. *I hope you don't mind me playing your piano*, she reflected silently. 'I haven't played for some time, either,' she explained to Nacho's housekeeper ruefully. 'I'm not even sure I *can* still play.'

Grace's heart squeezed tight when Maria touched her arm. 'I'm sure you can do anything you set your mind to, *señorita*.'

Grace could only hope Maria was right.

She sat for a long time without doing anything after Maria left. Putting off the moment, she guessed. The hall felt very quiet, very still, very empty. It was easy to imagine ghosts were listening. 'I don't want to let you down,' she murmured, reminding herself that all piano keys were set out in a logical sequence, so it should be no big deal that she couldn't see. The notes weren't going anywhere, and she could hear what she was playing just as well as she ever had. She just had to remember what Clark, the pianist at the club had told her. '*Close your eyes, Grace, and let the music flow...*'

What if it didn't flow?

It *would* flow, Grace told herself firmly. Nothing had changed since those nights at the club.

Everything had changed. Her fingers fumbled over the keys as if she was a toddler let loose on a piano. It didn't help that the instrument was so badly out of tune. She couldn't hear what she should be playing. She couldn't find her way into the tune—any tune. She couldn't trust her own judgement. Even the simplest nursery rhyme was beyond her reach.

This was ridiculous. She had to calm down and get over the fear. Dashing the tears away, she thought back to what they'd told her at the rehabilitation centre: she must always give herself time to think. Taking a deep breath, she tried again—first a scale, and then an arpeggio, and now a simple Chopin waltz, one of the slower ones she had always been able to play from memory. She started hesitantly, but her courage quickly grew. Clark Mayhew had been right. The music hadn't left her. It was still here in her head and in her fingers.

The hall was a natural amphitheatre, and even the suspect tuning seemed to add a poignant, haunting strain to the melody. The keys that had been sticking to begin with were working now, as if the piano was glad to be played again. Her heart began to soar as she played on. But then a door banged open and she jumped with alarm.

'Nacho?' She spun round on the stool.

Angry footsteps pounded across the hall towards her,

and she yelped with fright when Nacho slammed the piano lid down, narrowly missing her fingers.

'What are you doing?' she exclaimed, hugging herself defensively. His rage was buzzing around her like a swarm of angry bees.

'What am I *doing*?' he demanded hoarsely. 'Get away from the piano!' he roared as she ran her fingers along the edge of the lid with concern, feeling for damage. 'Get away from the piano, Grace.'

She was incapable of moving anywhere, and could only sit, stunned, wondering what had happened to her gentle lover from last night.

He couldn't believe Grace was still seated at the piano when he had insisted she must move away. His rational brain warned him that he was half mad with anger, grief, guilt, and that all of these were compounded by his concern for Grace, but the other part of him—the dark side that had once driven him to desert those he loved when he should have stayed to save them—said she must go. Just as Grace had made him forget the past last night, and the evil of which he was capable, she had brought it back to him today.

He would never have come back to the vineyards if it hadn't been to save his siblings' inheritance, and now he knew why. One by one he had forced himself to grow accustomed to all the familiar landmarks again, but the piano had always been at the root of the tragedy. And to hear it played again was torment beyond belief. He should have got rid of every piano in every house. Only the fact that if he had done so it would have created suspicion amongst his siblings had stopped him. He wouldn't do anything that might risk splitting his family when he had devoted his life to keeping that family together.

And Grace?

On the way to the house his head had been full of her. He hadn't been able to wait until this afternoon to see her. His only thought had been to be with her again. He had been aching to see her. But now he couldn't wait to send her away because he was frightened for her. He was frightened of the man he could be.

'I'm sorry,' she said with a helpless gesture. Grace's face was ashen. 'I'm not sure what I've done, Nacho.'

How could she be expected to know that when he'd walked into the house it was as if he had been thrown back in time to that fateful day when he'd heard his mother playing the piano? Or that what had happened next would shame him for ever? His brothers and sister would never forgive him if they knew what he'd done, and he was determined to keep their parents' memory intact. Lucia had been so young when they'd died. He wanted her to remember them like golden icons without fault or blemish, guardian angels watching over them.

'Nacho?'

Grace's voice was full of concern. *For him.* She was so unselfish. What did it matter if she was playing the piano?

'I didn't know you played,' he said distractedly.

'I didn't know I still could play,' she admitted.

Fresh guilt overwhelmed him when he heard her voice shaking and saw she was biting her lip. The tears in her eyes were proof enough that he must send her home, and quickly, before he destroyed her as he had destroyed his parents.

'Come away from the piano,' he said, as gently as he could.

'Of course,' she said, feeling for the edge of the seat. Every action she made now reminded him of how vulnerable she was, and how close he'd come to drawing Grace deeper into his dark world. He couldn't risk another tragedy.

'I'll ask Maria to help you collect your things so you can move back to the guest cottage,' he said. 'We have work to do this afternoon.' And thank goodness for it, he thought, longing for a return to something like normality.

'A tour of the vineyards?' she said, with some steel back in her voice.

'That's right,' he said, relieved that she seemed to have got over his shocking behaviour. 'And then, if you have all the information you need...'

'I can leave?' she said.

Her bewilderment stabbed him. 'Of course, if there's more research you have to do...'

'No,' she said, shaking her head. Drawing herself up, it was almost as if she drew a protective ring around herself. 'I'm sure I can complete my preliminary investigations this afternoon.'

But she couldn't sustain her composure and he found himself flinching when she seemed to fold in on herself.

'Can I ask you something, Nacho?' she said quietly.

'Of course.'

'What happened between last night and now?'

She didn't want to ask the question, but believed she deserved an answer, and when Nacho remained silent she drew the conclusion for herself. She could imagine him staring at her in bemusement. He was a man of the world who'd had sex with a woman. She was a woman who had made love with a man.

'What are you smiling about?' he said.

'I'm not smiling. I'm laughing at myself because I'm stupid.'

'You're not stupid, Grace.'

'Really?' she said. 'So I *didn't* read too much into last night, and imagine that we meant something to each other? Or is my piano playing just really bad?'

'This isn't funny, Grace.'

'You're telling me.' Her pain echoed round the hall. 'I think you owe me one thing,' she said. 'Can you tell me how you can be one person last night and another today? What have I done to make you so angry, Nacho?' She was all fired up and, turning to the piano, she made the lightest pass of her hand across the lid. 'I respect this instrument. I know it was your mother's, and I would never abuse her memory. I can't believe you think I would—'

'It's not that.'

'What, then? What have I done that's so terrible?'

Shaking her head, she let her anger burn out, and rested both her hands on the lid, bowing her head over them. He wished them both a million miles away. He wished he could be different. He wished Grace had never had to see him as he really was.

'I'm sorry,' she said, so softly he had to strain to hear her. 'I only wanted to find out if I could still play. You welcomed me into your home and I took advantage of your hospitality—no,' she said, stopping him with a raised hand when he tried to speak. 'I'm really sorry, Nacho. I didn't mean to remind you of such a difficult time in your life.'

A difficult time? It had been a murderous time, when he'd had murder in his heart.

'You weren't to know,' he said stiffly, cursing the day he had ever heard his mother play the piano.

Silence fell then, and a muscle flicked in his jaw as he stared at Grace. Her lips were still swollen from his kisses and her eyes were full of tears—tears *he* had put there. He had never wanted to comfort a woman more, but he knew that if he did that he would never let her go. *And he destroyed those he cared about.*

'Nacho?'

Grace's voice brought him back.

'Are you all right?' she asked him with concern.

She could still be concerned for him, he realised with incredulity. 'I'm fine,' he said brusquely, but his thoughts were in turmoil. He had been meaning to call Elias this very morning, to make some excuse so that Grace could stay. But now he knew he must send her away.

'At least speak to me,' she said.

'There's nothing more to say. You couldn't know about the piano,' he said stiffly. 'The lid should have been locked—'

'It was locked,' she said. 'I asked permission first, but please don't blame Maria.'

'It's no one's fault,' he managed somehow to grate out.

'Come on, Buddy.' Grace stood up.

'Wait—'

'No,' she said calmly. 'I'm here on business for Elias. So if you wouldn't mind…?'

He moved out of her way and the dog led her past. He watched Grace walk up the stairs with her head held high to collect her things. The irony occurred to him then. Unlike every other woman he had ever known, Grace really didn't need him.

As if to confirm this, she called back, without slowing her pace, 'Vineyards at two-thirty, Nacho.'

It was his turn to be on the back foot and wondering what last night had meant to Grace. 'I'll pick you up at two,' he said, calming the storm inside him.

'I'll make my own arrangements, thank you,' she called back.

* * *

She was confused by the piano incident, but wouldn't dwell on it. She knew from past experience that when she was as confused as this, as low as this, the only thing that would save her was launching herself straight back into life. It would be a life without Nacho in it, maybe, but she was going to do it by achieving one of her goals. Not a business goal, but a personal goal, and she would need Alejandro's help to do it.

What better time could there be to learn to ride independently, away from the safety of the corral, than when she was on her way to meet Nacho at the vineyard? Grace reflected, and she listened to Alejandro's instructions as he rode alongside her, with Buddy trotting at their heels.

To reassure both of them, Alejandro had explained, he was putting Grace's pony on a lead rein. 'So there are no unexpected hurdles for you to jump,' Alejandro had said, in the warm tone that always made her smile.

As if she hadn't jumped enough hurdles in Argentina already, Grace concluded, still feeling crushed and bruised after her encounter with Nacho. She had no answers for his behaviour, but now, with the breeze on her face like rare champagne, clean and clear with the fresh scent of blossom and lush green grass, she knew it was going to be a good day. She was determined it would be. The birds were singing, the frogs were croaking, and the wind played tag in the trees. What a great day, she told herself firmly. There was so much to enjoy. Why dwell on things she couldn't change?

If her heart would stop aching, maybe she could forget what had happened with Nacho.

'Nacho is also on horseback,' Alejandro explained, as if picking up her thoughts. 'That's why your pony's playing up. He can smell the stallion.'

Oh, good. Just when she thought she could forget

Nacho for five minutes he was back full force. 'Right,' she said, nodding her head sagely, as if the information Alejandro had just given her was useful rather than electrifyingly, terrifyingly and painfully upsetting.

'I called ahead to explain that you would be riding to meet him with me.'

Grace nodded her head, anxious now, although the whole purpose of this afternoon was to visit the vines with Nacho. But somehow, meeting him on horseback, surprising him that she was riding alone outside of the corral and without him behind her, felt a bit like waving a red rag to a bull. And she couldn't bear any more confrontation. If they couldn't be lovers then at least let them be friends—or, failing that, business associates who were capable of being civil to each other.

'Are we close?' she said, feeling her pulse speed up.

'Grace.'

Very close, she realised.

'Hello,' she said, taking care to strip her voice of all emotion.

'*Adiós, señorita!*'

'Are you leaving us, Alejandro?' Grace called out, feeling a sudden moment of panic at being left alone in her darkness with memory of Nacho's anger so fresh in her mind. The sound of galloping hooves was her answer, though Alejandro called something back as he left. 'What did he say?' she asked, not even sure Nacho was still there to answer her.

'Alejandro hopes that when you return to England you will leave your heart in Argentina.'

There was no emotion in Nacho's voice as he said this, and she couldn't see his expression to work out what he was thinking. 'Who knows?' she said, feeling stung. 'If the tour is successful today I might be back next year.

It would certainly be a pleasure to see Alejandro and Maria again.'

Another silence lengthened between them, and Grace found herself wishing for Nacho to break it. The horses were standing perfectly still for once, and she had lost track of where Nacho was in relation to her. There was nothing worse than this sense of being stranded somewhere she wasn't familiar with, and with a man who had shown such anger when she had done no more than play piano in his house.

'Nacho?' Her heart had begun to race with panic.

'I'm here,' he said. 'Let me help you to dismount.'

His voice was gentle, but though it reassured her, she wasn't ready to forgive him yet. She heard him spring to the ground close by, and now he was walking towards her, no doubt expecting her to wait until she could slide into his arms with relief. 'I know what to do,' she said. 'If you would just hold the pony steady for me?'

Her foot was *not* supposed to catch in the stirrup leather!

'Easy.' Nacho caught her before she hit the ground, but his only comment was, 'Swing your leg wider next time.'

So that was how it was going to be. She pulled herself together fast. 'Where are these new vines you want me to check?'

'This way,' he said.

'Which way?' she said, furious to feel her eyes welling up. 'I can't see where you're pointing.'

'So follow me,' he said. 'Here's Buddy's harness.' Freeing it from the saddle, where Alejandro had told her he had secured it, Nacho handed it to her. 'Would you like me to fasten it for you?'

'No, thank you. I can manage.'

'I dare say you can, but I don't have all day, Grace.'

She blinked, taken aback, but then realised she was so determined to do everything by herself it had never occurred to her that she might be holding other people up. 'I'll be as quick as I can,' she said, dipping down to secure the harness.

Forget heartache. Forget regret. Forget her feelings for the owner of this vineyard. They were irrelevant. She had always wanted to be accepted for who she was, with no allowances made for her being blind. Well, guess what? Nacho supported that wish of hers wholeheartedly. So, okay, now they understood each other. All that mattered now was making a successful survey of the Acosta vines for Elias. All that mattered now was business.

CHAPTER ELEVEN

GRACE was about ten minutes into the tour when she found a problem with the vines.

'What do you mean, you're not happy with the vines?' he demanded when she continued to frown.

'I mean you've got a problem,' she said.

'Well, I can't see anything wrong,' he argued impatiently as he scanned the lush wall of green vines.

'Neither can I,' Grace reminded him with an edge.

'So what *is* the problem?' he said, frowning as he imagined some small alteration to the hydration system, possibly. He exclaimed when she yanked off a yard of vine.

'*This* is your problem,' she said. 'You'll have to destroy this area and isolate it, then spray the rest of your vines with an organic pest control.'

'What the hell are you talking about? They look fine to me. A little dry, perhaps—'

'A *little* dry?' she said, crumbling one of the leaves in her fist and tossing the dust into the air. 'If I'm right, this leaf is providing bed and board for a bug. But as I can't see it I'll need you to confirm my suspicions. Well?' Unfurling another withered leaf, she held it out on her palm.

He cursed beneath his breath when he saw the tiny

bug nesting inside. 'You're right,' he confirmed. 'How could this have happened without anyone noticing?'

Grace's slender shoulders lifted in a shrug. 'This sort of infestation is practically impossible to detect in a forest of green until it takes hold—by which time it's usually too late to do anything about it. But if you run your hands over the vine you can feel the rogue leaves quite easily. I'm guessing your people have been checking them with a ride-by, or on foot?'

His jaw clenched as he accepted she was right.

'Well?' she said. '*Is* that what they do?'

He had to shake himself. He had been staring into Grace's upturned face, thinking she would be gone soon and safe from him, but now he was thinking, *Dios! She'll have to stay and see this thing through*. Torture for him, danger for her.

'Nacho?' she prompted.

'Yes, that's what they do,' he confirmed. 'I realise we'll have to change our procedures. It seems I owe you an apology, Grace.'

'It seems you do,' she agreed.

Touch had served her well again. If they had found this infestation in time, Grace had potentially just saved the vineyard. As the silence lengthened between them his gaze slipped to her lips. He could still taste her on his mouth and remember how she had felt beneath his hands—

'I'll make a call,' she said, crunching another leaf to powder in her hand.

Grace called a scientist who was an expert in viticulture the moment they got back to the house.

'She'll be here tomorrow,' Grace confirmed, ending the call.

'Then what?'

'If I'm correct, she will prescribe the correct spray to use, and then we wait.'

'For how long?'

Grace hesitated. 'A month or so.'

'Will you stay on?'

'I think I have to, don't you?' she said, in the same business-like tone. 'The result of the final survey will be crucial to both sides. Don't worry, I'll book into a hotel. Did I say something funny?' she demanded when he began to laugh.

'Only that the nearest hotel is around three hundred miles away. You'll have to stay here, Grace.'

She said nothing to this, and he felt bad laughing when Grace couldn't know the extent of the land they were standing on. She couldn't see that it stretched to the horizon, where it was bound by the snow-capped Andes, or that it extended for hundreds of miles on either side.

'You can stay on at the guest cottage.'

'Not if I'm in your way.'

'You won't be in my way, Grace.'

No, because Nacho would steer clear from now on, she imagined.

'That's settled, then,' she said, acting as if her heart hadn't been trampled on and business was all that mattered.

The expert arrived the next morning, as Grace had promised, flying in on Nacho's jet to the Acostas' private landing strip. He shook the woman's hand with relief and they strolled through the rows of vines deep in conversation.

'This is in no way finished yet,' the expert informed him. 'Grace has been correct in every detail, but we won't know for some time if the spray I have prescribed is effective. I suggest you keep Grace here and I'll come back in about a month—unless Grace needs me to return sooner.'

The irony of Grace suddenly being in charge didn't escape him. The thought of her staying on was both a relief and a concern, because he still wanted her desperately—even though he believed he was an inherent risk to her.

'At least the damage to the vines isn't irreparable,' Grace pointed out.

'And nowhere as bad as I feared,' he agreed, wondering if those dark circles beneath Grace's eyes meant she had tossed and turned all night like him.

'But you were right to call me,' the forensic viticulturist assured him, distracting him as she came to shake him by the hand again before leaving. 'It could have been a lot worse without Grace's prompt action, but if you remove those rogue vines and spray, the rest the problem should be eradicated.'

'And we should know this in around a month?' he confirmed, glancing at Grace, who showed no emotion.

'That's correct,' the scientist told him. 'Well…your jet's waiting to take me back,' she said, 'so I'll leave you two to organise the spraying and see you both again in a month.'

This was turning out to be the longest month of her life. Concern for the vineyards competed with the ache in her heart, resulting in a constant nagging pain. If it hadn't been for horse riding, and the kindness of Alejandro and Maria, she would have gone stark, staring mad, Grace concluded.

Nacho avoided her for much of the time, though every morning when she got up to check the vines to be sure the spray was doing its job she would invariably find he

was already there before her. He had organised teams of
workers to examine each plant, and she wouldn't have
been surprised to discover that he came here each night
to bathe each individual leaf in spray. The vineyard
meant so much to him.

This morning was no different from the rest, she re-
alised, patting his grazing horse as she walked past.
'Nacho?' she said, feeling her way along the row of vines.
She'd left Buddy with Nacho's horse to keep it company.
She found she moved faster on her own now she knew
every inch of the vineyards intimately.

'I *won't* let my people down,' Nacho exclaimed
fiercely, without pause for *hello, good morning* or *how
are you today?* 'This might have started as a project to
ensure the financial future of my brothers and sister and
their families, but these people...'

When Nacho paused, Grace guessed he was making
a gesture that encompassed all of the land and the cot-
tages on it.

'They mean everything to me, Grace,' he went on, the
passion mounting in his voice with every word. 'They
are fighting alongside us to keep this place running and
we can't let them down, you and I.'

The thought that they were fighting side by side made
her more determined than ever to see this through. She
could sense his desperation to preserve the livelihoods
of his staff, and for a brief moment they stood together—
one mind, one determination, one goal.

'What do you think of the progress so far?' he said.

She ran her hands over the nearest vine. The signs
were good, but she had to tell him honestly, 'It's too
soon to be sure yet.'

'You won't tell Elias?'

'I haven't yet.' Though putting off the moment was

getting harder as Elias grew ever more impatient for her report. 'I'll check the rest,' she said, moving past him as she reminded herself that checking the vines was what she was here for this morning.

'I won't get in your way,' he said.

And so another day without Nacho in her life passed, followed by another long, lonely night. A whole month of waiting anxiously, watching the vines and keeping their distance from each other with plenty of longing, yearning and worrying as they gave the spray time to work, interspersed with bouts of frustration and bewilderment on Grace's part at the change in Nacho. This last concern usually culminated in jaw-grinding anger. She wasn't a saint, and she didn't have a clue what she'd done wrong. Was playing the piano such a sin? Nacho had given her no inkling as to why he had changed so completely towards her between one day and the next. The end result? More sleepless nights, more anxious days.

And now, quite suddenly, or so it seemed, the expert was due back tomorrow.

They stood together as the scientist left, waiting until Alejandro had driven the Jeep away to the airstrip before either of them showed any emotion.

Nacho was the first to speak. '*Dios*, Grace, I can't believe it.'

'A clean bill of health,' Grace murmured, feeling her legs might give way with relief as she sent up fervent thanks.

Inside she was rejoicing, whilst still feeling the exhausting effects of a month of tension—not all of it brought about by waiting for the spray to work. A month of keeping her distance from Nacho hadn't lessened her feelings for him, but they couldn't go on like this. She'd be leaving soon, but if everything went well Elias would insist she made regular visits. She had to make her peace with Nacho even if she still wasn't sure what she'd done wrong. Whatever it was, she couldn't balk at this last hurdle.

'Truce?' she said, extending her hand in his general direction.

'Truce,' Nacho agreed, clasping it.

He seemed reluctant to let her go, and she couldn't bring herself to let him go. Moments passed—it could only have been a split second in reality—before they broke apart.

'So we're free for what's left of the day,' she said, feeling awkward suddenly. They hadn't had any spare time on their hands for a month. Every day since she had discovered that bug in the leaf had been ruled by hourly walk-pasts, checking, testing, spraying again, and waiting. Now they could relax and turn the maintenance programme over to Nacho's staff.

'I'm hungry,' he said.

She heard the frown in his voice and realised that this return to normality wasn't easy for either of them. 'We do need to eat,' she confirmed, thinking of the snatched meals both of them had taken in the kitchen whenever they got a chance.

'And I should say thank you to you,' Nacho remarked.

'Well, thank goodness you've got something to thank me for,' Grace said, smiling. She sensed they were both smiling for the first time in a month.

'Alejandro rode here with you?' he said as they walked back towards the horses.

'Yes, and then he went back for the Jeep. Could you hold Buddy's harness while I mount up?'

'Why don't I buckle Buddy's harness onto my saddle and then help you mount up?' Nacho suggested.

She smiled again—ruefully this time. 'I thought you'd know better than to ask by now.'

'And I thought you'd know better than to refuse,' he said.

She was still smiling when he helped her into the saddle.

'So where are you planning to take me?' she said, gathering up the reins.

'To eat.'

'That's not very helpful. Do I need to change?'

'You're fine as you are,' he said, thinking that Grace was more than fine, she was beautiful—a fact he had fought to ignore for the past month and lost. 'This is the first time I've taken you out,' he said, springing into the saddle.

And she could get *that* rogue thought out of her head right away, Grace informed her inner voice firmly. This was nothing like a first date.

Unfortunately, her heart refused to agree with this premise, and insisted on thundering painfully in her chest. She tried persuasive tactics: lunch would be a really great opportunity to cement their fledgling business relationship.

Oh, really?

Her heart went wild as her pony fell in step with Nacho's stallion. The relief and sheer exhilaration they both felt now the vineyard had been saved made this feel exactly like a first date.

'Is it far?' she said, hoping there would be a chance for her to calm down before they arrived.

'Not far at all. I hope you're not going to be disappointed. It's not much of a place for celebration. It's just a little *cantina* up in the hills, with a lot of local atmosphere attached.'

'Just as long as the food is good,' she said, suddenly realising how hungry she was. Had she even sat down long enough to eat a proper meal in a month?

'The food is excellent and the wine is even better.'

'From the Acosta vineyards?' she guessed.

Nacho confirmed this. 'And there's music, should you feel like dancing.'

As he spoke, Grace's dog positioned itself between them like some self-appointed chaperon.

'Okay, Buddy. Safety's always at the forefront of my mind, too.' He started to clip the lead rein on to the pony's bridle.

'If that's the rope,' Grace said, hearing the click of the catch, 'I don't need it.'

'Grace—'

'Alejandro says so,' she insisted, batting his hand away. What do you think I've been doing for the past month? I've ridden to the vineyards every day. I have to do this on my own. Alejandro trusts me. Don't you?'

Leaning over, he removed the rope. 'No cantering and no surprises, Grace.'

'I certainly hope not,' she agreed.

As Grace turned to say this and her gaze missed his face he remembered again everything she was, and everything he had been missing this past month while they'd been working. One thing was for sure: Grace never allowed anything to hold her back. He'd missed their verbal jousting.

'Hey, hold up,' he warned when Grace took off. 'If you trot as fast as that he'll bounce you right off.'

'And if you won't let me canter what else am I supposed to do? I'll be a mile behind you at this rate.'

He looked at the fixed set of Grace's mouth and re-alised it probably matched his own. 'Infuriating woman,' he muttered, bringing both horses to a halt. 'What part of *no* don't you understand?'

'Am I going too fast for you, Nacho?' Grace said with a defiant smile, lifting her chin.

'I think I can keep up,' he murmured. The look he gave her had stopped grown men dead in their tracks—but then he remembered. Nothing about Grace made it easy to remember she couldn't field those looks and bounce them straight back at him.

'Well?' she pressed. 'Are you ready to canter yet, Nacho?'

He barked a laugh. 'You're not good enough to take the lead yet.'

'But soon,' she said, laughing as she tossed the hair out of her eyes.

He saw no reason to doubt her.

CHAPTER TWELVE

'ARE you still there?' Grace mocked him.

'I'm still here,' he confirmed, noting how well she was managing the horse. Just seeing her in the saddle was enough to fire his blood. So much for not allowing Grace to get too close. He had always said half stubbornness and half instinct made a good rider, and Grace had both. 'You're making good progress,' he granted. If he gave her any more encouragement, knowing Grace, she'd bolt for the hills. 'Loosen the reins and make your hands softer. That's better.'

She blushed at his praise—which took his mind back to the last time he'd seen her face flushed, and led on seamlessly to how it had felt to have Grace's hands on his body. Thinking about that was enough to shake his resolve about sending her home now the vines had a clean bill of health.

'I told you it would be all right,' she called back to him. 'You have to start trusting me, Nacho.'

'And you have to learn to walk before you can canter.'

'Gallop, don't you mean?' she said, urging her pony on.

'Enthusiasm is great, but I'm still going to curb you.'

'I wish you luck with that,' she said, flinging the challenge at him as she rode even faster.

And risk her safety? *Never,* he determined as he urged his stallion to chase Grace's pony down.

'Spoilsport,' she said as he drew level.

'I'm saving you from yourself, Grace,' he said, taking charge of her reins.

She was excited and breathing heavily, and she stirred his blood like no one else. But he'd lived with his barriers too long to break them down now, despite how much he wanted her. 'Do as I say,' he warned, 'or this riding lesson is over. Do I make myself clear?'

'Perfectly,' she said, in a voice still full of defiance.

Was she supposed to like Nacho's stern tone quite so much? Grace wondered. She *liked* standing up to him. She *liked* having a wall to kick against and had missed it during their long month of separation. She settled for riding sensibly, knowing Nacho was probably right. They were both high on victory after the expert's verdict on the vines and feeling invincible right now.

She heard the *cantina* long before they arrived. She could hear the clop of shoes on a raised wooden floor and plates clashing above the racket of good-natured chatter. And just as Nacho had said, there was music—rustic and catchy. A local group, she guessed.

'Okay for you, Grace?' Nacho said, seeing her interest as he sprang down.

'The sounds take me back to the days when I was a waitress,' she admitted.

'Happy days?' he asked, taking her pony's reins over its head.

'Very,' she said, thinking about it. 'I miss the people—and don't forget I met Lucia while I was working as a cocktail waitress. Are you sure I don't look too scruffy?'

'You look great,' he said, helping her to dismount. 'I'll

take the horses and we'll leave Buddy here in the shade. I'll have some water and a steak sent out.'

She laughed. 'Are you trying to get round my best friend?'

'Could be...'

While they waited for their food they talked business—not as bad as it sounded, as they were two equals talking now. Grace had earned Nacho's respect, and their shared interest in saving the vineyard gave them plenty to talk about. And then they didn't talk business. They laughed—something neither of them had done for ages. Laughter shared was closeness too, Grace thought as they relaxed into each other's company. It had been far too long since they'd had a chance to relax.

And then the elderly owner of the *cantina* took Grace by surprise by suggesting that she dance with Nacho, forcing her to make up a couple of golden rules on the hoof: laughter? Yes. Dancing? No. She would never be ready for that. Dancing with Nacho? Being close to him again?

'I'm not sure that's wise,' she said diplomatically. 'I've got two left feet.'

'Fortunately I've got one of each,' Nacho murmured, drawing Grace away from the table.

And now she was on the dance floor, with Nacho's arms around her, remembering...remembering everything, Grace realised as she tried to catch her breath. The only certainty was that his remembered touch was nothing like the real thing. This was so much better, and she was instantly responsive to Nacho's sensitive hands.

To the music, Grace told herself firmly.

'Relax, Grace.'

How could she relax when she was remembering the morning after they'd made love, when Nacho had grown so cold and remote? How could she relax when she didn't have to see the effect Nacho had on other women to know he would be the centre of attention now? How could she relax when she felt like *this* about him?

'You dance well, Grace.'

How could anyone not dance well in Nacho's arms? Even locked in darkness she could feel the rhythm flowing through them. She moved instinctively with him, gaining courage with every step, though it was nothing short of a miracle that she could concentrate at all now she had discovered Nacho was wearing a tight-fitting shirt that left very little to the imagination of her all-seeing hands. It was a struggle to keep a clear head, and a struggle to know what to think when Nacho remained tantalisingly elusive. When she wanted him to drag her close he held her at a safe distance, and when she contrived to let the music bring them together naturally, his touch remained frustratingly impersonal. But, however clever Nacho might be at keeping them just that little bit apart, even he had no answer for the electricity between them—and that was as real and as exciting as it had ever been.

It was only when the music ended and they returned to the table that she realised they had developed a sort of shorthand between them. Nacho touched her arm and she knew when they were approaching her chair. Another touch and she knew roughly where that chair was, could feel for it and sit down. He had a sixth sense for when she wanted help and when it wasn't welcome.

When his shadow crossed her depleted vision she thanked him for the dance, though she guessed they both knew it had been a lot more than that. This time in the *cantina* had allowed them to rebalance their relationship, giving them chance to start over. *Maybe*...

'I really enjoyed that,' she admitted.

She felt the shift of air between them as he bowed ever so slightly in return. 'My pleasure, *señorita*,' he said coolly.

They were so close, so in tune, and yet something vital was missing. There was a chasm between them only the past could fill, and it would take some serious explaining on Nacho's part to do that, Grace realised as their food arrived and the past was something she couldn't force him to talk about.

Navigating a meal was always fraught with potential disaster. And now it turned out she had chosen the messiest food on the menu and was paying the price for it, Grace realised as Nacho rubbed one firm thumb-pad across the swell of her bottom lip.

'Crumbly *empanadas*,' he explained dryly when she drew a fast breath in.

So, not the irresistible attraction of her bee-stung lips?

After the release of tension at the vineyards and the fun they'd had since, chatting and dancing at the cantina, finishing the meal seemed to bring with it a new sort of tension. They had reached the *where-do-we-go-from-here*? point, Grace thought, feeling ready to scream by the time they walked outside. If Nacho wanted to start planning her homeward journey, he only had to say.

'About my flight home—' she said.

What happened next wasn't so much a conscious decision on his part as a reflex action, Nacho realised as he swept Grace off the ground and settled her on the saddle in front of him.

'You could have warned me,' she said, panting with shock as she laughed.

'Why?'

Grace only shook her head and smiled at his arrogance. 'What about my pony?' she said.

'They'll stable him here overnight. Don't worry, Grace, everything is taken care of.'

'Including me?' When he said nothing to this, she added, 'Should I be alarmed, Nacho?'

'Possibly,' he said, tightening his arm around her waist.

'And what about Buddy?' she exclaimed.

'He's coming with us.'

'Coming with us *where*?' she pressed. 'Look, you only have to say. I can pack and be ready to leave as soon as your jet is ready to take me—'

'I don't want to talk about your travel plans, Grace.' This couldn't go on any longer, he realized. Not when they'd been through so much together. 'I need to tell you why I want you to go home.'

'*Why* you want me to go,' she said.

The pain in Grace's voice shamed him after all she'd done for the Acostas, but he couldn't risk taking her into the dark place he inhabited. Just hearing that self-doubt creeping back into Grace's voice was proof of how easily he could wipe out everything she had achieved since her illness. He wanted to reassure her that she had done nothing wrong, that the fault lay with him. Whatever he might feel for Grace, the past would always stand between them. But if he didn't tell her the truth now he would destroy her too.

He rode past the guest cottage and on to the riverbank that held so many memories for him. It was the best place—in fact, the only place—to tell her what he must.

But as he dismounted and turned back to help her down, Grace launched herself from his horse. Almost falling as she reached the ground, she stumbled away from him.

'Grace—wait.'

Her dog, bewildered and uncertain for once, came to sit by his heels and looked up at him. 'Come on, Buddy,' he exclaimed, starting to run. Did she even know where she was going? Grace had left the path and was clambering down the embankment towards the river. Fear raged through him as she grew closer. 'Grace, stop! Come back!'

Memories tumbled on top of one another like an avalanche of guilt, burying him alive as he raced through brambles and over branches to get to her before it was too late. Grabbing her with relief, he hugged her to him as if he would never let her go.

'I'm all right,' she insisted angrily, her voice muffled against his chest.

'You almost fell into the river!'

'I didn't,' she said, still trying to push him away.

'You mustn't run off like that, Grace—'

'What's it to *you*?' she demanded.

'I care about you,' he said, releasing her.

'Then don't,' she said, appearing to attack her clothes rather than straighten them. 'How do you think I manage when you're not around?'

'Please just try and be sensible for once.'

'*Sensible?*' she exclaimed. 'Was I was sensible when I went to bed with you?'

He felt his heart wrench as her blank eyes searched his face. 'Grace—'

'Don't,' she said, shaking her head and turning away.

To hell with that. Catching hold of her wrists, he dragged her back again. 'I don't regret one single moment of making love to you, and I hope you don't regret it either. Well?' he ground out fiercely. '*Do* you regret it, Grace?'

'No,' she raged with matching fire, 'not for one second. But I don't understand how you blow hot and cold. You've barely spoken to me for a month, Nacho. We've achieved something incredible together at the vineyards, and we've had fun celebrating our victory at the *cantina,* and now, just when I think everything is back to normal between us, the curtain comes down.'

He had no answer for her. Well, he did, but it involved telling her about another time by the river that hadn't ended so happily.

Grace had gone still, and he stiffened as she folded like a leaf. Sinking to her knees on the damp earth, she whispered, 'I'm sorry, Nacho. This isn't about me. Please forgive me. I've grown selfish since I've lost my sight.'

With a roar of denial he swept her into his arms. Cupping her chin, he stared into her eyes even though he knew she couldn't see him. 'Selfish is the very last thing I'd call you, Grace. You worked to help save the vineyard and ensure its recovery along with everyone else. You were out every morning at dawn and you didn't stop working until the sun went down. You've been there for us every step of the way. You're the one who should be celebrating, Grace—for what you've achieved. We should all be celebrating.'

'So why aren't you?' she said.

He took a long pause. 'I have something to tell you first,' he said.

'About your past?'

He grimaced. 'I hate things that can't be changed,' he murmured, thinking back.

'You mean you hate things *you* can't change,' Grace argued gently.

He gave a faint smile of acknowledgement—one she couldn't see—and as the seconds ticked it gave him a chance to realise that even his past seemed insignificant when compared with what Grace had had to face.

'And you?' he said. 'What about you, Grace? Nobody ever gets round to asking about you.'

'You're changing the subject,' she said wryly.

'I know,' he whispered, drawing her back into his arms.

She resisted him briefly and weakly, and then she sighed and relaxed. 'So what do you want to know?' she said, resting her head on his shoulder.

'Let's start with everything,' he said.

She laughed as he drew her down onto the bank at his side. 'There's not much to say. I was an only child, a dreamer with a lot of time on my hands. I spent most of that time reading and playing the piano.'

'And your parents?'

'My parents were wonderful—my mother still is. I had a wonderful childhood, but then my father died and my mother remarried—happily, I'm pleased to say.' She shrugged. 'That's about it, I'm afraid.'

That was far from *it*, he thought. He left it a while and then asked, 'Did your father's death upset you greatly?'

'Of course.' She went quiet and then added, 'I felt terrible when we lost Dad, and guilty that I wasn't there for him when he died. I was playing at a concert,' she explained ruefully. 'It all seems so pointless now—'

'Not pointless, Grace. I'm sure your father would have been very proud of you.'

She pressed her lips together, half-smile, half-grimace. 'My mother met someone else quite quickly. He had his own family and they moved into our old house. My bedroom became someone else's bedroom while I was away—don't,' she said, sensing his concern on her be-half. 'It was time for me to move out—too late for me to become part of a new unit.'

'But surely when you became ill—?'

'Are you suggesting everyone should have dropped their own life and rallied round? Why would I expect them to?'

Because they're your family, he thought, knowing that was exactly what his family would do, realising how lucky they were to have such a tight family unit.

'By the time I became ill my mother was on a dozen committees—my stepfather was on even more. Why would I ask them to step in and sort out my life? No one could learn the things I had to learn except me. So what if I had a few more hurdles to jump than I anticipated?'

'Grace—' he scolded.

'I've got wonderful friends like Lucia,' she said, re-fusing to be kept down. 'I've got my health and a job I love—as well as the best guide dog in the world. I've got a fantastic life, Nacho. I wouldn't change a thing.'

'And you've still got your music,' he pointed out.

Grace went quiet. They both did. He had given her the cue she had been waiting for. 'Why did me playing the piano upset you so much?' she asked him bluntly. 'Were you reminded of your mother?'

'I never speak about my personal life,' he said, back-ing off from his earlier decision.

'Too late,' she said as she heard him brush grass and debris from his riding breeches. 'You promised to tell me why I must go. You can't go back on that now. You owe me that much.'

'I owe you a lot more,' he said.

'So tell me what you have done that's so terrible,' she said, confident she would find the right words to destroy

Nacho's demons. Goodness knew she had fought off enough of her own. 'Nothing you can say can shock me.'

'I killed my parents,' he said.

CHAPTER THIRTEEN

It was one of those moments when Grace realised she had no answers, no help to give. She felt as much at sea as she had when the doctor had told her she was going to go blind. A total inability to arrange her thoughts into any sort of useful order left everything a jumble in her mind. Feelings? She had those—and to spare. But when it came to practical answers she had none.

They sat in silence for a long time, and when the fog began to clear she asked the only question she could. 'Can you tell me what happened?'

Nacho took so long to answer she wondered at first if he hadn't heard her, but then he said, 'My late father's life has been well documented in the gutter press, so I guess you already know he wasn't a god.'

'And your mother?' she said carefully, sensing this was where the trouble lay—or why would the piano figure so prominently in Nacho's mind?

'She was left alone while my father was away playing polo.'

'And she was lonely?' Grace guessed, trying to imagine what it must have been like to be a young woman with small children in a foreign country, far away from those she loved. Isolating, but not insurmountable, she thought, remembering the friendliness she had encountered in Argentina. But it wasn't for her to read the past, or judge a woman she didn't know. 'We're not so different, you and I.'

'Meaning?'

'Meaning we both keep a lot hidden inside.'

'Everyone has secrets, Grace, but not everyone has your mountains to climb.'

'Don't worry about me,' she said and then she laughed. 'I've got a great set of crampons.'

She reached for his hand and almost missed it. He took her hand in both of his and linked their fingers. 'Turns out my mother wasn't the flawless icon I believed her to be.'

'You mean she was human?' Grace suggested wryly.

'More than,' he agreed, feeling a surge of contentment as she snuggled close to him. 'But I was naïve.'

'It was a long time ago,' Grace pointed out, pulling away and turning her head, as if she could look at him and receive confirmation of this. 'Are you mistaking young and idealistic for naivety?' she said. 'Tell me.'

'There's not much more to say.'

'Oh,' she said. 'So telling me that you killed your parents is not much…?'

She didn't press the point. She didn't need to. She turned her face to the river, where she heard some birds play-fighting—or maybe it was a mating dance. They were certainly making a lot of noise as they flew back and forth, scraping their wing-tips across the surface of the river as they dipped and soared. It was a special moment. It would be one of those rare events that wildlife photographers waited days to film.

And Grace couldn't see it.

'Tell me the rest, Nacho,' she said.

Turning his mind from Grace's constant battles he

thought back to the past, to the last time he'd heard his mother play the piano. 'On the day of the tragedy I was riding past the *hacienda* while my mother was having her music lesson. I couldn't wait to get off my horse and tell her how much I admired her musicianship. By the time I barged into the house she was in bed with her music teacher—a vain man, who made no secret of his contempt for the wild Acosta children.'

He paused, and even huffed a laugh as he remembered the next bit. It was hard to imagine he had been such a fool.

'Hearing my mother's cries, I burst into her bedroom to rescue her—only to realise they were cries of pleasure.' Grace wasn't smiling, he noticed. He was glad of that. He shrugged. 'That's it.'

'That isn't it,' Grace argued. 'That's no way *it,* Nacho.'

'There are no words—' There truly weren't.

She waited in silence.

'I didn't know my father was on his way home, or that he almost killed the music teacher when he found him with my mother before throwing him out. My mother screamed at my father and told him that she was leaving him for the music teacher and she left the house with him in a blaze of anger. None of us knew the river had burst its banks...'

'And then the flood came?' Grace prompted.

He gave a shuddering sigh as he thought back. 'They would have got away—but my mother insisted on going back into the house to get a ring my father had bought her. Maria told me that. When news reached us that she and her lover had been swept into the water the staff tried to launch a rescue. My father rushed out to try and save her, but the flood water was too fast and too deep. It swept all three of them to their deaths.'

'And where were you?' she said.

'Galloping as far and as fast as I could away from the house, with the devil on my back.'

'But you knew none of this until later,' Grace pointed out. 'You didn't kill your parents, Nacho, and you mustn't think that. The flood killed your parents. Nature killed your parents.'

'I could have saved them if I'd been here,' he insisted.

'Nacho,' she said, sitting back, 'you just have to accept there are some things you can't control.'

He was silent for a long time, and then he said, 'Like you, Grace?'

As the tension slowly eased between them she relaxed.

'You should stay,' he said. 'Stay on here, Grace. Help me to build the vineyards into something we can both be proud of.'

Hugging her knees, she smiled ruefully and shook her head.

'I'm asking you to stay,' he said. Taking both her hands in his, he broke the habit of a lifetime to plead for what he knew was right. 'I'm asking you to stay in Argentina with me. You don't have to go back to England. I'll take care of you.'

'No!' she exclaimed, pulling her hands free. 'Just listen to yourself, Nacho. I don't want anyone to *take care of me*. I'm not an invalid.'

'I phrased that badly.'

'No,' she said again—more fiercely than before. 'You phrased that exactly as you meant it to sound.'

'What's wrong with wanting to protect you and care for you?' he demanded. 'Do feelings frighten you, Grace?'

'No. *This* frightens me,' she said, sweeping a hand

across her eyes. 'Were you ever frightened of the dark, Nacho?'

He shook his head, feeling more ashamed at his ignorance of how Grace must be feeling than he had after his own tragedy.

'And if you lived in permanent darkness like me?' she said.

'I couldn't begin to imagine it,' he admitted.

'I used to think I'd know what it was like to be blind—back in the days when cheating was still possible and I put an eye mask on to perform a few simple tasks around the house. Have you ever tried balancing things on a tray with your eyes shut?'

'Grace—all I'm trying to say is that you don't have to be alone.'

'But I *am*,' she said, sounding distraught as she covered her face with her hands. 'I'm alone in *here*,' she insisted, shaking her head.

'What do you miss most?' he said fiercely, determined to shake her out of this. 'Come on, Grace—tell me!' Forced to resort to plucking her fingers from her face, he held them firmly in his as he demanded again, 'What do you miss the most, Grace?' He wanted her to taste the same freedom he did after dealing with the past—that sense of being like a helium balloon, flying high and free. 'Grace?' he prompted. 'Tell me.'

'Clouds,' she said suddenly.

He held his breath, certain she would come back to him.

'That's what I miss the most,' she said. 'I miss staring into the sky and deciding what the shapes are—I miss watching them scudding by to who knows where? I bet your mother used to look up and wonder if those same clouds were going to travel to where your father was. She must have been so lonely and frightened, Nacho.'

'And if *you* were alone here without friends?'

'I can't imagine that,' Grace said, remembering the young girl at the grape-treading and the kindness of Maria and Alejandro.

'You can't imagine being alone in this wilderness?' Nacho pressed.

She huffed a small laugh. 'Wilderness is a state of mind, surely? I've got the same view here as I do in London—that is to say nothing much. But that's okay,' she said, brightening as she thought about it, 'because I like people so much, and I like to think I can make friends anywhere. And don't forget your mother went back for her ring. She must have loved your father or why would she bother? And why would your father try to rescue your mother if he didn't love her?'

'You're such a dreamer, Grace.'

'Is that such a bad thing? Isn't it better to dream happy dreams than have nightmares? Life is fragile, but love is stronger. Sometimes I think we get those two things mixed up. Your parents were human and flawed, but at the end they proved they loved each other. If they were guilty of anything it was taking each other for granted. The real tragedy is that they were killed before they could make things right.'

'And what about us, Grace?'

'Us?'

Biting down on her lip, she looked as if she might cry. Only Grace's sheer force of will drove the tears back, he suspected.

'This is so unfair,' she said, lifting her face to his. 'You're not supposed to read my feelings like a book. I'm supposed to be the one who senses things.'

'So what do your senses tell you, Grace?'

Her eyes welled with tears. 'You make me feel too much,' she said in an angry voice.

'But that's a good thing, isn't it?'

She shook her head, as if he had missed the point entirely. 'Nacho, for goodness' sake, what do you think I am? I would *never* burden you with a blind woman—'

'Stop that.' Dragging Grace into his arms, he embraced her as if his life depended on it, only now realising what he had almost lost. 'Don't you *ever* say anything like that again,' he warned.

'Why not, when it's true?' she said. 'You've spent your life caring for other people. This is *your* time now, Nacho.'

'I'm not going anywhere,' he said, holding Grace tight against his chest. 'Still not,' he said when she made a feeble attempt to push him away.

'I'm warning you—'

'No, you're not,' he argued gently. 'You're asking for reassurance, and that's all I want to give you. I'm not very good at expressing myself, Grace, but in my eyes you're perfect. There's so much I want to show you.' He swore softly beneath his breath, realizing that even now he could get it wrong. 'So much I want you to experience,' he clarified, angry with himself for being so clumsy when words had never mattered more.

This wasn't about Grace being blind, or him wanting to smother or control her. He wanted to protect her when she couldn't help herself, and there were times when even the strongest woman couldn't do that. He wanted to be there for her in the darkness and in the light. He just wanted to be with her—and he wanted Grace to feel the same way about him.

'No, Nacho. I couldn't do that to you.'

She was tempted—God knew she was tempted. There was so much she had grown to love in Argentina—the kindness of the people, the scents and sounds of a new country, the rhythm of life on the vineyard...

And Nacho...

Nacho was a good enough reason as any to go away. She had always prided herself on being a realist, and an affair with Nacho could only leave her shredded and facing a whole new mountain to climb when the affair ended.

Was she a coward now? Too frightened to love?

Love wasn't even a word that was relevant where Nacho was concerned. Her feelings for him were complex. Sexual feelings had mixed with this recent bond of friendship, confusing her into believing what she felt had somewhere to grow. At best they were business associates and maybe friends. And what really frightened her about that was the more he encouraged her the more she might depend on him—losing her freedom, losing her will to fight.

'Grace?'

She turned towards the sound of his voice.

'So you're still with me?' he murmured, in that dark, husky, sexy voice.

'I'm still here,' she confirmed. 'I was just enjoying the sounds of the countryside while I can.'

'You can't wait to leave?'

'My life is in the crowded city. Your life is here on the pampas, with your vineyards and your horses.'

'You sound very sure.'

'I know I can't stay,' she said, determined she wouldn't burden him. Yes, in the light of what had happened today, the truly wonderful news at the vineyard, Nacho was naturally upbeat and could only see bright things in the

future—while she liked to think she was more of a realist who knew this burst of light would eventually fade
into darkness again.

'You can't stay or you won't?' Nacho demanded.

'I can't *and* I won't,' she said.

Ironically, the birdsong chose the moment Grace decided not to stay with him to reach its climax. The fact
that she had refused made no difference to the rowdy and
enthusiastic chorus. It was like the wrong soundtrack for
a film—discordant and inappropriate.

'So, you won't even stay to celebrate, when people
will surely want to thank you for what you've done?'

'It's you they should thank,' she said, wobbling a little
as she stood up on the uneven bank. Then she relented.
'I'll stay until I'm sure the vines have recovered—If
you want me to.'

'Of course I want you to. What would the celebration
be without you? Your prompt action saved the vineyard.
I'm going to invite everyone who works here and bring
the whole family over to make it something really special for you.'

'I said I'd stay until the vines had recovered. I said
nothing about staying on for a party.' She gave a small
smile. 'I'm only sorry I won't be here to share it with
you.'

'What are you talking about?' Defeat being snatched
from the jaws of victory described this moment perfectly.
'What happened to all that brave talk about seeing things
through to the end, Grace? You're all right with the bad
stuff, but not with the good—is that it?'

'That's not fair,' she protested. 'My job here is done.
As soon as I can make a report to Elias with a clear
conscience I have to get back to him. You'll get your
order,' she said.

His order? He had almost forgotten the damn order.

'I've got to go,' Grace insisted, moving away from him. 'I've got a life to live and a career to pursue.'

'And a duty to see this through!' he shouted after her.

Honouring his promise not to treat Grace as if there was something wrong with her meant watching and doing nothing as she crawled on her hands and knees up the bank, feeling for hazards on the ground along the way. He hated every loathsome second of it—but that was Grace, he accepted. That determined, stubborn, courageous blind woman was who she was, and if he couldn't accept it he should let her go.

He went after her.

'So what's your hurry?' he said. 'What are you so frightened of, Grace?'

'Nothing,' she said, straightening up to confront him, her determined stare missing his face by a mile.

'Then why are you shutting me out?'

'Why am I shutting *you* out? You've got a nerve after the way you've been behaving.'

'Do we need to go back over that?' he demanded, towering over her.

With an angry huff of frustration she felt for a space to get past him, with her arms outstretched like a child about to pin a tail on the donkey. The sight tore him up—but Grace was no child, and the bank was full of potential risk as she climbed rapidly, recklessly, away from him.

'Will you be satisfied when you've fallen into the river?' he demanded in a fury of concern.

She stopped and turned so abruptly he felt sure she'd tumble down the bank. He was aching with tension from standing ready to catch her if she slipped, but even that was nothing to the pain in his heart.

'What are you frightened of, Grace?' he said again.

'Me? Frightened?' she demanded, with an incredulous laugh in her voice.

'*Why* can't you risk giving any part of yourself to another person? *Why* do you always see that as giving up your independence? The Grace who recovered from the challenges you've faced should move on now, not close her mind to possibilities.'

'What possibilities?' she said impatiently. 'I've done everything I've been advised to do. I attended the rehabilitation centre religiously. I learned to read Braille. And thanks to your sister, I have Buddy to help me do practically anything a sighted person can do—'

'I'm talking about personal relationships,' he interrupted. 'What about those, Grace? No one could ever accuse you of falling short where practicalities are concerned.'

'All right!' she exclaimed angrily. 'So you didn't get it the first time. I don't want to be a burden, Nacho. Do you get it now?'

'I'm afraid I don't,' he said. 'Have you considered that it might be you who sees yourself as a burden and no one else does? Can you give me one example of when you've been a burden while you've been here? You have performed better than most experts in your field. And I certainly haven't heard anything to the contrary from my staff. They're very grateful to you, Grace, as I am. So I *don't* get all this nonsense about being a burden.'

Biting down on her lip, she shook her head, as if she couldn't believe he couldn't see the truth in front of his eyes. 'People are wary when they meet me for the first time—like they're not quite sure what I might ask them to do.'

'Stop right there,' he said, grabbing her arms. 'Is that

how Alejandro treated you? Or Maria? Or the old guy at the cantina? Are you saying that's how I am? Or is this all in your head, Grace? Are *you* the one who's guilty of prejudice here? You've had a traumatic time—I get that. And then a healing time of readjustment—I get that too. But now you're on your way, and it's time for you to move forward—not look back. You're so good at helping others. Why can't you help yourself? At least stay on for the party,' he insisted when she started to pull away. 'You helped to avert a catastrophe. You owe yourself that much, Grace.'

'I didn't do it for a pay-off.'

'I'm not saying you did, but you should be gracious enough to allow the people who work here to thank you.'

'Blackmail, Nacho?'

'Whatever it takes,' he said dragging her into his arms.

Nacho's kiss was fierce to begin with, but then it became long and gentle, and after all the passion flying between them what she really wanted now was just for him to hold her so she could stop fighting for a while.

'So what's your answer, Grace? I think I know where you're at,' Nacho added in a whisper against her hair. 'I'm an expert in knowing that when you start a fight it's very hard to draw back and almost impossible to take time out so you can see there could be another, even better way. You don't have to race back to London to find another dragon to slay. Why don't we play out what we've got here and see where it leads?'

'What about my career? I'm just getting started.'

'So go back to London after the celebrations, if that's what you want. I'll just make one more observation. Your knowledge of viticulture is bang up to date, and that's something we're badly in need of here.'

'Are you offering me a job?' she said, lifting her head.

'If you find that suggestion more acceptable than any other,' he said wryly, 'then yes, I am. You've certainly more than proved we need someone like you on the team, Grace.'

'And when my contract ends? This sounds like a short-term contract with long-term repercussions.'

'Why are you always so ready to be hurt? And stop avoiding the issue. Or are you frightened to face the truth?'

'What truth?' she said, frowning.

'That this isn't about the vineyards now. It's about you and me.'

Turning away from him, she hugged herself. 'I don't want to be hurt,' she blurted, burying her chin in her chest. 'I don't think I could handle it.'

'Who says I'm going to hurt you, Grace?' he argued, pulling her close again. 'You've been through a lot—more than I can imagine. Your emotional bank is drained. But you can fill it again and I can help you— if you'll let me.'

'What about Elias and my training? I can't just leave him in the lurch and come and work for you.'

'Can't you do both?' he said. 'I would have thought you could get around the world even faster for Elias with the Acosta jet at your disposal...'

'Are you serious?'

Nacho's answer was to draw her into his arms. 'Never more so,' he said.

Was it wrong to rest here, where she felt so safe? Was it dangerous to admit that together they might be stronger, and that that thought had nothing at all to do with her love of sight?

'You do know Elias is retiring soon?' Nacho said.

'He told you that?' Surprised, she placed her hands flat against his chest, where the beat of Nacho's heart was strong and steady.

'He did more than that,' Nacho explained. Taking her hands, he raised them to his lips, kissing each of them in turn. 'Elias called me and asked if I would be interested in buying his business.'

'What?' she breathed. She was stunned by this new information, but now she could see it made perfect sense for both men. 'Elias could retire in comfort while you would have the whole process covered from vine to glass.'

'An undreamed of advancement for the business,' Nacho confirmed. 'And with you by my side. Come and join me, Grace,' he challenged. 'The vineyards need you, the people who work here need you—I need you.'

'*You* need me?'

Nacho didn't touch her and he didn't speak. This was her decision to make alone. She had never wanted to be a wealthy man's woman, cosseted and protected from the realities of life, and she didn't want it now she was blind. She was used to fighting every day just to stay in the same place. But wasn't fighting for the livelihoods of the people who worked here a battle worth winning too? Wasn't confronting life head-on worth some effort? Or was she going to hide away now she'd reached a certain level in her recovery, and declare herself out?

'Just think of what you could achieve here, Grace— what we could *both* achieve. Don't let your blindness prevent you from taking this next step forward. You've learned to ride while you've been here. What's stopping you now? You can do anything you want to do.'

'What are you saying, Nacho?'

'I'm saying that I love you, and that I want you to stay with me always.'

'You *love* me?'

Terror suffused her. Not at the thought of all the work ahead of her, but at the thought of the biggest step of all… Love. Commitment to love for ever. Committing herself to Nacho. Risking her heart for something bigger than both of them. It was all she wanted, but now she could have it her courage had gone. He was right about her emotional bank being depleted. It was empty. She had nothing left to give him.

'This is where you belong. I belong in London. Please don't fight me on this, Nacho. My decision's made.'

He made no attempt to follow Grace as she struggled to the top of the bank. Her determination was, as ever, uncompromising. When she stumbled she picked herself up. When a tree branch slapped her in the face she pushed it away and moved on. He felt more emotion in those few seconds than he could ever remember feeling before. He had felt little since the day of the tragedy, and nothing came close to this.

But seeing Grace on the point of throwing away her life galvanised him into action, and in a couple of bounds he was ahead of her on the bank. There was only one certainty in his mind. The only woman he had ever loved wasn't going to walk out of his life for ever.

'I won't let you go,' he said fiercely.

'You can't stop me,' she warned, clearly frantic in her darkness.

'You don't have to fight all the time, Grace,' he said, holding her close. 'It's great to be in control—*Dios*, I should know. But it isn't a sign of weakness to share the load. Everyone has to ask for help from time to time, whether they can see or not. Give yourself a break,

Grace. Stand still for a moment and think about what you've accomplished.'

She turned her face towards him and his heart soared.

'Did you really just say you love me?'

'Yes, I did.' Reaching for Grace's hands, he knotted their fingers. 'And I'll never take you for granted,' he whispered fiercely, dragging her into his arms.

Concern for his mistress had brought Buddy snuffling round their feet. 'Not this time, boy,' he murmured as he swept Grace into his arms and carried her towards the cottage. 'I'll take over now…'

He carried Grace up the stairs into the small bedroom, where the windows were open to allow the early evening breeze to cool a room scented with day-warmed frangipani. He undressed her slowly, reverently, and then, stripping off his own clothes, he stretched out beside her on the crisp linen sheets.

'Just hold me,' she whispered.

To hold Grace in his arms was all he wanted. He could think of nothing he wanted more than to sleep with her and wake with her in the morning. To share tomorrow and the next day and the next with Grace. To live with her until they were both old and surrounded by their children and their children's children.

His kisses were slow and easy now, because they had all the time in the world. And when they sighed together, content, at home, complete, he asked her, 'Will you marry me, Grace?'

'I will,' she said, smiling against his mouth.

He felt a great surge of awe and pride that this incredible woman had chosen him. 'I love you,' he murmured after she'd fallen asleep.

'I love you too,' she whispered.

'So you weren't sleeping,' he said, kissing her again.

She nestled her head against his chest. 'You've done so much for me, Grace.'

'I've done so much for *you*?' she queried groggily.

'You've set me free,' he said.

EPILOGUE

ACROSS the world it was dubbed the wedding of the year, but for Grace it was the wedding of a lifetime—her lifetime and Nacho's.

A few carefully screened photographers were to be allowed in to record the event, with all the proceeds going to their new scheme to introduce blind youngsters to horse riding. The marriage ceremony was to be held at the *hacienda*, so it could be a double celebration in which everyone could join in.

It was a real family affair, with Nacho's sister-in-law—the celebrated wedding planner Maxie Acosta—in charge of the arrangements. To ensure Grace enjoyed her day as much as everyone else, Maxie had filled the sumptuously decorated marquee with delicately scented blossoms, and as Grace walked in on the arm of her new husband they crushed rose petals beneath their feet. Elias had been flown in on the family's jet at Nacho's personal invitation, and all the Acostas were there.

Lucia had helped Grace to choose her wedding dress—a dream of filmy silk chiffon, soft to the touch, edged with the finest Swiss lace embellished with tiny crystals and seed pearls because Grace liked the way they tickled her palm and Lucia said she glittered like a queen. There was even a new collar for Buddy, whose new best friend was Cormac, Nacho's Irish Wolfhound. Nacho's big dog had made the trip from the family's main *estancia* in the back of Ruiz Acosta's car.

Grace had only wanted a plain gold wedding band, but a man like Nacho could never be tamed to the extent where Grace would be allowed to instruct him on the subject of the type of jewellery to buy for his wife.

'And thank goodness for it,' Lucia exclaimed after the ceremony, as she examined Grace's diamond-encrusted wedding band. 'You can always have plain gold for everyday.'

Grace laughed indulgently as she hugged her new sister-in-law, glad that some things, like extravagant, fun-loving Lucia, would never change.

'Though I still can't believe Nacho went shopping,' Lucia said, frowning as she held Grace's hand up to the light.

'I think he had the jeweller come to him,' Grace confessed.

'And why not?' a husky voice demanded.

'Talk of the devil,' Lucia murmured dryly, leaving the newlyweds alone.

'I have a very special wedding gift for you,' he murmured, drawing Grace into his arms.

'But you've given me so much already' she said, quivering with love and desire when he found the sweet spot behind her ear.

'Come on,' he prompted, linking his arm through hers.

'Are we going into the *hacienda*?' she said, hearing the gravel path beneath their feet.

'Not for the reason you think,' he said as her breathing

quickened. 'We must be back in time for the first dance, or the wedding breakfast will grind to a halt.'

'But I don't need a gift,' Grace insisted, pulling back. 'I don't need anything but you. I wouldn't be able to see a gift anyway,' she pointed out with her unfailing logic.

'But you'll hear it,' he said. 'Sit…play.' Taking her by the hand, he led her to the piano stool. 'I finally got round to having all the pianos tuned,' he explained. 'They're all yours now, Grace. Everything I have is yours.'

He shouldn't be surprised at the sensitivity in those hands, Nacho realised, but the sounds Grace coaxed from a piano had to be heard to be believed. She made him want to listen to her all night. Well, almost all night, he accepted wryly as his gaze tracked up Grace's arms to the nape of her neck—so soft, so kissable.

'I'm sorry if I'm interrupting—'

He swung round in anger, hearing a woman's voice. Who would dare intrude at a time like this? 'Can I help you?' he asked frostily.

'I've come to take some photographs,' the diminutive photographer informed him boldly.

'Nacho,' Grace murmured, feeling his hackles rise. 'Can *I* help you?' she said, standing up.

'My apologies,' the girl said, speaking to Grace with more respect than she'd shown Nacho. 'I was supposed to check in with someone called Kruz Acosta?'

'My brother isn't here—as you can see,' Nacho cut in with an angry gesture. 'I imagine he's with the other guests in the marquee.'

'Would it be all right to take some photographs now I'm here?' the girl suggested. 'My name's Romily—Romily Winner, from *ROCK!* magazine. The magazine your sister-in-law Holly works for?' she prompted.

'Of course. I've been expecting you. I read your column. It's really good.'

'Thank you.'

'Nacho?' Grace prompted.

'I don't know it,' he said brusquely. 'But if you want some photographs you'd better get on with it. We're needed back at the marquee.'

'Perhaps if Grace could sit at the piano and you could stand behind her?' the girl called Romily suggested.

'Of course we will,' Grace accepted before Nacho could argue.

'So...that was interesting,' Grace said, when Romily had finished the photoshoot and left them. 'Do you think Holly is trying to set your brother up with Romily?'

'Who knows what goes through Holly's head,' he said with a shrug.

'What does she look like?' Grace asked him.

'I wouldn't have thought she was Kruz's type.'

'That's not much help,' Grace said with a laugh in her voice as they walked arm-in-arm to the door.

His lips pressed down as he shook his head, stumped for an answer. 'She looks...alternative.'

'Alternative? Now you *really* have to fill me in.'

'Piercings, tattoos, black eye make-up—leather clothes. As tiny as a whip, but more trouble than any man needs.'

'She sounds interesting,' Grace commented, her lips curving in an amused smile. 'Just what your rebel brother needs.'

'More trouble? I don't think so.' Nacho swung the big oak door wide, but before they stepped outside he brought Grace into his arms and kissed her. 'I suppose we *do* have to get back?' he said.

'To our own wedding breakfast? Yes, I think we must,' Grace said wryly. 'Let's make one condition.'

'Name it,' he said.

'As soon as we've cut the cake you and I come back here alone for dessert.'

'It's a deal,' Nacho agreed, dragging his wife into his arms for a hungry kiss.

* * * * *

THE UNTAMED
ARGENTINIAN

CHAPTER ONE

'Do you mind if I join you?'

A shiver of recognition ran down Bella's back as the man with the husky Latin American voice lifted the latch on the stable door and walked in. There was only one man who could breeze through security in Her Majesty's backyard: the Guards' Polo Club in Windsor. Nero Caracas, known as the Assassin in polo circles, played off ten, the highest ranking a polo player could achieve, and enjoyed privileges around the world others could only dream of. Impossibly good-looking, Bella had seen Nero commanding the field of play, and had lusted after him like every other hot-blooded woman, but nothing could have prepared her to be this close to so much man.

'So this is Misty,' he said, running an experienced palm down the pony's shoulder. 'She looks smaller close up—'

'Appearances can be deceptive.' Racing to the defence of her favourite pony, Bella forced her hands to go on oiling the mare's dainty hooves. She'd lived close to animals for so long she was as acutely tuned in to danger as they were and, though the mare seemed calm, Bella was on red alert.

'The match starts soon—'

And? Bella thought, still polishing. As trainer and one of the coaches of the British team, she knew only too well when the match started. Surely it was Nero, as captain of the opposing team, who should be elsewhere?

Nero's reputation preceded him. He had obviously thought he could drop in and his smallest wish would be granted with one eye on the timetable for a match in which he would captain the Argentinian team. No such luck. The Assassin could yield to the Ice Maiden on this occasion. And he did, but with a warning glint in his eye. 'I need to speak to you about Misty,' he said, running another appreciative glance over her pony.

'This isn't the time,' Bella said coolly, realising only when their stares clashed that she was running the same type of assessing look over Nero—experience had nothing to do with it. Her points of reference were in her head. And all the better for staying there, she thought, having taken in Nero's dark tan, close-fitting white breeches, plain dark polo shirt, wayward curls catching on his ferocious black stubble, not to mention the leather boots hugging his hard-muscled calves. It was safer, certainly.

'As you wish,' he said.

When he dipped his head, one professional acknowledging another, she saw the steel of challenge in his eyes. Nero Caracas was hardly the most sensible enemy for a woman in Bella's precarious financial position to make. The recession had taken a deep bite out of her resources and the polo world was too small, too incestuous to take chances. You failed in the eyes of one, you failed in the eyes of everyone. But she wouldn't fail, Bella told herself firmly, straightening up to confront this god of the game. 'Is that everything?'

Nero's lips pressed down. 'No,' he said with a shake

of his head. 'I think Misty would benefit from being ridden by a man who really appreciates her—'

'I can assure you that the captain of the English team appreciates Misty—'

'But does he ride her in a way that brings Misty pleasure?'

Did Nero Caracas have to make everything sound like an invitation to bed?

She glanced at her watch.

'Do I make you nervous, Bella?'

She laughed. 'Certainly not—I'm merely concerned that you're leaving yourself dangerously short of time.'

'My timing is split second,' Nero assured her.

Was that humour in his eyes? As the rugged Argentinian caressed Misty's neck, Bella lost herself for a moment. All muscles and tough, virile appeal, Nero Caracas was quite a man. Another woman, another time—who knew what might come of this meeting? Bella thought wryly, dragging herself round.

'En garde,' Nero murmured when she came to stand between him and the dapple grey polo pony. 'I would like you on my side, Isabella, not working against me for the competition.'

Bella gave him an ironic look. 'I'm very happy where I am, thank you.'

'Maybe I can change your mind—'

'I wish you joy of that—'

'If that's a gauntlet, I should warn you, Bella, I always pick them up.'

Too much man—too close—too desperately disturbing...

Irritated by the fact that her highly strung mare had remained calm when Nero had entered the stable, Bella demanded sharply, 'Anything else?'

Sensation overload, she registered dizzily as Nero's long dark stare made her heart go crazy. Nero Caracas was ridiculously attractive and had more charisma than was good for any man. No woman wanted to be reduced to a primal mating state by an unreconstructed male. A woman wanted control—something Bella possessed in vast amounts…usually.

Nero raised his hands in mock surrender. 'Don't worry, I'm going. But I'll be back to see you, Misty,' he crooned to the unusually compliant mare.

Bella's eyes flashed fire. 'When I'm not here, Misty is protected by the most stringent security measures.'

'Which I'll be sure to bear in mind—' Nero's Latin shrug could easily be translated as *So what?*

No one would keep him out. Nero Caracas could do anything he wanted, buy anything he wanted. Chatter around the yard suggested the famous Argentinian wanted to buy Misty, the polo pony Bella had foolishly allowed herself to love.

'You've done well with Misty, Bella,' Nero observed as he paused by the stable door. 'She's in prime condition—'

'Because she's happy with me—'

Nero's head dipped in acknowledgement of this, but the sardonic smile on his lips suggested he had more to offer any horse than she did.

She was at risk of losing Misty. The th   w k Bella like a bombshell. There was always press. e— honour in the game that demanded the best players were given the best polo ponies to ride. Misty was the best, and only a fool would stand in the way of a rider like Nero Caracas and expect to keep the career she loved intact.

'Until the next time, Bella—'

I wouldn't count on it, Bella thought, tightening her lips. There would be no *next time.* Misty was all she had left of her late father's yard—her late father's honour. While Misty was on the field people still talked of Jack Wheeler as the best of trainers, and forgot for that moment that Bella's father had been a gambler who had lost everything he had ever worked for. 'Misty only runs for those she trusts.'

'Like any woman.' Nero's smile deepened, carving an attractive crease in the side of his face. Coming back to the pony, he ran an experienced hand down Misty's near foreleg. 'Good legs,' he commented as he straightened up.

And she felt hers tingling too. The look Nero gave her left Bella in no doubt that everything in the stable had been assessed. She was way out of her depth here. If only Nero would go and everything could return to normal. 'Enjoy the match,' she said numbly, conscious of the power he wielded in the game.

'You too, Bella—' There was both humour and challenge in his voice.

'Misty will outrun your Criolla ponies from the Pampas—'

'We'll see.' Nero shot her an amused glance. 'My Criollo are descendants of the Spanish war horses. Their power is second to none. Their loyalty? Unquestioned. Stamina?' His lips pressed down in the most attractive way. 'Unrivalled, Bella. And it goes without saying that combat is in their genes.'

And Nero's, Bella thought. She'd watched him play, and had marvelled at his speed and agility, his hand-to-eye coordination, uncanny intuition, and the eager way Nero's ponies responded to him. She had never thought she would feel those subtle powers working on her. 'May the best man win,' she said, tilting her chin at a defiant angle as she rested a protective hand on Misty's neck.

'I have no doubt that he will,' the undisputed king of the game informed her.

She had always felt safe in the stables, with the scent of clean hay in her nostrils and the warmth of an animal she could trust close by, but that safety had just been challenged by a man whose voice was like a smoky cellar, deep and evocative, though ultimately cold. Whatever game it was, she must never forget that Nero Caracas always played to win. 'Win or lose today, Misty is not for sale—'

'I've completed my examination, and I like what I see,' Nero remarked as if she hadn't spoken. 'Of course, Misty would need to pass the vet's exam,' he went on thoughtfully, 'but if she fulfils her promise today, as I'm sure she will, I'd like to make you an offer, Bella. Name your price.'

'There is no price, Señor Caracas.' She wasn't going to roll over just because Nero Caracas said she must. 'I don't need your money.'

Nero angled his head. He didn't need to say anything to echo the thoughts of everyone else in the polo world, all of whom knew that couldn't be true. 'You might not need my money, *chica*,' he said with a faint mocking edge to his voice, 'but you must need something. Everybody does…'

'Is that a threat?' Was she to lose everything she had worked for? A flash of panic speared through her as the dark master of the game stared her down. Why should Nero answer when he was the centre of the polo universe, around which everything else revolved? He had more money, more skill on the field and a better eye for the horse than any man alive. Why was she challenging him when Nero Caracas could dash her career against the wall with a flick of his wrist?

'Relax,' he murmured. 'You work too hard and worry too much, Bella. Polo?' The massive shoulders eased in a shrug. 'It's only a game.'

Only a game?

'I look forward to seeing Misty play.' The dark eyes stared deeper into her soul than they had any right to and then he was gone.

Bella let out a shuddering breath and slumped back against the cold stone wall. How could she fight him? But fight him she would if Nero pushed her, Bella determined as one of her grooms came in and, after a few covert sideways glances, asked if Bella was all right.

'I'm fine… Fine,' Bella confirmed, wishing she was back at home with her dogs and horses, where life was uncomplicated, and where the children she encouraged to visit her stable yard learned how to care for animals in a blissfully down-to-earth setting. Mess with Nero and she would lose all that.

'Shall I take Misty to the pony lines?'

The girl glanced towards the stable door as she spoke, and Bella guessed she must have passed the master of the game on his way out. Nero threw off an aura of power and danger, which had made the young girl anxious. 'Yes, take her,' she confirmed, 'but don't let her out of your sight for a moment.'

'I won't,' the girl promised. 'Come on, Misty,' she coaxed, taking hold of the reins.

'Actually, I've changed my mind—I'll come with you.' She had intended to check the other ponies first, but she could do that at the pony lines. Nero Caracas turning up unannounced had really shaken her. He had reminded her that her life was a house of cards that could collapse at any time and that Nero Caracas never paid anyone a visit without a purpose in mind.

She would just have to fight his fire with her ice, Bella concluded, shutting the stable door behind them. She had done it before and come through in one piece. There was still talk about how her father's gambling had destroyed his career, which was one reason she still had the Ice Maiden tag. Life had taught her to keep rigid control over her feelings at all times. And Misty was more than just a pony; the small mare was a symbol of Bella's determination to rebuild the family name. She had promised her father before he died that she would always keep Misty safe. So could she fight off this bid from Nero Caracas?

She had to. Nero might be every woman's dream with his blacksmith's shoulders, wicked eyes and piratical stubble, but she had a job to do.

'Good luck, Bella,' the stable hands chorused as she crossed the yard.

Lifting her hand in recognition of their support, she hurried on, afraid to let Misty out of her sight now.

'The Argentine team is looking good,' one of the grooms observed, keeping pace with her for a few steps. 'Especially Nero Caracas—he's been living up to his nickname in the last few matches. The Assassin has cut a swathe through the competition—'

'Great. Thank you.' She didn't need reminding that Nero inhabited a brutal world. He might feel at home here, and play the role of gentleman in the prince's back-yard, but Nero lived in Argentina, where he bred and trained his ponies on an *estancia* the size of a country on the vast untamed reaches of the pampas.

The pampas.

This conjured up such fabulous images—terrifyingly wild and impossibly dangerous.

And the sooner he went back there, the sooner she could relax, Bella told herself firmly. They had reached the pony lines where the horses were tethered to wait their turn to enter the match. 'I'll never let you go,' she whispered, throwing her arms around Misty's firm grey neck. 'And I'd certainly never sell you on to some black-hearted savage like Nero Caracas. Why, I'd sooner—'

The images that conjured up had to stop there. Burying her face against Misty's warm hide, Bella tried and failed to blot out the image of her moaning with pleasure in Nero's arms. Daydreams were one thing, but she'd be sure to lock the stable door in future.

He never listened to gossip. He preferred to make up his own mind about people, places, animals, things—

And Isabella Wheeler.

The Ice Maiden's eyes had been wary and hostile to begin with, but not by the time he had left her. Why was Bella's luscious, long red hair cruelly contained beneath a net? It was preternaturally neat, but he had detected a wild streak beneath that icy veneer. He had seen enough ponies standing meekly in the corral, only to kick the daylights out of a groom if they weren't approached with respect. Control ruled Bella. She had earned the highest respect in equine circles, but still managed to remain an enigma, without a shred of gossip concerning her private life. How could she not present him with a challenge he found impossible to resist?

Mounting up, he gathered his reins and called his team around him for the pep talk. He was unusually wired and the men knew it. They stared at him warily whilst keeping a tight rein on their own restless mounts.

'No mercy,' he warned, 'but don't risk the horses. And take care of the grey the English captain will be riding. Depending on how the grey does today, I might want to buy her—'

Bella wouldn't sell her horse to him?

His determination to change that mounted as he remembered Bella would barely speak to him. The thought of unbuttoning that tightly laced exterior and seeing her eyes beg for pleasure instead of challenging him was all the encouragement he needed. He wanted her to relax for him. He wanted to discover who Bella Wheeler really was—

The light of challenge was so fierce in his eyes that his team, mistaking it for the fire of battle, wheeled away.

Bella would be different. Not easy, Nero thought as he took his helmet off to acknowledge the roar of the crowd when he galloped onto the field. Bella would not yield to him as easily as her pretty mare had. There was something else behind that composed stare. Fear. He wondered at it. She feared the loss of her pony—that he could understand, but there was something more. And there was another question: why did such a successful and attractive woman live the life of a celibate in what was a notoriously libidinous society?

Because Bella was different. She was an independent woman, and courageous. She had coped well with her father's disgrace, supporting Jack Wheeler to the bitter end and salvaging what she could of the business. But where a private life was concerned she seemed to have none, and planned to keep it that way, or why else would she dress so severely?

Bella was all business and no fun, Nero concluded, as if to show the slightest warmth or humour might put her at risk. Yet beneath that Ice Maiden façade he'd heard she was much loved by the children she invited to her stables. She could be useful to him. With that thought in mind, he replaced his helmet and lowered his face guard. Training his restless gaze on the stands he searched for Bella as he cantered up to start the match.

CHAPTER TWO

BELLA hated him. Nero Caracas had almost single-handedly annihilated the home team. Never mind that his three team-mates had played well, she held Nero directly responsible for trouncing the team whose ponies she had trained. She had one bittersweet moment when the prince, who was awarding the prizes that day, had named Misty pony of the match, but even that triumph was quickly smashed by the quick look Nero shot her—the look that said, *I'm having her. She's mine.* The look that had prompted Bella to flare back silently, *Over my dead body.*

Over your body, certainly, had been Nero's outrageously confident response, which he had laced with a wolfish grin. And now she was being forced into his company in the evening too. The prince had invited all the players and their trainers to dinner at the castle. It was not the type of invitation Bella could easily refuse. And why should she? The opportunity to eat dinner with the prince, to see round the royal castle—was she going to let Nero Caracas stand in the way of that? It was a signal from the prince himself that her father's yard was back in favour. Jack Wheeler's name would be spoken again with pride. And, realistically, her chance of being seated next to Nero was zero, Bella reassured herself. Protocol was everything in royal circles and she was sure to be seated with her team.

'I hope you don't mind that I put you next to me,' the prince said, smiling warmly at Bella, 'and that you're not sitting with your team…?'

'Of course not, Sir, it's an honour,' Bella replied graciously, trying not to care who was sitting across the table from her on the other side of the prince. Or the fact that Nero seemed unusually chummy with their royal host.

'The captain of the winning team and the owner and trainer of the pony of the match—it seemed an inevitable pairing to me,' the prince confided in his usual laid-back manner.

'Indeed, Sir,' Bella agreed, coolly meeting Nero's amused stare. What was going on?

'Your Royal Highness is, as ever, a most perceptive man,' Nero drawled, raising one sweeping ebony brow as he connected with Bella's narrow-eyed stare.

Bella Wheeler in a dinner gown. This was an image he had toyed with on his way to the castle. He had thought she might free her shiny auburn hair from its cruel captivity and reveal the young body that lurked beneath her workmanlike clothes. Instead, she was trussed up in a gown her grandmother would have approved of, and her hair was more tightly dressed than he had ever seen it. Did she have to make a statement every time they met? If it went on like this, he fully expected her to be wearing a sandwich board on the next occasion, proclaiming: Look, Don't Touch.

'So, Bella,' the prince said, distracting him, 'I've been hearing good things about you—and not just as far as training polo ponies goes. I'm thinking more of your work with children,' he explained.

Bella blushed. She didn't like to make a song and dance about the work she undertook in her free time.

'Have you ever thought of expanding your scheme?' the prince pressed.

Bella noticed Nero appeared to be equally intent on her answer. 'My polo commitments don't allow for it, Sir—'

'But you do what you can, which is more than most people even attempt,' the prince went on. 'And I've been hearing some very good things about you—'

Bella answered this with a modest smile.

As the meal continued her tension relaxed. She was imagining things, Bella reassured herself. Nero sitting across the table had made her edgy. There was no plan afoot between Nero and the prince. Her royal host was always well briefed, and was not only genuinely interested in the people he met but was an excellent conversationalist. Her father had been invited to the castle in his heyday, but this was Bella's first time and she wasn't going to waste it fretting about the prince's fanciful seating plan that saw spinster-and-contented-with-her-lot Bella Wheeler seated across the table from the world's most desirable man. She could only hope Nero had got her message—*Butt out of my life, Caracas. You're not wanted here.*

But she did want him. She wanted Nero with an ache so bad she could only hope the prince, who was undoubtedly a man of the world, hadn't picked up on it. Nero was a force of nature, a man who could have any woman in the world. What if he suspected how she felt about him? How professional would Nero think her then?

He'd think her a naïve fool. And he wouldn't be that far out. Right now, she was feeling as if she'd been parachuted in from Little Town in Nowhere Land to a life of such pomp and privilege she had to pinch herself to prove she wasn't dreaming. Thank goodness she'd found a gown at the back of the wardrobe suitable for dinner—ten years out of date, but conservative, which was all that mattered. She didn't like to draw attention to herself, which was another reason she appeared cold.

She stiffened and held Nero's gaze as he looked at her for one long potent moment, then turned away when the prince began talking to him. It was an opportunity to soak everything in—all the life-sized oil paintings on the ruby silk walls. Stout kings and thin kings, with glittering swords and crowns bearing testament to their wealth and power. Happy women and sad women, wearing sumptuous gowns, some of whom were surrounded by strangely disaffected children staring off bleakly into an unknowable future. With a shiver, she dragged her gaze away and began to study the vaulted ceiling instead. On a ground of rich cobalt blue, this was lavishly decorated with rosy-cheeked cherubs and cotton wool clouds and, coming back down to earth again, there was more crystal and silver on a dinner table made magical by candlelight than she had ever seen before. There must have been fifty people sitting at the table with them, and it was longer than a bowling alley to accommodate that number. A mischievous smile played around her lips when the royal butler and his team of efficient footmen strode silently by—some wild child inside her wanted to dance a crazy quickstep after them down the jewel-coloured runners that marked out their transit through the hall.

She could act serene, but inside her there was a wild

child longing to get out. Nero was as relaxed in this setting as he was on the polo field. How elegant and confident he appeared, lounging back in his chair, chatting easily to the prince—as well he might. Rumour said Nero lived in considerable style on his *estancia* back home, where he ruled his estate like his own private fiefdom. And if he had been devastating in match clothes, he was off the scale tonight in a beautifully cut evening suit. The dark cloth moulded his powerful frame to perfection, while the crisp white shirt and steel-grey tie showed off his tan.

Damn! He was watching her. She turned her attention quickly to her plate. She was safer with her ponies than with all these men. Men were strong and could physically overwhelm her, and Nero Caracas was the strongest of them all. When you'd fought and lost as badly as she had, you never forgot—

Yet here she was, wrapping her lips around the tines of her fork as if she wanted him to look at her.

Must she court danger at every opportunity?

It must be the Nero effect. She was never so foolish, but just sitting across from him was enough to make her act differently—made her monitor how she held herself and how she ate. She had even taken to sipping her drink demurely!

Damn this to hell! She was a professional woman, not some impressionable teenager. Straightening up, she made a special effort to engage the prince in a topic of conversation which she knew he would appreciate, but even the prince seemed to be on Nero's side.

'I'm surprised you haven't made an offer for the pony of the match, Caracas,' the prince observed after a few minutes of conversation which had fallen well within the bounds of what Bella considered safe.

Bella tensed. Must everything come back to this?

'But I have,' Nero said mildly. 'I would love to own Misty, but Ms Wheeler seems to have her doubts—'

'Doubts?' The prince's eyebrows shot up as he turned to stare at Bella. 'Señor Caracas has an enviable *estancia* in Argentina, with the best living conditions for polo ponies I've seen anywhere in the world—'

'And still Ms Wheeler doubts me.' Nero's eyes were glinting with humour as he attempted to capture Bella's stony stare.

'You must reconsider, Ms Wheeler,' the prince insisted. 'Nero is the best rider in the world, and as such he should have access to the best ponies.'

Should he? By whose right?

Bella flashed a furious look across the table, only to be met by Nero's relaxed, sardonic stare. Her heart thundered—and not with anger. She could have coped with that more easily than this lust-fuelled desire to engage in combat with him. But the prince's message was unmistakable. If she was intransigent she would lose his favour and, as the prince was one of the foremost sponsors of the game, everything she had worked so hard to build could quickly turn to dust. 'Your Royal Highness.' She appeared to agree—even adding a meek dip of her head, but inside she was fuming. She would not be forced to sell her most cherished possession—and Nero Caracas could stop pulling the prince's strings. There must be a way out of this and she would find it.

But then Nero foiled her by mentioning a project close to her heart and now, it appeared, close to his. He planned to work with children who wouldn't normally have the opportunity to ride. She'd been doing that for years, and had seen the benefits first hand.

'I want them to experience the freedom of the pampas,' Nero was explaining to the prince, 'and discover what life is like on my *estancia* in Argentina.'

She would like to find out too, Bella thought wryly. But then her suspicions grew when it became clear that the prince and Nero had been in negotiations for some time over this proposed scheme—long enough for Nero to persuade the prince to be its patron.

'There are many similarities to your own work,' the prince observed, turning to include Bella in their discussion. 'Perhaps you remember, I mentioned the possibility of spreading your good work a little further earlier this evening?'

She'd been set up, Bella thought angrily, noting the spark of triumph in Nero's eyes. And since when was Argentina *a little further*? It was half a world away. She must have paled as the prince indicated that one of the hovering footmen should refill her water glass.

'Sir, I cannot think of leaving England—especially so close to Christmas.' She was clutching at straws—and had broken royal protocol by speaking to the prince before he invited her to do so, but the prince, sensing her distress, was at pains to make amends. 'But Christmas in Argentina is so beautiful and warm. I'm sure that your concerns in this country could be addressed, and Nero would ensure paid professionals were on hand to help you with the day-to-day running of the scheme in Argentina.'

Had this already been decided?

Bella had never found it so hard in her life to hold her tongue, but to interrupt the prince a second time would be an unforgivable breach of etiquette.

'I understand your concerns,' the prince assured her. 'There's so much paperwork when schemes such as this are set up, but I don't see you being involved in that. I see you taking more of a hands-on role, Bella—teaching the children to ride, and sharing your love of horses with them.'

'But, Sir—' Bella's eyes implored the prince to understand that she couldn't leave her yard. She worked every hour of every day to be the best. She even turned to Nero for help, but he merely raised a sardonic brow.

'There would be ample reward,' the prince said, as if this would make a difference.

Bella flinched with embarrassment. 'It isn't the money, Sir—'

'Pride is a great thing, Bella, but we all have to be practical,' the prince replied. 'Nero's gauchos have centuries of knowledge that working closely with horses has brought them, just as we do. There's nothing wrong with sharing that knowledge amongst friends, is there?' The prince stared at her intently.

What could she say without appearing mean-spirited? 'You're quite right, Sir,' she agreed, avoiding Nero's sardonic stare.

'And you could take Misty with you,' the prince added, warming to his theme. 'I'm sure Nero would have no objections?'

Was this a joke? Bella wondered as the two men exchanged a knowing glance. And now Nero's stare was heating her face, but she couldn't pretend the cash on offer wouldn't be useful—

So Nero had won.

Misty could only benefit by being ridden by the greatest polo player in the world, and riding high in the prince's approval meant the future of her stable yard was assured. 'This doesn't mean I would sell Misty to you,' she assured Nero.

As the prince exclaimed with disappointment on

Nero's behalf, Nero said smoothly, 'I don't think we need to worry about that yet.'

But some time she would need to worry, Bella interpreted, tensing even as the prince relaxed. She was up against the might of Nero Caracas with no one, not even the prince, to back her up. 'I couldn't leave my work here,' she said firmly.

The prince sat forward as Nero offered what must have sounded to him like a reassurance. 'I would send a team to take over what is already an established scheme,' Nero said with a relaxed shrug. 'They would handle all your outstanding commitments.'

Was she the only one who could see the glint of irony in Nero's eyes?

Apparently, Bella thought as the prince sighed with approval. 'We would be in this together, Bella,' the prince confirmed, tying the knot between them even tighter. 'All I'm asking from you is that you share your expertise in the setting up of a similar scheme in Argentina to the one you already run in England.'

How reasonable that sounded, Bella thought as the prince turned his kind-hearted gaze on her face. Nero might as well have hog-tied her and served her up on a silver platter. Had his penetrating stare also worked out that he scrambled her brain cells and made her stomach melt? Almost certainly, she thought as his ebony brow lifted.

'Well, what do you think, Bella?' the prince prompted gently.

'Could I have some time to think about this, Sir?'

His Royal Highness hesitated.

'Not too much time,' Nero cut in, apparently oblivious to the rules of royal etiquette when it came to getting his own way.

* * *

After dinner a recital was to be held in the Blue drawing room, with the chance for everyone to freshen up first.

Freshen up? Bella raged silently, checking her hair was still securely tied back in the gilt-framed mirror hanging on the wall of the unimaginably ornate restroom. After listening to the prince's well-intentioned suggestions on one side, and batting off Nero's sardonic sallies on the other, she felt like a tennis ball being swiped between the two, frayed a little around the edges, but still ready to bounce—right over Nero, preferably.

Conclusion?

Her carefully controlled life was rapidly spiralling out of control.

Taking one last look around at all the beautiful things in the restroom—dainty chairs with soft leaf-green covers and the comforting array of traditional organic scent bottles lined up on a crystal tray for visitors to sample—she had the strongest feeling that if Nero had anything to do with it, it would be some time before she would be making a return visit here.

In this same anxious mood she opened the door and managed to bump straight into him.

'Ill met by moonlight,' Nero murmured with amusement as Bella exclaimed with alarm.

Her breath echoed in the silence as she stared up at Nero's strong, tanned hand on the wall by her face. 'Excuse me, please—'

He didn't move.

'I said—'

'I heard what you said.'

'Then would you let me pass, please?' She would fight off the effects of that deceptively sleepy stare.

'What's your hurry, Bella?'

'We should be getting back to the recital...'

Nero hummed.

Bracing herself, she looked up. Moonlight was indeed bathing them both in a strange sapphire light as it poured in through one of the castle's many stained-glass windows. The effect was wonderful for Nero's dark skin and thick black hair—she guessed her own face was a watery blue and her red hair a strange shade of green. Heating up under Nero's amused scrutiny, she launched a counter-attack. 'What were you doing at dinner with the prince and all that talk of a scheme?'

'It wasn't talk, Bella—'

'And I suppose it wasn't a ruse to make me sell Misty to you, either?'

'The scheme will continue, with or without your help, Bella.'

In his severe formal clothes, in this most refined of settings, Nero Caracas looked like a dark angel and more dangerous than ever. 'You led the prince to think I might sell Misty—and that my compliance with the scheme was a given.'

Nero's lips pressed down in a most attractive way. 'There's no mystery,' he said with a shrug. 'I offered to pay whatever price you ask for the pony. I doubt you'll find anyone who will match my offer.'

Or match Nero's compelling aura, or his physical strength, Bella thought, fighting off the seductive effect. It was impossible to be this close to Nero Caracas without feeling something, she reasoned, willing her voice to remain steady. 'I told you once—and this is the last time—Misty isn't for sale.'

'And what if the prince wants to buy her?'

Stunned by the idea, Bella gasped.

'Don't tell me that thought hasn't occurred to you,'

Nero murmured in his lazy South American drawl. 'And if the prince does want your mare, how can you refuse him?' Nero gave her a moment to soak this up, before adding dryly, 'Perhaps I can save the situation for you.'

Bella's eyes narrowed. 'What would it cost me?'

'Oh, come now, Bella. You know Misty would be happier with me than the prince.'

Check. And mate. Nero had cut the legs from under her. Forget the threat he posed in the personal sense— polo ponies lived to play the game and Misty adored the high-powered cut and thrust of the international arena. It was common knowledge that the prince had practically retired from the game, which meant Misty would hardly be played at all, whereas as one of Nero's pampered ponies, Misty would get every opportunity to indulge the passion the small mare lived for.

'Having doubts?' Nero prompted, pouncing on her hesitation.

'None,' she lied. 'I only wish you had some scruples.'

Nero laughed. Throwing back his head, he revealed the long, firm column of his throat. 'Your innocence is touching, Bella.' Dipping his head, he stared her in the eyes to drive the point home. 'I have no scruples when it comes to the game.'

Which game?

In the heat of the moment, she grabbed his arm. 'Just keep the prince out of this.' Feeling the heat and muscle beneath her hand, she quickly released her grip. Inhaling sharply, she shook herself round. Nero was an experienced man. You didn't come up against him without getting burned. This was all a game to him and if she had any sense she'd put some much needed space between them…

Nero's hand slammed against the wall at the side of her face.

'Get out of my way,' Bella raged with shock, green eyes blazing.

'So I am right,' Nero murmured, standing back.

'Right about what?' she said angrily, thoroughly discomfited.

'There is fire beneath that ice of yours,' Nero murmured.

Bella inhaled sharply as Nero stroked back a strand of her hair that had escaped its stern captivity. 'You can stop congratulating yourself on your perception,' she said coldly. 'It doesn't seem to have helped you where Misty is concerned.'

Nero's mouth curved disconcertingly. 'You seem very sure of that, Bella.'

'I am.' Her voice was shaking, but in some strange way she was enjoying this. Nero made her feel alive. She should thank him for goading her.

'Temper, temper,' Nero murmured, reading her.

She stood aloof, but they were still so close she could feel his heat warming her, and his spicy scent invading her senses and making her dizzy. Nero was enjoying this too, Bella realised with a rush of concern and excitement mixed.

And have you chosen to overlook that small thing called consequences?

How she hated her inner voice for intruding at a time like this, but she couldn't ignore it. Her fighting spirit might have made a comeback, but her ability to trust a man still had a long way to go.

CHAPTER THREE

THE corridor was silent until the sound of doors closing made them both turn. 'Oh, dear,' Nero observed dryly, 'it appears we've missed the recital.'

'And what will the prince have to say about that?' Bella murmured defiantly.

Nero sighed in response but didn't look a bit repentant. 'It seems we're both in trouble.'

More than he could know, Bella thought, brewing up a storm.

Nero lounged back against the wall with footmen playing silent sentry as he waited for the music to end. The moment the doors were opened again, the prince summoned them both over.

She might as well give up now, Bella thought as the prince said how happy it made him to indulge a friend. She had just smiled her thanks when the prince made it clear that friend was Nero. 'As you know, I have agreed to be the patron of Nero's charity,' the prince confided in her, 'but as I have so many calls on my time I would like you, Bella, to represent me.'

'Me, Sir?' Of course she was surprised but, crucially, the prince had taken the decision about going to Argentina out of her hands.

'I can't think of anyone better qualified,' he continued.

'You are the best trainer I know, Bella. And when the polo season comes to an end, what better use of your time could there be than introducing more young people to the joys of riding? See what you can do over there, Bella—what you can both do,' the prince added, gazing at Bella and Nero in turn. 'Though I should warn you, Bella, that when you leave the northern hemisphere behind and experience the very different world you are going to, you might want to stay there. Passions run high on the pampas—isn't that so, Caracas?'

'Exactly so, Your Royal Highness.' Nero's amused gaze switched to Bella.

'I know you'll enjoy the teaching, Bella,' the prince continued, turning serious again. 'And if you would do this one thing for me, I would feel I was still there, in some way. I'm afraid I can't spare anyone from my own staff. But who knows the relationship between man and horse better than you?' he added persuasively. 'It will mean you spending quite some time in Argentina, Bella, but I feel certain you will enjoy that as much as I did.'

How could she refuse now?

By taking in the triumph in Nero's eyes, possibly? Bella thought tensely. Or the amused tug at the corner of his mouth? How she wished she could snatch some reason out of the air why she couldn't go, but she couldn't afford to risk offending the prince. There was no escape, she concluded. 'I would consider it a great honour to assist you in any way I can, Sir.'

'Excellent. I'm glad that's settled,' the prince said, beaming. 'And now... If you will both excuse me?'

'Of course.' At last she could look at Nero. His expression was exactly what she had expected. And she hoped hers left Nero in no doubt that she would do this, but only because the prince had asked her. Working as an adviser for Nero's charitable scheme was a privilege; she was too polite to even think of the word to describe working alongside a man who challenged every sensible boundary she had ever put in place.

'You'll be my guest, of course,' Nero explained, all business now his triumph was in the bag. 'Working and living on the pampas will be very different to anything you are used to here, but I am confident that in time you will grow to love it.'

In time? Bella swallowed deep. There were so many undertones to that apparently innocent statement she could only be glad the well-meaning prince hadn't stayed to hear them. 'I wouldn't be able to stay very long...'

'But long enough for the project to be established. The children need you, Bella.'

'As does my yard and my horses. I have my own scheme, Nero.'

He checked her at every turn. 'You'd break your word to the prince?'

'Had you already decided this plan between the two of you? Was my agreement to the prince's proposal merely a formality?'

Nero smiled faintly. 'You're so suspicious, Bella.'

'With good reason, I think,' she flashed.

'I will hold myself personally responsible for maintaining the high standards you have set at your yard in the UK. As I told both you and the prince, I will send my most trusted team to ensure you have nothing to worry about—financially, or otherwise.'

Was he serious? The systems she had set in place to take care of things should she be incapacitated by illness, or be taken out of the picture in some other way, would ensure the yard ran smoothly. If she chose to do this, it was Nero she was worried about, working in close proximity to him being the major problem. 'I have made enough money to keep everything ticking over nicely, thank you. I don't need any help from you!'

'Your reputation does you much credit, Bella,' Nero snapped. 'It seems you are your father's daughter, after all.'

Bella blenched. 'What's that supposed to mean?'

Nero's powerful shoulders eased in a shrug. 'You can't make a decision and stick to it.'

'How dare you—'

'How dare I speak the truth?' Nero's eyes drilled into her. 'If you break your word as easily as this, Bella Wheeler, I'm not sure I want you as part of my scheme.'

For a moment she didn't trust herself to speak. Nero had blatantly manipulated her, but if she lost her temper and blackened her father's memory even more she would never forgive herself. Taking a deep steadying breath, she buried her pride. 'You give me your word that my work in England wouldn't suffer?'

'I do,' Nero assured her in a clipped voice.

'And my visit to Argentina would be conditional on coming home as soon as the scheme is set up.'

'I can't imagine why I would want you to stay beyond that.'

Her heart beat with outrage. Nero really knew how to cut her with words, she realised, smiling prettily for the prince as Nero escorted her out of the royal presence.

'This is a win-win situation, Bella,' Nero insisted as they strolled across the room. 'I'm surprised you can't see it.'

'How do you reach that conclusion?'

'The prince secures you as his representative. My

project secures your experience. And you get to keep your pony.'

'In spite of your scare tactics, my ownership of Misty has never been in doubt. So what do you get out of it?' Bella demanded suspiciously.

'I get to keep Misty on my yard—and even ride her—if you will allow me to?'

Nero's tongue was firmly planted in his cheek, Bella suspected. And his face was close enough to make her lips tingle. 'Do you really need my permission?' she countered. And would she be able to resist seeing the world's best polo player mounted on the best pony? Nero's laughing eyes and the curve of his sensuous mouth reflected his confidence that this would be the case.

'Most important of all, Bella, the children benefit,' Nero said, turning serious.

And that was the one thing she couldn't argue with. 'Believe me, your project is the only reason I'm saying yes to Argentina.'

'But of course,' Nero agreed smoothly. 'What other reason could there be for a respectable woman to visit my *estancia*?'

'I can't imagine,' Bella said frostily, smiling her thanks as a royal footman opened the outer doors for them.

'And where will you go now?' Nero asked her as a driver brought his ink-black four-wheel-drive up to the foot of the steps for him.

'Back to the stables for one last check on the horses.'

'As I'm going there myself, why don't I give you a lift?'

'I prefer to walk, thank you.'

'In an evening dress?'

'It's a pleasant evening, and I need the fresh air.'

'Well, if you're sure?'

'I am.' Her mind was still whirling with the fact that she had agreed of her own free will to walk into the lion's den—and not here on familiar turf, but Argentina, and the wild, untamed pampas, where she would be staying on Nero's *estancia*. She needed some fresh air to come to terms with that alone—lots of it.

'Then good night,' Nero murmured, his eyes glittering with triumph. 'I'll see you tomorrow when we will firm up your travel arrangements.'

Life had suddenly become very interesting, Nero reflected as he gunned the engine and drove away from the castle. Word had it that Isabella Wheeler lived in an ivory tower whose walls had never been breached, but he'd caught flashes of internal fires raging out of control. She reminded him of one of his spirited mares. They took their time to trust and were always looking for trouble, but that was because they had lost the freedom of the pampas, something they would never forget. What had Bella Wheeler lost that caused her such torment? Rumour said there was some mystery surrounding her. He could confirm that. Bella said one thing and her eyes, the mirror of Bella's soul, said something different. She was lying by omission. She was hiding something big.

Bella's outwardly contained manner intrigued him almost as much as her unnaturally well-groomed appearance irritated him. It wasn't often he met a woman who had her own life, her own successful career and wasn't looking for anything material from him. Far from it, Nero reflected wryly. If he had to categorise Bella after getting to know her a little better, it would still be under the heading: Ice Maiden. He had never met a woman who went all out to make herself as unobtainable and as aloof as she could and, the irony was, Bella didn't realise what a desirable prize that made her. He'd seen the way men looked at her as they dreamed of loosening her tight-fitting breeches. He knew how he felt about her. And, judging by the way Bella responded to him, she wasn't exactly immune to him either.

He wanted her. She wanted him. There should have been a very easy solution, but there wasn't, and he was going to find out why.

When she had satisfied herself that everything at the stables was as it should be, Bella's thoughts turned to her grooms. Some of them were very young and she felt responsible for them. Hearing that a couple of the girls hadn't returned to the small bed and breakfast where Bella had rented them rooms, she set out to look for them. She knew exactly where they would be. After the match a large, luxurious nightclub had set up camp in a marquee in the grounds. It was *the* place to be, the girls had assured her. Bella had seen pictures on the news and could understand their excitement. The huge white tent was decorated like something out of *Arabian Nights* with exotic silken drapes in a variety of jewel colours and dramatic water features shooting plumes of glittering spray into the air. A dance floor had been erected in the middle of the tent and one of the top DJs had been booked to keep the excitement of the polo match alive until dawn.

She was only halfway across the field when the bass beat started pounding through her. She was really out of her comfort zone. Even before the prince's invitation, she had refused the young grooms' invitation to join them. She had made all sorts of excuses—she was too old, too boring—and had laughed when they had protested she was neither. It was never easy to mix business with pleasure, even had she wanted to, but like an old mother hen, she was determined to make sure her girls were safe tonight.

She was off to a good start, having the right credentials, apparently. A member of the security staff recognised her and showed her straight in through the VIP entrance. The noise was amazing and there was such a crowd it was a while before she spotted the girls, by which time she had been sucked deep into the throng and men were speaking to her, offering her drinks and wanting to dance with her. She was here for business purposes, she told them frostily, tilting her chin at a determined angle as she headed for the girls.

The heat was overwhelming inside the tent after the chill night air. What with the press of people, the noise, the screams of laughter, the relentless beat, the flash of chandeliers and the glittering, garish splendour of it all, it was no wonder she was disorientated to begin with. Shaking off the faint sense of danger approaching, she pressed on, determined not to leave until she knew the girls had arranged to get home safely.

'Bella!' they exclaimed the moment they caught sight of her.

Before she knew it, she was on the dance floor.

'Meet…'

She didn't hear the rest—there were too many names and far too many new faces. She smiled and jigged around a bit, trying to string a few steps together on a heavily overpopulated dance floor on which there was hardly room to move, let alone dance. And she felt silly in her strait-laced dinner gown amongst so many cool young girls.

'Are you sure you're all okay?' she asked, drawing one of them aside. 'Have you made plans for later, or shall I call a taxi for you?'

'My brother's here,' the girl explained, angling her chin towards a tall, good-looking youth. 'No worries, Bella. Woo-hoo! Enjoy yourself!' And, grabbing hold of Bella's wrist, the girl dragged her back onto the dance floor.

And why not? Bella reasoned, glancing round. Everyone was here for a good time, and one dance wouldn't hurt. She didn't want to be a killjoy, and there was such an air of celebration it felt great to be part of it. There was certainly nothing to be concerned about—even if that persistent prickle down her spine refused to go away.

'Come on—you can't go now. You've only just arrived,' the girls insisted, gathering round Bella, who was still glancing anxiously over her shoulder, hardly knowing what she was looking for. They formed a circle round her so she couldn't escape, which made her laugh, and soon she was dancing again and everyone was shooting their arms in the air. After some persuasion, Bella did too. It was fun. It felt good to let go. Her hair tumbled down and swung around her shoulders. She tossed it back, making no attempt to tidy herself for once. She was just happy to lose her inhibitions—happy to lose herself in the music, and the moment.

Until it all came crashing down.

So this was where Miss Bluestocking hung out when she wasn't preaching death to desire and all-natural female responses. Those responses were only curbed when he was around, it seemed. Her glorious hair was flying free, and was as spectacular as he had always imagined it would be, and she was dancing with all the abandon he had suspected she might possess—a fact that wasn't lost on the men around her, though Bella appeared to be oblivious to the interest she was arousing.

The crowd parted like the Red Sea as he strode up to her. He stopped in the centre of the dance floor in front of the one person oblivious to his approach. Currently gyrating with her eyes closed and her hands reaching for the sky, the so-called Ice Maiden was mouthing lyrics to the raunchy track and grinding her hips in time to the beat with extremely un-maidenly relish. 'What the hell are you doing here?' he rapped for the sheer pleasure of seeing the shock in her eyes.

'Nero!'

'Yes, Nero,' he confirmed. 'So this is why you re-fused my offer of a lift.'

She pretended not to understand him, and was pleasingly flushed and unsettled as she smoothed back her hair. He showed her no mercy. Instead, he tugged her into his arms.

'What are you doing?' she demanded, struggling to find her severe face as their bodies brushed and finally connected.

'Oh, I'm sorry,' he mocked as she let out a shocked breath. 'I didn't realise you had come here to lead a temperance rally. I thought you were dancing...'

She manoeuvred herself so their lower bodies were no longer touching. 'You don't understand—'

'Oh, I think I do,' Nero argued, drawing her close again as the uptempo track segued into a slower number. 'I understand things such as this very well.'

'I mean you don't understand me,' she said, going as stiff as a board. 'This isn't what it seems—'

'This is exactly what it seems,' he argued.

'I'm only here to...'

'Check out the ponies?' he reminded her in a deceptively mild tone.

'I'm here to check up on my girls,' Bella argued hotly. 'Not that it's any business of yours what I choose to do with my free time.'

'Not yet it isn't.'

Nero's powerful hands were on her arm and on her waist, making it hard to think straight. And he was radically changed. No more the suave aristocrat in an impeccably tailored suit, Nero had found time to change his clothes and in a tight-fitting top and well-worn jeans that sculpted his hard, toned muscles it was no wonder the crowds had parted for him. He looked like an invading warrior. His shoulders were massive. His biceps were ripped. His thick, inky-black hair tumbled over his brow, while his sharp black stubble seemed more piratical than ever, giving him the appearance of some brigand on a raid. Worse—he had caught her off guard, obliterating her carefully constructed image for the sake of one reckless dance.

'So why are you here?' she demanded, determined to turn the tables on him. 'Looking for entertainment, Nero?'

'I was looking for you,' he fired back. 'I expected to find you at the stables so we could discuss your travel plans for tomorrow. Imagine my surprise when one of the stable lads told me where you'd gone.' As one inky brow rose it coincided with a move that brought them into even closer contact. 'I wouldn't have missed this for the world,' he murmured as she gasped. 'Imagine my surprise at finding Miss Butter-Wouldn't-Melt in Sodom and Gomorrah.'

'I was dancing with my friends!'

Nero shot a glance around at the men staring open-mouthed at Bella. 'Really?' He guessed none of them had seen Bella Wheeler breaking free before. The flickering light played into his hands, giving everything a hellish glow. Flashing and reflecting off the glitter balls hanging from the ceiling, the coloured lights made the mass of dancing figures seem contorted as if they were taking part in some primitive orgiastic rite. This was as far removed from the hushed sanctuary of the stable yard as it was possible to imagine. 'I would never have guessed this was your scene,' he murmured, twisting the knife. 'I understood you preferred an innocent stroll in the clean night air.'

He loved the way she writhed in his arms. She even balled her tiny hand into a fist, but thought better of using it on him, and gradually, in spite of all her best efforts, the stiffness seeped out of her and she softened in his arms.

'That's better,' he commented as she responded to the persuasive beat.

'Don't think I'm dancing with you because I want to.'

'Of course you aren't,' he agreed, soothing her as they moved to the music. There were only two things a man and woman could do to a rhythm when they were as close as this, and dancing was step one.

She couldn't have been more humiliated. Of all the things to happen, Nero discovering her midbellow in the middle of a raunchy song... How often did she let herself go?

Try never.

And that cringing feeling she got when some man she didn't know touched her—where was that? Nero felt amazing, not that she was touching him unnecessarily.

And then the music quietened and faded, and she waited for him to release her…

Was he going to kiss her?

Nero was staring down as if he might. They were alone in the middle of a packed dance floor. Closing her eyes, she drew in a shaking breath. Nero dipped his head…

The wait went on too long.

'See you tomorrow, Bella.'

She was left standing in confusion. Nero had walked off. People were staring at her.

With as little fuss as possible, she left the floor, making sure she took a different route. He was playing games with her, and she had no one to blame but herself. She could have brought that encounter to an end at any time. Why on earth hadn't she?

CHAPTER FOUR

IT WAS dawn when Nero rang the next morning. Bella was already at the stables. It had nothing to do with a restless night; this was her usual routine. 'Yes?' she said coolly. Answering the phone was easier than facing him.

'Travel plans,' Nero said briskly in the same no-nonsense tone.

'I'm listening.' And with some relief, she realised. After last night, she wouldn't have been surprised if Nero had left the country without another word.

The conversation that followed never strayed from the point, with Nero doing most of the talking. Bella was a highly respected professional, but Nero was the owner of countless polo ponies as well as being a top international player, so their respective positions in the game put him firmly in the driving seat. 'You will travel with me to Argentina,' he informed her. 'The horses will follow later when I'm satisfied everything is ready for them.'

Before she could ask if she would have any part to play in this, Nero went on to say that he would wind down in Buenos Aires before travelling to his *estancia*, which would give Bella chance to recover from the flight.

What form would Nero's wind-down take? And how much did she hate herself for wondering if she would even see him in Buenos Aires? She was still brooding about it when she ate breakfast with a group of red-eyed grooms.

It was ridiculous to care. This was business, Bella told herself firmly as she paid the bill and checked out of the small bed and breakfast hotel where she and the grooms had been staying. And she could hardly ask Nero what his intentions were—unless she wanted to appear desperate, of course.

Nero had been all male disapproval last night, but a spark had flared between them. She had acted cool at the castle, only for him to discover her dancing the night away, apparently surrounded by men. He had chosen not to notice the girlfriends dancing with her. Nero hadn't seen anything beyond the heat of the night, the throb of the music and the fact that everyone but him was in the same abandoned state. Nero would keep his word and honour their business arrangement, but he wouldn't forget. That pride of his would never allow it.

As she walked up the steps of Nero's private jet, Bella felt she was leaving everything certain behind and entering a world far beyond the scope of her imagination. There was a uniformed flight attendant to show her round while Nero joined his copilot in the cockpit. Everything in the interior of the plane was of the best— thick cream carpets, pale leather armchairs, just like a topclass hotel. Señor Caracas had his own private suite, the attendant explained, but Bella could take her pick from any of the other four options on board. She was still reeling from this information when the attendant added that Señor Caracas would meet her for breakfast the next morning as this was an overnight flight, and that in the meantime if she needed anything at all she only had to call him.

Was Nero avoiding her? Thinking back to her wild abandonment the previous evening, Bella went hot with embarrassment. It was so unlike her to expose herself like that—to become the butt of speculation.

But she'd done nothing wrong, Bella told herself firmly. Meanwhile, she should enjoy this. Her bedroom was small, but beautifully fitted with polished wood and a comfortable-looking bed dressed with crisp white linen. Thanking the attendant as he put her small suitcase down on the soft wool carpet, she vowed to put last night behind her and start again. This was just a short and fascinating interlude, after which she would return to her old life and Nero would carry on with his as if they'd never met.

And on that prescription she spent a restless night, tossing and turning, and waking long before the steward had arranged to call her. Having showered and dressed neatly in jeans and a long-sleeved top, she went to find breakfast. Nero was already lounging at the table in the salon, also dressed casually, his damp hair suggesting he was fresh from the shower. He greeted her politely above the hum of the engines and put down his newspaper.

Beyond that…nothing.

Nero was aloof, but knowing, Bella thought, flashing him a covert glance as she gave her order to the hovering steward. He had perfected the art of saying nothing and conveying too much, she thought, feeling her cheeks blaze red. Nero knew she had wanted him the other night—knew she had expected him to kiss her. It hadn't changed his mind about their business arrangement, but it had changed Nero's manner towards her, giving him more the upper hand than ever. He had formed an opinion about her and, mistaken though that opinion was, she didn't feel like offering an explanation for having fun in her free time.

He stared at Bella thoughtfully. She was discreetly dressed with her hair scraped back from a make-up-less face. Did she think he was going to throw her to the floor and have his evil way with her? After the other night he'd got her message loud and clear, as if he needed a reminder. As if he was interested.

But he was interested, which gave him a problem. And the more Bella played him, the more interested he became.

Bella wasn't sure what to expect when the plane landed. She had thought plenty about their destination and had bought every travel guide going, though beyond describing the pampas she had learned nothing about Nero's ranch. She couldn't wait to see where he lived and realised it was a measure of the power Nero wielded, as well as the security surrounding him, that only wild speculation could be rooted out regarding the lifestyle of one of the world's most private men. The first surprise came when they landed. She hadn't really thought about the practicalities of leaving a private jet. It proved to be a real eye-opener. Her passport was checked on board and a sleek black saloon was waiting for them on the tarmac at the foot of the steps.

The first thing Bella noticed as she exited the aircraft was how beautifully warm it was after the chill of London. The sky was blue and as she walked down the steps the spicy scent of Argentina blotted out the sickly fumes of aviation fuel. Waving the chauffeur away, Nero opened the passenger door for her and as soon as she was comfortably settled inside he shut the door and walked round to the driver's side. The checkpoint at the exit might not have existed. The bar was quickly raised and they were waved on their way by a guard who saluted them as if they were royalty. Which, in many ways, Nero was, Bella reflected, shooting him a sideways glance. The king of polo was looking more than usually splendid this morning and, in spite of all her strongest warnings to self, she felt her senses roar. Dark and dangerous described Nero to a T and who didn't like to dabble their toes in danger from time to time...?

'Are you going to buckle your seat belt any time soon?'

Nero's voice was rough and husky and she nearly jumped out of her seat to be caught in the middle of some rather raunchy thoughts about him. She buckled up without reply and gave herself a telling off. Better she leave the danger to those sophisticated women—the 'stick chicks' as they were known in polo circles. Far better for someone like her to stay in the stables with the ponies, Bella concluded wryly.

They were soon speeding down the highway towards the city. It was impossible to relax in such a confined space with Nero sitting beside her. He broke the silence only once to explain that he had booked her into a hotel in the centre of Buenos Aires where she would have the chance to recover from the thirteen-hour flight.

'Thank you,' she said, falling silent again. Nero didn't want conversation, and she didn't have the first clue how to start one with him. Without their mutual interest in horses or the kindly prince to prompt her, she was lost.

Nero drove as he played polo, at speed and with

confidence, and there was enough testosterone bouncing round the small cabin of his high-powered car to drown in. If a man could increase his sex appeal just to taunt her, then that was exactly what Nero had done. The relentless march of his sharp black stubble had won the razor war and he looked every bit the tough, tanned lover, wearing jeans that clung to his hard-muscled thighs and sleeves rolled back on his casual shirt to expose his powerful forearms.

What would working for him be like? Bella wondered. Everything in Nero's life was his way or no way. It remained to be seen what would happen when he worked alongside a woman who felt exactly the same way about her ponies.

As they drove on through the unprepossessing outskirts of the city Bella's personal concerns shrank to nothing in the shadow of the shanty town stalking the highway. No wonder Nero wanted to share his good fortune with youngsters who had so little. What she was seeing now would make it easy to forget her personal feelings about Nero and throw everything she'd got behind his scheme.

'It's known as Villa 31,' he said, noticing her interest in the depressing sprawl. 'It's been here fifty years or more, and it's still growing. No point dwelling on it,' he added. 'We have to *do* something.'

Narrowing his eyes, Nero stared ahead as they sped past the chaotic urbanisation, but he was seeing a lot more than the road, Bella guessed.

It was late afternoon when they arrived in the centre of Buenos Aires, by which time shadows were falling over the graceful buildings. This was another side of the coin, Bella thought, as she peered out of the car window at the romantic soul of Argentina. No wonder Buenos

Aires was known as the Paris of South America, or
that Nero was so proud of his homeland. The sun was
still putting up a good fight and as it sank had turned
the ancient stone a rosy pink, though as the day waned
she thought Nero seemed to grow in force and intent
like a creature of the night. It was as if this return to
his homeland had stirred fresh passion in him, and as it
swirled around them in the confined space of the car it
infected Bella too. She had never felt so acutely aware,
or so excited by the prospect of what lay ahead of her.

Nero had joined the heavy traffic on a grand twelve-
lane boulevard with a soaring monument at the end of
it. 'El Obelisco,' he explained, his glance sparking a
lightning flash down Bella's spine. 'The tapering obelisk
celebrates four hundred years of the founding of our
capital city. There is so much beauty here,' he murmured, resting his stubble-shaded chin on one arm as he
waited for the traffic to move. 'As you will learn, Bella,'
he said, turning to lavish a longer look into her eyes,
'Argentina is a country of huge contrasts and monumental passions.'

The passion she already knew about, but the pride in
Nero's voice made Bella envy his sense of belonging.
She felt her body thrill at his attention, and it was all she
could do to stop her imagination taking over. The most
she could reasonably hope for, she told herself sensibly,
was that this trip heralded a fresh start between them. If
they could put their differences behind them she could
experience something of the diversity of Argentina with
Nero as her guide.

'Everything is on such a vast scale,' she commented,
dragging her stare away from the huge phallic monument. It was a relief to let her gaze linger on what ap-

peared to be a glorious fairy-tale chateau lifted straight out of some lush green valley in France.

'That's the French embassy,' Nero explained. 'It's a fantastic example of Belle Epoque architecture, don't you think?'

Bella nodded, relieved to be talking about something innocent after the way her thoughts had been turning.

'It was built in the golden age before the First World War when the world was still innocent,' Nero mused.

Bella turned to keep the magical building in sight. 'And yet it looks so right here—'

'Where nothing is innocent,' Nero murmured.

Silence hung between them for a while and then it became clear they were leaving the centre behind and entering an area with a uniquely quaint beat rather than a city atmosphere. 'I thought you might like the cobbled streets and Bohemian atmosphere...'

Was Nero teasing her? It was never easy to tell. Whatever his motive, it was clear he had booked the strait-laced Ice Maiden into one of the hottest areas of the city. The narrow streets were still crowded with pedestrians and there was a wide choice of clubs and bars and interesting little shops.

'I hope you approve, Bella?'

'I'm certainly intrigued.' She was longing to explore.

'Here we are.' Nero drew the vehicle to a halt outside a small chic boutique hotel. 'I chose this particular hotel because it's far enough away from the action for you to get some sleep, but close enough, should you wish to sample it,' he added with a touch of irony.

'I'll be far too busy sleeping,' she countered, turning away from Nero's mocking stare.

She was acutely aware of his strong hands on the

wheel and the determined jut of his chin. Nero was in control for now and she had to step up to the plate or go home, and she had no intention of going anywhere until her job was done. Nero might think he could control every woman as he controlled his polo ponies, but not this woman. And with that silent pep talk over Bella felt a lot more confident. 'Thank you for the lift.'

Leaning across, Nero stopped her opening the door, which was enough in itself to blank her mind of all her fragile resolutions. 'Allow me,' he said, staring into her eyes.

Oh, that long, confident Latin stare—when would she ever learn to deal with it? Bella wondered as Nero opened the door for her. She hadn't missed the ironic twist of his mouth. Nero thought she was easy meat and simply acting tough. He was right about one of those—she was acting. She was in a strange country with a man she hardly knew, and she felt vulnerable. Only when they reached Nero's *estancia* and she was working with her horses in a setting she understood would she be totally at ease again.

She stood for a moment on the cobbles in the warm gardenia-scented air. She just wanted to soak everything in. She could hear music playing in the distance. This was even better than the Buenos Aires she had dreamed about. And was that really a couple dancing in the street?

'Tango—the lifeblood of Buenos Aires,' Nero informed her in his deep, husky voice.

Bella's heart was beating off the scale—surely Nero must hear it? She hadn't even realised he'd come to stand so close beside her. Sensibly, she moved away. She had to keep all her wits about her on this trip. This was only page one of her Argentinian adventure, and the book promised to be as exciting and surprising as the country Nero called home.

CHAPTER FIVE

DETERMINED to maintain her cool, Bella fixed her gaze on the hotel entrance as she started up the steps. The polished wooden door had black wrought-iron decoration of a type that seemed to be fashionable in the area. Nero was definitely right about the area's appeal. The cobbled streets and colonial buildings, coupled with Bohemian chic *and* the tango, gave it an irresistible charm.

She gasped as Nero held her back.

'Don't you want to stay and watch the dancers for a moment?'

Night was closing fast and shadows elongated the dancing couple into lean, languorous shapes. They were dancing without inhibition—not for an audience, but for themselves. They were unaware that they had been captured in the spotlight of a street lamp in the middle of the city. Staring intently into each other's faces, the dancers inhabited their own erotic world of fierce stares and abrupt movements, finishing in sinuous reconciliation. The tango was the dance of love, Bella realised.

'There is a *milonga*, a neighbourhood dance hall where people go to dance tango—quite famous, actually—just across the street,' Nero explained, bringing Bella back down to earth again. 'That couple will almost certainly be practising for their performance tonight.'

'I'd love to see them dance,' Bella murmured, transfixed by their skill. The man was resting the woman over his arm so that her hair almost brushed the pavement, and the woman was slim and lithe, and dressed for a night of dancing such as Bella couldn't even begin to imagine—and had certainly never experienced.

And was never likely to, she told herself sensibly, but how she envied the woman her confidence and her style. She was wearing the highest stiletto heels and the sheerest black tights with a fine seam up the back, and her dress was the merest whisper of black silk that flicked and clung to her toned, tanned body. The man was taller, but he too was lean and strong. He guided and directed his partner in a way that seemed to have no answer to it until she snapped her legs around him, and that spoke of another truth—that a woman with the right sort of confidence could tame any man.

Right, Bella thought as she watched them, but not this woman, not me. And not this man, she reflected, stealing a glance at Nero. No wonder she was a stranger to this type of dancing. Pulling herself round, she turned to follow the porter into the hotel.

'Do you want to go there later?'

She stopped dead, completely dumbfounded by Nero's question. She felt a shiver of awareness streak down her back. She must have misheard him, surely? 'I'm sorry?' She turned to face him.

'Perhaps you're too tired to go out tonight?' Nero suggested dryly.

Nero was inviting her to join him at the tango club? The mocking challenge in his voice sent warning tingles down her spine. But wasn't this what she had wanted?

On the simplest level she longed to see something of Buenos Aires while she had the chance. Let's not even go near the complicated level, Bella concluded. But hadn't Nero said that tango was the lifeblood of the city? 'As long as I don't have to dance,' she said, feeling happy now she had put a condition on accepting his invitation.

'Don't worry,' he said dryly, 'I've seen you dance.'

A curl of excitement unfurled inside her as Nero met her stare. 'I'll pick you up at ten,' he said.

Now what had she done? Bella wondered as Nero got back into his car and roared away. One thing was sure; she was playing a far more sophisticated game than she was used to.

Up in her hotel room, with its state portrait of a very beautiful and glamorous Eva Peron smiling down, Bella's problems were mounting. She had packed three sets of riding gear for this trip, an unflattering old-fashioned swimming costume that covered up far more than it revealed, a matching cover-up, a pair of shorts, some work clothes, jeans, sneakers, boots, a pile of T-shirts, some serviceable underwear and a couple of sweaters. At the very last minute she had added a neat pencil skirt with a pair of chunky-heeled shoes, a tailored blouse and jacket, just in case she needed to attend a business meeting during her visit. Tango costume, it was not.

Though as she wouldn't be dancing…

She definitely wouldn't be dancing, Bella told herself firmly, remembering how it had felt to be held in Nero's arms at the polo party. And, as strictly speaking this was a business outing with her boss, the pencil skirt would be perfect. Tying her hair back neatly, she told her heart to stop behaving so erratically and, with a final check in the mirror, she drew a deep breath and left the room.

Nero was leaning against the wall at the foot of the stairs. Surrounded by an adoring crowd, he was signing autographs. Yet another reminder that she was out of her depth here. Thank goodness for her sensible business outfit. There was no danger she could be mistaken for one of Nero's girlfriends looking like this. In fact, she should be able to reach the front door without anyone noticing her—

'Bella?'

Wrong. Nero was at her elbow. Or, rather, she was at his. He was so much taller than she was. He was like a solid wall of muscle protecting her from his fans, all of whom seemed intent on getting a piece of him. But all he had to do was speak a few words in his own language and with a collective sigh of understanding the crowd fell back.

'What did you say to them?' Bella asked, impressed.

'I told them you were here so you could learn to dance—' Nero's powerful shoulders eased into a typical Latin shrug. 'I explained that you come from a place where dancing is practically unheard of, and that this is a mercy mission on my part. They understood completely.'

I bet they did, Bella thought. She tilted her chin as Nero held the door for her and walked past him with what she sincerely hoped was a businesslike expression on her face—in the manner of a woman whose intention was to do anything but dance her way into danger tonight.

The tango club was situated on the top floor of an old building. Vast and echoey, the white-flagged floors had turned grey with age and the tiled staircase was of the same vintage, but the people hadn't come to admire the architecture. They were being drawn upstairs by the heady pulse of music, which floated down from an open doorway on the upper landing.

Bella was soon to discover that the whole of the attic space had been transformed into a dance hall. The air was warm and sultry, and the room was lit by candlelight which gave it a golden shadowy hue. The scent of wax melting was added to the faint overlay of perfume and warm clean bodies—and something else…something heady and alluring, which Bella flatly refused to identify as emotion, let alone passion.

Wooden chairs surrounded tables covered with welcoming red-and-white cloths—though no one seemed to be eating as far as Bella could tell—they all were too intent on watching the tango demonstration. The room was packed and hushed. A couple was about to start. A table was quickly found for Bella and Nero, who murmured something in Spanish to a waiter before ushering her ahead of him. She was so drawn to the upcoming performance she almost stumbled—and would have done if Nero hadn't steadied her. 'Sit, Bella,' he prompted.

She sank down on the hard wooden chair, tingling from his touch. This next couple seemed to be the one everyone had been waiting for—and this wasn't the glitzy entertainment Bella had seen on TV back home, but something earthy and sensual, and unashamedly erotic. The moment the accordionist began to play she was drawn into another world. The couple on the dance floor held each other's gaze intently as they moved with feline languor to the steady beat of the music—though this could change in a heel tap into something fierce and aggressive. As the rhythm rose in a climactic wave Bella realised that these dramatic changes from slumbering passion to outright conflict and back again to soothing gestures were exactly what the spectators had come to see. There was no doubt the woman gave as good as she got—pushing her partner away with a blistering glare, only for him to snatch her back again.

This was how her life could be, Bella reflected whimsically, leaning her chin on the heel of her hand. Instead of safe and bland, she could change it in an instant to risk and danger and attack—

Nero returned her to reality with a jolt, asking her what she'd like to drink. 'Water, please.' She didn't trust herself with anything stronger.

How far out of her comfort zone was she now? Bella thought as the performance heated up. If there was one thing she had already learned in Argentina, it was that the tango was the vertical expression of horizontal desire, and she'd have preferred something a touch safer for her first outing with the boss.

Her boss...

It could be worse, she reflected dryly, taking him in. Nero had dressed for the evening in slim black trousers that complemented his incredible physique. His powerful shoulders tapered to his narrow waist, which was cinched by a leather belt. His shoes were black and highly polished, and his shirt was white and crisp—

And he was dressed for dancing, Bella realised with a sudden blaze of panic. Nero was an athlete—one of the world's top athletes. And the tango at this level couldn't be attempted by anyone who didn't enjoy peak fitness. 'Do you dance?' she said weakly as the crashing finale and riotous applause brought the display they'd been watching to a close.

'I love to dance,' Nero assured her, putting down his

glass of wine. 'I love anything where I have to use my body.'

She didn't doubt it, Bella thought, swallowing deep as one of the startlingly beautiful young girls in the club sashayed towards their table. How could she compete with this? Was that why Nero had brought her here? To humiliate her? Was this Nero's revenge for not allowing him to buy Misty?

She was clutching her glass so hard she would break it if she wasn't careful, Bella realised. Then some demon got into her and, throwing caution to the wind, she sprang to her feet. 'I'll dance,' she said wildly, only to find her voice blasting through a momentary silence.

People stared at her. The young girl stared at her. How ridiculous she must seem in her office clothes when everyone else around her was dressed…well, not for the office.

'Bella?'

Tall and imposing, Nero was holding out his hand to her. The music was thrumming with an almost irresistible beat. She did a quick inventory. Her skirt had a slit up the back and everything that should be covered was covered—

And she was nothing if not game. She hadn't come to Argentina to be pushed around, or to be pushed into the shadows. Adopting the typical haughty stare of a female tango dancer, she tilted her chin as a challenge to Nero to follow her to the dance floor.

'Are you sure about this?' he murmured.

The sexy sibilant syllables tickled her ear as she whispered back, 'Absolutely certain—'

She wasn't sure about anything—her own sanity was most in question. But she had excelled in Scottish country dancing at her all-girls school.

'In that case…'

Snatching her to him, Nero managed in the shadows of the dimly lit club to look more saturnine and menacing than he ever had. She tilted her chin a little higher to acknowledge the round of somewhat hesitant applause. 'You'd better lead,' she conceded.

'Oh, I'll lead,' Nero assured her.

'And take it slowly, please—'

'I will,' he promised, sounding amused.

And then her palm was flat against Nero's strong, warm hand and a whole universe of new feelings opened up to her. It would pass, Bella told herself confidently. She was only going to dance with him. What was the worst that could happen? She could make a fool of herself. Something told her that Nero would never allow that to happen. And for just once in her life she wanted to unselfconsciously do something she had watched and admired others do. 'I just have to make sure I don't tread on your feet,' she said awkwardly as they waited for the music to begin.

'Relax,' Nero murmured. 'Just imagine that you're a pony I am breaking in.'

What? 'I'd rather imagine I'm a woman and you're a man who is very kindly teaching me an unfamiliar dance.'

'Oh, I think you'll be familiar with this dance,' Nero murmured.

Bella gulped. She had to be the only person here who wasn't familiar with the dance of love. But how could she not respond to Nero's hand in the small of her back, or the insistent pressure of his thigh? He could be so subtle and so persuasive and, though she wasn't doing anything clever like flicking her leg through his, she was moving to the music. Nero's control of the dance was absolute, and yet his control was so light she could understand why his polo ponies were so responsive to him. Was it wrong to want a little more pressure? Was it really possible that Nero had such an incredible level of sensitivity, or such a sense of rhythm, and such an acute insight into what pleased her most?

'You dance well,' he said as a smattering of applause greeted their first experiment. 'You have a natural flair.'

Only thanks to him, she thought.

'And now let's try and put a little more passion into it. Look at me, Bella. Look at me as if you hate me.'

At least something was easy.

'That's good. Now soften a little…entice me…'

She could do that too—but not too much. A brush from Nero's body was like a lightning bolt to her system. No one was required to weld themselves to their teacher, Bella reassured herself. She would call upon her under-used acting skills instead. Raising a brow, she stared at Nero beneath her eyelashes. Lifting her ribcage, she adopted a more dramatic pose—a move that got her a little more applause.

'Easy,' Nero growled in her ear when she attempted to lead him. 'This is only your first lesson.'

'Then there will have to be many more,' she assured him, growing in confidence and feeling invincible as more couples joined them on the floor.

Perhaps the right word was invisible…

Whatever. She was beginning to think the ability to dance the tango was a prerequisite for living in Argentina. 'From what I've seen tonight, I'm going to need those lessons,' she admitted.

'You certainly will,' Nero agreed. 'And I'll be sure to find someone good to teach you.'

As Bella went stiff and pulled away Nero drew her back again, inch by steady inch. And, yes, she should put an end to this, but why, when Nero kept each move so slow and deliberate and she could easily follow him, and he never once made her feel that he was mocking her, or that he would step over the all-important boundary from stylised dancing into something more threatening and real? He always maintained a space between them and, though some people undoubtedly found tango as intoxicating as sex, she had realised it was the promise of sex rather than the act itself, and as a woman who didn't like admitting how inexperienced she was, that held enormous appeal. Unlike the frenzied bouncing in the marquee at the polo ground, this was dance as art.

Nero loosened his grip when the music faded and led Bella back to their table. 'You're full of surprises, Bella Wheeler,' he said, narrowing his eyes as he gave her a considering look. Raising his hand, he called the waiter over to bring them another drink.

'Just some more water, please.' She had more surprises locked away inside her than Nero could possibly guess at, and she was going to keep a clear head while she was in Argentina to make sure she kept it that way.

CHAPTER SIX

KEEPING a clear head guaranteed Bella an early night. Nero delivered her to the door of her hotel and, with a brisk nod, bid her good night. Put him out of your head, she told herself next morning. She was ready to explore.

The Sunday traffic was every bit as crazy as when she had arrived, but she welcomed the noise and bustle of a new day, thinking this was the most exhilarating introduction to a city as fascinating as Buenos Aires that she could possibly have. And she certainly wasn't going to sit in her hotel room wondering what Nero was doing. He had said he would call for her at eleven that morning to take her to his *estancia*. Where he was or what he did before then was Nero's business.

And she didn't care a jot.

Liar, Bella thought as she left the hotel. But she was determined to make the most of her short stay in one of the world's most vibrant and beautiful cities. This was just one of the places Nero called home, and she was curious to explore it. Buenos Aires was full of personality and charm, the staff in the hotel had assured her. Everywhere she went she would find *porteños*, as the residents of Buenos Aires were called, performing the tango on the streets. Crowds gathered, music played, and dancers dressed for the occasion would entertain you, they told her with a smile.

She didn't have to look far before she discovered a small square at the end of the street where an impromptu dance floor had been created simply by laying board down on the cobbles. The sun was warm, the sky was blue, the setting was exquisite and she joined the crowd to watch. Colourful gardens surrounded her and the central fountain in the tiny square provided a pleasant overlay to the music. A small white rococo church with steeples like plump figs added to the charm of the setting. She was really in South America now, Bella thought, feeling excited and rather cosmopolitan. Shading her eyes, she watched the dancers and soon she was lost in their skill, and in the music, and was hardly aware that someone had walked up behind her.

'How easy it would be to relieve you of this,' a husky male voice very close to her ear said disapprovingly.

'Nero!' Her heart lurched violently. So much for playing it cool. The heat of the dance was all around them—most of it in her cheeks when Nero held up the wallet he had taken from her handbag.

'Your handbag was open,' he explained. 'Lucky for you the hotel told me where I could find you. I hope you're packed and ready to leave?'

'Of course.' She was thrown immediately from carefree tourist into awkward sort-of-employee, and had to move quickly on from that mind-set to professional woman whose only purpose in being in Argentina was to do a worthwhile job for the prince of her country. She held out her hand for the wallet and Nero gave it to her. Stuffing it back into her shoulder bag, she fastened the catch securely. 'Do you make a habit of this?' she demanded.

'Do you make a habit of leaving your wits behind when you travel?' Nero countered.

They stared at each other. The dance between them had begun. Tango must be catching, Bella thought dryly. 'Shall we?' she said, keen to break eye contact.

'By all means.'

She turned for the hotel. That husky Argentine accent was the sexiest in the world, she decided as she led the way.

And she'd soon get used to Nero's voice and let it wash over her, Bella told herself firmly, quickening her step. But however prim she tried to act, Buenos Aires worked against her. There was too much passion here—too many dancers expressing their feelings on this Sunday morning, swirling, spinning, legs flicking, arms raised at acute angles—men in spats, women dropping as if into a dead faint in their partners' arms, only to revive so they could continue the fight. It was exhausting just watching them.

'Tango gets into your blood,' Nero commented when they reached the steps of Bella's hotel.

Then she must be sure not to let it get into her own blood, Bella thought. 'I'll just ask the porter for my suitcase. I left it ready in the lobby when I checked out.'

'Your case has already been taken to the airport.'

'The airport?' Bella's throat dried. Was Nero sending her home? Were her services no longer required?

'I take it you won't mind being my only passenger?' he demanded.

She must have looked at him blankly. 'In the jet,' he prompted.

'You'll be flying a jet to the *estancia*?' she confirmed.

'Yes. Is something wrong with that?'

'No, of course not.' Didn't everyone have a selection of private jets from which to choose?

The cockpit of Nero's executive jet was yet another confined space in which Bella was forced to sit too close to Nero. Of course, she could have sat in the back where there were comfortable leather seats, and entertainment as well as refreshments on tap, but she had given way to a childish urge to sit next to the pilot.

And taste a little of that danger she was growing so fond of?

She had always been fascinated by the concept of flight, Bella argued primly with her inner voice.

And fascinated by Nero.

Why pretend? She had an overriding desire to sit next to Nero.

He checked the buckles on her seat belt and helped her to fit the headphones securely. 'Okay?'

Her senses soared to answer him before she could. He smiled deep into her eyes. Nero saw everything, Bella realised, turning quickly to stare out of the window. By the time he had completed his pre-flight checks she could hardly breathe for arousal. He was totally in control, and his self-assurance filled her with confidence—and not just as to how well Nero would fly a jet.

'There's no need to be nervous,' he said, turning to look at her.

'I'm not nervous,' she protested, consciously relaxing her grip on the seat. Just sitting next to him was making her nervous. Going to Nero's *estancia*, where the only way out was by private plane, or goodness knew how long a road trip, was nothing short of insanity.

'Don't look so worried, Bella; I'll take care of you.'

That was what she was afraid of. 'The only thing

wrong with me,' she said as Nero lined up the jet for take-off, 'is that I like to be in control. Sitting in the copilot's seat doesn't suit me.'

'But it suits me very well,' Nero assured her, breaking off to acknowledge instructions from the control tower. Having been given the all-clear, he opened the throttle and released the brake and in seconds, or so it seemed, the small jet rocketed into the clear blue sky.

There was no turning back now, Bella thought as the jet soared through the first bank of cloud.

After a couple of hours the clouds parted to reveal a very different world from the towering skyscrapers and sprawling urbanisations of Buenos Aires. Nero's private airstrip was little more than a thin stripe of bleached earth on what seemed to be an endless carpet of green and russet and gold, stretching towards a horizon where misty mountains clawed at the cobalt sky with jagged fingers.

The Pampas. Bella's heart leapt with an intoxicating mixture of excitement and fear. The thought of riding here—of living here—with so much space, and so close to nature—

'Wait until you breathe the air,' Nero murmured.

Pollution-free and as heady as the most refined wine, Bella guessed.

'Here,' Nero told her as he banked the jet steeply. 'Take a look out of the side window and you'll see the *estancia*.'

Bella gasped as the g-force hit her.

'Nervous now?' Nero suggested with a wicked grin.

'Not at all,' Bella lied as the jet levelled off.

'You'll need steady nerves while you're working here. Life is tough on the pampas, Bella.'

'I'm not here for easy,' she told him frankly. 'I'm here to do the best job I can.' Her gaze turned to the hundreds of horses on the ground below.

'We had a lot of foals born this year.'

'Incredible,' Bella murmured. Everyone knew Nero was a wealthy man, but this was a polo establishment on an unimaginable scale.

'I'll fly you over the house before we land.'

Her stomach flipped as the plane dropped lower. The house Nero was referring to was an elegant colonial-style building the size of a small town, and now they were only a hundred feet or so above it she could see the long shaded verandas and a formal garden as vast as a park. There was even a polo field at one end of the cultivated grounds, with a stand and clubhouse, while in the central courtyard of the main building a fountain spurted diamond plumes into the air. Behind the house there was a glistening lake with a fabulous sandy beach and one—no, two swimming pools…

'One is for the horses,' Nero said when he saw her looking. 'We use it for treatment and for strengthening exercises, though we ride in the lake for preference—'

Bella exclaimed with pleasure, but then her usual common sense kicked in. What on earth had she been thinking when she had agreed to this? Nero's vast estate was like a country in its own right. She would be as isolated here as if she had been shipwrecked with him and they were stranded on a desert island with the ocean surrounding them. Unless she could find some way to ignore the electricity that constantly sparked between them, this could turn into a very tense and challenging stay.

Nero landed the jet skilfully with scarcely a bump. As he slowed to a halt and cut the engines Bella's concerns gave way to excitement. 'Oh, just look at that,' she exclaimed as she stared out across the miles of rolling grass. 'I can't wait to get out there and smell the air.'

'Feel the sun, and ride the horses,' Nero added with matching enthusiasm. 'It's beautiful, isn't it?'

When the door of the jet swung open Bella was greeted by a gust of warm, fragrant air. She was so excited she didn't even shrug off Nero's steadying hand when he helped her down the steps. There was always that small adjustment from sitting and floating to stepping out onto terra firma—add her eagerness to that and she was like a wild pony who, for that moment at least, was glad of Nero's reassuring presence. A wind had kicked up, blowing her hair about, and the ground was dusty and hard beneath her feet, but the warmth of her welcome was in no doubt at all.

'This is Ignacio,' Nero explained, introducing an elderly man standing by the utility vehicle waiting to take them to the ranch. 'My estate manager and right-hand man.'

Now she really was on the pampas, Bella thought, feeling a thrill of excitement as the elderly man stepped forward to shake her hand. She took in the slouched hat and red bandana, the voluminous trousers worn with leather chaps to protect the gaucho's legs from the constant friction of riding a horse. 'Welcome to Estancia Caracas,' he said in heavily accented English, bowing briefly over Bella's hand.

'*Buenas tardes*—good afternoon,' Bella replied, feeling more than welcome.

'We have heard many good things about your work with the English horses,' Ignacio added graciously.

'And battled the proof of it on the polo field,' Nero said as both men laughed.

'You're too kind. Your work with horses is second to none in Argentina.' Nero's estate manager had skin like beaten leather and was as wrinkled as a turtle, but his raisin-black eyes were full of kindness and warmth, and his handshake was firm. 'I'm so pleased to meet you, Ignacio. *Mucho gusto.*'

Ignacio grunted appreciatively at Bella's attempt to speak his language and said something in rapid Spanish to Nero that elicited a noncommittal hum.

Whether Nero was pleased or not by her clumsy effort, she had made one friend, Bella thought, judging by the warmth in the elderly gaucho's eyes as he invited her to sit in the vehicle for the short drive to the house.

She found everything thrilling, even the bumpy ride during which Ignacio pointed out the colourful ducks flying in arrow formation against the flawless blue sky, and then Nero spotted one of the giant hares native to the pampas as it bounced across the road. 'Look, Bella,' he said, grabbing hold of her arm in his excitement.

That touch was most thrilling of all, she thought, and the sights were pretty spectacular. And now Nero's powerful arm was resting across the seat in front of her. The only decoration he wore was a steel wristwatch that could probably tell their position in relation to the moon, but his sheer physical presence was what overwhelmed her.

'Good, huh?'

She jumped alert as he prompted her. 'Amazing,' she murmured, staring into his eyes. This time she had to force her stubborn gaze outside the vehicle.

They entered Estancia Caracas through an arched

entrance that reminded Bella of old cowboy films where the gates loomed large and impressive in what was otherwise a barren landscape. A long, well-groomed drive led the way to the sprawling hacienda—though this was a hacienda with a capital H—far larger and better kept than seemed humanly possible in such a wild and remote area, she decided as Ignacio turned into a cobbled courtyard the size of a football pitch.

'Wow,' Bella murmured. Nero's home was seriously fabulous.

They got out and she paused for a moment. The breeze was tickling the leaves on the eucalyptus trees and the only other sound was the distant whinnying of a horse. The courtyard was full of flowers—vivid cascades tumbling down the walls and draping in lush swags over the balconies. 'You must find it so hard to leave here,' she murmured.

'And so good to come back,' Nero agreed. 'Shall we?'

'Yes, of course.' The walls of the hacienda were painted in a muted shade of chalky terracotta, while the smooth cobbles beneath her feet were a deeper shade of golden red. Everything looked so warm and welcoming beneath the cobalt sky.

'Is this not what you had expected?' Nero demanded as Bella exclaimed with pleasure as she trailed her fingertips across some clusters of blossom.

Of such a hard, rugged man? 'No,' she admitted. 'I don't know what I expected, really.'

'So what do you think now?'

'That you have mastered the art of living in harmony with your surroundings,' she said honestly.

Nero seemed pleased by this analysis and introduced Bella to María, his cook and housekeeper, and María's sister, Concepcion, both of whom were waiting to greet him outside the door. The older ladies' faces were wreathed in smiles. They were so obviously delighted to see him Bella could only conclude Nero must have been an engaging child.

Perhaps she was being a little unfair to him, Bella conceded as the women bustled ahead, turning constantly to check that Nero hadn't left them again. The large hallway was paved in fabulous terracotta marble, softened by cinnamon-coloured rugs. The walls, painted a warm cream, were hung with antique mirrors and pictures. Probably family heirlooms, Bella guessed, apart from a painting of a wild horse, which was more recent and drew her attention immediately.

'Do you like it?' Nero asked, noticing her interest.

'I love it,' she enthused. Gadamus was an American artist noted for his freestyle technique with an airbrush and there was nothing cosy about this picture. There was nothing cosy about her life any longer, Bella thought as she glanced at Nero.

'So, what do you like about it?' he probed.

'The brutal realism,' she said, holding his gaze.

'You're drawn to danger and risk?' Nero suggested.

'It appears so,' Bella agreed coolly. She refused to be over-faced by all this quiet money, or by a man of such power and charisma.

'We'd better not keep María and Concepcion waiting,' Nero pointed out, making her a mocking bow.

They understood each other completely, Bella thought, though her confidence in handling Nero was short-lived. His touch on her arm shot the breath from her lungs as he held the door for her and they traded the shady lobby for an interior courtyard.

She quickly recovered to take in the peaceful haven

where the only disturbance was the sound of water gushing in the fountain to a background of birdsong. The air was scented with blossom, which reminded Bella that Christmas in Argentina was very different to the same season in England. The prince had warned her that she would be leaving the cold northern hemisphere for something very different. How right he was. This was another world altogether…

'You have a beautiful home, Nero.' And she was allowing herself to invest far too much interest and emotion.

The interior of the house made it even harder for Bella to disengage her feelings. There was a grand hall with a sweeping staircase, and the lake they had flown over was the focus of all the main rooms. From the windows of each elegant salon she could see beautifully tended lawns sweeping away to a golden beach and, in the far distance, snow-capped mountains.

'Do you approve?' Nero demanded dryly.

'I've never seen anything like it,' Bella admitted. 'But I'm here to work,' she managed in a firmer tone.

'Of course.'

Nero held the door for her and as she passed in front of him he made her feel so very small and vulnerable. Why must every part of her respond to him so urgently? Her mind must remain set on business, she told herself firmly.

'This is my den,' Nero explained, showing her into a smaller wood-panelled room. 'But you must make yourself at home here.'

Bella felt her smile must be little short of incredulous. Making herself at home here would take a little longer than she intended to spend in Argentina. 'I don't know how you can ever bear to leave,' she exclaimed impulsively.

'That's only because you haven't seen my place in Buenos Aires yet,' Nero informed her dryly.

And was never likely to, she thought. Hey ho.

CHAPTER SEVEN

'You must be hungry,' Nero suggested, leading the way to the kitchen. 'I know I am,' he said.

Nero's lips were pressing down so attractively she would have followed him anywhere, Bella mused wryly.

The kitchen took up a large part of the ground floor, and was another design triumph. State-of-the-art appliances sat comfortably next to well-worn settles and pieces of riding equipment. And, judging by the boots, gloves and polo helmet resting on a small side table next to an easy chair, this was the heart of the home and Nero's preferred space. The seat and the back of the chair wore the imprint of his body, Bella noticed, dragging her gaze away.

'What do you think?' Nero asked.

Censored. Dreams she could have, but she wasn't sharing them with him. 'Something smells good,' she said, inhaling appreciatively. And such smells they were—aromatic broth steaming busily on top of the old range cooker, the scent of freshly baked bread and ground coffee. Bella's mouth was watering by the time María and Concepcion had invited them to sit at the large scrubbed table.

'Perhaps you would like María to show you to your

bedroom first—so you can freshen up before you eat?' Nero suggested. 'Whenever you're ready, come down, we'll eat and then I'll take you on a tour of the stables.'

'Perfect. Though the bunkhouse would suit me fine,' Bella protested as María led the way into the hall.

'The bunkhouse?' Nero raised an amused brow. 'I'm not sure the gauchos would take too kindly to you moving in. And how could I deny María and Concepcion the pleasure of your sunny nature?' he added dryly.

Was she really such a stuck-up, starchy old maid? She must appear so, Bella realised. If only she could learn how to relax without giving Nero the wrong idea.

Her bedroom was beautiful, full of the scent of flowers freshly picked from the garden and deliciously feminine. She would never have indulged herself to this extent with all the lace and frills and flowers at home. It proved to be another occasion when she had to drag herself away.

She hadn't realised how hungry she was and devoured the delicious meal María placed in front of her. When she finally sat back with a contented sigh she noticed Nero watching her.

'Ms Wheeler?' he said formally, standing to hold her chair. 'Would you care to see the stables now?'

She flashed him a quick smile. 'Thank you, Señor Caracas. I would love to see the stables…'

The prince hadn't exaggerated. Nero's stables were unlike anything she'd seen before—six-star accommodation for horses with amenities second to none. For a moment Bella almost lost her confidence. Everything she was used to back home was so low-key compared to this. Nero's yard was the Bugatti Veyron Super Sport to her banged-up Mini of a polo yard.

But she produced great horses, Bella reminded herself.

It was Nero who shook her out of these concerns when he reminded her that the youngsters would be arriving soon, and that Ignacio wanted to show Bella the ponies he thought suitable for novices. These were retired ponies who couldn't take too much weight and whose exercise regime had been drastically reduced. 'As long as we make sure their mouths can't be dragged—and I have a cure for that,' Bella said, explaining her process with the reins to Nero. Before she knew it, she was right back where she belonged, chatting easily to him about horses. This was one area at least in which there were no tensions between them.

The stables were cleaner than many hotel rooms Bella had stayed in; sweet-smelling hay was banked high and her imagination took flight in the shadowy stall. 'We'd better get on,' she said abruptly, giving Nero one of her tight-lipped smiles.

'Why so tense, Bella?'

'I'd like to see the clinic,' she said, concerned that Nero could read her mind.

He shrugged. 'As you wish.'

Nero's shadow fell over her as he opened the stable door. He made her feel so small and feminine, which was something quite new for Bella. And she would ignore it, she determined.

And that was easy, Bella thought wryly as Nero led the way across the yard. He had changed out of his casual travel clothes into close-fitting breeches, which he was wearing with a deep maroon polo top. The contrast of colours against Nero's tanned skin made for a compelling picture. The wide spread of his shoulders and the hard, tanned chest just visible at the neck of his top didn't hurt either. And she wouldn't have been looking at his breeches if she hadn't been admiring his fabulous knee-length black leather boots. She noted with concern than the placket at the front of his breeches appeared to be under some considerable strain...

'This way,' Nero prompted.

'Of course,' she said, tipping her chin at a professional angle as she followed him.

'I have a polo match next week.'

'Next week?' So soon? And the children were arriving when?

She could cope. She would cope.

'Ignacio thought you would enjoy preparing the ponies with him.'

'I would,' Bella agreed, quickly burying her concerns. 'That's what I'm here for.' She thrilled at the challenge.

'I want the kids to get straight into it as soon as they arrive,' Nero explained, 'and this friendly match with a neighbouring *estancia* will be their first proper introduction to polo, so everything must go smoothly.'

'And it will.' She only had one concern left. Did Nero know the meaning of a *friendly* match? Somehow, Bella doubted it. 'A week isn't a lot of time to prepare the ponies.'

'My ponies are always ready.'

She didn't doubt it. Proud. Hard. Driven—didn't even begin to describe this man. Competition was everything to Nero and, just as she had suspected, this would be anything but a friendly match—and those ponies had better be ready.

It wasn't just the way Nero looked, it was the way he

moved, Bella reflected, allowing him to walk ahead of her so she could assess him like prime breeding stock. She might be the Ice Maiden, happily set on her spinster ways, but that was no curb on admiring a perfect male physique. She was a professional, wasn't she? Bella thought as Nero turned to flash a quick glance her way to make sure she was following. What else did she do all day at work if not stare thoughtfully at muscle and flesh to make sure the beast in question was in tiptop form and had the stamina to do what was required of it without injury? This beast was definitely at the peak of fitness, and Nero's stamina had never been in question.

'That was a heavy sigh,' Nero commented, hanging back to keep pace with her. 'Not tired already, I hope, Bella?'

'Not tired at all. In fact, I can't remember feeling quite so energised.'

'Excellent.' Nero's lips pressed down with approval. 'The pampas air is obviously good for you.'

Something was, Bella thought as her mouth formed the Ice Maiden line.

'This is the hospital and recovery block,' Nero explained as they approached a smart white building.

He held the door open and she walked in under his arm. Heat curled low inside her in a primitive response to Nero's size and virility. The untamed pampas had loosed something elemental inside her. It was just as well the facilities inside the clinic were exceptional and she could quickly become absorbed in these.

'We can carry out operations here if we have to,' Nero explained. 'Vets live on site. There is also a doctor and a nurse in residence to care for the two-legged members of the team. The distances are so vast here we can't rely on help reaching us in time.'

Wasn't that the truth? she thought.

'Bella?'

'Wonderful,' she said, refocusing. 'May I see the facilities for the children now?'

'I can assure you they will be well catered for.'

Bella met and held Nero's proud gaze. 'I wouldn't be doing my job if I left out one of the most crucial parts of it.'

'As you wish.'

Even Nero's back had something to say about her thoroughness. Nero was a fierce, passionate man to whom pride meant everything, and he didn't take kindly to having his establishment judged by anyone, especially her. But pride was important to Bella too, at least where doing the best job possible was concerned.

'I trust this meets with your approval?' he said, opening the door to the first wooden chalet.

How prim and boring he must think her, Bella realised as she took a look around. If she were a child staying here she would be in seventh heaven—there was even a view of the ponies grazing in the paddocks through the windows. 'It's wonderful.' She turned to find Nero with his arms braced either side of the doorway, displaying his formidable physique as he leaned into the room. 'Did you plan the finishing touches while we were in Buenos Aires?' she said, noticing the recent magazines and the latest teen films stacked by the TV.

'I had nothing better to do.'

Nero's tongue was firmly planted in his cheek, Bella suspected. 'What?' she demanded when he raised a brow. 'I didn't spend all my time in Buenos Aires learning to dance the tango...'

'How very noble of you, Bella. And how reassuring for me to know our evening out wasn't wasted.'

She groaned inwardly. What a dull companion he must think her. 'I'll take some shots for the prince,' she said, finding her phone.

'I trust your report will be favourable?'

'How could it not be when you've thought of everything—even fire extinguishers.'

'You won't need one,' Nero murmured under his breath.

The Ice Maiden had never regretted her tag more—and this time there was plenty of room for her to pass Nero at the door without touching him. He was standing well clear.

'Would you like to see the ponies we have chosen for you to look at?'

'I'd love to.'

'So you do trust our judgement?'

'Ignacio's reputation precedes him.'

'As does mine, I have no doubt,' Nero observed dryly as they walked along the dusty path together.

This time she thought it better to say nothing.

CHAPTER EIGHT

As Bella had expected, Nero and Ignacio had judged the ponies perfectly. 'These will be a match made in heaven,' she said, 'and will give the kids loads of confidence.' She was conscious of Nero brooding at her side and wondered what was on his mind.

'We'd better go,' he said, pulling his booted foot from the fence rail. 'The first group of kids will be arriving soon, and I've no doubt you'll want to settle them in.'

'It's you they'll want to see,' Bella pointed out. Whether he chose to accept it or not, Nero was a national hero. 'It's no secret that half the kids we're expecting to join the scheme would have scoffed at the idea of leaving the city for the wilds of the pampas if there hadn't been a certain attraction named Nero Caracas waiting here for them.'

'Are you attempting to flatter me?' Nero laughed. 'I should warn you, I am immune to it.'

In the same way that familiarity bred contempt? Bella thought. 'I'm merely stating a fact.'

'Then allow me to reassure you,' Nero murmured as they walked back to the hacienda side by side, 'I'll be with you every step of the way.'

Oh, good, Bella thought wryly as her glance crashed into Nero's. 'I'm sure the children will appreciate that.'

'And you will too, I hope?'

The mocking note in Nero's voice hadn't escaped her. 'That goes without saying,' she said.

'Your wish is my command, Bella.'

And if she believed that then she was well on her way to becoming a doormat. Nero would tolerate her involvement at Estancia Caracas for the sake of his scheme and the prince's goodwill—and nothing more. She would have to work harder than she ever had in her life to make this work, Bella realised as Nero snapped his whip against his boots. At least she'd be too tired to dream about him at night. If brooding Nero intended to shadow her she would just have to act out a part—someone confident in her personal as well as her professional life—someone sophisticated who could handle Nero's high-powered sex appeal and take it all in her stride.

Someone else?

There was no one else. There was just Bella Wheeler, the Ice Maiden, and Nero Caracas, the Assassin. Oh, good.

They parted in the kitchen to shower and freshen up. When Nero came downstairs again it amused him to see María stuffing *empanadas*, the delicious little stuffed pastries, inside Bella's mouth as she crossed the kitchen on her way out, and pressing even more pastries into her hands as she tried to get through the door. Someone had made a friend.

'Sorry,' Bella garbled, chewing down a mouthful as he left the house to join her.

'Don't apologise,' he said, stealing a pastry from her hands. 'Hmm, delicious,' he agreed, smacking his hands together to get rid of the crumbs.

She risked a smile.

'What are you wearing?' he demanded.

'Dungarees—I thought, settling kids in, carrying cases...'

He shrugged.

'You don't agree?'

'There are others here who can carry cases. Wasn't it you who said we're the inspiration? And, as in this instance, I agree you're right, and so I dressed the part.' Nero ran a hand down his black polo shirt with the team emblem—The Assassin's skull and crossbones boldly embroidered in white on black over his heart. His hand moved on down his close-fitting breeches, tough riding boots and the knee protectors he customarily wore during a match. 'This is all about first appearances, you said—give the kids something to remember?'

'I see what you mean...' She frowned, but swiftly rallied. 'I suppose none of them would have a clue who you were if you were waiting for them wearing jeans.'

He met the innocent look with the faintest of smiles. 'You're probably right,' he agreed mildly.

'So, as I'm short of a Hammer House of Horrors polo shirt, what do you suggest I wear?' she asked.

Holding the concerned gaze, he put a curb on his amusement. 'What would you think if you were greeted by a woman in dungarees?'

Bella shrugged. 'The grooms were too busy caring for the horses to hang around waiting for my coach?' she suggested, reasoning that the grooms were all young—and, however scruffy they got in the course of their work, all attractive. The kids would only think an older woman in dungarees a poor substitute who probably knew nothing about horses, anyway.

'And?' Nero pressed, dipping his head to stare her in the eyes.

'The owners and trainers had better things to do?'

'And how would that make you feel?'

'Okay,' she agreed. 'You've made your point.'

'As you made yours,' Nero pointed out wryly.

He was right. If Bella had been one of the kids arriving on the coach she would like to think her arrival counted for something—enough, at least, for the people who ran the course to be waiting to greet her. 'I'll go and put something else on.'

Nero glanced at his watch. There was just enough time for Bella to change her clothes. He watched her return to the house, straight-backed, with a brisk stride. He anticipated the transformation with interest.

'Much better,' he approved when she cocked a brow before mutely running her hands down her neatly packaged frame.

Much, *much* better, he thought as his body responded with indecent enthusiasm to Bella's transformation. This was far better than dungarees, and a vast improvement on her working breeches. It was even better than Bella in a straight-laced evening dress.

'Would you like me to do a twirl?' she asked with a heavy dose of sarcasm.

'I've seen you dance, remember? So I know twirls aren't your strength.' He held her gaze. He loved holding her gaze. And so they stared at each other—staring into each other's eyes, neither one of them prepared to back down.

Until the sound of a coach approaching forced them both to glance away. But even as he stood ready to welcome the children he was keenly aware of the extremely attractive woman standing at his side dressed in nononsense breeches and a crisp white tailored shirt.

* * *

The children were settling in, but there was no time to relax. While his team of gauchos took the children through safety procedures and introduced them to the ponies, it was time for Nero and Bella to turn their thoughts towards the polo match. 'Let's get started, shall we?' he said, heading off towards the stables.

Bella pulled a wry face as she tucked a strand of rebellious hair back into position. 'I hope you don't live to regret involving me in this.'

He did too.

'Are you sure you're not going to find this too much? Teaching reckless kids and even wilder ponies?' He stared into her eyes, wanting to study Bella more deeply. He was a practical man. Sometimes lust intruded. Usually he would take a practical view of what was on offer—make his decision—yes or no, and then move on. Bella was too vulnerable for that. She might be acting the role but, like any actress, Bella's woman-of-the-world façade came off with the costume.

'I'm sure,' she said, meeting his gaze confidently. 'I have some experience of…coping.'

She spoke without emotion, and then he remembered Bella had three younger siblings—brothers, none of whom were interested in horses or their father's yard, and all of whom had gone on to university, thanks to Bella's riding boot up their backside. The children had lost their mother at an early age, and when their father had gone to pieces it had been left to Bella to set things on an even keel. There was more to this Ice Maiden than most people even guessed at and, remembering what he'd seen of her other side on the dance floor, he said, 'I hope you'll make time for your tango lessons. Or will they have to be put on hold for now?'

Her timing was perfect. There was a short pause,

and then, 'Why should they be put on hold?' she asked, 'Ignacio has promised to hone my technique, so the next time you and I hit the dance floor, I'll be ready for you.'

'Oh, will you?' he said.

So Ignacio was going to teach Bella the tango, was he? First María, and now Ignacio—what was happening here? 'You want to watch Ignacio,' he said, narrowing his eyes in mock suspicion. 'Many a good tune is played on an old fiddle.'

Bella laughed, letting herself go for the first time in a long time, but then she angled her chin to stare into his eyes. 'Are you jealous, Nero?'

He huffed and turned away.

'Could we have a drink before we start thinking about the polo match?' she asked, catching up with him in the yard.

'Water okay for you?'

'Perfect,' she said.

He led the way into the barn. Opening the door, he let it swing shut behind them. They were instantly enclosed in warm silence. Walking over to a sink in the corner, he filled a container with the crystal-clear water that flowed straight from the glacier via an underground stream to the hacienda. 'We'll take this with us,' he said, offering the container to Bella first.

She drank deeply and then handed it to him. He did the same. As he wiped the back of his hand across his mouth he caught her staring at him. His mouth curved with amusement as he read her thoughts. They had shared a drink from the same container. It was the closest their mouths had come to touching—up to now.

She was within touching distance of Nero. There was something magical about a hay barn. Perhaps it was the mountains of dried grass soaking up the sound, or the dust motes floating on sunbeams giving the impression of a shimmering golden veil between them. It was a soft—a ridiculously soft—frame, in which Nero appeared violently masculine.

'Bella?' he murmured.

'Could I have another drink?' She reached for the canister. Their fingers touched as Nero handed it to her and a bolt of electricity shot up her arm.

'We'd better fill it again before we leave,' he said as she lowered the container from her lips. Holding her gaze, he removed it from her hand and placed it on the side. She drew in a sharp breath as Nero's hands rested lightly on her arms.

'What are you frightened of, Bella?'

She couldn't look at him even though the temptation to let go just this once was overwhelming. 'I'm not frightened.'

'Prove it,' Nero said quietly, and behind his customary irony Bella sensed a deeper layer of concern.

'Shouldn't we be getting on?' She glanced across the honeyed space—the chasm between them and the door. Nero was like a sleeping tiger, breathing steadily and yet keenly aware at the same time. She had never played the mating game before, but she knew the signs. The look in Nero's eyes—the attractive tug at one corner of his mouth. Nero liked her. No. It was a lot more than that…

'Bella, Bella,' he murmured.

She swayed a little closer.

But something was wrong…something was out of sync. It felt as if she was edging along a tightrope with the promise of the most wonderful reward at the end of it with snapping sharks waiting in the waters below. At no point had Nero touched her—in fact, he had pulled back, and now one brow was raised in sardonic enquiry. 'What was that about?' he said.

Softening had been an insane lapse of judgement on her part—that was what it had been, Bella thought. She shared a professional relationship with Nero and that was all.

Until he dragged her close and rasped, 'You have no idea what you're playing with.' And, as she stared up at him in mute bewilderment, he added, 'I advise you very strongly to think before you act, Bella. You think you know me? You think you can play your schoolgirl games with me?'

'Don't worry,' she flashed, bouncing back onto the attack as she broke free. 'There's not the slightest chance I will ever play games with you.' And, when Nero laughed, she added, 'You're not as irresistible as you seem to think you are.' And that was meant to be her exit line, but Nero snatched her back again. 'Let go of me,' she warned him.

'You don't want this?' Nero smothered her cry of protest the most effective way he could. Brushing his lips across hers until the need poured out of her in whimpers of anger and frustrated tears, he took possession of her mouth in a fierce salty kiss.

Balling her hands into fists, she thrust them against his chest. She soon learned that fighting Nero was pointless. She should have hated him for this victory, but how could she when she wanted him, and when every encounter in the past was as nothing compared to this? The taste of him…the spice and scent of warm clean man…the feelings flooding through her veins…the heat pooling in her heart, her body, her senses…the need building up inside her…the urge to claim him as her mate.

When Nero kissed her the world and all its complications fell away. There was nothing left but sensation and the absolute conviction that this was right.

'*Dios*, Bella!' He thrust her away.

Shaken to the core, she was panting, while Nero towered over her, looking down as if he hated her. 'What if I was a different man, Bella? Don't you know what a dangerous game this is?'

'It's a game you're playing too,' she whipped back, hand across her mouth as if that could hide the proof of her arousal. She had to turn away to catch her breath before she could come back at him. Gripping the edge of the sink as if her life depended upon it, she drew a deep calming breath. Nero was right. They were both equally to blame for this. She had wanted him, but this was wrong. They were both wrong.

On the outside at least, she was utterly calm by the time she turned round again. 'We shouldn't keep Ignacio waiting,' she said coolly.

Nero opened the barn door and she walked through. And now it was back to business, Bella told herself firmly. She must forget this as if it had never happened. Or lose her credibility.

Her work provided the lifeline. The sound of churning water saved her. It distracted her and she exclaimed with interest when their route to the polo yard took them past the hydrotherapy spa. 'Can I take a closer look?'

'Of course.' Nero hung back while she went to watch the pony having its treatment. Rubber matting on the floor and side walls prevented accidental injury, and the spa stall was just large enough for the horse to feel safe as the healing salts in the chilly water bubbled around its legs. 'This is fantastic,' she commented.

'The low temperature increases the pony's circulation

and speeds up the curative process,' Nero explained, coming to stand beside her.

She breathed a sigh of relief. Thank goodness they had found something of interest in common that didn't put either her reputation or her heart at risk. 'I don't have anything like this in England.' She flashed a glance at Nero, and then remembered how things stood between them.

'I'm sure you'll find everything you need here, Bella.'

'I'm sure I will,' she said, determined to ignore the shiver of arousal that rippled down her spine.

CHAPTER NINE

As PART of the final matching process between horse and rider for the upcoming polo game, Nero was mounted and ready to give a riding demonstration. This was primarily for Bella so he could show her each pony's paces and quirks, though the newly arrived youngsters from the city had been invited to watch too.

This was why they were here, Bella thought as she watched the rapt faces around her. Nero might look like a movie star, but they all knew he wasn't playing a role, and he was doing more than show the paces of each horse. He was making the kids hungry—making them aspire to do better—to be the best they could be, so they could make a difference in the world in which they lived. But for now, Nero could turn a polo pony on a sixpence. He could gallop, skid to a halt in a cloud of dust within inches of the fence and make them all scream. He could prompt a pony to weave and turn, back up, rear round and change direction constantly, without appearing to move a muscle. And he did all this with the nonchalance of a Sunday ride in the park.

Nero was cool—really cool. He wasn't just the master of the game or even the horse he happened to be riding. Nero was master of himself, and that was sexy. He was powerful, and yet he coaxed a wild animal to be part of a team, and to do that he had to be sensitive and almost primal in his understanding of the relationship between two living things—and almost preternaturally refined in the delicacy of the adjustments he made to draw differing responses from the horse. It didn't take much to start wondering how that sensitivity of his might translate in bed.

And she had to stop thinking like that right away. She joined in the applause when Nero cantered round the ring acknowledging the appreciation of his audience with one hand raised. Staring at his strong tanned hand and imagining how it would feel resting on her naked body—firm, yet light and intuitive when it came to dealing pleasure. She had to stop that too.

'Did you draw any conclusions?' Nero demanded, reining in his horse in front of her.

'Plenty,' Bella managed as her throat went suddenly dry.

'Good.' Slipping his feet out of the stirrups, Nero eased his powerful limbs. 'I look forward to hearing your comments when I've helped the boys take the ponies back.'

'Right.' She nodded as he wheeled the pony away, but she was still rather more drawn by his muscular thighs straining the seams of his breeches than by any conclusions she had made on the work front. 'Get real, Bella,' she muttered impatiently under her breath.

Nero and Ignacio received her comments with approving nods. At least she hadn't lost it where horses were concerned. But that didn't address the bigger problem, Bella mused as Nero started to walk off with Ignacio. Staying in the house with him meant she saw Nero every day. She couldn't afford to slip up again like she had in the barn. 'I'll see you later,' she called to the two men as she headed off in the opposite direction.

She could be happy here, Bella realised as she walked along the path between the paddocks and the warm breeze ruffled her hair. It was the type of life people dreamed of, with the added spice of Nero close by. Reaching the house, she was already anticipating the welcoming smiles from María and Concepcion. The warmth of family, she thought as she opened the kitchen door. Kicking off her boots, she lined them up on the mat. Walking across the room, she left her helmet and riding gloves where Nero left his. It was maybe the closest she'd come to him since their kiss...

Seeing her smile fade momentarily, the two beaming women hijacked her with a piece of chocolate cake. 'Mmm—delicious,' Bella exclaimed, biting deep.

'More,' the two women insisted, cutting her a second slice.

'I'll miss you both so much when I go home,' she told them both in halting Spanish whilst fending off their attempts to force-feed her. She'd tried to learn more of the language, wanting to get closer to the people she was living with. She had only been in Argentina a short time, but it had made a huge impression on her. It wasn't just the facilities here, or even the challenging ponies...

It must be something in the air, Bella decided wryly, sucking crumbs off her fingers as she headed for the door. Nero *and* the pampas? That was quite a combustible combination for anyone to handle...

So she'd leave it for someone with more relationship smarts than she had.

And now she was jealous of that unknown someone.

She must remember not to let her feelings show, Bella

realised as María chased her to the door in an attempt to feed her more reviving chocolate cake. Laughing and holding up her hands in submission, she took the cake, dropped a kiss on María's cheek and ran upstairs to her bedroom.

Trailing her fingertips across the beautiful hand-worked quilt, Bella's gaze was drawn as it had been the first time she'd walked into the room, to an oil painting over the fireplace. Bella's mother had been soft and kind, but the woman in this portrait had Nero's fierce stare and was dressed like a gaucho in men's clothes. The only nod to femininity was the froth of chiffon at her neck.

Bella lay on the bed, staring at the portrait. The strong character of the woman in the painting blazed out at her. That must have been one formidable lady, Bella thought, taking in the determined set of the woman's jaw, the unflinching gaze, and the line already cutting a cruel furrow down one side of her full red lips. The likeness to Nero was uncanny. And I bet she had a sardonic smile too, Bella mused. The woman in the painting looked as if she could cut any man down to size with either a whip or her tongue. It pleased Bella to recognise the country-side in the background, though the *estancia* appeared much smaller. No wonder the ranch had grown, she thought, smiling as she took in the woman's planted fist on top of the sturdy fencing. The portrait spoke volumes about Nero's ancestry and why he was so attached to the *estancia*. With people like that in his family, how could he not be?

Nothing much had changed, Bella reflected as she went to take a shower. Estancia Caracas might be huge now and home to a very rich man, but Nero was as much a warrior as the woman in the painting. Had no softening influences touched him? What about his parents? Had they been written out of the picture? He never spoke about them. What sort of childhood had he had? And would she ever know?

It seemed unlikely, Bella thought as she soaped herself down. Nero wouldn't confide in her, and she could hardly question his staff.

One idyllic day melted into another, with Bella growing ever closer to Nero's staff until she felt like a real member of the team, and the youth scheme was going even better than she had dared to hope. Ignacio lightened everything, making her laugh and drip-feeding her information about Nero, as if the elderly gaucho wanted her to know what made his boss tick. The portrait in her bedroom was Nero's grandmother, he explained.

No surprise there, Bella thought dryly. She only had one regret left. She hardly saw Nero. They ate at different times, and he never seemed to be around when she was teaching. Whether he was too busy preparing for the polo match or whether he was avoiding her, she had no idea. It was none of her business what Nero was doing with his time. If she had any sense at all, she wouldn't miss him.

But she did.

The night before the ponies were due to arrive from England Bella slept fitfully. When she did manage to doze off, the young woman in the portrait seemed to come alive. With a fist planted on her hip and her strong jaw jutting at a determined angle, it felt as if she was sizing Bella up.

At one point Bella shot up with a start and switched the lights on. The room was empty. Of course it was empty, but when the cockerel crowed she realised it was time to get up. Leaping out of bed, she pushed back the heavy curtain. Excitement flashed inside her at the sight of a dust cloud that could only herald the horseboxes arriving from England.

Nero was already out in the yard.

If there was one thing guaranteed to bring Nero out, it was horses.

Heedless of how she looked or what she was wearing, Bella tugged her old dungarees over her pyjamas, adding a baggy sweater for extra warmth. There was no time to scrape her hair back, though she did pause in the bathroom to run a toothbrush over her teeth before racing out of the room and pelting downstairs. Tearing through the kitchen, startling María and Concepcion along the way, she burst through the door just in time to jog alongside the lead vehicle until it slowed to a stop in the stable yard.

'Leave this to the drivers, Bella,' Nero said sharply as she began to reach for the locks.

She was elated at the sight of Nero and feeling purposeful at the thought of the horses so close at hand. And determined to have her own way.

'I said leave it,' Nero snapped.

Moving in front of her, he said, 'This is men's work.'

'Men's work?' Bella demanded. 'Would your grandmother have said that?'

Nero's face froze and in that split second Bella said firmly, 'Excuse me, please,' and moved past him.

Bella was certain his expression could put a layer of ice on the lake, but Misty was in the back of this transporter and no one was getting in her way.

'Why don't you go back to the house and let us handle this?' Nero suggested in a more persuasive tone. She looked at his hand covering hers. 'I'll let you know when Misty's settled.'

'I'd like to do that myself. I want to welcome my own horse and check her over. I won't be going back to the house until I've checked all the ponies over,' she assured him. Planting her fists on her hips, she stared at him and he stared at her, neither of them moving.

'Shall we get on with this?' Nero suggested dryly as the back of the trailer was unhitched.

'Together,' she insisted.

Nero's lips tugged a little as he stretched the ironic stare. 'Together,' he agreed finally.

Good. This might be Nero's *estancia*, but the ponies were her responsibility too. They'd had a long drive, and a transatlantic flight and—

And standing up to Nero excited her. Her heart was pounding. And, much as she loved her work, she couldn't put all this excitement down to the arrival of her favourite horse.

Nero took charge of the lead horse, a towering bay called Colonel, one of his favourites, Bella remembered, while she took happy charge of Misty. It was inevitable they walked to the stables together—or, more accurately, walked to the small paddock outside the clinic where the ponies would wait their turn to be checked over by the vet.

'They'll be here for a few days of observation,' Nero explained as Misty whickered and nuzzled Bella. 'We'll keep her close for a few days, allow her to get acclimatised, and then you can ride her whenever you want.'

Bella's jaw must have dropped. It was the first time anyone had ever stepped in and told her what she could or couldn't do with her ponies. 'When I judge it right, I'll ride her.'

'With the vet's approval.'

'In consultation with the vet.' She had her hand balled into a fist, Bella realised, and it was resting on the top of the fence in a disturbing mirror pose of the woman in the painting in her room. And, just like Nero's grandmother, she wasn't about to back down.

The sight of Bella, even in those wretched dungarees, stirred all sorts of unwelcome feelings inside him. Those feelings had only increased when she'd drawn battle lines between them. Why must Bella make his life so complicated? Why couldn't she just fall into line?

Like the girls who put him to sleep? The girls who had nothing to talk about? The girls who might as well have lived on another planet? Was that the type of person he would like to change Bella into?

Okay. He'd felt her passion in the barn. It was all or nothing for Bella. Sex without commitment would never be enough for her. Sex with commitment was something he had never contemplated. That didn't stop his happy contemplation of her naked body beneath the shapeless clothes as they led the horses towards the veterinary station. On the surface, Bella was ignoring him, but there was a current snapping between them as she whispered sweet nothings in her pony's ear. She was probably instructing Misty to obey no one but Bella—

And who could he blame for bringing Bella here?

No one but himself.

By the eve of the polo match all the horses had passed the vet's stringent tests, which was a relief. Bella had taken it upon herself to exercise Misty the moment the small mare was given the all-clear and now Nero was down at the corral with the other men, with his boot lodged on one of the wooden struts of the enclosing fence as he watched some of the new yearlings being put through their paces. He was aware of Bella coming up on his right. He felt her presence the moment she left the house and walked across the yard. He could feel her quiet determination and confidence. Both were justified. When it came to her job, Bella had no equal—other than himself, and Ignacio, of course. When it came to caring for the ponies, Bella's energy, intuition and love for them was second to none—except, perhaps, his.

He could see her now without turning—her hair would be scraped back beneath a net under the hard hat she always wore for riding. He turned his head to confirm he wasn't wrong—giving himself the excuse that he didn't want any injuries on his conscience…

Of course she was wearing a hard hat. Perversely, he wanted to see her with her red hair flowing free now.

'Nero.' She acknowledged him briskly without breaking step.

He dipped his head briefly in response. He wouldn't see her again until she supervised the quick changes from one pony to the next between the chukkas that divided the game. Bella would be working with Ignacio, which was a great honour for her. Ignacio traditionally worked alone. But Bella was different, his elderly friend had told him.

'She has the heart of a gaucho—'

He looked at Ignacio, standing by his side.

'She reminds me of your grandmother…'

Nero hummed and curbed his smile. Those few words were probably the longest speech he'd ever heard from Ignacio on any subject that didn't include a horse. They were both staring at Bella, but he was remembering the grandmother who had brought him up, and whose portrait now hung in Bella's bedroom. In her youth,

Annalisa Caracas was said to possess the beauty of a pampered aristocrat. Nero knew she had the courage of a frontierswoman and rode like a man. Born to great wealth, Nero's father had considered a life of ease his natural right and had allowed the *estancia* to slip into ruin, forcing his own mother to come out of retirement and turn it round. It was lucky for him *and* the ranch that his grandmother had stepped in, and Annalisa Caracas was firmly placed on a pedestal in his mind.

Yes, Annalisa Caracas had been quite a woman.

He was jolted out of these thoughts by Ignacio nudging him. Bella had just mounted up and was turning her small mare towards the freedom of the pampas. He shook his head and huffed a laugh as the gauchos cheered when she set Misty at the fence instead of taking her through the gate. The small mare sailed over and then tossed her head, and in spirit so did Bella.

This was the first time in a long time, Nero realised, that he had stood with the other men to watch a woman ride.

CHAPTER TEN

THE polo match loomed ever closer and excitement was reaching fever pitch on the ranch. But it was more than excitement, Bella realised. It was as if they were preparing for the battle of the century. No piece of turf or rail had been left unchecked and her young charges were bursting with excitement. A sense of purpose had gripped everyone on the *estancia*—yet these were people whose world revolved around horses and polo, and who should surely take this *friendly* game in their stride?

Friendly game? Some hope, Bella mused. The team representing the neighbouring *estancia* were also world-class players, and although she didn't usually get worked up where testosterone-pumped males indulging in feats of macho lunacy were concerned, this was different. This was polo. But today even her great love for the game wasn't enough to stop her being anxious for Nero.

As the day wore on people arrived from far and wide. The match had brought the great and good of Argentina in helicopters, private jets and impressive cars, but there was also a large contingent of unsophisticated vehicles—trucks, horseboxes, battered Jeeps, cars with cracked suspension, rusting wheel arches and dubious paint jobs, along with a clutch of horse-drawn carts, as well as whole families riding in convoy on their ponies, trailing mules behind them, loaded with supplies. Polo meant fiesta on the pampas. It was both an excuse for a party as well as an all too rare get-together for far-flung families. All these people needed shade and water and food, as well as the other facilities associated with a small mobile city, and Bella and the rest of the staff had worked tirelessly to ensure that the event was a success. She was thrilled to think that everyone had come to see Nero Caracas, their national hero, lead his team. Nero represented everything that was proud and fine and wonderful about Argentina—her adopted country, Bella reflected as she stared out across the pampas. That was exactly how she felt about Nero's homeland—as if she belonged here.

And that was enough daydreaming when there was work to be done. The air of expectation gripping the crowd had made the ponies skittish—particularly Colonel, the pony on which Nero had decided to finish the match. In Bella's opinion, it would have been better to use Colonel in the first, or at least one of the earlier chukkas, rather than keeping the high-spirited horse until the end of the match, but Nero had overruled her saying his old faithful only needed time to calm down.

If only she could learn to calm down when it came to Nero, Bella reflected as he strode towards her down the pony lines. Surely, she should have got used to how he looked by now, but the sight of him still thrilled her—she still filled her eyes with him as she might have feasted them on a work of art. Nero was brutally beautiful, but he was more than that, she thought as her heart banged painfully in her chest. Oh, to hell with it—he was the sexiest man alive!

'Ready?' he said briefly.

'Ready,' Bella confirmed.

They had both checked the ponies numerous times. They were both professionals doing the job they did best, but that didn't cut off the electricity between them, or reduce her concern for Nero's safety in what was certain to be a fiercely competitive match.

And then the polo groupies arrived. Argentina was no different to the UK when it came to girls managing to look as if they had just stepped out of the fashion pages of some glossy magazine in this most workmanlike of settings. And here they were, complete with high heels and short flirty skirts, picking their way across a carpet of cobbles and horse manure. If she'd tried wearing shoes like that she'd have been up to her ankles in muck by now. She had to hand it to them, Bella thought as they clustered round Nero, the girls were groomed to the max. She couldn't blame them for their fascination. Polo was a savage game for rugged men, and horses as high-spirited could be found anywhere in the world. But as the girls fluttered round, and Nero, the king of the game, continued to ignore them and got on with his swift, practised preparations, she almost felt sorry for them. Almost, but not quite. Bella understood the tensions of the match and didn't expect Nero to pay her any attention, but the girls didn't understand that and thought all they had to do was look pretty and stick around long enough for Nero to turn and reward them with a smile...

He'd better not reward them with anything, Bella thought, feeling unusually moody as Nero turned to ask her for his stick. She passed it to him and, resting it over his shoulder, he cantered away without another word.

Taking her heart with him.

Don't be ridiculous, Bella told herself sternly. What was the point of giving her heart to Nero when he'd sooner have a bag of carrots for his ponies?

There was a tense air of expectation around the field of play. Everyone was geared up for action at the highest possible level and the game promised to be riskier than Bella had imagined. It soon became clear that, as she had suspected, this was no civilised knock-about between old friends, but a long-standing grudge match with no quarter offered by either side. There was battle fever between the players and, though Bella expected to feel on edge, she had not imagined longing for the match to finish so she could be sure Nero was safe.

Just let them all get through it in one piece, Bella thought as her gaze fixed on Nero. More the warrior than ever, with his tanned face grim beneath his helmet and his thick black hair curling beneath it, his muscles pumped and flexing and his strong hands on the reins, Nero looked invincible as he cantered round the field. That light grip was so deceptive. There was such power and certainty in it...and his powerful thighs, so subtly yet firmly controlling and directing his pony's movements.

She was jealous of a horse now?

The referee was speaking to each team. Silence fell other than the champing of bits. Anthems were played. The ball was positioned. Ponies jostled, and Nero hooked the first play clear.

The players thundered down the field with Nero taking an early lead. He was easily the most skilful rider. But even Nero wasn't invulnerable, and he couldn't evade all the opposing team's dirty tricks.

The other team's sole aim appeared to be to ride Nero off the field, and when two horses came cannoning towards him Bella screamed out a warning along with the rest of the crowd.

Nero would never risk his horse. Nero would rather risk himself—

A collective sigh rose from the crowd as Nero corkscrewed out of trouble, but it had been a narrow escape and, as the game continued, Bella grew increasingly anxious. The opposition wasn't interested in playing the game, they just wanted to create havoc with Nero in the centre of it. This wasn't about an elbow in the ribs or a well-placed knee in an attempt to unseat him, every action they took was designed to put Nero Caracas out of the game for good.

Yet Nero had never appeared stronger or more in control, Bella thought, taking comfort from his confidence as he leapt effortlessly from the back of one pony to the next between chukkas. This required split-second timing between groom and rider, with the groom having the next pony ready when the tired pony came cantering in, and no way was she going to let anyone have this responsibility—this was hers, and for once in his life Nero didn't have time to argue with her.

There was no basis for her sense of dread, Bella reasoned sensibly as the next chukka got underway. This was sport at the highest level and she couldn't expect it to be soft or easy. She should just relax and enjoy it. To see Nero at full stretch like this was a rare indulgence. She was watching out for risks around him, anticipating trouble even before it occurred. Nero shared this sixth sense and he used it to wheel and dodge his way out of trouble, while he controlled the field of play and kept his pony safe.

She was beginning to relax and enjoy the match, and shouted herself hoarse with the rest of the crowd when Nero whacked a ball halfway down the pitch and went charging after it. The other riders were in hot pursuit, but not fast enough to stop Nero smacking a goal between the posts. Rapturous applause greeted him as the teams changed ends, and within moments Nero had galloped in at the end of the chukka to change his shirt. Tugging it over his head, he displayed an obscene wealth of muscle to which Bella had to appear unmoved. And as if that wasn't bad enough, she now had to tell Nero something he wouldn't want to hear. 'I've substituted Colonel.'

'No—' Nero was scowling at the horse whose reins she was holding. 'Colonel doesn't have many matches left in him and I won't deny him this game.'

'But he's in a lather, Nero.' She shot an anxious glance towards the big bay it was taking two men to hold.

'It's your job to calm him down.'

And while she was still absorbing this piece of arrant nonsense, Nero mounted up.

'Colonel has been waiting for this moment, haven't you, boy?' he crooned, and she had to grit her teeth as the pony became both instantly alert and instantly cooperative.

'You'll never tame him, Bella.'

Was Ignacio talking about Nero or the pony? she wondered. 'It's a fantastic match,' she said distractedly. Even with Ignacio at her side, she had to brush off her growing sense of unease.

'Don't look so worried,' Ignacio said, following her gaze onto the field. 'Nero and Colonel have a special bond.'

She hoped so.

'I just wish this game didn't have to be quite so violent,' she confessed, voicing her fears.

'When you have some of the best players in the world on the field, competition is only to be expected,' Ignacio told her with a shrug.

Yes, but this was more than competition, Bella thought. This was war.

She'd never had this much invested in a match before, Bella reasoned as she leaned on the fence to watch. Ignacio had remained with her as if he sensed she needed company. There was only one man Ignacio was interested in watching, and that was Nero. She realised Ignacio couldn't have cared more deeply for Nero if he had been his own son.

'We're ahead,' Ignacio cheered as Nero swung his polo mallet and fired off another goal. The applause was deafening, but this became the cue for the game to become even rougher, and the crowd groaned when one of the riders was unseated.

Bella stared anxiously onto the field and only relaxed when she could see that both pony and player were unharmed. Her gaze flew to Nero, whose expression was thunderous beneath his helmet. She guessed he was furious at the risks the opposing team were taking with their horses. He glanced towards her and patted Colonel's neck as if he wanted to reassure her that they were both okay. She had to admit Colonel had never looked more alert or more impatient to enter the fray again. And Colonel's rider had never looked so savage, or so brutally attractive. She found a smile, though her eyes must have betrayed her concern and, with a brief nod, Nero wheeled away.

They were well into the first play when the ball

changed direction suddenly and a tightly bunched group
of riders came thundering down the field towards Bella
and Ignacio. Everything happened so fast—Ignacio
grabbed her arm and threw her clear but, in doing so, he
lost his balance as well as valuable seconds, while tons
of horseflesh continued crashing towards them. Nero
rode straight into the melee to save them. People were
screaming as Bella went back to catch hold of Ignacio.
Shoving him to the ground beneath her, she protected
him with her body. For a moment it was all a terrible
confusion of flailing hooves and rearing horses, with the
additional obstacles of boots, feet, thighs, bridles and
polo mallets. How they survived it, Bella would never
know. Her first clear thought was seeing Ignacio safe
on the other side of the fence as Nero swept her from
the ground and threw them both clear of the mayhem.
'Thank God,' she gasped against his chest.

When she turned to look, everything was slowly returning to normal. Reins were being gathered up, boots
stuck back in stirrups and horses were being turned by
their riders to calm them and give each other space. It
was only then that Bella realised Colonel was still on
the ground. 'I told you not to ride him,' she cried out as
grief and shock exploded inside her.

Dumping her on her feet, Nero returned to his horse.
'Get away from him,' he snapped when Bella would have
joined them.

Ignoring Nero's instruction, she quickly checked
Colonel over. 'I think he's winded.'

'And you know this for sure?' Nero's voice was ice.
His eyes were unforgiving.

For some reason, Nero blamed her for this, Bella
realised. 'I'm using my professional judgement,' she
said as calmly as she could.

He flashed something at her in Spanish that sounded ugly. It didn't need a translation. She understood him perfectly.

'Get out of my way,' he snarled, moving to block her out.

'We should help Colonel up as soon as we can,' she said, glancing around to enlist the help of Ignacio and the other gauchos.

'Are *you* going to lift him?' Nero rapped without turning to look at them as he knelt at his horse's head. 'Where's the vet?'

'Coming—he's coming,' Ignacio soothed in their own language.

Bella looked round with relief as the vet came running up.

Ignacio grabbed her arm. 'I want to thank you, Bella, for what you did—'

'Thank you,' she replied, holding Ignacio's gaze. 'We helped each other. It could have been so much worse—' Though she doubted Nero would see it that way, Bella thought, staring at him, shoulders hunched and tense as he crouched over his horse.

The game had been suspended and uneasy murmurs swept the crowd while the vet made his examination. When he had finished, Nero drew him aside so they could talk in private.

Knowing no boundaries when it came to the animals under her care, Bella followed them. She waited until there was a pause in the conversation, and then she touched Nero's arm. 'This wasn't your fault, Nero.'

The look Nero gave her should have warned her to leave it, but she was too upset by the fact that Nero had risked Colonel by riding the horse into the collision to save her. 'Thank you.'

'For what?' Nero's fierce black eyes drilled deep into her confidence.

'For saving me.'

The aggressive stare narrowed. Did Nero regret his actions? Turning away, he resumed his conversation with the vet in rapid Spanish, leaving Bella on the sidelines until Ignacio offered to translate for her.

Thank goodness Colonel wasn't so badly injured he would have to be destroyed. For all their power and bulk, horses were such fragile animals, but iced bandages followed by a stint in the hydrotherapy unit would be enough on this occasion.

They all stood round as a team, supervised by the vet, arranged a sling to hoist Colonel onto the recovery vehicle. Nero stood apart from the rest as the transport drove slowly away. The space between them might as well have been a continent, Bella thought.

Once the field was clear the game would be restarted. It was good news for a crowd relieved to discover there had been no serious casualties. Applause followed Colonel in his transporter across the field, though Nero remained staring after it with an expression that suggested the sky had just fallen in. 'It will be his last match,' he said to no one in particular.

And Nero blames me for that, Bella realised.

CHAPTER ELEVEN

'THE game is about to restart, Nero,' Bella prompted gently.

Nero didn't turn until the transporter had disappeared and then he said, 'Where's my next horse?'

She flinched at the tone of his voice. There wasn't an ounce of compassion in it. Nero was angry with himself, but he blamed both of them for bringing Colonel's career to an abrupt close.

And she was also badly shaken, Bella realised as she offered to bring a fresh horse up. A near fatal accident had almost taken out Ignacio, an elderly man she considered her friend now. Waiting for the vet's verdict had left her in pieces. *And the children!* How must they be feeling? 'I'm sorry—you'll have to excuse me,' she said, waving to one of the grooms.

'Where the hell do you think you're going?' Nero rapped. 'Do you have any idea what just happened?'

'Yes, and I'm sorry, but the kids from the scheme have been watching all this and they will be just as shocked as we are.' Without waiting for Nero's reply, she left him and ran. The sooner the children were reassured, the sooner she could get back to work.

Every cloud had a silver lining, Bella thought as she returned to the pony lines. None of the kids had realised the dangers of polo, and those who had dismissed the sport as girlie had been transformed into fervent fans, insisting polo was every bit as dangerous as motor racing and a lot more exciting to watch. Strange how fate worked sometimes, she thought wryly. And now there was just Nero to deal with. Her smile faded as she started to run.

'So you've turned up at last,' he said as he checked the bridle on the grey.

'Didn't the groom look after you?' Bella shot a quick smile of reassurance at the hapless girl whose bad luck it was to have her good work double-checked by Nero.

'You're in charge, Bella,' Nero said sharply, springing into the saddle. 'You should be here to supervise the grooms. This is not what I expect of you in a top-class game.'

'What else could I do?' Her voice was raised to match Nero's.

Grooms turned to stare as Nero demanded harshly, 'What were you doing on the polo field in the first place? This isn't a walk in the park, Bella, as you should know. How could you, of all people, be so irresponsible? What kind of example do you think you're setting for those kids you care so much about?'

She realised Nero couldn't have seen what had happened. He didn't know that Ignacio had almost been trampled. From Nero's angle as he rode up to save her, he would only have seen Bella staggering back as the group of horses collided with the fence, and had formed his own opinion. She was hardly going to mention that she had pushed Ignacio clear. She would just have to take this unfair reprimand on the chin. And smile sweetly. Until Nero turned his back.

'I'm not interested in excuses,' he barked, clearing

a space around them as he turned his horse to keep the high-spirited animal's energy in play. 'You never go near the fence again—and that's an order. And from a purely common sense point of view,' he added in a scathing tone, 'if you see horses galloping towards you, you back away. You don't rush to meet them!'

The air of battle was on him. She understood that. After a lifetime in polo, Bella knew that what appeared to be a society sport was, as the children from the city had so correctly identified, dangerous and demanding, and the top-class athletes who played the game were as driven and as fiercely competitive as their ponies.

So she'd make allowances. But she wouldn't be a doormat. 'I can only apologise,' she said, wanting to cool things down before Nero galloped off again. 'I'll go now and make sure that your next pony is properly warmed up.' The words were compliant, but there was something in her voice that warned Nero to drop it. Having said her piece, she spun on her heel and strode away.

He had felt stirred up in the middle of a match before, but never like this. But then he had never knowingly risked a horse before. And, of all horses, it had to be his old faithful, Colonel. His anger followed Bella to the pony lines, where he watched her working with her usual efficiency as if nothing untoward had taken place. Even that infuriated him. She was like no woman he had ever known before. He had risked everything for her. Why?

Bella's reckless behaviour had forced his hand. If she wanted to risk her life that was up to her, but in future he'd keep his horses safe. He galloped grim-faced onto the field. Defeat wasn't an option. Blaming Bella for her reckless actions wasn't enough. He blamed the opposing team for riding their loyal ponies as if they owed them nothing, but, most of all, he blamed himself.

Raising his helmet in a salute to the crowd, Nero acknowledged the applause as he led his team on the winners' gallop round the field. Only loyalty to the fans and to his team-mates was keeping him back. He badly wanted to be in the equine clinic with Colonel. He was desperate to check that everything possible was being done for the horse—and that shock hadn't set in.

Bella was waiting as he cantered off the field. She looked as cool as ever, while he was in turmoil. Kicking the stirrups away, he threw his leg over his pony and sprang down, thrusting the reins into her hand in the same movement. 'Ice immediately,' he ordered.

'I know,' she soothed.

The grooms were already waiting, he noticed, with iced bandages to cool the pony's overheated muscles. It was a pity they couldn't cool his overheated mind at the same time.

'Nero, you must take a drink too,' Bella insisted, holding out a water bottle with the tempting bloom of ice still visible on its surface.

Ignoring her, he moved past her.

She chased after him and thrust it into his hands. 'Drink,' she insisted, glaring at him.

'Can't you take a hint?' he demanded roughly, but he drank the water all the same.

He could feel Bella's concern following him all the way to the clinic. He'd told her from the outset that life here was tough. She knew the game. She knew the risks—

But she had never seen him like this before. *Too bad.* There was no room on the *estancia* for passengers. His grandmother had taught him that at a very young age.

'Nero, wait!'

Bella was running after him?

She not only ran after him, she ran ahead of him and stopped in front of him. 'What the hell?' He raked his hair.

'You won't do Colonel any good if you blaze into his stable in this state of mind.' She stood unmoving, glaring at him. 'I won't let you go in there.'

'Oh, won't you?' he said roughly, reaching out to move her away.

She slapped his hands down. 'Don't you dare touch me,' she raged at him white-lipped. 'While I'm here, those ponies are my responsibility as much as yours and I won't let you visit the clinic while you're like this!'

'Are you questioning my judgement?' he roared.

'Right now?' she roared back at him. 'Yes, I am.'

He walked round her. Had he really expected the Ice Maiden to tremble and quake like a virgin?

'I know why you're angry, Nero,' she said, running to keep up with him.

'Oh, do you?' he said.

'Colonel was reaching the end of his playing days, and you think you hastened that...' And when he made a sound of contempt it only prompted her to add fiercely, 'You did no such thing, Nero. You rode into danger to save the situation.'

'I had no option,' he flashed. 'I did what anyone else would have done under the same circumstances.'

Bella very much doubted it.

'If you will excuse me, I have an injured horse to check up on.'

'Then I'm coming with you,' she insisted, chasing after him.

'You've done enough damage for one day,' Nero

rapped, barging through the gate without holding it open for her. 'May I suggest you go back to the pony lines and confine yourself to bathing legs? Just make sure you don't get kicked by the ponies when you do so. We don't need any more slip-ups today.'

She fell back, allowing Nero to stalk off. He was without doubt the most obnoxious, pig-headed, arrogant man she had ever met. There wasn't a soft bone in his body or a kind thought in his head. Nero cared for nothing but his horses. He was truly incapable of a single caring feeling for his fellow man.

Which should have made him correspondingly unattractive, but unfortunately it had no effect in that direction.

It just made him more of a challenge, Bella realised, pulling out her phone and calling ahead to give the clinic a storm warning. Nero, a challenge? Yes, and professionally she could handle him, but in every other way Nero was destined to torment some other woman with more experience than Bella would ever have.

Having reassured himself that all was well with Colonel and that the horse was resting quietly, Nero returned to the *estancia* to eat and freshen up. There was no sign of Bella. He glanced up from the dining table every time he heard a door open or close. María and Concepcion were unusually subdued, as if the drama on the pitch had affected them too. He still couldn't work out why, for the first time in his life, he'd risked a horse. He ended up with the only answer he found palatable—he would have done the same for anyone. Human life was worth any risk he could take. There was nothing remotely personal about it. The fact that Bella was involved was mere coincidence.

He was in the shower when Ignacio rushed to tell him that Colonel had developed potentially fatal colic. He ran straight from his shower to the stable, barely pausing to dry himself, pulling on his jeans as he ran.

Bella had taken over the vigil in Colonel's stable from Nero the moment he had left the yard. He didn't know she was there. She wanted no fuss. And she certainly didn't want another row with him. She had agreed with Ignacio that, for all their sakes, it was better if she did this discreetly. And so it was Bella who had called the vet and sent for Nero. There was nothing more she could do, Bella realised, leaving a bowed and shaking Colonel in the care of Ignacio and the vet. Walking swiftly from the yard to avoid a confrontation with Nero, she saw him running from the house. She doubted he would even have noticed her.

She called in on Misty and spent some time with her own pony. The yard was quiet and there was no way she could know what was going on. When she left Misty's stable, she leaned her face for a moment against the cool stone wall. It was so peaceful in the stable yard after the high octane drama on the polo field. Squeezing her eyes tightly shut, she knew it was ridiculous to feel this way. She had too much emotion invested in a man who didn't have the slightest interest in her beyond her knowledge of horses. When he'd sucked that dry Nero would be happy to let her go.

And these tears were for Colonel, Bella thought impatiently, dashing them away. Straightening up, she lifted her chin. She'd check on her human charges next. The kids knew nothing of what was happening to Colonel at the clinic, and Ignacio had asked her to keep it that way. 'Not everyone has our resilience, Bella,' her elderly friend had counselled her gently. 'We don't know these children like you and I know each other, and we can't risk undoing the work we've already done with them.'

She'd felt proud at that moment, and touched that a man she admired had included her in his summary. Events had thrown her together with Ignacio and in a short space of time they had become close friends. The gaucho's friendship warmed her now and gave her courage. And Ignacio was right about the children, Bella thought as she walked briskly towards their chalets. Normally, she wouldn't dream of keeping anyone in the dark and would have come straight out with it, but these kids had a lot on their plates already, and it was up to everyone on the *estancia* to introduce them to different types of hardship sensitively. A party had been arranged for them tonight and she didn't want to spoil that for them. Without knowing the outcome of Colonel's colic, she had to consider that a drama on the pitch was one thing, but a tragedy might ruin the children's adventure on Estancia Caracas almost before it had begun. She'd tell them when she had some firm news.

The children greeted her warmly and she left them in the best of moods with the young counsellors the authorities had chosen to accompany them. She had another cause in mind now. Leaning back against the smooth sweet-smelling wood of the chalet she had so recently visited with Nero, she stared down the road leading to the clinic wondering what was happening with the sick pony.

What gave her the right? Bella thought. She was hardly qualified to offer therapy to anyone. She hadn't felt like this for years—so defensive. Perhaps she should take her own advice and leave Nero to it. This was a deeply personal crisis for a cold, sardonic man to whom horses meant everything. She really shouldn't intrude.

Nero had made it clear that he didn't welcome her interference.

It wasn't like her to give up either, Bella thought as she walked back to the house in the darkest of moods. Nero's feelings were standing in her way, and she was still fighting with herself when she pushed open the door of the hacienda. She'd have an early night. Things would look better in the morning. Whatever was going to happen with Colonel would happen, with or without her intervention.

She took a bath and went to bed, burying her head under the pillows, refusing to think about anything. At least that was the theory, but she was restless and sleep eluded her. She shot up with a start and glanced at her watch. 3:00 a.m. Whatever was going to happen to Colonel would have happened by now. She just had to know what that was. Nero would have been in bed hours ago.

Now the decision was made, she was filled with a sense of urgency. Not even waiting to tie her hair back, she tugged on a pair of jeans and a warm sweater and ran through the house, pulling on her boots at the door.

The clinic was unlocked and she took the narrow corridor with its faint smell of disinfectant and wet animals leading to the yard. Colonel's stable was easy to find. It was the only one with a dim light burning inside and the half-door left open. 'Hello, Colonel.' Bright eyes and pricked ears told her all she wanted to know. Colonel had recovered. And then something else stirred in the stable. She peered in cautiously. Nero was asleep on the hay, sprawled out with two dogs and the stable cat curled up alongside him. Her heart stirred. She pulled away as quietly as she could, not wanting to disturb him. Pressing her back against the door, she closed her eyes tightly. A man with so much love to give couldn't be all bad, could he?

She just didn't know when to give up, Bella thought as she walked back to the house. But why should she give up? A girl could dream, couldn't she? she mused, climbing the stairs. Nero was a product of his environment as much as she was of hers. So what if he was cranky? She was cranky herself. Add defensive, mistrustful, wary and aloof—oh, yes. She was a barrel of laughs.

First thing in the morning, she tacked Misty up and walked her round to the clinic yard, just to see, Bella told herself. There was no sign of Nero, and the veterinary nurse told her that Colonel had been released into the small paddock attached to the clinic where they could keep an eye on him. Colonel's leg was still strapped but the colic had passed, and the vet thought it best to keep him moving.

Thanking the nurse, she kept Misty on a loose rein and walked her as far as the boundary fence to stare out across the pampas. During her stay Bella had grown accustomed to its wild splendour, but today it looked so empty and not enticing at all. Take the romance out of it, and it was just mile upon mile of flat, open countryside, ringed with white-capped mountains showing faintly purple in the distance.

She turned at the sound of a horse's hooves. If there was one thing she should be accustomed to by now it was the sight of Nero on horseback. So why was her pulse going crazy? He'd been monstrous to her yesterday!

He had slept with his sick horse, she remembered, and was wearing the red bandana of a gaucho tied around his forehead, which was a very sexy look indeed with all that thick black hair tumbling over it.

'Where are you going?' he demanded, reining to a halt. 'Or are you just coming back?' His dark glance ran over her breeches which, clean of dust and mud, gave him the answer. Resting his fists on the pommel of his saddle, Nero raised an imperious brow. 'So where are you going?'

'Good morning to you too,' she said, turning Misty.

'Wait—'

The small mare recognised the note of command in Nero's voice even if Bella was determined to ignore it and Misty stopped dead, waiting for her next instruction. Not wanting to confuse her, Bella turned a cool glance on Nero's face. 'Yes?' she said.

'You need to be careful of the *yarara* if you're thinking of riding out,' he said in a voice devoid of emotion.

'The *yarara*?' Bella frowned, thinking only of the safety of her pony now.

'Poisonous snakes. It's the season for them,' he said before turning away.

'Wait,' she called after him.

Nero turned his horse. 'They won't bite unless you frighten them, but they will spook the horses.'

'Thanks for the warning.'

'Don't mention it,' he said. 'Just be sure you don't linger by any low-lying shrubs, or go rooting under rocks.'

'Is that it?'

'Should there be more?'

They confronted each other as if they were squaring up for a fight. Bella broke the silence first. 'If you've got something to say to me, Nero, just spit it out. It won't take me long to pack.'

'Pack?' he demanded with an angry gesture. 'Your work isn't finished here.'

Before she had a chance to react to that, Nero ground his jaw and finally admitted, 'I was wrong yesterday.' He raised a brow as if daring her to disagree, while she waited for a chorus of angels singing *Hallelujah!* 'I shouldn't have shouted at you,' he said, 'especially after Ignacio told me what you had done. That was very brave of you, Bella.'

'I don't want your praise!'

'Well, you shall have it.'

'I'll be sure to keep away from the *yararas*,' she said, turning Misty abruptly.

'Bella—'

She ignored him and the moment they were through the gate she urged Misty into a gallop. Nero caught up with her easily. 'You know emotions are heightened on the polo field.'

'I also know that's no excuse,' she called back. 'Your rudeness to me—'

'My rudeness?' Nero refused to take offence as he cantered easily alongside.

'You shouted at me!'

'And you shouted back.'

She rode without speaking, but all she could think about was Nero sleeping in the stable with his motley crew of animals and his sick horse.

'You came to find me in the stable,' he said, riding with all the nonchalance of a gaucho born in the saddle, 'so I can't have been so bad.'

'I was worried about your horse.'

'And me, just a little bit?'

'Not at all.' And, with a shout of encouragement, she gave Misty her head.

'But you will agree that it's good news about Colonel?' Nero caught up with her again and rode alongside as if they were trotting sedately in Windsor Park rather than indulging in a flat-out gallop across the pampas.

'It is good news,' she said. 'The best.' And there was only so long she could hold the frown for. 'Did you get much sleep?' she asked, trying not to sound too interested.

'Not much,' Nero admitted, slowing his horse. 'You?'

'Some,' Bella admitted, walking Misty towards the welcome shade of some trees. 'I woke in the night and wanted to check up on him. I thought you'd be asleep in bed,' she confessed.

Reaching for his water bottle, Nero took a long, thirsty slug. 'Do you have water?' he said, holding the canister out to her.

She wasn't falling for that again. 'I do,' she said, patting her saddlebag.

'Hey,' Nero called after her as she nudged Misty forward to hide her glowing cheeks. 'You forgot to tie your hair back, Bella.'

She was already feeling for the hairband on her wrist when it occurred to her he was teasing.

'What are you frightened of?' Nero challenged as she tied it up again, bringing his horse level with Misty. 'Are you worried you might show a softer side?'

'I'm only worried about getting my hair tangled when I ride,' she said mildly. 'And you're hardly in a position to talk about a softer side.'

Nero acknowledged this with a shrug. 'But I'm not frightened,' he said.

And she was? Yes, she was, Bella acknowledged silently—of some things, some men, but most of all she was frightened of losing control—of letting go. She hid these thoughts behind a counter-attack. 'You're the Assassin, remember. What do you know about fear?'

'Only a fool doesn't know fear,' Nero countered, 'but I'm not afraid. There's a big difference, Bella.'

With those dark eyes searching hers, she was glad of her shirt buttoned to the neck and the severe no-nonsense cut of her riding breeches. No way could this encounter be mistaken for anything other than it was—a purely chance meeting of the world's top polo player riding out on his ranch with a visiting professional who would soon be returning home.

CHAPTER TWELVE

FULFILLING her role as a professional judge of horse-flesh, Bella turned her attention from Nero to his horse. He was riding a magnificent black stallion, far bigger than any of the polo ponies in his yard. She guessed this must be a descendant of the Spanish war horses Nero had told her about. His mount certainly looked pretty impressive with its fancy scarlet saddlecloth, silver bit and the silver headband to keep its thickly waving forelock back. Nero wore silver spurs, and when the horse danced impatiently as he turned it in circles to calm it she saw that his belt was decorated with silver coins, and the typical gaucho dagger Ignacio had told her was called a *facon* was firmly secured in the back. More interestingly, Nero hadn't shaved and looked more dangerous than he ever had.

'How about a race?' he challenged with a curving grin.

'You are joking. Misty barely reaches the withers of that fire-breathing monster.'

'Then I'll give you a head start,' he said.

'Don't patronise us, Caracas.'

Nero's answer to this was a tug of his lips and a Latin shrug. 'If you're not up to it—'

Bella barely needed to touch Misty with her heels. The mare got the message and bounded forward.

A contest? Bella thought with relish. She was up for that. Let the best horse win!

'Hey,' Nero shouted after her as he took up the chase. 'Your hair's come loose, Bella!'

Bella's hair would feel like skeins of silk beneath his hands and her kisses hot. The thought of challenging the Ice Maiden to a race had got his juices flowing, Nero realised, reining back to slow his stallion. It would be the easiest thing in the world to overtake her, but that would mean the end of the chase—and, as any hunter knew, the thrill of the chase was everything—something to be drawn out and appreciated, so that the final outcome might be relished all the more. And seeing Bella crouched low over her pony as she rode with absolute determination to win this contest made him think the final outcome mustn't be too long coming.

They rode like the wind with no boundaries in front of them other than the snow-capped mountains more than half a day's ride away. The thrill of the chase excited Bella and, as the wind blew her hair back from her face, she felt this was the first time she had felt completely free since landing in Argentina—maybe the first time she had ever felt so free. The thunder of hooves warned her that Nero was close behind, the challenge in his eyes that if he caught her she would pay the consequences. She wouldn't give up without a fight. Goaded into renewed effort, she crouched low over Misty's neck as they streaked like an arrow across the pampas, but it was only a matter of time before the renowned agility of her polo pony lost out to the brute strength of Nero's stallion. Feeling the hunter relentlessly closing the distance between them stopped the breath in her throat.

There was something so controlled about it—so confident. Hot, hectic panic overwhelmed her and blazed a trail down her spine that spread across her back like cracking glass. There was nowhere to run—nowhere to hide—just miles of flat plain ahead of them. She would need a half mile head start to get away from him, and any moment now Nero would gallop past them. The anticipation of that was infuriating, and terrifying, and thrilling.

But Nero didn't overtake her. He must be holding back, Bella realised. Misty was fast but the polo pony was a sprinter, while a long gallop like this was little more than an easy hack for Nero's stallion. He should have disappeared ahead of them in a cloud of dust by now. Beneath her, Misty was straining to gallop faster. Having the stallion so close behind had unleashed a primitive flight mechanism in the mare. Misty's flared nostrils and laid-back ears were as telling as the arousal flooding Bella when she realised Nero had no intention of riding past her; he was wearing her down, knowing she was as unlikely to put her horse at risk as he was. Nero understood her a little too well.

Feeling Misty starting to flag, she steered her towards a covert of some gum trees. It was still a victory, Bella reasoned, slapping Misty's neck in praise as they slowed down. They had still won the race, and she had decided the finish line.

She was shivering with excitement by the time she reined to a halt. At least she'd made a good choice in stopping here—not only was it cooler, but an underground stream had thrust its way through the soft, fertile earth so the horses could drink their fill. Kicking her feet free of the stirrups, Bella dropped to the ground. She heard the chink of a bridle close behind her and

then heard Nero spring down to the ground close by.
'Well?' she demanded, swinging round, hands on hips.
'Are you going to congratulate me?'

'You have my respect,' Nero conceded in a husky
tone. 'You have a good pony, Bella, and you have trained
her well.'

'Well, thank you, kind sir,' she said dryly. 'Forgive
me if I'm wrong, but something in your tone suggests
you believe you could have overtaken me any time.'

'And you don't think that's the case?' Nero raised
one sweeping ebony brow.

A rush of excitement thrilled though her. She loved
this game, loved the opponent best of all.

'You surely don't think you could outrun me?' Nero
mocked.

She countered this with an amused huff. 'I did outrun
you.'

'And now you want me to grovel in defeat?' Nero
suggested.

Her gaze dropped to his lips, adrenalin still raging
through her. 'No. I want more than that.'

She thought she was safe taunting him? Nero's head
only dropped minutely, as if he were thinking about
this. The next thing she knew, she was in his arms.

The heat of the chase had made her crazy, Bella concluded as Nero's mouth crashed down on hers—crazy
for Nero. A lifetime of wondering and longing, and ultimate disappointment and embarrassment, was all worth
it for it to end like this in a fierce pampas kiss—not a
vain old man's kiss, but a gaucho's kiss—a real man's
kiss—a kiss that was certain and firm, and teasing, and
exciting, and so much more than she had ever dreamed
a kiss could be.

Fire met fire. They should have burned each other

out. Not a chance. Sharp black stubble scored soft, pale skin. Pain was pleasure. The hot, experienced South American and the cool, inexperienced Englishwoman. Surely, it should have been unmitigated disaster—it wasn't. It was fire and ice, heat and need, action and pressure, gripping, grasping, seizing, holding, punctuated by groans of ecstasy and growls of intent. And all the time the heat was mounting. Even the horses had moved away. Who'd have thought it? The Ice Maiden had finally melted and met her match.

No... No!... *No!* What was she thinking? Theirs was a professional relationship. She had to recover the situation somehow!

Which hardly seemed likely when her body was an out of control, wanton, craving force. And if she was any other woman, it might be possible to go right ahead with this and deal with the consequences later, in a cool and professional manner. But she would never recover her self-respect if she didn't get out fast. She didn't have the savvy, the nous, the tools...

'Please—' Pulling away, she combed her hair with her fingers into some semblance of order. 'Forgive me...' She added a light laugh that sounded as insincere as it was. 'I don't usually get carried away like this.' All this in a cut-glass accent as foreign to her as Nero's South American drawl. 'The excitement of the chase...' She glanced at Nero to judge his reaction, only to find she had missed the mark by a mile or so. His face was a mask of sardonic disbelief.

'You'd like to talk about the scheme now?' he suggested.

'Yes, yes, I would,' she exclaimed with relief, blanking the sarcasm in his voice.

There was time to see little more than a flash of

movement—amused eyes and a tug of Nero's lips—before she was in his arms again. 'I don't want to talk,' he murmured. To prove the point, he teased her with his tongue and with his teeth, brushing the swell of her bottom lip with kisses until she was struggling to breathe and arousal hit every erotic zone at once, leaving her whimpering with need, and longing for release. But he hadn't taken possession of her mouth yet and, when he did, plunging deep into her moist warmth in a blistering approximation of what he could be doing to her, she responded as he must have known she would, by arcing upwards, seeking contact in a frenzy of excitement.

And Nero's answer to this loss of self-control?

He pulled away, leaving her in a daze.

She had been dazzled by the master of control. It was this foreign land and their exotic surroundings, Bella reasoned, the unfamiliar trees rustling a very different tune, and the small, angry stream bursting through the ground on its way to the sea. She was lost in a terrifyingly wild open space on a scale she couldn't even begin to describe.

All this was her fault, Bella convinced herself, tying her hair back in a signal to them both that this mistake was well and truly over.

Who was she trying to kid? She certainly wasn't fooling Nero who, having had time to process the data, was now regarding her with barely controlled amusement. 'Don't tie your hair up on my account,' he said.

'Lady Godiva of the pampas?' Bella grimaced as she pretended to consider this. 'I don't think so, do you?'

'Depends on whether you think I want to see you naked.'

She flinched inwardly. 'Believe me, you really don't.'

Nero knocked some dried grass from his breeches. 'Concerned you might disappoint me?'

'Concerned?' She laughed it off. 'Why should I be? And, anyway, as you won't get the chance to find out...'

'You're supposing I want that chance.'

But he did, Bella thought as she went to find Misty. And, more worrying that that, so did she.

She drew a sharp breath as Nero caught hold of her arm. 'Why do you always pull back from the brink, Bella?'

'I don't.'

'Don't lie to me—I sensed the change in you while I was kissing you.'

Her hand was already at her mouth. 'The change in me?' she repeated, pretending surprise though the proof that she had been violently aroused was emblazoned on her lips.

'You know what I mean,' Nero insisted.

Brazening it out and holding his gaze, she snapped, 'Do I?'

'I've seen you on the dance floor, Bella, and I've seen you retreat into your shell. What I don't understand is why you don't just let go for once—take a risk, taste life,' Nero tempted, refusing to have his good mood squashed by Bella's sudden change of heart.

'And if I did?' She laughed. 'I only get it wrong.'

'Do you think you're the only one who makes mistakes, Bella?' Nero demanded.

She had just thrown the reins over Misty's head and was about to put her foot in the stirrup when Nero held her back. 'When I was a little boy, idiot was my middle name. I was always getting into trouble. I never did what I was told.'

'Am I supposed to be surprised?' Bella said wryly, leaning back against Misty's flank. 'From what I can see of your grandmother from her portrait and from what Ignacio told me about her, I'm guessing she soon sorted you out.'

Nero laughed. 'You could call it that. She warned me that if I was determined to run wild, I should have a real challenge.'

Bella stroked Misty's neck. 'How old were you?'

'I was about nine when my grandmother took me for this particular ride on the pampas. We were both riding crazy horses.'

'Do you breed any other type?' Bella laughed.

'We didn't take a lot of food.' Nero's eyes grew thoughtful. There was a self-deprecating curve to his lips, as if he couldn't believe how badly he'd been sucked in. 'You think you know everything when you're nine— you're immortal and invincible.' Refocusing, he went on. 'Grandmother told me she wouldn't be out long enough for us to need much in the way of food.'

'I bet she did,' Bella said, her eyes twinkling. 'And you weren't suspicious?'

'Why should I be?' Nero frowned. 'This is my grandmother we're talking about.'

'Exactly,' Bella said wryly.

And now Nero was laughing too. 'I should have known when she asked if I had plenty of water with me, but I was very trusting in those days.' His lips pressed down as he rasped his chin.

'I guess we were both destined to learn our lessons young,' Bella commented. 'So your grandmother abandoned you on the pampas?'

'Yes, she did,' Nero confirmed. 'We made camp. She made sure I had something to eat, and then, while

I was lying back relaxing, no doubt planning my next mischief, she sneaked off.'

'And you didn't hear her ride away?'

'My grandmother had learned the ways of the gaucho. She tied cloths over her horse's hooves and led him away. By the time I looked around and wondered where she'd gone she was probably back at the ranch.'

'How long did it take you to find your way home?'

'Two days.'

'And what did your grandmother say when you finally turned up?'

'We never spoke of it—she wasn't exactly noted for showing her feelings.'

Like Nero, Bella thought.

'But she had—shown her feelings, I mean,' he murmured as he thought about it. 'In her way.' He grinned. 'Anyway, after that, Ignacio started playing a larger part in my life, or perhaps I started listening. I knew now that I would need all the tricks Ignacio could teach me to make sure I was never caught out again—like knowing where to find food and water on the pampas. How to catch a runaway horse. How to understand women...'

'Ah, the hardest lesson of all.'

'And one I'm still brushing up on,' Nero admitted with an engaging grin.

'And were you still a bad boy after this period of study?'

'What do you think?'

'I think you channelled your energies in a different direction.'

Nero shrugged and grinned back. 'I couldn't possibly comment.'

'So Ignacio has played a really crucial role in your life.'

'Ignacio and my grandmother were my formative influences. Everything I am, I owe to them. And that's enough of me,' he said. 'I want to hear more about you. I want to know if you mean to live up to your Ice Maiden tag for the rest of your life, Bella.'

'Maybe.' Bella shrugged. 'It hasn't done me any harm so far.'

'Hasn't it?' Nero challenged. 'Why would you choose to be that way, Bella, when there's so much life to live?'

She thought about it for a moment, 'Because I feel safer.'

'Safer?' Nero demanded. 'What happened to make you feel unsafe?'

'It was nothing,' she insisted with a flippant gesture.

'Nothing? There must be something to make you so defensive.'

'It's just so stupid,' Bella exclaimed with frustration, not wanting to talk about it. 'And the more time goes by, the harder it is to get past it.'

'Try me,' Nero said.

'It's not that easy,' Bella said wryly, twisting with embarrassment.

'It's never easy to open up and share things you hide deep inside. And if you've held on to something for a long time you can't expect it to come pouring out. Everyone fears they'll be judged, Bella, or that they're making too much of what happened, but that can't be the case with you, because you're so strong in every other area of your life except this.'

'All right,' she blurted suddenly, as if he'd lanced a wound. 'If you must know, when I was a teenager one of my father's friends made a pass at me.'

'And you kept it quiet all these years?'

'No one likes to be made a fool of twice. I didn't think anyone would believe me.'

'Why not?'

She shrugged unhappily, forced to remember. 'He had status. I had none.'

'Status?' Nero demanded as if the word had burned his tongue.

'I was just a kid around the stables back then. I'd always thought of myself as one of the boys. I grew up with brothers, remember, and so all that girlie stuff passed me by. I wasn't sure how to dress or to put make-up on without feeling silly, so my confidence wasn't exactly sky-high to start with.'

'What you're telling me sounds more serious than make-up and clothes, or even an acute lack of self-confidence. This sounds more like a breach of trust with long-reaching consequences,' Nero argued firmly.

'Anyway,' Bella continued offhandedly, 'when he left me he spread a rumour around the polo club that I was frigid. People started laughing at me. I didn't know why at first, but when it finally dawned on me...'

Nero cursed viciously beneath his breath. 'Forget him. Forget all those people. They're not worth remembering, Bella.'

'How can I forget them when that's my world?'

'That's your workplace. Your world is something different. At least,' Nero added wryly, 'I hope it is. What happened wasn't your fault, Bella. You were young and naïve, but you got over it. You're a survivor and you're strong. You built something wonderful with the legacy your father left you. I think you can afford to give yourself some credit for that.'

'You make it all sound so romantic—so excusable,

but I must have led that man on for him to try in the first place.'

Nero interrupted her with a vicious curse. 'How did you lead him on?' he demanded. 'With your youth? With your innocence? The man who did this to you isn't worthy of being called a man. His behaviour is not excusable. And being strong isn't romantic, Bella, it's a necessity. Being strong is what life requires and demands of you. When you're pushed to the limit you grow stronger and, whether you know it or not, that is what has happened to you, so instead of letting the past drag you down, take a look at what you have learned from it, and how it has lifted you up.'

'I couldn't fight him,' she said, lost in the past now. 'He was so much stronger than I was…'

'You don't need to tell me any more.'

'In the end he gave up.'

'Not for want of trying,' Nero said angrily. Bella's bewildered gaze had shocked him and the realisation of what she had been hiding all these years cut him like a knife. 'You must have been terrified.'

'Terrified? Yes,' she said faintly as she thought back. 'When he started laughing at me and calling me frigid and ugly, I was at my lowest point—beaten. But later, when I got over the shock of what had happened, I felt angry. When people joined in with his mocking comments—laughing about me and my father—it changed me for good, Nero. It turned me into a fighter. It made me determined that no man or woman would ever control me. And when my father's business failed I went to work for him. I wanted to help him rebuild—not just the business, but his good name. I wanted to prove to the world that Jack Wheeler still counted for something.'

'The Wheeler name counts for a lot,' Nero cut in.

'And that's thanks to you, Bella. Whatever problems your father had in the past have been eclipsed by your work in his name.'

He took her in his arms, feeling instantly protective, along with a whole host of less worthy feelings towards the man who had assaulted her. Without a mother to advise her, or close female friends to coax her out of her defensive shell, she had battled this nightmare alone. No wonder she found it so hard to trust anyone. Bella was the most thoughtful person he knew and only her complete lack of vanity and self-absorption had allowed so much time to pass before she unburdened herself. He was touched and honoured that she had chosen him when she chose to do so.

'Nero?'

He stared down into her wounded eyes. 'I wish I'd known all this before, Bella.'

'Well, you know now,' she said with the same flippant gesture, still trying to make light of it.

Speaking gently, he captured her hand and held her close. 'I want you to promise that you're going listen to what I'm going to say to you, because you need to hear this.' He waited until she relaxed. 'While you were struggling to take control of your life, you imposed sterner rules on yourself than anyone else would have done. You've been unforgiving where Bella Wheeler is concerned and you need to ease up. Let the past go, Bella. Let the bad parts fall away. You've got too much to give to keep yourself imprisoned in this Ice Maiden cage.'

She was hugging herself, Bella realised, releasing her arms. 'How can I do that when it still hurts every time I remember?'

'It will hurt less now you've told someone,' Nero promised.

'But it hurts now.'

'These are old wounds, Bella, and you just poked them with a stick.'

She had never felt able to share the past with anyone, or to talk freely about herself before, yet Nero had made her do that, Bella realised. For all his savage masculinity, he possessed some deep curative power. He was using it now to calm Misty. The little mare was impatient to leave and was showing off in front of Nero's stallion with head tosses and jaunty prancing, but one quiet word from Nero and she was still.

Bella was so busy admiring Nero's horse-whispering technique, he surprised her. Instead of mounting up, he turned his back and, ripping his shirt free of his gaucho breeches, he loosened his belt and pulled the waistband of his breeches down revealing the most terrible scars.

'Oh, my God,' Bella exclaimed in shock. 'Who did that to you?' The cruel score of whip marks was livid red and unmistakable. This was calculated cruelty on a scale that made her own long-held internal wounds pale into insignificance.

'This is my father's work,' Nero said without emotion. Adjusting his clothing, he fastened his belt. 'I was eleven years old before the beatings stopped.'

Around the time his parents had been killed and Nero's grandmother had moved in to take care of him, Bella realised. No wonder Nero had pushed himself and the ranch to the limit. Nero was as driven as she was in his own way. 'Your grandmother must have been horrified to discover what had been happening to you in her absence.'

'It was something we never talked about.'

'But it must have hurt her terribly if she loved you—'

'Love?' Nero murmured, appearing distracted for a moment. 'I adored my grandmother, but love was something else we never discussed,' he admitted wryly.

That made her sad. The way Nero dismissed love was an ominous sign, Bella thought, even if it was understandable. As a child, he had been denied love by his violent, drunken father and, with a child's stoical acceptance of what couldn't be changed, had learned to live without love.

'Things happen,' he said with a shrug. 'I'm only showing you these scars to let you know they haven't changed me—my father hasn't won, and neither must you allow what happened to you to rule your life and hold you back.'

'You can't compare what happened to me with someone beating a child!'

'And, bad as that was, somewhere out there will be children beyond number who have suffered far worse. That is why we are launching our schemes, Bella. You may not have thought it through as I have and come to that conclusion, but that is why you and I are so driven, and why you must use the past as a stepping stone rather than a barrier.'

The past hadn't changed him, Bella realised as Nero turned away to check the girth on his horse, but it had formed the man he was. Would Nero ever settle down, or would he never be able to trust enough to take the risk of loving anyone?

It all made sense now, Bella thought as she calmed Misty—her chats with Ignacio and the gaucho's closed face whenever she'd tried to ask him about Nero's father.

Estancia Caracas was a closed community where everyone knew everything that was going on.

'Bella?'

Refocusing, she put her foot in the stirrup and swung
lightly into the saddle. 'Nothing's easy, is it, Nero?'

His mouth curved into a grin. 'You want easy, you
could always go back to England.'

She shot him a level stare. 'And leave a job half-
done?'

'Follow me back to the *estancia*, Bella.'

'Until we reach the straight,' she agreed. Challenging
glances met and held. They had learned a lot about each
other in a very short time, Bella thought, which, if they
were to work together successfully, was no bad thing.
'Well?' she pressed. 'What are you waiting for?'

'I'm giving you a head start,' Nero told her with an
ironic look. 'It's only fair.'

'Fair?' She laughed. 'I'll give you fair. I'll have a cup
of coffee waiting for you when you get back.'

'Do you seriously think you're going to arrive before
me?' Nero vaulted onto his horse. '*Hasta la vista*, Bella.
I'll be in the bath by the time you get back.'

He stayed just far ahead of her to know she was safe.
There was no point exhausting the horses, and he had
nothing to prove. Neither did Bella. She had more than
proved herself, Nero thought wryly. Everything he had
sensed about Bella was true—except that her hunger for
fulfilment went even deeper than he had thought. That
was one problem he could solve. Her hair had felt like
heaven beneath his hands—and her body, neatly packaged in practical yet severe riding clothes, had given him
a provocative hint of the softly yielding flesh beneath.

She had stopped him because of lack of confidence,

he knew that now. Confidence could make a person, just as the lack of it could break you, he mused, easing the pace when he heard her pony falling back.

He liked her all the more for her unflinching acceptance of his scars. But Bella was as stubborn as the grandmother who had raised him. Like his grandmother, Bella would never admit to any inner weakness, believing it made her seem less in control. Unfortunately for Bella, he'd grown up with a woman like that. He knew what was going on.

He slowed the stallion to a brisk trot as they approached the yard. He didn't want to hurt Bella, but nothing had changed. He still wanted her.

CHAPTER THIRTEEN

SHE blamed it on the tango. Her neatly ordered life had always made sense before, but the tango made her confront her passions and accept that she was human. And it did all that—with a little help from Ignacio—in the first thirty-two bars. She wasn't exactly a new person by that stage, but she had certainly loosened up, and by the end of the dance Ignacio had managed to prove to her that as much as control was necessary to succeed, so was passion.

As in tango, so in life? One thing was certain, she couldn't go on the way she had been, marking time.

A number of parties had been arranged for the days following the polo match, and so she didn't lose face completely, Ignacio had agreed to tutor her in private dance lessons. The barn had a number of uses, Bella had discovered, and not all of them contained the dangers inherent in meeting Nero alone there. Ignacio came equipped with an ancient portable machine to play their music and proceeded to train her with the same mixture of firmness and patience with which he schooled the polo ponies. She'd never be an expert, she accepted, but she was a lot better than she had been by the time Ignacio had finished with her.

'Don't be frightened to let yourself go, Bella,' Ignacio

advised. 'And then the contrast when you draw yourself back will be sharper. You'll have people trembling on the edge of their seats,' he assured her when she laughed at her pathetic attempt. 'Bravo!' he exclaimed with gusto when she got it right.

Would Nero tremble on the edge of his seat? Somehow, Bella doubted it.

Nero felt her arrive at the party and his gaze followed her across the room. She looked incredible. The transformation from Ice Maiden to Tango Queen was complete, and was all the more impressive because of the contrast it drew between cool Bella and too-hot-to-handle Bella.

Too hot for any other man to handle, Nero determined, making his move. He bridled when he noticed the hungry stares of all the men present following her across the room. 'Bella.' He ground his jaw as one of the good-looking young stable lads got there first and led her onto the floor. He narrowed his eyes when he noticed Ignacio raise a glass to him at the far side of the room. Ruthless old rogue.

Nero grinned and then he laughed. It appeared Ignacio still had some lessons to teach him. And he'd obviously been busy with Bella too—boy, could she dance. They were queuing up to dance with her—boys who had hardly started shaving, some of them. And, of course, Bella being Bella, was only too happy to dance with all of them. She had so much joie de vivre waiting to burst out of her—something he'd only caught a glimpse of at the polo party in London. He raised a glass to Ignacio, who bowed his head in acknowledgement of the praise as Bella continued to dance with boys from the project, boys from the stable.

Men too.

He was at her side in moments.

She stared up at him. Her lips were full and red. Lipstick she never wore outlined them, enhanced them, made them gleam. 'Nero,' she murmured provocatively.

Her hair was severely drawn back, but he would forgive her that at a tango party, as the style was appropriate for the occasion. Her eyes were smoky and made even more lustrous by make-up. She looked and smelled fabulous—like a warm pot of passion just waiting for him to drown in. And the dress... What a dress. Low-necked and split to the thigh in shimmering silver, it was an exquisite example of the type of dress a professional tango dancer would wear.

María's daughter, he thought immediately. Carina was a famous tango dancer in Buenos Aires and about the same size as Bella. He had already noticed that María had made sure all the girls on Bella's scheme had the prettiest dresses to wear, and Bella's outfit was yet another example of his staff showering approval on her. He'd heard rumours that Ignacio had been teaching Bella to dance, and knew for a fact that Ignacio had found smart clothes for all the city boys to wear. But it was Bella, and only Bella, he was interested in now. There was a new confidence in her eyes, and the outfit, with those fine black stockings with the sexy seam up the back, had changed her, like an actress walking onto a stage she owned. If he waited for Bella to be without a partner, he'd be waiting all night.

And so he cut in. 'I'm claiming the winner's prize,' he told Nacho, owner of the neighbouring ranch, who just happened to be the most notorious playboy in Argentina and who was still stinging from losing the polo match to

Nero. Their black stares met in a fierce, no-holds-barred challenge.

'Would you like a partner who can show you how it's done?' Nero demanded when Bella hesitated.

'Get in line, Caracas,' she told him with a glint of humour in her seductive, smoky eyes.

'Nero doesn't wait for anything,' Nacho murmured, yielding as good manners dictated he must.

Nero stared with triumph into Bella's eyes. Remembering their last outing on the dance floor, he offered benevolently, 'I'll lead.'

'Into trouble?' she murmured.

Those lips!

Those lips were his. Firing one last stare at Nacho, he led her onto the floor.

It was like holding an electric current in his arms—dangerous, hot and impossible to contain or let go. 'Don't worry,' he soothed in a soft, mocking voice as she looked up at him, 'I'll be gentle with you.'

'And I with you,' she assured him as they waited for the music to begin.

He noticed how poised she was. She was a very different woman to the one who had taken the floor so awkwardly with him in Buenos Aires. Could this be the same woman who was almost, but not quite touching her flattened palm to his?

It was only Bella's hand, but he wanted it. He wanted her hand in his… He wanted all of her.

She evaded him as the music began and, with a provocative flash of her emerald eyes, she whipped out of his reach in a turn he wouldn't have imagined her to be capable of executing. He snatched her back again and held her close, staring down, imposing his will.

Raising a brow, she thrust him away.

His eyes assured her that he accepted the challenge and, when he drew her close this time, she had no option but to move with him. She fought him at first, and then she relaxed. They were attracting attention, he noticed. Or, rather, Bella was attracting interest. She was his perfect partner. The fact that they were dancing together, and quite so intensely, was drawing a lot of attention. He noticed Ignacio watching them from the shadows. The jigsaw didn't take much piecing together. Ignacio knew Nero had finally met his match and had enjoyed tutoring Bella so she could more than hold her own when they next met on the dance floor.

Hold her own? Bella was incredible. She set the air on fire, and everyone had gathered round to watch. Sensually and emotionally, she was transformed. It was like dancing with a different Bella—a confident woman who had found herself and knew what she wanted out of life—and she wanted more than polo. There were other gaps in Bella's education, gaps that only he could fill.

'Where are we going?' Bella demanded as Nero strode with her across the yard. She dug her heels in, refusing to go another step with him until he explained why he had taken her away from the party.

'I don't care to play out my private life in front of an audience.'

'I thought you didn't care what people thought.' She fought him, but his grip only tightened on her arm.

'I don't.' Nero stopped dead, his breathing heightened as he stared down at her. 'You look fabulous tonight, Bella.' And just when her eyes widened at the thought that he was paying her a compliment, he added, 'You could hardly think you were going to fade into the background in a dress like that?'

'Are you jealous, Nero?'

'Jealous?' Heat rose in his eyes.

'Do you regret dancing with me when there were so many more important women at the party?'

'What?' Nero looked genuinely bemused.

'Or don't you like my dress?'

'It certainly draws attention.'

A glint of humour was in his eyes and the glance he lavished on her now made the blood sizzle in her veins.

'And men were staring at me?' She struck a pose to stir him even more. As if she was on a mission to push Nero to his limits, she couldn't stop. Even his growled response and his grip on her arm had no effect. 'You were happy to call me the Ice Maiden along with everyone else, but now I show another side and you don't like it.'

'That's not true,' Nero said huskily, 'I like it a lot.'

'How much?' She shivered deliciously as Nero's thunderous expression changed to a challenging smile. He was playing with her, Bella realised as he released his grip on her arm. He was treating her like one of his ponies in the corral—drawing her to him, then casting her into the void without him so she craved nothing more than his attention. 'I'm going back to the party.'

'I don't think so.'

Balling her hands into fists, she thrust them against his chest, but from the waist down they were connected. There was so much passion between them now they could set the barn on fire. Had Nero planned to goad her all along? He did very little in life without a very good reason. Nero was the consummate seducer—of horses, women—everyone he met. Ice Maiden? Nero cared nothing for that tag. He had always known how to make her burn.

They should have made it to the house—to a bed-room—to a bed.

They'd made it halfway across the stable yard when Nero dragged her close and trapped her between his hard body and the barn door. With his hands planted flat on the door either side of her face, he nuzzled her ears, her lips, her cheeks, her neck, sending heat shooting through her veins to her core. Her breasts felt heavy and a pulse throbbed hungrily between her legs. And when she managed to focus at all it was only to see all sorts of wickedness in Nero's eyes.

She was drowning in arousal by the time Nero dipped his head to brush her bottom lip with his mouth. As his warmth and strength enveloped her, all it took was his lightest touch to fire her senses. The will to move—to leave him—the will to do anything remotely sensible had completely deserted her. She claimed one small victory, hearing him groan deep in his chest when he deepened the kiss and her tongue tangled with his. A lifetime of avoiding men had left her hungry, and now she found it ironic that the most masculine man she had ever met had freed something inside her, allowing her female powers to have their head.

Their kisses grew more heated, more urgent, until the barn door creaked behind them. Shouldering it open, Nero drew her inside. The silence was intense. It shielded them from the noise of the party, and when he dropped the great iron bar across the door she knew that no one could disturb them.

Kissing her, Nero backed her towards the sweet-smelling bed of hay. She kept hold of his shirt as she sank down, dragging him with her. This might be a dream that lasted one night, but she had no intention of waking yet. She softened as Nero pressed her to the ground. Each of his touches was a caress, and each glance a promise to keep her safe…

Unfastening the straps on her dancing shoes, he tossed them aside.

'I'm not wearing very much beneath my dress,' she explained haltingly, having a sudden fit of the same self-consciousness that had dogged her all her life.

'Excellent,' Nero approved, lowering the zip on her dress.

'Nero—' She flinched as he pushed her bra straps down.

'You're not frightened of me, are you?'

'You? No,' she answered. She was more frightened of the way she felt about him. 'I'm not frightened of anything.'

'Only a fool doesn't know fear,' Nero reminded her as his kisses moved to her shoulder and then the swell of her breast. And when she sighed in his arms, he took her bra off and tossed it away. 'If I ruled the world—'

'You'd be unbearable?' she suggested, rallying determinedly between gasps of pleasure.

'It would be a crime to construct lingerie out of reinforced canvas,' Nero advised her as he teased her nipple with the tip of his tongue. 'How did you fit that ugly contraption beneath this divine dress?'

'With the greatest difficulty,' Bella admitted.

'Are you a virgin?'

'What sort of question is that?' she demanded.

'It's a perfectly reasonable question. And if you are, now would be a good time to tell me. Come on, Bella, your answer can only be yes or no—'

'Or yes…and no,' she said, stalling.

Nero frowned as he shifted position. 'I think you'd better explain.'

When had she ever found it easy to discuss intimacy—or met a man who cared enough to ask? 'Of course I'm not a virgin. At my age?' she added with an awkward laugh.

Nero shrugged this answer off. 'Plenty of women your age are virgins—they haven't met the right man—they're flat-out not interested. It isn't a crime, Bella.'

Right. But she hadn't thought to hear Nero say it. She had always believed it was almost as taboo for a woman to admit to being a virgin at her age as it was to admitting she slept around.

'So what's your reason?' he prompted gently.

Surrender. That was Bella's reason. Loss of control. Putting her trust in someone else. She had never trusted anyone enough to be able to completely let go. But how to tell Nero that? 'People can control your life,' she murmured.

'Only if you let them,' Nero murmured between tender kisses. 'I would never do that. I have too much respect for you, Bella.'

She searched his eyes as Nero stroked her hair back. 'You have to let the past go,' he insisted gently. 'Learn from it, by all means, but move forward.'

'I have moved forward,' she said fiercely.

'Hey.' Nero was laughing softly as he brought her into his arms. 'No one's achieved more than you, tiger woman.'

'I had to...I had to defend my father.'

'Your hero?' Nero prompted, understanding.

'He was always my hero,' Bella admitted, eyes shining as she remembered all the wonderful times she had shared with a man who was flawed in the eyes of the world, but just about perfect where she was concerned. 'I had to stand my ground.'

'And fight?' Nero supplied. 'I know something about that,' he said wryly.

'I had to show all those people, Nero.'

'And you did,' he reassured her. 'Now it's time for you to think about Bella Wheeler for a change…'

And as he kissed her she thought that might, at long last, be possible—except there would always be that same thing holding her back—Bella's hidden flaw. 'I can't,' she said, pulling free from Nero's embrace.

'You can't?' Nero's ebony brows rose, though his eyes were as warm and as passionate as they had ever been.

'You asked me if I was a virgin,' she reminded him. 'And I don't know how to answer you because if I say I am, I'm not… What I mean is, I have and I haven't…'

'And when you did it was a bad experience—and that's what you remember?'

'Enough not to try it again,' Bella admitted, trying to be wry and funny at the same time, with the inevitable result that she ended up stumbling over the words. Her cheeks were glowing redder by the second. Closing her eyes, she tried again. 'What I'm trying to say and not making a very good job of is that I have…once, but I've never reached the ultimate conclusion that everyone else raves about.' She opened her eyes again. 'So you tell me, Nero. What does that make me?'

'A woman I want,' he murmured, drawing her into his arms. 'And if you haven't had an orgasm before, you're about to. So buckle your seat belt, Ms Wheeler—you're coming with me.'

And when she made some mild protest, Nero ignored her and removed her dress as if they had all the time in the world, and every inch he brought it down he replaced the whisper of silky fabric with his sensitive hands, or with his lips, or the nip of his teeth. Naked and exposed, her heart opened but, vulnerable though she was, she had gone too far now to turn back. The truth was, she didn't want to turn back.

Cradling her in his arms, Nero freed her hair and arranged it around her shoulders so that it framed her face. 'You're beautiful, Bella Wheeler,' he murmured.

She wasn't, but Nero made her feel so, and for the first time in her life she felt like a desirable woman. That feeling gave her strength and, unbuttoning his shirt, she pushed it from his shoulders, pausing only to admire the firm tanned flesh. At what moment had this hard, rugged face become hers to kiss? She brushed the curve of her smooth cheek against Nero's sharp black stubble and shivered with the promise of all the knowledge in his dark eyes that he would use to bring her pleasure.

Dipping his head, he took her lips again. 'No doubts?' he murmured, making her quiver as his hot breath touched her ear.

'None,' she said shakily. Torn between passion and fear of the past coming back to haunt her, she blocked out her past experiences and believed only in a very different future with the man she loved. Lacing her fingers through Nero's hair, she bound him to her.

Sensing her disquiet, Nero soothed her with a kiss, and when that kiss became heated he turned her, bringing her across his thighs so he could kiss his way up the back of her knees, her thighs and her buttocks until he reached the small of her back. As he cupped them, her buttocks responded with delight to each kiss and nip and stroke. She groaned with anticipation, forgetting everything but this, and even opened her legs a little to encourage him. Nero turned her so he could watch the pleasure building in her eyes as he stroked her into a frenzy of arousal. His hand found her heat and moved with an exquisite understanding of her need, but he drew it away, smiling faintly when he saw her disappointment. 'Not yet,' he cautioned.

'But soon,' she begged, writhing against him.

Nero suckled first on one breast and then the other. The heat of his mouth, the lash of his tongue and the rasp of his stubble all conspired to heighten sensation until she was completely lost in the moment. Laughing softly, Nero kissed the corner of her mouth until she turned to look at him, when he deepened the kiss and, drawing her into his arms, lay down with her on the hay.

'Now,' she begged him, easing down on the hay so that his kisses must find her belly and now the inside of her thighs. Shameless and determined, she thrust her hips towards him in a blatant invitation, crying out in triumph when Nero parted her legs with the wide spread of his powerful shoulders. Throwing her head back she gasped with approval.

But it still wasn't enough.

'I submit,' Nero murmured, when she moved over him and held him down.

'That's good,' she said, kissing his face, his neck, his shoulders, and then his chest.

'Don't stop now,' he teased her.

She had no intention of doing so, though she felt a jolt when she kissed the hard planes of his belly. He was so toned, so perfect. Nero was a playground of pleasure. And it was his turn to exclaim softly when she stroked his thighs, before cupping the swell of his erection beneath the straining fabric of his breeches. She measured and nursed it, and wondered if she could encompass it in one hand. There was only one way to find out…

'Feel free,' Nero murmured as she trailed one finger-tip down the cool steel zip.

'Shameless,' she mocked him softly as he locked his arms behind his head.

'You'd better believe it.'

Freeing the fastening at the top of his zip, she eased it down and he sprang free. Question answered: two hands. Lowering her head, she closed her mouth around him.

CHAPTER FOURTEEN

FOR a moment Nero was completely lost. He couldn't move, he couldn't think; the pleasure was far too intense. Bella had really surprised him. She was bolder than he had imagined, and instinctively sensual. She traced the acutely sensitive tip with her tongue, sucking and licking until he was forced to move—had to move if he wanted to please her.

Without losing the delicious contact of Bella's mouth on him, he kissed his way down her body until he reached the plump swell of her arousal. When she whimpered and threw herself back in the hay he stripped off the last of his clothes. Spreading her thighs wide, he found the heat at her core again and, laving it delicately with his tongue, he gradually increased the pressure. She was already moist and so swollen with arousal that when he parted her plump lips to claim the most intimate part of her, she widened her thighs and urged him on. When Bella's mouth and tongue began their work again, the exchange of pleasure between them was like nothing he had ever known.

Nero brought her to the brink so many times she wondered how he knew when to draw back. Was it second sight? Intuition? Whatever it was, she was pleased he possessed the skill. And, as for her fears of falling short as a woman—what fears? By the time Nero moved over her she couldn't have taken fright if she'd tried. She had never felt anything like this—had never thought herself capable of such intense sensations. Could it really get any better?

Nero brought her beneath him, positioning her as he teased her with just the tip of his pulsing erection. She loved the way he cushioned her buttocks with his hands. 'Oh, please,' she begged him. 'Don't make me wait this time.'

She heard herself add to this a brazen request in words that to her knowledge she had never spoken out loud before. Nero didn't seem shocked. He stared into her eyes and kissed her as he eased inside her, filling her completely. 'Yes, oh, yes,' she cried as he stretched her beyond what seemed possible. He waited until she relaxed before he moved again, and when he did she whimpered with surprise that such pleasure was possible as he thrust deeply before slowly withdrawing again.

'No,' she cried out, ordering him back immediately.

Nero laughed softly as her fingers bit into his shoulders and her teeth closed on his skin. She was soon gasping for breath as he started moving to a steady and dependable rhythm, taking her higher and closer to the promised goal with each firm stroke. Could it be possible to hover so near the edge and still feel safe? The tango might have brought her here, but this was the best dance on earth. She was rocking on a plateau of pleasure with a great dam waiting to burst behind her eyes and in her mind.

'Look at me, Bella,' Nero commanded.

As he claimed her attention she obeyed, and with one final thrust he gave her what she had waited a lifetime to achieve. Briefly, it took her out. Shooting stars invaded her head as pleasure exploded inside her. Sensation ruled and she embraced it hungrily, screaming out her release as the violent spasms gripped her, and they went on and on until she was completely spent and left to float gently on a tide of lazy waves.

'More?' Nero suggested dryly.

'Why are you smiling?' Bella demanded groggily, barely able to summon up the strength to speak.

'Once is never enough,' Nero murmured against her lips.

'You're so right,' she agreed on a contented breath. 'That was so good, I think you'd better do it all over again just so I can be sure I wasn't dreaming.'

Laughing softly, he brought her on top of him. 'It's your turn now. Ride me, take your pleasure. Use me as you will.'

She laughed into his eyes, feeling safe and strong— so safe she missed the flicker of something out of sync in Nero's eyes. She was still buzzing with how it felt to be liberated sexually—to be free and fulfilled. Nero had shown her that this was how it should be—and how it would be from now on. He was unique. Fate had brought them together. They shared so much—and not just this, she thought as she began to rock to a primal rhythm. They shared careers, and a whole raft of other interests... Nero was a friend she trusted, and now he was her lover. Could anything be more perfect?

Bella sucked in a sharp breath as Nero's hands began to control her movements. While one guided her hips, encouraging her, the other moved skilfully at pleasuring her. Her mouth opened in a gasp of surprise as Nero quickly brought her to the brink again. Lost to all rational thought, she allowed him to finish what he had so expertly begun and in the final moment before she took the plunge into pleasure she screamed out his name, and might even have whispered that she loved him.

Holding her safe in his arms, Nero stroked her hair until she fell into a contented sleep, while he stared unseeing into the shadows at the far end of the barn.

Bella slept soundly until a sharp ray of sunshine breached her closed eyelids. Stretching contentedly, she reached out a questing hand. The prickle of hay greeted her. It took her a moment to get her thoughts in order to process this. Party... Nero... Last night... Incredible.

And all these disjointed thoughts were bound by one certainty. She was in love. Nero was the man she loved. Thanks to him, she was transformed from Ice Maiden into something unimaginably different, Bella thought with a happy sigh, and last night Nero had put the seal on her love by proving that he felt the same. They had laughed and learned about each other and, trusting each other completely, had made the most spectacular love together.

So where was he?

She called his name, not really expecting a reply. Nero would be down at the stables with the horses. Considerately, he'd left her to sleep. He'd even brought a blanket from the house to cover her. Drawing it close, she sighed a second time. Did life get any better than this? She moved with remembered pleasure, but found it impossible to settle. The silence hung heavily all around her, making the barn feel incredibly empty, making her feel shut out.

So it was time to get up, she reasoned sensibly. She couldn't lie here all day with just a blanket covering her. Nero had folded her clothes. They were so neatly stacked there was something alarming about it. She couldn't put her finger on it exactly, but it could be interpreted as making order out of chaos. Last night had been chaotic and passionate—and amazing. Did Nero think so too? Or was he trying to make sense of the passion that had consumed them both?

And now she was overreacting as usual, Bella reassured herself. The Ice Maiden with her frozen shell and vivid inner life—she could put all that behind her now. Last night had changed everything—and she refused to think anything bad. Sitting up, she dragged the blanket round her and smiled like a contented kitten. She ached all over—in the most pleasant way. The impossible had happened. She had something going on with Nero, something deep and special. She felt like a real woman for the first time in her life, well loved and completely fulfilled. The Ice Maiden had gone for ever. Bella Wheeler had a new life now. Hurrying to get dressed, she threw on her clothes, brushed off the hay and didn't even bother to tie back her hair. What was the point when she'd leap straight in the shower when she got back to the house? And, anyway, well-loved women didn't bother with scraping their hair back. Flinging open the barn door in this new mood of abandon, she closed it quickly and then opened it a crack. Nero had his back to her and he was discussing something with a couple of gauchos. One of them was holding Misty, saddled and ready for him to ride.

Well? That was part of the deal. She brushed off any lingering qualms.

Once Nero gets used to riding Misty, he will never be able to let the pony go.

Nero should ride Misty—she wanted him to ride her pony. He'd been far too considerate so far, never trespassing on her enjoyment of riding her favourite horse—always giving way while she had been staying on the *estancia*.

Stealing another look out of the door, Bella's heart picked up pace. Nero was so poised, so utterly in command. The dark blue top emphasised his tan, and he was freshly showered with his hair still damp. Clean breeches, highly polished boots, and muscular legs it seemed incredible to her now she had been kissing only hours before. The conversation in rapid Spanish was indecipherable but, judging by Nero's gestures, he was telling the gauchos to take Misty back to the stables and get the mare ready for *Inglaterra*—she could hardly mistake that.

To hell with what people thought of her. Quickly, she slung the high-heeled sandals over her wrist and left the barn barefoot in her tango dress to confront Nero.

The men had gone, taking Misty with them. Nero was standing alone with one hand on the back of his neck and his head bowed as if the woes of the world were on his shoulders.

Swallowing deep, she could feel her own life splintering in front of her eyes. There was no pretending she didn't know what was going on. They had grown too close for the smallest nuance in Nero's behaviour to escape her. Her time in Argentina was at an end. They had always known this was a temporary arrangement. The scheme for the children was a success—they all wanted to come back and had promised to recommend the project at Estancia Caracas to their friends, which was all Nero or Bella had wanted. The prince would be pleased too, Bella told herself numbly. She had fulfilled her duty. 'Nero... Good morning,' she said lightly.

'Bella.' He turned, but the light in his eyes was swiftly dimmed.

He had made her strong, and now it was time for her to be strong for Nero—for both of them. 'So the time has come,' she said without emotion, angling her head to one side. Damn it, the smile wouldn't come. 'It's been—'

'Don't,' he said shortly.

'It's time for me to go, Nero,' she said as if she were encouraging him. She turned then and walked towards the house without a backwards glance. She had always known, deep down, Nero wasn't going to ask her to stay. Nero Caracas was a free spirit whose life had taught him that he could only be happy on his own. He had given her all that he could.

And that was a lot, Bella reflected as the shadow of the hacienda fell over her. Nero had made her believe in herself and in her inner strength, and in the beauty that came from a woman who was happy in her own body, and he had cemented that belief by making love to her. Nero Caracas, the Assassin, polo hero, national icon, the world's most eligible bachelor and most beddable man, the heartbreaker of Argentina. Why was she surprised that it hadn't worked out? She was a professional career woman, Bella told herself firmly, ignoring the tears battering the back of her eyes. Tilting her chin at a determined angle, she told herself firmly that polo was her life, not polo players—whoever they were, they were incidental—*which wasn't enough to stop her heart feeling as if someone had smashed it into tiny pieces with a polo mallet.*

She just needed a minute to settle her thoughts and then she'd get on with the rest of the day. The rest of the day? What about the rest of her life?

* * *

Nero spent the rest of the morning arranging transport to England for Bella and her horse. They'd use his private jet, of course, and with one of his own vets in attendance. He couldn't do more for Bella. He could never do enough for her.

And thoughts like those were where it all started to go wrong. He could see the future in Bella's eyes, while his was firmly lodged in his head. It was the same plan he'd had all along—be the best, make his grandmother and Ignacio proud—there was no room in his life for anything but the ranch and polo.

Nero's eyes softened briefly, and then grew resolute again when he remembered the hearts and flowers in Bella's eyes and the cold, clear thoughts in his. Rather than soften towards him, she would have done better to remain the Ice Maiden, for his heart was still the same piece of stone. He'd seen what families could do to each other—and knew he didn't want that. He wouldn't inflict that on any woman. What? And break her like a horse? Would he strip away Bella's successful career and dim that flare of emerald fire in her stare? What gave him the right to do these things when she had done everything he and the prince had expected of her and more? Could he take her pony? No.

Could he love her?

The only thing he knew about love was that it was corrosive and destroyed everything in its path. He refused to even think about it. He and Bella had enjoyed a great short-term professional relationship and that was it.

He should never have seduced her. He should never have enjoyed her. He would never stop thinking about her. His only option was to send her away before he wrecked everything for her. She must go back to

England, where she could continue her valuable work and pick up her successful career. Work was something he understood. Work meant building, as he had rebuilt the ranch. Love destroyed. These were some lessons a boy growing up never forgot. He wanted Bella, but what could he offer that wouldn't take her from the life she had built for herself half a world away?

Nothing more needed to be said, Bella reflected, which was both strange and sad. She had to go and Nero had to stay. She had started her packing straight after her shower. By the time she went downstairs Nero was in the kitchen drinking coffee as if it were any other day. It was every other day, but it was radically, horribly changed by the unbearable tension between them. She felt fresh and clean, neatly ordered and ready for work—with a yawning hole in her chest where her heart used to be.

'Thank you, María,' she said with a warm smile when Nero's housekeeper passed her a steamy cup of freshly brewed coffee. She turned away fast. She couldn't bear to see that look in María's eyes. How did María know? Was everyone on the pampas psychic?

This definitely wasn't the usual relaxed morning in the kitchen, Bella registered, feeling the tension rise to unsustainable levels. Nero finished his coffee. Putting his newspaper down, he stood, reminding her of how small she'd felt in his arms, and how protected.

'When you've got a minute, we should discuss your travel arrangements,' he said.

'Of course,' she said briskly, 'but I want to talk to the children first. And Ignacio. I want them to hear I'm leaving from me.' She swung round, conscious of María standing close behind her as if hovering, waiting to give comfort. 'And of course I'd really appreciate a few minutes of your time, María—I'm going to miss you all so much.'

Instead of answering this, María enveloped Bella in a hug.

And now they both had tears in their eyes.

'I'll be at the stables,' Nero said as he wheeled away.

As the jet soared into the sky Bella stared out of the window, feeling as though she was joined to Argentina by an umbilical cord and that cord was being stretched tighter and tighter until finally it snapped. There was just a solid floor of cloud beneath her now. She could have been anywhere—going anywhere.

Turning away from the window, her throat felt tight as she answered politely when the flight attendant asked her if she had everything she needed. Not nearly, Bella thought. The man quickly left her, as if he could sense that she was nursing some deep wound.

She stared unseeing at the dossier in front of her. These were the papers and photographs and the quotations from the children, which she had collected to show the prince. She could have sent most of it by e-mail, but wanted…needed, maybe, concrete evidence of her time in Argentina.

She'd miss the children, Bella thought, focusing on a group shot. She'd miss everyone. Ignacio, dressed for the occasion in full gaucho rig, positively exuding a sense of adventure and exoticism. The kids with their cheeky grins—long-time enemies, some of them, with their arms around each other, smiling for the camera—teams now, not gangs. María and Concepcion, their laughing faces so kind and smiling. And Nero. Nero towering over everyone in his polo rig, looking every bit the glamorous hero with the wind ruffling his thick black hair and his fist planted firmly on the fence beside him. No wonder control was so important to him. He'd seen where the lack of it had led, and what restoring it and going forward could achieve.

And she wasn't going to cry.

Who knew bottled up tears could hurt so much?

Picking up the champagne the flight attendant had poured for her, she raised a glass to absent friends.

CHAPTER FIFTEEN

LIFE went flat the moment Bella left Argentina. The atmosphere inside the *estancia* was instantly sombre, and the mood in the stable yard was scarcely any better.

'Everyone misses her,' Ignacio complained, stating the obvious.

'Do I need telling this?' Nero scowled at his old friend, who simply shrugged.

The last of the children in this year's scheme had just left, and the two of them had stayed behind to wave them off, but all the children had wanted to know was: Where was Bella? When was Bella coming back? Would she be here next year?

'Maybe,' was the best he could offer them, swiftly followed by, 'she's very busy.'

It had felt like a cop-out to him and he hadn't fooled anyone. To make things worse, Bella had left a jokey video for them all to watch. It had made the children laugh—and not just because of Bella's halting Spanish. He had stood at the back with his arms folded and his eyes narrowed as Ignacio ran the film—preparing to close a chapter and turn the page, but even he had smiled. No, it was more than that. He'd been drawn in. He'd grown wistful. He'd wanted things he couldn't have.

And now he felt wretched. The moment the lights had

come up he had acted as if this was just another day. But nothing would ever be the same again. Who could have predicted Bella would remember her first uncertain days on the *estancia* and could communicate the mistakes she'd made in such a hilarious and self-deprecating way in order to make the kids feel better?

Bella had given them all something to think about, Nero reflected, turning for the stables to saddle up his horse.

He stopped dead inside the stable yard. 'Ignacio. Is something wrong?' He had never seen his old friend dumbstruck before. Ignacio was known for being taciturn but nothing like this. Nero's heart raced with apprehension. 'Which horse is it?' he demanded, expecting the worst.

'You'd better see for yourself,' Ignacio told him, standing back.

'She left you a note,' one of the grooms told him, pressing a letter into his hand.

'Not now,' he said, in a rush to see whichever horse had succumbed to illness or injury. But then he halted. 'Who left me a note?'

'Bella,' the young lad said.

Ripping the envelope open, Nero scanned the contents rapidly: *She'll have a better chance with you—a better life.* Both the letter and the envelope drifted to the ground as he threw the stable door open. 'Misty...'

The sight of the little horse in his stable overwhelmed him. Sentiments he had never allowed himself to feel came flooding in. Bella had sacrificed part of her heart for him—and for the little horse she loved. 'How did this happen?' he asked Ignacio with a tight throat. 'How could the transporter leave my yard with the wrong horse?'

'Bella?' Ignacio said wryly. 'Bella insisted on over-seeing all the arrangements for Misty's transport personally.'

'Of course she did…' A faint smile broke through Nero's frown. And she would have done so knowing that no one would argue with that.

'No. I can't do it.' Bella shook her head.

'But you must,' Bella's second in command insisted.

Agnes Dillon was an older no-nonsense woman who had worked for Bella's father as a young girl and now worked for Bella. 'The British team has asked for you by name. The prince has too. You're going to be supervising the royal stable yard, for goodness' sake, Bella—doesn't that mean anything to you?'

For the England-Argentina international? Yes, that meant something to her. All she could see in her head was Nero—the same man who had sent her a cryptic message saying: *Bella, what have you done?* But there was nothing to be done about it now. Staying longer than she had intended in Argentina meant she had come straight back home to a match. 'I suppose I could take the day off sick,' she mused out loud.

Agnes's wiry grey bun bobbed. 'You're never sick,' she pointed out, rejecting this idea.

'Then I'll take a holiday.'

'On the day of the most crucial match in the polo calendar?'

'Okay, I don't do either of those things,' Bella conceded while Agnes shoved her hands into the pockets of her faded raspberry-coloured cords and waited. 'I'll work in the background.'

'People expect to see you, Bella. Your place is on the

pony lines at an international. What's the matter with you?' Agnes demanded. 'You haven't been the same since you came home.'

No. She had been restless and anxious and angry that Nero hadn't sent her more news about Misty. She couldn't bring herself to phone him, but her call to Ignacio had confirmed that Misty was in the best of spirits and was being ridden every day in preparation for the season. And, yes, Nero would be riding her. Misty would be his first choice in all the matches. It would have been nice to hear this from Nero.

'Did something happen in Argentina, Bella?'

Bella looked long and hard into Agnes's eyes. 'No. Nothing,' she insisted fiercely, as though trying to convince herself.

Agnes shrugged in the way people did when they knew not to press.

'Okay, we've got work to do.' Bella shut her mind to everything else. 'I should get my horse ready. I'm planning to ride one of the newly trained horses in the last chukka in the women's match.'

Bella could feel Agnes's concern on her back as she walked away. If only the older woman knew! How would she handle seeing Nero again when she'd thought of him every waking moment since leaving Argentina?

She'd handle it because that was her job, Bella told her herself impatiently, mounting up. Her team was at the top of the tree when it came to horse management. Man management she'd leave to the specialists, Bella concluded, seeing a group of stick chicks wandering off to the bar. They had no interest in watching women play, but when the Argentinians arrived, like the answer to every woman's sex-starved dream, they'd be back.

* * *

The Argentinian contingent rolled into town like a conquering army—four-wheel drives with blacked-out windows, vans, trucks, flashy sports cars with exotic-sounding names, a couple of fire-fed motorbikes and what seemed like a constant parade of sleek new horse transporters. The glamour quotient in the prince's polo yard shot into the stratosphere as the polo guys and their skimpily clad groupies emerged to stroll nonchalantly about while the polo ponies with their massive entourage decanted exuberantly from their motorised stalls, tossing their heads as if to say, *Clear a path; we're the real stars of the show!*

With so much testosterone flying about, it was no wonder Bella had her work cut out keeping her young grooms in check. The brash new Argentinian horse transporters were like nothing they had ever seen before. The Argentinian horses breathed fire. And the men...

The less said about the men, the better, Bella thought, heart thundering as the swarthy marauders with their flashing eyes, deep tans and athletic frames took possession of every inch of space. Even Agnes had come over all coy and girlie.

Whereas she was attending solely to business, Bella reassured herself, checking each horse into the yard on her clipboard, ignoring the fact that her heart was beating a frantic *so-where-is-he?* tattoo. She was doing very well until a deep voice penetrated her thoughts.

Whirling around, she saw him at once. Nero must have been riding shotgun at the back of the parade, but now he had moved in to help bring a particularly fractious pony down one of the transporter ramps. Seeing him with his muscles pumped at full stretch kept her rooted to the spot for a moment. Nero was so much more than she remembered. He meant so much more to her than she had even realised.

But when a horse threatened to run amok, safety was paramount. With the carefully choreographed re-union between one professional and another that she had planned forgotten, Bella dropped her clipboard on the ground and ran to help.

Everyone else had backed away when she ran in. Corded muscles stood out on Nero's arms. He had looped the rope around his waist but, as the horse shrieked its disapproval and reared up again, something in Nero's stillness caught its attention. Rolling white eyes fixed on Nero's while flattened ears pricked up as Nero began crooning reassurances in his deep, husky voice. It was a sound that touched not only the horse, but Bella somewhere deep too. She loved this man. Love wasted, maybe, but she would always love him. She drank in Nero's resolute face and loved him all the more. Her heart and her eyes were full of him. Nothing in her life had ever come close to this feeling.

Finally, the horse was calm enough to lead away. Nero would allow no one but himself to take the risk of leading her and Bella hurried ahead of him to open the stable door. Her heart was stripped bare for Nero to trample on and only her professionalism allowed her to put her own feelings to one side and do what her train-ing, her life had taught her. It was cool and shadowy inside the stable. She had prepared everything for just this eventuality. There was always one horse, sometimes more than one, spooked by the journey and the new sur-roundings, and Bella's aim was to soothe the frightened animal with the fresh sweet scent of hay and clean, cool water. Nero was also the consummate professional and, having seen his troupe safely into the yard, he wouldn't allow himself to acknowledge the world outside until everyone was safe.

Slipping the harness off the horse, he handed it to her. They hadn't spoken a word to each other yet, but there was an incredible level of tension between them. It was like an electric current joining them. They didn't need to speak, Bella realised as they quietened the highly strung horse between them. In this area of their lives, at least, they would always be as one.

Satisfied that the horse was calm, they left quietly. Bella turned for one last look over the top of the stable door.

'All's well that ends well. Isn't that what you say in your country, Bella?'

Nero's muscular forearms were resting on the lower half of the door as he turned to look at her. Holding his luminous gaze, she sensed rather than saw the hard mouth soften. 'Hello, Nero.'

Warmth stole into his eyes. 'Hello, Bella...'

Their naked arms were almost touching, but while Nero might have stepped straight out of the pages of a fashion magazine and smelled divine, Bella was conscious that she smelled of horse and in her workmanlike outfit of faded top and muckers—the boots she wore around the stables—with hoof oil smeared across her stable breeches, she was hardly a contender for groupie of the year. She hadn't wanted to look as if she was trying too hard when Nero and the Argentinians arrived, but there were degrees, she realised now.

'How are you, Bella?'

How was she? She had planned to be calm and professional. 'I'm well... And you?' Such few words to express a whole world of feeling.

'I'm very well, thank you,' Nero replied formally.

Nero hadn't moved. He was just staring at her as if he wanted to imprint every fraction of her face on his mind. 'Bella, what you did—'

'I should go. I have all your documentation here,' she said, clinging to business. She handed him the pack she had prepared earlier. He didn't even look at it. 'I'll come down to the stables later when you've had time to settle in,' she said, turning to go. 'If you need anything at all before then, please don't hesitate to call me. You'll find my number in the folder, along with all the others I thought you might find useful.' She was looking into his eyes. She should have seen. She should have known.

The breath caught in her throat as Nero put his hands on her shoulders. 'No more talking, Bella.'

She weakened against him. When Nero kissed her it felt so good, so right. The scent of him, the touch, the taste, the strength. She felt protected all over again.

And knew how dangerous that could be. It was better, safer, to be alone.

'No,' Nero exclaimed fiercely when she tried to pull away. 'I won't let you go this time. I've missed you too much, Bella. I didn't know what I was losing, or what I stood to gain,' he added with a glint of the old humour.

She would not—could not—give way to the maelstrom of feelings boiling inside her. 'You thought I was teaching you something?' Nero murmured, staring deep into her eyes. 'But you taught me more, Bella. You made me realise how proud my grandmother would be of the ranch as it is now, how the team she founded has gone on and prospered.'

'How proud she would be of you,' Bella amended softly. 'Don't put yourself down, Nero.'

'Says the expert on such matters,' Nero observed

huskily, brushing her lips with his mouth. 'You showed me that history doesn't have to repeat itself, and that a life alone is a lonely life.'

'I've missed you,' she breathed, nuzzling into him.

'Of course you have,' Nero agreed with all the old confidence, dropping another kiss on her mouth. His eyes were dancing with laughter and the familiar crease was back in his cheek.

'You're impossible,' she said.

Nero shrugged. His mouth curved. 'I won't deny it, but I've missed you, Bella—more than you know.'

For the first time in his life he felt a little up in the air. He'd put his heart on the line and Bella had been called away. He knew she wasn't a woman to be ordered around or someone who would fit in to suit—not that he wanted that, but Bella was at the other extreme. This was a woman with her life totally mapped out.

Was there a place for him in that life? He had never thought to ask the question before. It was clear that Bella belonged here as much as he belonged in Argentina. Could two lovers half a world apart ever be together for longer than the polo season? With a vicious curse under his breath, he watched her stride away. And then he shook his head a little ruefully. She was cool. He had to give her that. He admired her composure, just so long as the Ice Maiden didn't make a bid to come back.

'Hey, Ignacio,' he called. His face lit up at the sight of his closest ally and dearest friend.

'Can't stop,' Ignacio informed him in rapid Spanish. 'I'm going to see Bella. Can't be late; she's expecting me!'

He was jealous of Ignacio now? He felt shut out, Nero realised as Ignacio hurried off in the same direction

Bella had taken. At least he knew where he stood in the pecking order now. Try nowhere for size.

'Can I help you?'

He looked down into the concerned face of an older woman he remembered from previous visits. 'Agnes,' he said, remembering her name. They shook hands. 'It's good to see you again. Bella has made sure I have everything I need, thank you.' Except for the one thing he wanted, Nero thought as his glance strayed after Bella.

He was still grinding his jaw with frustration when he went to check on the ponies. He had wanted to say so much more to Bella, but she hadn't given him the chance. He had wanted to thank her for the movie she'd left for the kids and tell her how they had used it for each new intake—and that they would need a new film for next year. He had thought about their reunion constantly since she'd left, but he had pictured something very different—fireworks, not business. It was always duty first for Bella.

But now duty called him too. Work soothed him. The ponies always soothed him. And Bella would be back at his side as soon as she had finished whatever it was she had left him to do.

Bella wasn't back at his side, later that day or the next. Having made discreet enquiries, he learned she was evaluating the fitness of borderline match-ready ponies. Ignacio was his usual taciturn self and, in spite of Nero's subtle and not-so-subtle prompting, Ignacio refused to let anything slip about his own reunion with Bella. So had they talked about him at all? Or was work really all that mattered to Bella? And why was he feeling so indignant when it was the same for him? He had a week of non-stop training and preparation until the match ahead of him.

The day of the game matched his mood, with grim grey skies and rolling clouds of ink-lined pewter. He had only dozed on and off through another lonely night. How was Bella? Had she slept well? Selfishly, he hoped not. He hoped, like him, she hadn't slept properly all week.

Peering out of the window of his hotel, which was located on the fringes of the polo club, he had a good view of the pitch. Slippery, he determined, and the weather wasn't going to get better any time soon. He let the curtain fall back.

Drying off after an ice-cold shower, he switched on the news in time to catch the weather forecast. Thunder predicted later. Brilliant. Just what the horses didn't like. Bella would need all the help she could get to keep them calm. Sensing electricity in the air, they would be restless. It was one thing staying out of Bella's private life, but where work was involved her safety was his concern. And at work was the only time he'd seen her this week, at a joint team briefing. And each time when tension snapped between them she found some excuse to hurry away.

The time had come to change that for good.

Bella enjoyed her time with Ignacio, asking him questions about Nero's wild youth. Of course, she knew there were areas where she shouldn't trespass. Nero had told her about his parents—his father, in particular, and she wouldn't stretch the elderly gaucho's patience by delving into a past that he wouldn't care to remember, but he did give one reason why Nero had difficulty expressing his feelings. 'It's the gaucho's way,' Ignacio told her.

Ignacio had been a huge influence on Nero's life, stepping in and teaching him all his grandmother's tricks, as well as a few of his own. But there were other reasons for Nero's solitary path through life, his horrific childhood for one. When he should have known love and protection, Nero had faced cruelty and uncertainty. But if she could put her past behind her—

'Are all the ponies match-ready?'

She jumped guiltily at the sound of Nero's voice. 'All the ponies on this side of the yard have been passed by the vet.'

Without a word, Ignacio gathered up his grooming tackle and left them.

'What do *you* think, Bella?' Nero pressed.

'I think the weather conditions are treacherous and likely to get worse,' she said, holding Nero's fierce stare. 'I think the ponies are in great condition, but you need to take care. The ground will be slippery and your ponies don't like the wet, whereas our English ponies are used to damp conditions.' Her heart was pounding with concern and with longing.

'And your English ponies are unlike every other breed on the planet in that they're used to thunder, are they?' Nero demanded. With a sceptical huff, he flicked a look at the sky.

'We'll just have to hope the storm holds off.'

'Well, whatever happens, no more heroics from you. No more straying onto the pitch. For whatever reason,' Nero insisted, dipping his handsome head to stare her in the eyes. 'Do you understand me?'

'I thought we had that squared away.'

'We have, but I haven't forgotten.'

She let out a shaking breath as he strode away. Would things ever be relaxed and easy between them again?

Since his return it felt as if Nero had seized hold of her life and tossed it into the path of a hurricane.

Yes, and when he left she'd be in the doldrums again. Even if they hardly spoke now, she dreaded him leaving. She dreaded facing another endless span of unbearable longing. Resting her face against the warm, firm neck of the pony she'd been grooming, Bella vowed not to waste another second of her life thinking about Nero. Time was such a fragile, fleeting thing, and he would soon be going home to Argentina.

CHAPTER SIXTEEN

THE thunder held off, though Bella had been right about the ponies. The ground was wet and more than one pony had gone lame after skidding to a halt. The pony Nero was riding in this chukka had cast a shoe. 'Where is she?' he demanded when he rode in. 'Where's Bella?'

'She's with the grooms, warming up the ponies,' Agnes explained as he swung down from the saddle.

'She should be here.' He gazed up and down the pony lines, searching for her. 'It's her job to be here.' He pulled off his helmet as the horn sounded, announcing the end of the first half.

Meanwhile, Agnes was wringing her hands, which was most unlike her. 'What's the matter, Agnes?'

'We're short of horses, or I'd have another one brought up for you right away.'

'Don't worry; it's not your fault. These are unusual weather conditions. The match should have been cancelled.'

'Such an important match?' Agnes appeared horror-struck.

'Why not?' he said. 'It's only a game.' Words he thought he'd never hear himself say twice in one lifetime. He turned to see Bella leading Misty towards them. 'What are you doing?' he said suspiciously. 'I heard you'd run out of horses.'

'Not quite,' Bella said as she patted the pony's neck.

'You have to be joking. I'm not risking Misty. I brought her back to England where she belongs—with you. Have you seen the weather conditions? It's carnage out there.' And his emotions were all over the place. Bella was offering him her pony, a symbol of everything she cared about. 'I won't ride her,' he said decisively.

'She's equal to anything out there.'

'The brutality?'

'She'll keep you safe, Nero.'

There was so much in Bella's steady gaze, he seized her in front of everyone and brought her close. They stared into each other's eyes for a moment, for a lifetime, for eternity. 'Don't you ever stay away from me again,' he ground out.

'It's been a week,' she teased him.

'A week too long,' he argued, kissing her with hungry passion. He cursed impatiently as the horn sounded, calling him back onto the field.

'I'll be waiting for you,' she called after him, levelling that same steady stare on his face.

'I'll take care of her,' he promised, vaulting onto Misty's back. As he settled his helmet on his head he was suddenly aware that Bella and he were the focus of everyone's attention, from the grooms to Ignacio, and from the stick chicks to the prince, who had come to inspect his horses. 'I love you, Bella Wheeler,' he called out as everyone cheered. 'I've always loved you and I always will.' And he didn't care who heard.

'I love you too,' she said, her face as bright as the sun peeping through the clouds. 'Stay safe!'

Removing his helmet, he saluted her with a bow. He'd

won the only match he cared about. He hadn't a clue how Bella and he were going to make it work; he only knew they would.

They drank a toast to the victory of Nero's team. It was a massive victory, as the prince was the first to admit. He could hardly blame Bella for allowing the captain of the Argentinian team to ride her best pony, when it was the prince who had suggested that the best polo player in the world ought to be matched with Misty. He just hadn't factored the timing into his thinking, the prince admitted wryly. Just as he hadn't realised what a wonderful job Bella had done in Argentina, he added, thanking her for the portfolio of her stay she'd compiled for him. 'You must go back there,' the prince insisted. 'Agnes and my team can hold the fort for you here.'

'You're too kind, Sir,' Bella said, glancing at Nero.

The moment the prince's back was turned, Nero grabbed hold of her hand. 'You, me. Quiet time, now,' he insisted, leading Bella away. 'You can't refuse a royal command,' he reminded her, tongue in cheek, 'though I don't need the prince to prompt me.'

Bella curbed a smile. 'I've got something for you,' she said softly.

'And I've got something I want to tell you,' he said, drawing her to a halt in the grand, ornately plastered hallway of the Polo Club.

'Present first,' Bella insisted. Ignacio had told her that although Nero was the most generous of men, he frowned on his staff spending their hard-earned money on him. And, as he had no living relatives, Nero didn't exactly get a full Christmas sack. Bella intended to change that.

Nero looked suspicious. 'Is Ignacio in on this?'

'If he is I wouldn't tell you.'

'Will I like it?'

'Oh, I think so,' she said confidently.

He must be patient, Nero thought as Bella led him back across the polo ground towards the stables. What he had to say to her had waited long enough—it could wait a little longer. Bella touched him more than any woman ever had. Like now, when she was clutching her breast above her heart as she took him across the yard towards an emerald-green paddock that stretched down to the river. The paddock was home to a herd of spirited young colts, currently racing around, testing each other.

'The grey,' Bella said, pointing. 'That's Misty's first colt. He was born before I even met you, but he's two years old now, ready to start polo training.'

She stared up at him. 'He's a fine pony.' Nero's eyes narrowed as he watched the young horse go through his paces. 'A little wild, but courage and daring is what I always look for.' His gaze was drawn to Bella. 'You've done well,' he said, 'really well.'

'I named him Tango. For you.'

He inhaled sharply. 'For me?'

'It's my gift to you,' she explained, 'for your…hospitality in Argentina.'

He was incredulous. No one had ever given him anything of such great value before. He threw her a crooked smile. 'I'm glad you enjoyed yourself.'

'Oh, I did. And now at least you can breed some decent animals from those Criollas of yours,' she teased him, tilting her chin at the familiar challenging angle.

'Cheeky,' he warned, but he was laughing too. He wondered if he had ever been so happy in his life.

'Hopefully, a few years down the line your polo

ponies will be able to keep their feet when they come to England.' She turned serious. 'Tango has a great bloodline, Nero, and I think he'll be happy with those pretty mares of yours on the pampas.'

'Bella, I don't know what to say.'

'Don't say anything.'

'What can I give you in return?'

'I don't want anything in return—I never have.'

'May I give you my heart?' He stared down, realising that this was the single most important question he had ever asked in his life, and that Bella's answer would change both their lives for ever.

The solution was simple. The solution had been in front of them all the time, which was probably why they hadn't seen it and the prince had, Bella realised as she tried on the wedding dress in the thirty-third shop in at least the sixth country on the polo tour. But this one was perfect, which was just as well, since it was essential she found one before Nero came back to drag her out of the shop. Patience was not one of his virtues. A special licence and the two of them was all that was required—Bella had different ideas. She wanted photographs for their children to remember. So here she was in the most exclusive wedding store in Rome.

As the murmuring attendants fussed around her, Bella allowed herself a moment of quiet reflection. After their wedding, she would be back in Argentina with Nero in time for the new intake of children on the scheme and for the polo season there. They would then both travel back to the northern hemisphere in time to manage Bella's projects. But, more important than all of this, Nero insisted, was the life they built together. Remembering the portrait of his grandmother, Bella knew she would be following her heart to the pampas, just as Nero would be following his head when he came to England to play polo for the prince.

She was jolted out of these thoughts by Nero throwing the assistants into a panic by striding unannounced into a wedding boutique that suddenly seemed far too small to hold both Nero Caracas and the chosen wedding dress. Barring the entrance to her cubicle, the brave women held him at bay.

'Get me out of this,' Bella exclaimed, already tearing at the laces.

The women only just managed to remove the gown in time and hide it as Nero threw back the curtain.

'Don't test me, Bella.'

The women scattered, leaving them alone.

Bella levelled a stare on Nero's face as his fierce expression mellowed into a lazy gaze. 'Do you like it?' she asked, modelling the new underwear he'd bought her.

'It's a great improvement on industrial weight serge and heavy engineering.'

And she would never have bought such inconsequential scraps of lace for herself, or dreamed of wearing such things before she met Nero but, thanks to him, the damage of the past was nothing more than a reminder of how lucky they were to have found each other.

'We are in the city of lovers,' Nero murmured, running the knuckles of one hand very lightly down her cheek, 'so I shall test you later, to see if the new lingerie is having the required effect.'

'Excellent,' Bella agreed softly. 'The Ice Maiden is already melting in anticipation of your prolonged attention.' Catching hold of his hand, she kissed it whilst holding his gaze.

'You're my world, Bella,' Nero said, turning suddenly serious as he cupped her face between his hands. 'And after this tour we're going to stay home in Argentina and raise ponies together.'

'*What?*' And then she saw the laughter in his eyes.

'Did I say ponies?' Nero murmured.

'You know you did. Nero—stop,' she begged him as his kisses migrated from her mouth to her neck and from her neck to her breast. 'We're not alone.'

'When in Rome…' he murmured, clasping her to him.

'But the women in the shop…'

'Have seen it all before.'

'We can't.'

'No, you're right,' Nero agreed, leaving her weak and trembling as he removed his hand. 'We may need some time, so I'm going to make you wait until we get back to the hotel. All those years of work and no play have made Bella a very naughty girl indeed.'

'And you, of course, are absolutely innocent,' she commented wryly.

'No, *chica*,' Nero murmured against her mouth, 'I'm a very bad man indeed.'

All Bella could hear was the beating of her heart. 'Yes, yes…*Yes*!' she agreed in a heated whisper, 'Promise we can keep it that way…'

* * * * *

TAMING THE
LAST ACOSTA

For Joanne, who holds my hand
when I'm in the dentist's chair.

CHAPTER ONE

TWO PEOPLE IN the glittering wedding marquee appeared distanced from the celebrations. One was a photojournalist, known as Romy Winner, for whom detachment was part of her job. Kruz Acosta, the brother of the groom, had no excuse. With his wild dark looks, barely mellowed by formal wedding attire, Romily—who preferred to call herself no-nonsense Romy—thought Kruz perfectly suited to the harsh, unforgiving pampas in Argentina where this wedding was taking place.

Trying to slip deeper into the shadows, she stole some more shots of him. Immune to feeling when she was working, this time she felt excitement grip her. Not just because every photo editor in the world would pay a fortune to get their hands on her shots of Kruz Acosta, the most elusive of the notorious Acosta brothers, but because Kruz stirred her in some dark, atavistic way, involving a violently raised heartbeat and a lot of ill-timed appreciation below the belt.

Perhaps it was his air of menace, or maybe it was his hard-edged warrior look, but whatever it was she was enjoying it.

All four Acosta brothers were big, powerful men, but rumours abounded where Kruz was concerned, which made him all the more intriguing. A veteran of Special Forces, educated in both Europe and America, Kruz was believed to work for two governments now, though no one really knew

anything about him other than his success in business and
his prowess on the polo field.

She was getting to know him through her camera lens at
this wedding of Kruz's older brother, Nacho, to his beautiful
blind bride, Grace. What she had learned so far was less than
reassuring: Kruz missed nothing. She ducked out of sight as
he scanned the sumptuously decorated wedding venue, no
doubt looking for unwanted visitors like her.

It was time to forget Kruz Acosta and concentrate on work,
Romy told herself sternly, even if he *was* compelling viewing to someone who made her living out of stand-out shots.
It would take more than a froth of tulle and a family reunion
to soften Kruz Acosta, Romy guessed, as she ran off another
series of images she knew Ronald, her editor at *ROCK!*, would
happily give his eye teeth for.

Just one or two more and then she'd make herself scarce…

Maybe sooner rather than later, Romy concluded as Kruz
glanced her way. This job would have been a pleasure if
she'd had an official press pass, but *ROCK!* was considered a
scandal sheet by many, so no one from *ROCK!* had received
an invitation to the wedding. Romy was attending on secret
business for the bride, on the understanding that she could
use some of the shots for other purposes.

Romy's fame as a photographer had reached Grace through
Holly Acosta, one of Romy's colleagues at *ROCK!* The three
women had been having secret meetings over the past few
months, culminating in Grace declaring that she would trust
no one but Romy to make a photographic record of her wedding for her husband, Nacho, and for any children they might
have. Inspired by the blind bride's courage, Romy had agreed.
Grace was fast becoming a friend rather than just another
client, and this was a chance in a million for Romy to see the
Acostas at play—though she doubted Kruz would be as ac-
commodating as the bride if he caught her.

So he mustn't catch her, Romy determined, shivering with

awareness as she focused her lens on the one man in the marquee her camera loved above all others. He had a special sort of energy that seemed to reach her across the crowded tent, and the menace he threw out was alarming. The more shots she took of him, the more she couldn't imagine that much got in his way. It was easy to picture Kruz as a rebellious youth who had gone on to win medals for gallantry in the Special Forces. All the bespoke tailoring in the world couldn't hide the fact that Kruz Acosta was a weapon in disguise. He now ran a formidably successful security company, which placed him firmly in charge of security at this wedding.

A flush of alarm scorched her as Kruz's gaze swept over her like a searchlight and moved on. He must have seen her. The question was: would he do anything about it? She hadn't come halfway across the world in order to return home to London empty-handed.

Or to let down the bride, Romy concluded as she moved deeper into the crowd. This commission for Grace was more of a sacred charge than a job, and she had no intention of being distracted by one of the most alarming-looking men it had ever been her pleasure to photograph. Running off a blizzard of shots, she realised Kruz couldn't have stood in starker contrast to the bride. Grace's gentle beauty had never seemed more pronounced than at this moment, when she was standing beneath a flower-bedecked canopy between her husband and Kruz.

Romy drew a swift breath when the man in question stared straight at her. Lowering her camera, she glanced around, searching for a better hiding place, but shadows were in short supply in the brilliantly lit tent. One of the few things Grace could still detect after a virus had stolen her sight was light, so the dress code for the wedding was 'sparkle' and every corner of the giant marquee was floodlit by fabulous Venetian chandeliers.

Mingling with the guests, Romy kept her head down. The

crowd was moving towards the receiving line, where all the Acostas were standing. There was a murmur of anticipation in the queue—and no wonder. The Acostas were an incredibly good-looking family. Nacho, the oldest brother, was clearly besotted by his beautiful new bride, while the sparks flying between Diego and his wedding planner wife Maxie could have ignited a fire. The supremely cool Ruiz Acosta clearly couldn't wait to get his firebrand wife, Romy's friend and colleague Holly, into bed, judging by the looks they were exchanging, while Lucia Acosta, the only girl in this family of four outrageously good-looking brothers, was flirting with her husband Luke Forster, the ridiculously photogenic American polo player.

Which left Kruz...

The only unmarried brother. So what? Her camera loved him, but that didn't mean *she* had to like him—though she would take full advantage of his distraction as he greeted his guests.

Those scars... That grim expression... She snapped away, knowing that everything about Kruz Acosta should put her off, but instead she was spellbound.

From a safe distance, Romy amended sensibly, as a pulse of arousal ripped through her.

And then he really did surprise her. As Kruz turned to say something to the bride his expression softened momentarily. That was the money shot, as it was known in the trade. It was the type of unexpected photograph that Romy was so good at capturing and had built her reputation on.

She was so busy congratulating herself she almost missed Kruz swinging round to stare at her again. Now she knew how a rabbit trapped in headlights felt. When he moved she moved too. Grabbing her kitbag, she stowed the camera. Her hands were trembling as panic mounted inside her. She hurried towards the exit, knowing this was unlike her. She was a seasoned pro, not some cub reporter—a thick skin came with

the job. And why such breathless excitement at the thought
of being chased by him? She was hardly an innocent abroad
where men were concerned.

Because Kruz was the stuff of heated erotic dreams and
her body liked the idea of being chased by him. Next question.

Before she made herself scarce there were a few more shots
she wanted to take for Grace. Squeezing herself into a small
gap behind a pillar, she took some close-ups of flowers and
trimmings—richly scented white roses and lush fat peonies
in softest pink, secured with white satin ribbon and tiny silver bells. The ceiling was draped like a Bedouin tent, white
and silver chiffon lavishly decorated with scented flowers,
crystal beads and fiery diamanté. Though Grace couldn't
see these details the wedding planner had ensured she would
enjoy a scent sensation, while Romy was equally determined
to make a photographic record of the day with detailed de-
scriptions in Braille alongside each image.

'Hello, Romy.'

She nearly jumped out of her skin, but it was only a famous celebrity touching her arm, in the hope of a photograph.
Romy's editor at *ROCK!* loved those shots, so she had to make
time for it. Shots like these brought in the money Romy so
badly needed, though what she really longed to do was to
tell the story of ordinary people in extraordinary situations
through her photographs. One day she'd do that, she vowed
stepping forward to take the shot, leaving herself dangerously exposed.

The queue of guests at the receiving line was thinning as
people moved on to their tables for the wedding feast, and
an icy warning was trickling down her spine before she even
had a chance to say goodbye to the celebrity. She didn't need
to check to know she was being watched. She usually managed to blend in with the crowd, with or without an official
press pass, but there was nothing usual in any situation when
Kruz Acosta was in town.

As soon as the celebrity moved on she found another hiding place behind some elaborate table decorations. From here she could observe Kruz to her heart's content. She settled down to enjoy the play of muscle beneath his tailored jacket and imagined him stripped to the buff.

Nice...

The only downside was Grace had mentioned that although Kruz felt at home on the pampas he was going to open an office in London—'Just around the corner from *ROCK!*,' Grace had said, as if it were a good thing.

Now she'd seen him, Romy was sure Kruz Acosta was nothing but trouble.

But attractive... He was off-the-scale *hot*.

But she wasn't here to play make-believe with one of the lead characters at this wedding. She had got what she needed and she was out of here.

Glancing over her shoulder, she noticed that Kruz was no longer in the receiving line.

So where the hell was he?

She scanned the marquee, but there was no sign of Kruz anywhere. There were quite a few exits from the tent—he could have used any one of them. She wasn't going to take any chances, and would head straight for the press coach to send off her copy. Thank goodness Holly had given her a key.

The press coach wasn't too far. She could see its twinkling lights. She quickened her step, fixing her gaze on them, feeling that same sense of being hunted—though why was she worried? She could look after herself. Growing up small and plain had ruled out girlie pursuits, so she had taken up kickboxing instead. Anyone who thought they could take her camera was in for a big surprise.

He had recognised the girl heading towards the exit. There was no chance he would let her get away. Having signed off the press passes personally, he knew Romy Winner didn't appear on any of them.

Romy Winner was said to be ruthless in pursuit of a story, but she was no more ruthless than he was. Her work was reputed to be cutting-edge and insightful—he'd even heard it said that as a photojournalist Romy Winner had no equal—but that didn't excuse her trespass here.

She had disappointed him, Kruz reflected as he closed in on her. Renowned for lodging herself in the most ingenious of nooks, he might have expected to find Ms Winner hanging from the roof trusses, or masquerading as a waitress, rather than skulking in the shadows like some rent-a-punk oddity, with her pale face, thin body, huge kohl-ringed eyes and that coal-black, gel-spiked, red-tipped hair, for all the wedding guests to stare at and comment on.

So Romy could catch guests off-guard and snap away at her leisure?

Maybe she wasn't so dumb after all. She must have captured some great shots. He was impressed by her cunning, but far less impressed by Señorita Winner's brazen attempt to gate-crash his brother's wedding. He would make her pay. He just hadn't decided what currency he was accepting today. That would depend on his mood when he caught up with her.

Romy hurried on into the darkness. She couldn't shake the feeling she was being followed, though she doubted it was Kruz. Surely he had more important things to do?

Crunching her way along a cinder path, she reasoned that with all the Acosta siblings having been raised by Nacho, after their parents had been killed in a flood, Kruz had enjoyed no softening influence from a mother—which accounted for the air of danger surrounding him. It was no more than that. Her overworked imagination could take a rest. Pausing at a crossroads, she picked up the lights and followed them. She couldn't afford to lose her nerve now. She had to get her copy away. The money Romy earned from her photographs kept her mother well cared for in the nursing home where she had lived since Romy's father had beaten her half to death.

When Romy had first become a photojournalist it hadn't taken her long to realise that pretty pictures earned pennies, while sensational images sold almost as well as sex. Her success in the field had been forged in stone on the day she was told that her mother would need full-time care for the rest of her life. From that day on Romy had been determined that her mother would have the best of care and Romy would provide it for her.

A gust of wind sweeping down from the Andes made her shudder violently. She wondered if she had ever felt more out of place than she did now. She lived in London, amidst constant bustle and noise. Here in the shadow of a gigantic mountain range everything turned sinister at night and her chest tightened as she quickened her step. The ghostly shape of the wedding tent was far behind her now, and ahead was just a vast emptiness, dotted with faint lights from the *hacienda*. There were no landmarks on the pampas and no stars to guide her. The Acosta brothers were giants amongst men, and the land they came from was on the same impressive scale. There were no boundaries here, there was only space, and the Acostas owned most of it.

Rounding a corner, she caught sight of the press coach again and began to jog. Her breath hitched in her throat as she stopped to listen. Was that a twig snapping behind her? Her heart was hammering so violently it was hard to tell. Focusing her gaze on the press coach, with its halo of aerials and satellite dishes, she fumbled for the key, wanting to have it ready in her hand—and cried out with shock as a man's hand seized her wrist.

His other hand snatched hold of her camera. Reacting purely on instinct, she launched a stinging roundhouse kick—only to have her ankle captured in an iron grip.

'Good, but not good enough,' Kruz Acosta ground out.

Rammed up hard against the motorcoach, with Kruz's head in her face, it was hard for Romy to disagree. In the unforgiving flesh, Kruz made the evidence of her camera lens seem pallid and insubstantial. He was hard like rock, and so close she could see the flecks of gold in his fierce black eyes, as well as the cynical twist on his mouth. While their gazes were locked he brought her camera strap down, inch by taunting inch, until finally he removed it from her arm and placed it on the ground behind him.

'No,' he said softly when she glanced at it.

She still made a lunge, which he countered effortlessly. Flipping her to the ground, he stood back. Rolling away, she sprang up, assuming a defensive position with her hands clenched into angry fists, and demanded that he give it up.

Kruz Acosta merely raised a brow.

'I said—'

'I heard what you said,' he said quietly.

He was even more devastating at short range. She rubbed her arm as she stared balefully. He hadn't hurt her. He had branded her with his touch.

A shocked cry sprang from her lips when he seized hold of her again. His reach was phenomenal. His grip like steel. He made no allowance for the fact that she was half his size, so now every inch of her was rammed up tight against him, and when she fought him he just laughed, saying, 'Is that all you've got?'

She staggered as Kruz thrust her away. She felt humiliated as well as angry. Now he'd had a chance to take a better look at her he wasn't impressed. And why would he be?

'How does a member of the paparazzi get in here?'

Kruz was playing with her, she suspected. 'I'm not paparazzi. I'm on the staff at *ROCK!*'

'My apologies.' He made her a mocking bow. 'So you're

a fully paid-up member of the paparazzi. With your own executive office, I presume?'

'I have a very nice office, as it happens,' she lied. He was making her feel hot and self-conscious. She was used to being in control. It was going too far to say that amongst photojournalists she was accorded a certain respect, but she certainly wasn't used to being talked down to by men.

'So as well as being an infamous photojournalist *and* an executive at *ROCK!* magazine,' Kruz mocked, 'I now discover that the infamous Romy Winner is an expert kick-boxer.'

Her cheeks flushed red. Not so expert, since he'd blocked her first move.

'I suppose kick-boxing is a useful skill when it comes to gate-crashing events you haven't been invited to?' Kruz suggested.

'It's one of my interests—and just as well with men like you around—'

'Men like me?' he said, holding her angry stare. 'Perhaps you and I should get on the mat in the gym sometime.'

'Over my dead body,' she fired back.

His look suggested he expected her to blink, or flinch, or even lower her gaze in submission. She did none of those things, though she did find herself staring at his lips. Kruz had the most amazing mouth—hard, yet sensual—and she couldn't help wondering what it would feel like to be kissed by him, though she had a pretty good idea...

An idea that was ridiculous! It wouldn't happen this side of hell. Kruz was one of the beautiful people—the type she liked to look at through her lens much as a wildlife photographer might observe a tiger, without having the slightest intention of touching it. Instead of drooling over him like some lovesick teenager it was time to put him straight.

'Kick-boxing is great for fending off unwanted advances—'

'Don't flatter yourself, Romy.'

Kruz's eyes had turned cold and she shivered involuntarily. There was no chance of getting her camera back now. He was good, economical with his movements, and he was fast.

Who knew what he was like as a lover...?

Thankfully she would never find out. All that mattered now was getting her camera back.

Darting round him, she tried to snatch it—and was totally unprepared for Kruz whipping the leather jacket from her shoulders. Underneath it she was wearing a simple white vest. No bra. She hardly needed one. Her cheeks fired up when he took full inventory of her chest. She could imagine the kind of breasts Kruz liked, and perversely wished she had big bouncing breasts to thrust in his face—if only to make a better job of showing her contempt than her embarrassingly desperate nipples were doing right now, poking through her flimsy top to signal their sheer, agonising frustration.

'Still want to take me on?' he drawled provocatively.

'I'm sure I could make some sort of dent in your ego,' she countered, crossing her arms over her chest. She circled round him. 'All I want is my property back.' She glanced at the camera, lying just a tantalising distance away.

'So what's on this camera that you're so keen for me not to see?' He picked it up. 'You can collect it in the morning, when I've had a chance to evaluate your photographs.'

'It's my work, and *I* need to edit it—'

'Your unauthorised work,' he corrected her.

There was no point trying to reason with this man. Action was the only option.

One moment she was diving for the camera, and the next Kruz had tumbled her to the ground.

'Now, what shall I do with you?' he murmured, his warm, minty breath brushing her face.

With Kruz pinning her to the ground, one powerful thigh planted either side of her body, her options were limited—until he yanked her onto a soft bed of grass at the side of the cinder path. Then they became boundless. The grass felt like damp ribbons beneath her skin, and she could smell the rising sap where she had crushed it. Overlaying that was the heat of a powerful, highly sexed, highly aroused man.

She should try to escape. She should put up some sort of token struggle, at least. She should remember her martial arts training and search for a weakness in Kruz to exploit.

She did none of those things. And as for that potential weakness—as it turned out it was one they shared.

As she reached up to push him away Kruz swooped down. Ravishing her mouth was a purposeful exercise, and one at which he excelled. For a moment she was too stunned to do anything, and then the sensation of being possessed, entered, controlled and plundered, even if it was only her mouth, by a man with whom she had been having fantasy sex for quite a few hours, sent her wild with excitement. She even groaned a complaint when he pulled away, and was relieved to find it was only to remove his jacket.

For such a big man Kruz went about his business with purpose and speed. His natural athleticism, she supposed, feeling her body heat, pulse and melt at the thought of being thoroughly pleasured by him. Growing up with a pillow over her head to shut out the violence at home had left her a stranger to romance and tenderness. Given a choice, she preferred to observe life through her camera lens, but when an opportunity for pleasure presented itself she seized it, enjoyed it, and moved on. She wasn't about to turn down *this* opportunity.

Pleasure with no curb or reason? Pleasure without thought of consequence?

Correct, she informed her inner critic firmly. Even the leisurely way Kruz was folding his jacket and putting it aside was like foreplay. He was so sexy. His powerful body was sexy—his hands were sexy—the wide spread of his shoulders was sexy—his shadowy face was sexy.

Kruz's confidence in her unquestioning acceptance of everything that was about to happen was so damn sexy she could lose control right now.

A life spent living vicariously through a camera lens was ultimately unsatisfactory, while this unexpected encounter was proving to be anything but. A rush of lust and longing gripped her as he held her stare. The look they exchanged spoke about need and fulfilment. It was explicit and potent. She broke the moment of stillness. Ripping off his shirt, she sent buttons flying everywhere. Yanking the fabric from the waistband of his pants, she tossed it away, exclaiming with happy shock as bespoke tailoring yielded to hard, tanned flesh. This was everything she had ever dreamed of and more. Liberally embellished with tattoos and scars, Kruz's torso was outstanding. She could hardly breathe for excitement when he found the button on her jeans and quickly dealt with it. He quickly got them down. In comparison, her own fingers felt fat and useless as she struggled with the buckle on his belt.

'Let me help you.'

Kruz held her gaze with a mocking look as he made this suggestion. It was all the aphrodisiac she needed. She cried out with excitement when his thumbs slipped beneath the elastic on her flimsy briefs to ease them down her hips. His big hands blazed a trail of fire everywhere they touched. She couldn't bear the wait when he paused to protect them both, but it was a badly needed wake-up call. The fact that this man had thought of it before she had went some way to reminding her how far she'd travelled from the safe shores she called home.

Her body overruled the last-minute qualms. Her body was one hundred per cent in favour of what was coming. Even her tiny breasts felt swollen and heavy, while her nipples were cheekily pert and obscenely hard, and the carnal pulse throbbing insistently between her legs demanded satisfaction.

Kruz had awakened such an appetite inside her she wouldn't be human if she didn't want to discover what sex could be like with someone who really knew what he was doing. She was about to find out. When Kruz stretched his length against her she could feel his huge erection, heavy and hard against her leg. And that look in his eyes—that slumberous, confident look. It told her exactly what he intended to do with her and just how much she was going to enjoy it. And, in case she was in any doubt, he now spelled out his intentions in a few succinct words.

She gasped with excitement. With hardly any experience of dating, and even less of foreplay, she was happy to hear that nothing was about to change.

CHAPTER TWO

SHE EXCLAIMED WITH shock when Kruz eased inside her. She was ready. That wasn't the problem. Kruz was the problem. He was huge.

Built to scale.

She should have known.

Her breath came in short, shocked whimpers, pain and pleasure combined. It was a relief when he took his time and didn't rush her. She began to relax.

This was good... Yes, better than good...

Releasing the shaking breath from her lungs, she silently thanked him for giving her the chance to explore such incredible sensation at her leisure. Leisure? The brief plateau lasted no more than a few seconds, then she was clambering all over him as a force swept them into a world where moving deeper, harder, rougher, fast and furious, was more than an imperative: it was essential to life.

'You okay?' Kruz asked, coming down briefly to register concern as she screamed wildly and let go.

It seemed for ever before she could answer him, and then she wasn't sure she said anything that made sense.

'A little better, at least?' he suggested with amusement when she quietened.

'Not that much better,' she argued, blatantly asking for more.

Taking his weight on his arms, Kruz stared down at her.

It didn't get much better than this, Romy registered groggily, lost in pleasure the instant he began to move. She loved his hard, confident mouth. She loved the feeling of being full and ready to be sated. She even loved her grassy bed, complete with night sounds: cicadas chirruping and an owl somewhere in the distance hooting softly. Kruz's clean, musky scent was in her nostrils, and when she turned her head, groaning in extremes of pleasure, her bed of grass added a piquant tang to an already intoxicating mix. She was floating on sensation, hardly daring to move in case she fell too soon. She didn't want it to end, but Kruz was too experienced and made it really hard to hold on. Moving persuasively from side to side, he pushed her little by little, closer to the edge.

'Good?' he said, staring down, mocking her with his confident smile.

'Very good,' she managed on a shaking breath.

And then he did something that lifted her onto an even higher plane of sensation. Slowly withdrawing, he left her trembling and uncertain, before slowly thrusting into her again. Whatever she had imagined before was eclipsed by this intensity of feeling. It was like the first time all over again, except now she was so much more receptive and aroused. She couldn't hold back, and shrieked as she fell, shouting his name as powerful spasms gripped her.

When she finally relaxed what she realised was her pincer grip on Kruz's arms, she realised she had probably bruised him. He was holding her just as firmly, but with more care. She loved his firm grip on her buttocks, his slightly callused hands rough on her soft skin.

'I can't,' she protested as he began to move again . 'I truly can't.'

'There's no such word as *can't*,' he whispered.

Incredibly, he was right. It didn't seem possible that she had anything left, but when Kruz stared deep into her eyes it was as if he was instructing her that she must give herself up to sensation. There was no reason to disobey and she tumbled promptly, laughing and crying with surprise as she fell again.

It turned out to be just the start of her lessons in advanced lovemaking. Pressing her knees back, Kruz stared down. Now she discovered that she loved to watch him watching her. Lifting herself up, she folded her arms behind her head so she had a better view. Nothing existed outside this extreme pleasure. Kruz had placed himself at her disposal, and to reward him she pressed her legs as wide as they would go. He demanded all her concentration as he worked steadily and effectively on the task in hand.

'You really should try holding on once in a while,' he said, smiling against her mouth.

'Why?' she whispered back.

'Try it and you'll find out,' he said.

'Will you teach me?' Her heart drummed at the thought.

'Perhaps,' Kruz murmured.

He wasn't joking, Romy discovered as Kruz led her through a lengthy session of tease and withdraw until her body was screaming for release.

'Greedy girl,' he murmured with approval. 'Again?' he suggested, when finally he allowed her to let go.

Bracing her hands against his chest, she smiled into his eyes. For a hectic hook-up this was turning into a lengthy encounter, and she hadn't got a single complaint. Kruz was addictive. The pleasure he conjured was amazing. But—

'What?' he said as she turned her head away from him.

'Nothing.' She dismissed the niggle hiding deep in her subconscious.

'You think too much,' he said.

'Agreed,' she replied, dragging in a fast breath as he began to move again.

Kruz didn't need to ask if she wanted more; the answer was obvious to both of them. Gripping his iron buttocks, she urged him on as he set up a drugging beat. Tightening her legs around his waist, she moved with him—harder—faster—giving as good as she got, and through it all Kruz maintained eye contact, which was probably the biggest turn-on of all, because he could see where she was so quickly going. Holding her firmly in place, he kept her in position beneath him, and when the storm rose he judged each thrust to perfection. Pushing her knees apart, he made sure they both had an excellent view, and now even he was unable to hold on, and roared with pleasure as he gave in to violent release.

She went with him, falling gratefully into a vortex of sensation from which there was no escape. It was only when she came to that she realised fantasy had in no way prepared her for reality—her fantasies were wholly selfish, and Kruz had woken something inside her that made her care for him just a little bit. It was a shame he didn't feel the same. Now he was sated she sensed a core of ice growing around him. It frightened her, because she was feeling emotional for the first time with a man. And now he was pulling back—emotionally, physically.

No wonder that niggle of unease had gripped her, Romy reflected. She was playing well out of her league. As if to prove this, Kruz was already on his feet, pulling on his clothes. He buckled his belt as if it were just another day at the office. She might have laughed under other circumstances when he was forced to tug the edges of his shirt together where she had ripped the buttons off. He did no more than hide the evidence of her desperation beneath his tie. How could he be so chillingly unfazed by all this? Her unease grew at the thought that what had just happened between them had made a dangerously strong impression on her, while it appeared to have washed over Kruz.

And why not? What happened was freely given and freely taken by both of you.

'Are you okay?' he said, glancing down when she remained immobile.

'Of course I am,' she said in a casual tone. Inwardly she was screaming. Was she really so stupid she had imagined she would come out of something like this unscathed?

Even inward reasoning didn't help—she was still waiting for him to say something encouraging. How pathetic was that? She had never felt like this before, and had no way of dealing with the feelings, so, gathering up her clothes, she lost herself in mundane matters—shaking the grass off her jacket, pulling on her jeans, sorting her hair out, then smoothing her hands over her face, hoping that by the time she removed them she would appear cool and detached.

Wrong. She felt as if she'd come out the wrong end of a spin dry.

Her thoughts turned at last to her camera. It was still lying on the bank, temptingly close. She had learned her lesson where lunging for it was concerned, but felt confident that Kruz would give it to her now. It was the least he could do.

Fortunately Kruz appeared to be oblivious both to her and to her camera. He was on the phone, telling his security operatives that he was patrolling the grounds.

She eased her neck, as if that would ease the other aches, most of which had taken up residence in her heart.

Hadn't she learned anything from the past? Had Kruz made her forget her father's rages and her mother's dependency on a violent man?

Kruz hadn't been in any way violent towards her—but he was strong, commanding, and detached from emotion. All the things she had learned to avoid.

She was safe in that, unlike her mother, she had learned to avoid the pitfalls of attachment by switching off her emotions. In that she wasn't so dissimilar from Kruz. This was just a brief interlude of fun for both of them and now it was over. Neither of them was capable of love.

Love?

He swung round as she made a wry sound. Love was a

long road to nowhere, with a punch in the teeth at the end. So, yes, if she was in any doubt at all about the protocol between two strangers who'd just had sex on a grassy bank, she'd go with cool and detached every time.

'Right,' he said, ending the call, 'I need to get back.'

'Of course,' she said off-handedly. 'But I'd like my camera first.'

He frowned, as if they were two strangers at odds with each other. 'You've had your fun and now you're on your way,' he said.

She'd asked for that, Romy concluded. 'Well, I'm not going anywhere without it,' she said stubbornly. It was true. The camera was more than a tool of her trade, it was a fifth limb. It was an extension of her body, of her mind. It was the only way she knew how to make the money she needed to support herself and her mother.

'I've told you already. You'll get it back when I've checked it,' he said coldly, hoisting the camera over his shoulder.

'You're my censor now?' she said, chasing after him. 'I don't think so.'

The look Kruz gave her made her stomach clench with alarm.

'You can sleep in the bunkhouse,' he said, 'along with the rest of the press crew. Pick up your camera in the morning from my staff.'

She blinked. He'd said it as if they hadn't touched each other, pleasured each other.

They'd had sex and that was all.

Except for the slap in the face she got from realising that he saw it as no reason to give up her camera. 'By morning it will be too late—I need it now.'

'For what?' he said.

'I have to edit the photographs and then catch the news desk.' It was a lie of desperation, but she would do anything to recover her camera. 'There is another reason,' she added, waiting for a thunderclap to strike her down. This idea had only just occurred to her. 'I need to work on the shots I'm donating to your charity.'

As if he'd guessed, Kruz's eyes narrowed. 'The Acosta charity?'

'Yes.' She had a lot of shots in the can, Romy reasoned, quickly running through them in her mind. She had more than enough to pay for her mother's care and to keep herself off the breadline. She had taken a lot of shots specifically for Grace's album, and he couldn't have those, but there were more—plenty more.

Had she bought herself a reprieve? Romy wondered as she stared at Kruz. 'I've identified a good opportunity for the charity,' she said, as the germ of an idea sprouted wings.

'Tell me,' Kruz said impatiently.

'My editor at *ROCK!* is thinking about making a feature on the Acostas and your charity.' Or at least she would make sure he was thinking about it by the time she got back. 'Think of how that would raise the charity's profile,' she said, dangling a carrot she hoped no Acosta in his right mind could refuse.

'So why didn't Grace or Holly tell me about this?' Kruz probed, staring at her keenly. 'If either of them had mentioned it I would have made sure you were issued with an official pass.'

'I *am* here on a mission for Grace,' Romy admitted, 'which is how I got in. Grace asked me not to say anything, and I haven't. It's crucial that Nacho doesn't learn about Grace's special surprise. I hope you'll respect that.' Kruz remained silent as she went on. 'I'm sure Grace and Holly were just too wrapped up in the wedding to remember to tell you,' she said, not wanting to get either of her friends into trouble.

Kruz paused. And now she could only wait.

'I suppose Grace could confirm this if I asked her?'

'If you feel like interrogating a bride on her wedding day, I'm sure she would.'

One ebony brow lifted. Whether Kruz believed her or not, for the moment she had him firmly in check.

'The solution to this,' he remarked, 'is that *I* take a look at the shots and *I* decide.'

As he strode away she ran after him. Dodging in front of him, she forced him to stop.

He studied Romy's elfin features with a practised eye. He interpreted the nervous hand running distractedly through her disordered hair. The camera meant everything to her, and if there was one thing that could really throw Ms Winner he had it swinging from his shoulder now. She was terrified he was going to disappear with her camera. She worked with it every day. It was her family, her income stream, her life. He almost felt sorry for her, and then stamped the feeling out. What was Romy Winner to *him*?

Actually, she was a lot more than he wanted her to be. She had got to him in a way he hadn't quite fathomed yet. 'Is there some reason why I shouldn't see these shots?' he asked, teasing her by lifting the camera to Romy's eye level.

'None whatsoever,' she said firmly, but her face softened in response to his mocking expression and she almost smiled.

Testing Romy was fun, he discovered, and fun and he were strangers. With such a jaundiced palette as his, any novelty was a prize. But he wouldn't taunt her any longer. He wasn't a bully, and wouldn't intentionally try to increase that look of concern in her eyes. 'Shall we?' he invited, glancing at the press coach.

She eyed him suspiciously, perhaps wondering if she was being set up. She knew there was nothing she could do about it, if that were the case. She strode ahead of him, head down, mouth set in a stubborn line, no doubt planning her next move. And then she really did throw him.

'So, what have you got to hide?' she asked him, swinging round at the door

'Me?' he demanded.

Tilting her head to one side, she studied his face. 'People with something to hide are generally wary of me and my camera, so I wondered what *you* had to hide…'

'You think that's why I confiscated it?'

'Maybe,' she said, not flinching from his stare.

That direct look of hers asked a lot of questions about a man who could have such prolonged and spectacular sex with a woman he didn't know. It was a look that suggested Romy was asking herself the same question.

'Are you worried that I might have taken some compromising pictures of you?' she said. There was a tug of humour at one corner of her mouth.

'Worried?' He shook his head. But the truth was he had never been so reckless with a woman. He sure as hell wouldn't be so reckless again.

'Kruz?' she prompted.

His name sounded soft on her lips. That had to be a first. He smiled. 'What?'

'Just checking you know I'm still here.'

He gave her a wry look and felt a surge of heat when she tossed one back. He wasn't an animal. He was still capable of feeling. His brother Nacho had made him believe that when Kruz had been discharged from the army hospital. It was Nacho who had persuaded him to channel his particular talents into a security company, saying Kruz must need and feel and care before he could really start living again. Nacho was right. The more he looked at Romy, the more human he felt.

Did Kruz *have* to stare at her lips like that? Here she was, trying to forget her body was still thrilling from his touch, and he wasn't making it easy. She was a professional woman, trying to persuade herself she would soon get over tonight—yet all he had to do was look at her for her to long for him to take hold of her and draw her into an embrace that was neither sexual nor mocking. She had never wanted to share and trust and rest awhile quite so badly.

And she wasn't about to fall into that trap now.

'Shall we take a look?'

She looked at Kruz and frowned.

'The pictures?' he prompted, and she realised that he had not only removed the key to the press coach from her hand, but had opened the door and was holding it for her.

That yearning feeling inside…?

It wasn't helpful. Women who felt the urge to nurture men would end up like her mother: battered, withdrawn, and helpless in a nursing home.

She led the way into the coach. Her manner was cold. They were both cold, and that suited her fine.

Romy's mood now was a slap in the face to him after what they'd experienced together, but he had to concede she was only as detached as he was. He was just surprised, he supposed, that those much vaunted attributes of tenderness and sensitivity, which women were supposed to possess in abundance, appeared to have bypassed her completely. He should be pleased about that, but he wasn't. He was offended. Romy was the first woman who hadn't clung to him possessively after sex. And bizarrely, for the first time in his life, some primitive part of him had wanted her to.

'Are you coming in?' she said, when he stood at the entrance at the top of the steps.

His senses surged as he brushed past her. However unlikely it seemed to him, this whip-thin fighting girl stirred him like no other. He wanted more. So did she, judging by than quick intake of breath. He could feel her sexual hunger in the energy firing between them. But Romy wanted more that he could give her. He wanted more of Romy, but all he wanted was sex.

CHAPTER THREE

SHE MADE HER way down the aisle towards the area at the rear of the coach set aside for desks and equipment. Her small, slender shape, dressed all in black, quickly became part of the shadows.

'I know there's a light switch in here somewhere,' she said.

Her voice was a little shaky now the door was closed, and the tension rocketed between them. He could feel her anticipation as she waited for his next move. He could taste it in the air. He could detect her arousal. He was a hunter through and through.

'Here,' he said, pressing a switch that illuminated the coach and set some unseen power source humming.

'Thank you,' she said, with her back to him as she sat down at a desk.

'You'll need this,' he said, handing over the camera.

She thanked him and hugged it to her as if it contained gold bars rather than her shots.

He had more time than he needed while she logged on. He used it to reflect on what had happened over the past hour or so. Ejecting Romy from the wedding feast should have been straightforward. She should have been on her way to Buenos Aires by now, then back to London. Instead his head was still full of her, and his body still wanted her. He could still hear her moaning and writhing beneath him and feel her beneath his hands. He could still taste her on his mouth, and he could remember the smell of her soap-fresh skin. He smiled in the shadows, remembering her attacking him, that tiny frame surprisingly strong, yet so undeniably feminine. Why did Romy Winner hide herself away behind the lens of a camera?

A blaze of colour hit the screen as she began to work. What he saw answered his question. Romy Winner was quite simply a genius with a camera. Images assailed his senses. The scenery was incredible, the wildlife exotic. Her pictures of the Criolla ponies were extraordinary. She had captured some amusing shots of the wedding guests, but nothing cruel, though she *had* caught out some of the most pompous in less than flattering moments. She'd taken a lot of pictures of the staff too, and it was those shots that really told a story. Perhaps because more expression could be shown on faces that hadn't been stitched into place, he reflected dryly as Romy continued to sort and select her images.

She'd made him smile. Another first, he mused as she turned to him.

'Well?' she said. 'Do you like what you see?'

'I like them,' he confirmed. 'Show me what else you've got.'

'There's about a thousand more.'

'I'm in no hurry.' For maybe the first time in his life.

'Why don't you pull up a chair?' she suggested. 'Just let me know if there any images you don't feel are suitable for the charity.'

'So I'm your editor now?' he remarked, with some amusement after her earlier comment about censorship.

'No,' she said mildly. 'You're a client I want to please.'

He inclined his head in acknowledgement of this. He could think of a million ways she could please him. When she turned back to her work he thought the nape of her neck extremely vulnerable and appealing, just for starters. He considered dropping a kiss on the peachy flesh, and then decided no. Once he'd tasted her...

'What do you think of these?' she said, distracting him.

'Grace is very beautiful,' he said as he stared at Romy's shots of the bride. He could see that his new sister-in-law was exquisite, like some beautifully fashioned piece of china. But did Grace move him? Did she make his blood race? He admired Grace as he might admire some priceless *objet d'art*, but it was Romy who heated his blood.

'She is beautiful, isn't she?' Romy agreed, with a warmth in her voice he had never noticed before. She certainly didn't use that voice when she spoke to him.

And why should he care?

Because for the first time in his life he found himself missing the attentions of a woman, and perhaps because he was still stung, after Romy's enthusiastic response to their lovemaking, that she wasn't telling him how she thrilled and throbbed, and all the other things his partners were usually at such pains to tell him. Had Romy Winner simply feasted on him and moved on? If she had, it would be the first time any woman had turned the tables on him.

'This is the sort of shot my editor loves,' she said as she brought a picture of him up on the screen.

'Why is that?'

'Because you're so elusive,' she explained. 'You're hardly ever photographed. I'll make a lot from this,' she added with a pleased note in her voice.

Was he nothing but a commodity?

'Though what I'd *like* to do,' she explained, 'is give it to the charity. So, much as I'd like to make some money out of you, you can have this one *gratis.*'

As she turned to him he felt like laughing. She was so honest, he felt…uncomfortable. 'Thank you,' he said with a guarded expression. 'If you've just taken a couple of shots of me you can keep the rest. '

'What makes you think I'd want to take more than one?' *Youch.*

What, indeed? He shrugged and even managed to smile at that.

Romy Winner intrigued him. He had grown up with women telling him he was the best and that they couldn't get enough of him. He'd grown up fighting for approval as the youngest of four highly skilled, highly intelligent brothers. When he couldn't beat Nacho as a youth he had turned to darker pursuits—in which, naturally, he had excelled—until Nacho had finally knocked some sense into him. Then Harvard had beckoned, encouraging him to stretch what Nacho referred to as the most important muscle in his body: the brain. After college he had found the ideal outlet for his energy and tirelessly competitive nature in the army.

'There,' Romy said, jolting him back from these musings. 'You're finished.'

'I wouldn't be too sure of that,' he said, leaning in close to study her edited version. He noticed again how lithe and strong she was, and how easy it would be to pull her into his arms.

'I have a deadline,' she said, getting back to work.

'Go right ahead.' He settled back to watch her.

The huge press coach was closing in on her, and all the tiny hairs on the back of her neck were standing erect at the thought of Kruz just a short distance away. She could hear him breathing. She could smell his warm, sexy scent. Some very interesting clenching of her interior muscles suggested she was going to have to concentrate really hard if she was going to get any work done.

'Could you pass me that kitbag?' she said, without risking turning round. She needed a new memory card and didn't want to brush past him.

Her breath hitched as their fingers touched and that touch wiped all sensible thought from her head. All she could think about now was what they had done and what they could do again.

Work!

She pulled herself back to attention with difficulty, but even as she worked she dreamed, while her body throbbed and yearned, setting up a nagging ache that distracted her.

'Shall I put this other memory card in the pocket for you?' Kruz suggested.

She realised then that she had clenched her hand over it. 'Yes—thank you.'

His fingers were firm as they brushed hers again, and that set up more distracting twinges and delicious little aftershocks. Would she ever be able to live normally again?

Not if she kept remembering what Kruz had done—and so expertly.

Her mind was in turmoil. Every nerve-ending in her body felt as if it had been jangled. And all he'd done was brush her hand!

Somehow she got through to the end of the editing process and was ready to show him what she'd got. She ran through the images, giving a commentary like one stranger informing another about this work, and even while Kruz seemed genuinely interested and even impressed she felt his aloofness. Perhaps he thought she was a heartless bitch after enjoying him so fully and so vigorously. Perhaps he thought she took *what* she wanted *when* she wanted. Perhaps he was right. Perhaps they deserved each other.

So why this yearning ache inside her?

Because she wanted things she couldn't have, Romy reasoned, bringing up a group photograph of the Acostas on the screen. They were such a tight-knit family...

'Are you sure you want to give me all these shots?'

'Concerned, Kruz?' she said, staring at him wryly. 'Don't worry about me. I've kept more than enough shots back.'

'I'd better see the ones you're giving me again.'

'Okay. No problem.' She ran through them again, just for the dangerous pleasure of having Kruz lean in close. She had never felt like this before—so aware, alert and aroused. It was like being hunted by the hunter she would most like to be caught by.

'These are excellent,' Kruz commented. 'I'm sure Grace can only be thrilled when she hears the reaction of people to these photographs.'

'Thank you. I hope so,' she said, concentrating on the screen. Grace's wedding was the first romantic project she had worked on. Romy was better known as a scandal queen. And that was one of the more polite epithets she'd heard tossed her way.

'This one I can't take,' Kruz insisted when she flashed up another image on the screen. 'You have to make *some* money,' he reminded her.

Was this a test? Was he paying her off? Or was that her insecurity speaking? He might just be making a kindly gesture, and she maybe should let him.

She shook her head. 'I can't sell this one,' she said quietly. 'I want you to have it.'

The picture in question showed Kruz sharing a smile with his sister, Lucia. It was a rare and special moment between siblings, and it belonged to them alone—not the general public. It was a moment in time that told a story about Nacho's success at bringing up his brothers and sister while he was still very young. They would see that when they studied it, just as she had. She wouldn't dream of selling something like that.

'Frame it and you'll always have a reminder of what a wonderful family you have.'

Why was she doing this for him? Kruz wondered suspiciously. He eased his shoulders restlessly, realising that Romy had stirred feelings in him he hadn't experienced since his parents were alive. He stared at her, trying to work out why. She was fierce and passionate one moment, aloof and withdrawn the next. He might even call her cold. He couldn't pretend he understood her, but he'd like to—and that was definitely a first.

'Thank you,' he said, accepting the gift. 'I appreciate it.'

'I'll make a copy for Lucia as well,' she offered, getting back to work.

'I know my sister will appreciate that.' After Lucia had picked herself off the floor because he'd given her a gift outside of her birthday or Christmas.

The tension between them had subsided with this return to business. He was Romy's client and she was his photographer—an excellent photographer. Her photographs revealed so much about other people, while the woman behind the lens guarded her inner self like a sphinx.

DAMN. She was going to cry if she didn't stop looking at images of Grace and Nacho. So that was what love looked like...

'Shall we move on?' she said briskly, because Kruz seemed in no hurry to bring the viewing session to an end. She was deeply affected by some of the shots she had captured of the bridal couple, and that wasn't helpful right now. Since she was a child she had felt the need to protect her inner self. Drawing a big, thick safety curtain around herself rather than staring at an impossible dream on the screen would be her action of choice right now.

'That was a heavy sigh,' Kruz commented.

She shrugged, neither wanting nor able to confide in him. 'I just need to do a little more work,' she said. 'That's if you'll let me stay to do it?' she added, turning to face him, knowing it could only be a matter of minutes before they went their separate ways.

This was the moment she had been dreading and yet she needed him to go, Romy realised. Staring at those photographs of Grace and Nacho had only underlined the fact that her own life was going nowhere.

'Here,' she said, handing over the memory stick. 'These are

for you and for the charity. You *will* keep that special shot?'
she said, her chest tightening at the thought that Kruz might
think nothing of it.

'So I can stare at myself?' he suggested, slanting her a
half-smile.

'So you can look at your family,' she corrected him, 'and
feel their love.'

Did he *have* to stare at her so intently? She wished he
wouldn't. It made her uncomfortable. She didn't know what
Kruz expected from her.

'What?' she said, when he continued to stare.

'I never took you for an emotional woman,' he said.

'Because I'm not,' she countered, but her breath caught in
her throat, calling her a liar. The French called this a *coup de
foudre*—a thunderbolt. She had no explanation for the longing inside her except to say Kruz had turned her life inside
out. It made no sense. They hardly knew each other outside
of sex. They didn't know if they could trust each other, and
they had no shared history. They had everything to learn
about each other and no time to do so. And why would Kruz
want to know more about her?

They could be friends, maybe...

Friends? She almost laughed out loud at this naïve suggestion from a subconscious that hadn't learned much in her
twenty-four years of life. Romy Winner and Kruz Acosta?
Ms Frost and Señor Ice? Taking time out to get to know each
other? To *really* get to know each other? The idea was so
preposterous she wasn't going to waste another second on
it. She'd settle for maintaining a truce between them long
enough for her to leave Argentina in one piece with her camera.

'Thanks for this,' Kruz said, angling his stubble-shaded
chin as he slipped the memory stick into his pocket.

She felt lost when he turned to go—something else she
would have to get used to. She had to get over him. She'd

leave love at first sight to those who believed in it. As far as she was concerned love at first sight was a load of bull. Lust at first sight, maybe. Lack of self-control, certainly.

Her throat squeezed tight when he reached the door and turned to look at her.

'How are you planning to get back to England, Romy?'

'The same way I arrived, I guess,' she said wryly.

'Did you bring much luggage with you?'

'Just the essentials.' She glanced at her kitbag, where everything she'd brought to Argentina was stashed. 'Why do you ask?'

'My jet's flying to London tomorrow and there are still a few spare places, if you're stuck.'

Did he mean stuck as in unprepared? Did he think she was so irresponsible? Maybe he thought she was an opportunist who seized the moment and thought nothing more about it?

'I bought a return ticket,' she said, just short of tongue in cheek. 'But thanks for the offer.'

Kruz shrugged, but as he was about to go through the door he paused. 'You're passing up the chance to take some exclusive shots of the young royals—'

'So be it,' she said. 'I wouldn't dream of intruding on their privacy.'

'Romy Winner passing up a scoop?'

'What you're suggesting sounds more like a cheap thrill for an amateur,' she retorted, stung by his poor opinion of her. 'When celebrities or royals are out in public it's a different matter.'

Kruz made a calming motion with his hands.

'I *am* calm,' she said, raging with frustration at the thought that they had shared so much yet knew so little about each other. Kruz had tagged her with the label paparazzi the first moment he'd caught sight of her—as someone who would do anything it took to get her shots. Even have sex with Kruz Acosta, presumably, if that was what was required.

'Romy—'

'What?' she flashed defensively.

'You seem…angry?' Kruz suggested dryly.

She huffed, as if she didn't care what he thought, but even so her gaze was drawn to his mouth. 'I just wonder what type of photographer you think I am,' she said, shaking her head.

'A very good one, from what I've seen today, Señorita Winner,' Kruz said softly, completely disarming her.

'*Gracias*,' she said, firming her jaw as they stared at each other.

And now Kruz should leave. And she should stay where she was—at the back of the coach, as far away from him as possible, with a desk, a chair and most of the coach seats between them.

She waited for him to go, to close the door behind him and bring this madness to an end.

He didn't go.

Leaning over the driver's seat, Kruz hit the master switch and the lights dimmed, and then he walked down the aisle towards her.

CHAPTER FOUR

THEY COLLIDED SOMEWHERE in the middle and there was a tangle of arms and moans and tongues and heated breathing.

She kicked off her boots as Kruz slipped his fingers beneath the waistband of her jeans. The button sprang free and the zipper was down, the fabric skimming over her hips like silk, so that now she was wearing only her jacket, the white vest and her ridiculously insubstantial briefs. Kruz ripped them off. Somehow the fact that she was partly clothed made what was happening even more erotic. There was only one area that needed attention and they both knew it.

Her breathing had grown frantic, and it became even more hectic when she heard foil rip. She was working hectically on Kruz's belt and could feel his erection pressing thick and hard against her hand. She gasped with relief as she released him. She was getting better at this, she registered dazedly, though her brain was still scrambled and she was gasping for breath. Kruz, on the other hand, was breathing steadily, like a man who knew exactly where he was going and how to get there. His control turned her on. He was a rock-solid promise of release and satisfaction, delivered in the most efficient way

'Wrap your legs around me, Romy,' he commanded as he lifted her.

Kruz's movements were measured and certain, while she was a wild, feverish mess. She did as he said, and as she clung to him he whipped his hand across the desk, clearing a space for her. She groaned with anticipation as he moved between her legs. The sensation was building to an incredible pitch. She cried out encouragement as he positioned her, his rough hands firm on her buttocks just the way she liked them. Pressing her knees back, he stared into her eyes. Pleasure guaranteed, she thought, reaching up to lace her fingers through his hair, binding him to her.

This time...this one last time. And then never again.

She was so ready for him, so hungry. As Kruz sank deep, shock, pleasure, relief, eagerness, all combined to help her reach the goal. Thrusting firmly, he seemed to feel the same urgency, but then he found his control and began to tease her. Withdrawing slowly, he entered her again in the way she loved. The sensation was incredible and she couldn't hold on. She fell violently, noisily, conscious only of her own pleasure until the waves had subsided a little, when she was finally able to remember that this was for both of them. Tightening her muscles, she left Kruz in no doubt that she wasn't a silent partner but a full participant.

He smiled into her eyes and pressed her back against the desk. Wherever she took him he took her one level higher. Pinning her hands above her head, he held her hips firmly in place with his other hand as he took her hard and fast. There was no finesse and only one required outcome, and understanding the power she had over him excited her. Grabbing his arms, she rocked with him, welcoming each thrust as Kruz encouraged her in his own language. Within moments she was flying high in a galaxy composed entirely of light, with only Kruz's strong embrace to keep her safe.

It was afterwards that was awkward, Romy realised as she pulled on her jeans. When they were together they were as close as two people could be—trusting, caring, encouraging, pleasuring. But now they were apart all that evaporated, disappeared almost immediately. Kruz had already sorted out his clothes and was heading for the door. They could have been two strangers who, having fallen to earth, had landed in a place neither of them recognised.

'The seat on the jet is still available if you need it,' he said, pausing at the door.

She worked harder than ever to appear nonchalant. If she looked at Kruz, really looked at him, she would want him to stay and might even say so.

'I won't be stuck,' she said, assuming an air of confidence. 'But thanks again for the offer. And don't forget I'm only an e-mail away if you ever need any more shots from the wedding.'

'And only round the corner when I get to London,' he said opening the door.

What the hell...? She pretended not to understand. Say anything at all and her cool façade would shatter into a million pieces. When tears threatened she bit them back. She wasn't going to ask Kruz if they would meet up in London. This wasn't a date. It was a heated encounter in the press coach. And now it was nothing.

'I'll put the lights on for you,' he said, killing her yearning for one last meaningful look from Kruz.

'That would be great. Thank you.' She was proud of herself for saying this without expression. She was proud of remaining cool and detached. 'I've got quite a bit of work left to do.'

'I'll leave you to it, then,' he said. 'It's been a pleasure, Romy.'

Her head shot up. Was he mocking her?

Kruz was mocking both of them, Romy realised, seeing the tug at one corner of his mouth.

'Me too,' she called casually. After all, this was just another day in the life of a South American playboy. It didn't matter how much her heart ached because Kruz had gone, leaving her with just the flickering images of him on a computer screen for company.

* * *

Glancing back, he saw Romy through the window of the coach. She was poring over the monitor screen as if nothing had happened. She certainly wasn't watching him go. She was no clinging vine. It irked him. His male ego had taken a severe hit. He was used to women trying to pin him down, asking him when they'd meet again—if he'd call them—could they have his number? Romy didn't seem remotely bothered.

The wedding party was still in full swing as he approached the marquee. He rounded up his team, heard their reports and supervised the change-over for the next shift. All of these were measurable activities, which were a blessed relief after his encounter with the impossible-to-classify woman he'd left working in the press coach.

The woman he still wanted

Yeah, that one, he thought.

The noise coming from the marquee was boisterous, joyous, celebratory. Shadows flitted to and fro across the gently billowing tent, silhouettes jouncing crazily from side to side as the music rose and fell.

And Romy was on her own in the press coach.

So what? She was safe there. He'd get someone to check up on her later.

Stopping dead in his tracks, he swung round to look back the way he'd come. He'd send one of the men to make sure she made it to the bunkhouse safely.

Really?

Okay, so maybe he'd do that himself.

Romy shot up. Hearing a sound in the darkness, she was instantly awake. Reaching for the light on the nightstand, she switched it on. And breathed a sigh of relief.

'Sorry if I woke you,' the other girl said, stumbling over the end of the bed as she tried to kick off her shoes, unzip her dress and tumble onto the bed all at the same time. 'Jane

Harlot, foreign correspondent for *Frenzy* magazine—pleased to meet you.'

'Romy Winner for *ROCK!*'

Jane stretched out a hand and missed completely. 'Brilliant—I love your pictures. Harlot's not my real name,' Jane managed, before slamming a hand over her mouth. 'Sorry—too much to drink. Never could resist a challenge, even when it comes from a group of old men who look as if they have pickled their bodies in alcohol to preserve them.'

'Here, let me help you,' Romy offered, recognising a disaster in the making. Swinging her legs over the side of the bed, she quickly unzipped her new roomie's dress. 'Did you have a good time?'

'Too good,' Jane confessed, shimmying out of the red silk clingy number. 'Those gauchos really know how to drink. But they're chivalrous too. One of them insisted on accompanying me to the press coach and actually waited outside while I sent my copy so he could escort me back here.'

'He waited for you outside the press coach?'

'Of course outside,' Jane said, laughing. 'He was about ninety. And, anyway, it didn't take me long to send my stuff. What I write is basically a comic strip. You know the sort of thing—scandal, slebs, stinking rich people. I only got a look-in because my dad used to work with one of the reporters who got an official invitation and he brought me in as his assistant.'

Looking alarmed at this point, Jane waved a hand, keeping the other hand firmly clamped over her mouth.

Jane had landed a big scoop, and Romy was hardly in a position to criticise the other girl's methods. This wasn't a profession for shrinking violets. The Acostas had nothing to worry about, but some of their guests definitely did, she reflected, remembering those prominent personalities she had noticed attending the wedding with the wrong partner.

'Are you sure you're okay?' she asked with concern as Jane got up and staggered in the general direction of the bathroom.

'Fine…I'll sleep it off on the plane going home. The gauchos said their boss has places going spare on his private jet tomorrow, so I'll be travelling with the young royals, no less. And I'll be collected from here and taken to the airstrip in a limo. I'll be in the lap of luxury one minute and my crummy old office the next.'

'That's great—enjoy it while you can,' Romy called out, trying to convince herself that this was a good thing, that she was in fact *Saint* Romy and thoroughly thrilled for Jane, and didn't mind at all that the man she'd had sex with hadn't even bothered to see her back to the bunkhouse safely.

He stayed on post until the lights went out in the bunkhouse and he was satisfied Romy was safely tucked up in bed. Pulling away from the fencepost, it occurred to him that against the odds his caring instinct seemed to have survived. But before he could read too much into that he factored his security business into the mix. Plus he had a sister. Before Lucia had got together with Luke he had always hoped someone would keep an eye on her when he wasn't around. Why should he be any different where a girl like Romy was concerned?

London. Monday morning. The office. Grey skies. Cold. Bleak. Dark-clad people racing back and forth across the rainswept street outside her window, heads down, shoulders hunched against the bitter wind.

It might as well be raining inside, Romy thought, shivering convulsively in her tiny cupboard of an office. It was so cold.

She was cold inside and out, Romy reflected, hugging herself. She was back at work, which normally she loved, but today she couldn't settle, because all she could think about was Kruz. And what was the point in that? She should do something worthwhile to make her forget him.

Something like *this*, Romy thought some time later, poring over the finished version of Grace Acosta's wedding journal. She had added a Braille commentary beside each photograph, so that Grace could explain each picture as she shared the journal. Romy had worried about the space the Braille might take up at first but, putting herself in Grace's place, had known it was the right thing to do.

Sitting back, she smiled. She had been looking forward to this moment for so long—the moment when she could hand over the finished journal to Grace. She wasn't completely freelance yet, though this tiny office at *ROCK!* had housed many notable freelance photographers at the start of their careers and Romy dreamed of following in their footsteps. She hoped this first, really important commission for Grace would be the key to helping her on her way, and that she could make a business out of telling stories with pictures instead of pandering to the insatiable appetite for scandal. Maybe she could tell real stories about real people with her photographs—family celebrations, local news, romance—

Romance?

Yes. Romance, Romy thought, setting her mouth in a stubborn line.

Excuse me for asking the obvious, but what exactly do you know about romance?

As her inner critic didn't seem to know when to be quiet, she answered firmly: *In the absence of romance in my own life, my mind is a blank sheet upon which I will be able to record the happy moments in other people's lives.*

Gathering up her work, Romy headed for the editing suite run by the magazine's reining emperor of visuals: Ronald Smith. *ROCK!* relied on photographs for impact, which made the editor one of the most influential people in the building.

'Ronald,' Romy said, acknowledging her boss as she walked into his hushed and perfumed sanctum.

'Well? What have you got for me, princess?' Ronald demanded, lowering his *faux*-tortoiseshell of-the-moment spectacles down his surgically enhanced nose.

'Some images to blow your socks off,' she said mildly.

'Show me,' Ronald ordered.

Romy stalled as she arranged her images on the viewing table. There was no variety. Why hadn't she seen that before?

Possibly because she had given the best images to Kruz?

Ronald was understandably disappointed. 'This seems to be a series of shots of the waiting staff,' he said, raising his head to pin her with a questioning stare.

'They had the most interesting faces.'

'I hope our readers agrèe,' Ronald said wearily, returning to studying the images Romy had set out for him. 'It seems to me you've creamed off the best shots for yourself, and that's not like you, Romy.'

A rising sense of dread hit her as Ronald removed his glasses to pinch the bridge of his nose. She needed this job. She needed the financial security and she hated letting Ronald down.

'I can't believe,' he began, 'that I send you to Argentina and you return with nothing more than half a dozen shots I can use—and not one of them of the newly married couple in the bridal suite.'

Romy huffed with frustration. Ronald really had gone too far this time. 'What did you expect? Was I supposed to swing in through their window on a vine?'

'You do whatever it takes,' he insisted. 'You do what you're famous for, Romy.'

Intruding where she wasn't wanted? Was that to be her mark on history?

'It was you who assured me you had an in to this wedding,' Ronald went on. 'When *ROCK!* was refused representation at the ceremony I felt confident that you would capture something special for us. I can't believe you've let us down. I wouldn't have given you time off for this adventure if I had known you would return with precisely nothing. You're not freelance yet, Romy,' he said, echoing her own troubled thoughts. 'But the way you're heading you'll be freelancing sooner than you want to be.'

She was only as good as her last assignment, and Ronald wouldn't forget this. She had to try and make things right. 'I must have missed something,' she said, her brain racing to find a solution. 'Let me go back and check my computer again—'

'I think you better had,' Ronald agreed. 'But not now. You look all in.'

Sympathy from Ronald was the last thing she had expected and guilty tears stung her eyes. She didn't deserve Ronald's concern. 'You're right,' she said, pulling herself together. 'Jet-lag has wiped me out. I should have waited until tomorrow. I'm sorry I've wasted your time.'

'You haven't wasted my time,' Ronald insisted. 'You just haven't shown me anything commercial—anything I can use.'

'I'm confident I can get hold of some more shots. Just give me chance to look. I don't want to disappoint you.'

'It would be the first time that you have,' Romy's editor pointed out. 'But first I want you to promise that you'll leave early today and try to get some rest.'

'I will,' she said, feeling worse than ever when she saw the expression on Ronald's face.

Actually, she did feel a bit under the weather. And to put the cap on her day she had grown a nice crop of spots. 'I won't let you down,' she said, turning at the door.

'Oh, I almost forgot,' Ronald said, glancing up from the viewing table. 'There's someone waiting for you in your office.'

Some hopeful intern, Romy guessed, no doubt waiting in breathless anticipation for a few words of encouragement from the once notorious and now about to be sacked Romy Winner. She pinned a smile to her face. No matter that she felt like a wrung-out rag and her only specialism today was projecting misery and failure, she would find those words of encouragement whatever it took.

Hurrying along the corridors of power on the fifth floor, she headed for the elevators and her lowly cupboard in the basement. She could spare Ronald some shots from Grace's folder. Crisis averted. She just had to sort them out. She should have sorted them out long before now.

But she hadn't because her head was full of Kruz.

'Thank you,' she muttered as her inner voice stated the obvious. Actually, the real reason was because she was still jet-lagged. She hadn't travelled home in a luxurious private jet but in cattle class, with her knees on her chin in an aging commercial plane.

And whose fault was that?

'Oh, shut up,' Romy said out loud, to the consternation of her fellow travellers in the elevator.

The steel doors slid open on a different world. Gone were the cutting edge bleached oak floors of the executive level, the pale ecru paint, the state-of-the-art lighting specifically designed to draw attention to the carefully hung covers of *ROCK!* In the place of artwork, on this lowly, worker bee level was a spaghetti tangle of exposed pipework that had nothing to do with minimalist design and everything to do with neglect. A narrow avenue of peeling paint, graffiti and lino led to the door of her trash tip of a cupboard.

Stop! Breathe deeply. Pin smile to face. Open door to greet lowly, hopeful intern—

Or not!

'Language, Romy,' Kruz cautioned.

Had she said a bad word? Had she even spoken? 'Sorry,' she said with an awkward gesture. 'I'm just surprised to see you.' *To put it mildly.*

It took her a moment to rejig her thoughts. She had been wearing her most encouraging smile, anticipating an intern waiting eagerly where she had once stood, hoping for a word of encouragement to send her on her way. Romy had been lucky enough to get that word, and had been determined that whoever wanted to see her today would receive some encouragement too. She doubted Kruz needed any.

So forget the encouraging word.

Okay, then.

Standing by the chipped and shabby table that passed for her desk, Kruz Acosta, in all his business-suited magnificence, accessorised with a stone-faced stare and an overabundance of muscle, was toying with some discarded images she had printed out, scrunched up and had been meaning to toss.

They were all of him.

CHAPTER FIVE

OKAY, SHE COULD handle this. She had to handle this. Whatever Kruz was here for *it wasn't her.*

She had to make sure he didn't leave with the impression that he had intimidated her.

And how was she going to achieve that with her heart racing off the scale?

She was going to remain calm, hold her head up high and meet him on equal ground.

'I like your office, Romy,' he murmured, in the sexy, faintly mocking voice she remembered only too well. 'Do all the executives at *ROCK!* get quite so much space?'

'Okay, okay,' she said, closing this down before he could get started. 'So space is at a premium in the city.'

The smile crept from Kruz's mouth to his eyes, which had a corresponding effect on her own expression. That was half the trouble—it was hard to remain angry with him for long. She guessed Kruz probably had the top floor of a skyscraper to himself, with a helipad as the cherry on top.

'What can I do for you, Kruz?' she said, proud of how cool she sounded.

So many things. Which was why he'd decided to call by. His office was just around the corner. And he'd needed to… to take a look at some more photographs, he remembered, jolting his mind back into gear.

'Those shots you gave me for the charity,' he said, producing the memory stick Romy had given him back in Argentina.

'What about them?' she said.

She had backed herself into the furthest corner of the room, with the desk between them like a shield. In a room as small as this he could still reach her, but he was content just to look at her. She smelled so good, so young and fresh, and she looked great. 'The shots you gave me are fantastic,' he admitted. 'So much so I'd like to see what else you've got.'

'Oh,' she said.

Was she blinking with relief? Romy could act nonchalant all she liked, but he had a sister and he knew all about acting. He took in her working outfit—the clinging leggings, flat fur boots, the long tee—and as she approached the desk and sat down he concluded that she didn't need to try hard to look great. Romy Winner was one hell of a woman. Was she ready for him now? he wondered as she bit down on her lip.

'We've decided the charity should have a calendar,' he said, 'and we thought you could help. What you've given me so far are mostly people shots, which are great—but there are too many celebrities. And the royals... Great shots, but they're not what we need.'

'What do you want?' she said.

'Those character studies of people who've worked on the *estancia* for most of their lives. Group shots used to be taken in the old days, as well as individual portraits, and that's a tradition I'd like to revive. You make everyone look like members of the same family, which is how I've always seen it.'

'Team Acosta?' she suggested, the shadow of a smile creeping onto her lips.

'Exactly,' he agreed. He was glad he didn't have to spell it out to her. On reflection, he didn't have to spell anything out for Romy. She *got* him.

'What about scenery, wildlife—that sort of thing?' she said, turning to her screen.

'Perfect. I think we're going to make one hell of a calendar,' he enthused as she brought up some amazing images.

Hallelujah! She could hardly believe her luck. This was incredible. She wouldn't lose her job after all. Of course a charity would want vistas and wildlife images, while Ronald wanted all the shots Kruz wanted to discard. She hadn't been thinking straight in Argentina—*for some reason*—and had loaded pictures into files without thinking things through.

'So you don't mind if I have the people shots back?' she confirmed, wondering if it was possible to overdose on Kruz's drugging scent.

'Not at all,' he said, in the low, sexy drawl that made her wish she'd bothered to put some make-up on this morning, gelled her hair and covered her spots.

'You look tired, Romy,' he added as she started loading images onto a clean memory stick. 'You don't have to do this now. I can come back later.'

'Better you stay so you're sure you get what you want,' she said.

'Okay, I will,' he said, hiding his wry smile. 'Thanks for doing this at such short notice.'

She couldn't deny she was puzzled. He was happy to stay? Either Kruz wanted this calendar really badly, or he was... what? Checking up on her? Checking her out?

Not the latter, Romy concluded. Kruz could have anyone he wanted, and London was chock-a-block full of beautiful women. Hard luck for her, when she still wanted him and felt connected to him in a way she couldn't explain.

Fact: what happened in the press coach is history. Get used to it.

With a sigh she lifted her shoulders and dropped them again in response to her oh, so sensible inner voice. Wiping a hand across her forehead, she wondered if it was hot in here.

'Are you okay?' Kruz asked with concern.

No. She felt faint. Another first. 'Of course,' she said brightly, getting back to her work.

The tiny room was buzzing with Kruz's energy, she thought—which was the only reason her head was spinning. She stopped to take a swig of water from the plastic bottle on her desk, but she still didn't feel that great.

'Will you excuse me for a moment?' she said shakily, blundering to her feet.

She didn't wait to hear Kruz's answer. Rushing from the desk, she just made it to the rest room in time to be heartily sick.

It was just a reaction at having her underground bunker invaded by Kruz Acosta, Romy reasoned as she studied the green sheen on her face. Swilling her face with cold water, she took a drink and several deep breaths before heading back to her room—and she only did that when she was absolutely certain that the brief moment of weakness had been and gone.

He was worried about Romy. She looked pale.

'No... No, I'm fine,' she said when he asked her if she was all right as she breezed back into the room. 'Must have been something I ate. Sorry. You don't need to hear that.'

He shrugged. 'I was brought up on a farm. I'm not as rarefied as you seem to think.'

'Not rarefied at all,' she said, flashing him a glance that jolted him back to a grassy bank and a blue-black sky.

'It's hot in here,' he observed. No wonder she felt faint. Opening the door, he stuck a chair in the way. Not that it did much good. The basement air was stale. He hated the claustrophobic surroundings.

'Why don't you sit and relax while I do this?' she suggested, without turning from the screen.

'It won't take long, will it?'

She shook her head.

'Then I'll stand, thank you.'

In the tiny room that meant he was standing close behind

her. He was close enough to watch Romy's neck flush as pink as her cheeks.

With arousal? With awareness of him?

He doubted it was a response to the images she was bringing up on the screen.

He felt a matching surge of interest. Even under the harsh strip-light Romy's skin looked as temptingly soft as a peach. And her birdwing-black hair, which she hadn't bothered to gel today, was enticingly thick and silky. A cluster of fat, glossy curls caressed her neck and softened her un-made-up face…

She was lovely.

She felt better, so there was no reason for this raised heartbeat apart from Kruz. Normally she could lose herself in work, but not today. He was such a presence in the small, dingy room—such a presence in her life. Shaking her head, she gave a wry smile.

'Is something amusing you?' he said.

'No,' she said, leaning closer to the screen, as if the answer to her amusement lay there. There was nothing amusing about her thoughts. She should be ashamed, not smiling asininely as it occurred to her that she had never seen Kruz close up in the light other than through her camera. Of course she knew to her cost that close up he was an incredible force. She was feeling something of that now. She could liken it to being close to a soft-pawed predator, never being quite sure when it would pounce and somehow—insanely—longing for that moment.

'There. All done,' she said in a brisk tone, swinging round to face him.

It was a shock to find him staring at her as if his thoughts hadn't all been of business. Confusion flooded her. Confusion wasn't something she was familiar with—except when Kruz was around. The expression in his eyes didn't help her to regain her composure. Kruz had the most incredible eyes.

They were dark and compelling, and he had the longest eyelashes she'd ever seen.

'These are excellent,' he said, distracting her. 'When you've copied them to a memory stick you'll keep copies on your computer, I presume?'

'Yes, of course,' she said, struggling to put her mind in gear and match him with her business plan going forward. 'They're all in a file, so if you want more, or you lose them, just ask me.' *For anything,* she thought.

'And you can supply whatever I need?'

She hesitated before answering, and turning back to the screen flicked through the images one more time. 'Are you pleased?'

'I'm very pleased,' Kruz confirmed.

Even now he'd pulled back he couldn't get that far away, and he was close enough to make her ears tingle. She kept her gaze on the monitor, not trusting herself to look round. This was not Romy Winner, thick-skinned photojournalist, but someone who felt as self-conscious as a teenager on her first date. But she wasn't a kid, and this wasn't a date. This was the man she'd had sex with after knowing him for around half an hour. When thousands of miles divided them she could just about live with that, but when Kruz was here in her office—

'Your compositions are really good, Romy.'

She exhaled shakily, wondering if it was only she who could feel the electricity between them.

'These shots are perfect for the calendar,' he went on, apparently immune to all the things she was feeling.

She logged off, wanting him to go now, so her wounded heart would get half a chance to heal.

'And on behalf of the family,' Kruz was saying. 'I'm asking you to handle this project for us.'

She swung round. Wiping a hand across her face, she wondered what she'd missed.

'That's if you've got time?' Kruz said, seeming faintly

amused as he stared down at her. 'And don't worry—my office is just around the corner, so I'll be your liaison in London.'

Don't worry?

Her heart was thundering as he went on.

'I'd like to see a mock-up of the calendar when you've completed it. I don't foresee any problems, just so long as you remember that quality is all-important when it comes to the Acosta charity.'

Her head was reeling. Was she hearing straight? The Acosta family was giving her the break she had longed for? She couldn't think straight for all the emotion bursting inside her. She had to concentrate really hard to take in everything Kruz was telling her. A commission for the Acosta family? What better start could she have?

Something that didn't potentially tie her in to Kruz?

She mustn't think about that now. She just had to say yes before she lost it completely.

'No,' she blurted, as the consequences of seeing Kruz again and again and again sank in. 'I'd love to do it, but—'

'But what?' he said with surprise.

Answering his question meant looking into that amazing face. And she could do that. But to keep on seeing Kruz day after day, knowing she meant nothing to him... That would be too demoralising even to contemplate. 'I'd love to do it,' she said honestly, feeling her spirit sag as she began to destroy her chances of doing so, 'but I don't have time. I'm really sorry, Kruz, but I'm just too tied up here—'

'Enjoying the security that comes with working for one of the top magazines?' he interrupted, glancing round. 'I can see it would take guts to take time out from *this*.'

She wasn't in the mood for his mockery.

'No worries,' he said, smiling faintly as he moved towards the door. 'I'll just tell Grace you can't find the time to do it.'

'Grace?' she said.

'Grace is our new patron. It was Grace who suggested I approach you—but I'm sure there are plenty of other photographers who can do the job.'

Ouch!

'Wait—'

Kruz paused with his hand on the door. She remembered those hands from the grassy bank and from the press coach, and she remembered what they were capable of. Shivering with longing, she folded her arms around her waist and hugged herself tight.

'Well?' Kruz prompted. 'What am I going to say to Grace? Do you have a message for her, Romy?'

How could she let Grace down? Grace was trying to help her. They had had a long talk when Romy had first arrived in Argentina. Grace had been so easy to talk to that Romy had found herself pouring out her hopes and dreams for the future. She had never done that with anyone before, but somehow her words came easily when she was with Grace. Maybe Grace's gentle nature had allowed her to lower her guard for once.

'I'll do it,' she said quietly.

'Good,' Kruz confirmed, as if he had known she would all along.

She should be imagining her relief when he closed the door behind him rather than wishing he would stay so they could discuss this some more—so she could keep him here until they shared more than just memories of hot sex on someone else's wedding day.

'Romy? You don't seem as pleased about this work as I expected you to be.'

She flushed as Kruz's gaze skimmed over her body. 'Of course I'm pleased.'

'So I can tell Grace you'll do this for her?'

'I'd rather tell her myself.'

Kruz's powerful shoulders eased in a shrug. 'As you wish.'

There was still nothing for her on that stony face, but she

was hardly known for shows of emotion herself. Like Kruz, she preferred to be the one in control. A further idea chilled her as they locked stares. Romy's control came from childhood, when showing emotion would only have made things worse for her mother. When her father was in one of his rages she'd just had to wait quietly until he was out of the way before she could go to look after her mother, or he'd go for her too, and then she'd be in no state to help. Control was just as important to Kruz, which prompted the question: what dark secret was he hiding?

Romy worked off her passions at the gym in the kickboxing ring, where she found the discipline integral to martial arts steadying. Maybe Kruz found the same. His instinctive and measured response to her roundhouse kick pointed to someone for whom keeping his feelings in check was a way of life.

The only time she had lost it was in Argentina, Romy reflected, when something inside her had snapped. *The Kruz effect?* All those years of training and learning how to govern her emotions had been lost in one passionate encounter.

She covered this disturbing thought with the blandest of questions. 'Is that everything?'

'For now.'

Ice meets ice—today. In Argentina they had been on fire for each other. But theirs was a business relationship now, Romy reminded herself as Kruz prepared to leave. She had to stop thinking about being crushed against his hard body, the minty taste of his sexy mouth, or the sweet, nagging ache that had decided to lodge itself for the duration of his visit at the apex of her thighs. If he knew about that she'd be in real trouble.

'It's been good to see you again,' she said, as if to test her conviction that she was capable of keeping up this cool act.

'Romy,' Kruz said, acknowledging her with a dip of his head and just the slightest glint of humour in his eyes.

The Acosta brothers weren't exactly known for being monks. Kruz was simply being polite and friendly. 'It will be good to be in regular contact with Grace,' she said, moving off her chair to show him out.

'Talking of which…' He paused outside her door.

'Yes?' She tried to appear nonchalant, but she felt faint again.

'We're holding a benefit on Saturday night for the charity, at one of the London hotels. Grace will be there, and I thought it would be a great opportunity for you two to get together and for you to meet my family so you can understand what the charity means to us. That's if you're interested?' he said wryly.

She stared into Kruz's eyes, trying to work out his motive for asking her. Was it purely business, or something else…?

His weary sigh jolted her back to the present. 'When you're ready?' he prompted, staring pointedly at his watch.

'Saturday…?'

'Yes or no?'

He said it with about as much enthusiasm as if he were booking the local plumber to sort out a blocked drain. 'Thank you,' she said formally. 'As you say, it's too good a chance to miss—seeing Grace and the rest of your family.'

'I'm glad to hear it. There may be more work coming your way if the calendar is a success. A newsletter, for example.'

'That's a great idea. Shall I bring my camera?'

'Leave it behind this time,' Kruz suggested, his dark glance flickering over her as he named the hotel where they were to meet.

She couldn't pretend not to be impressed.

'Dress up,' he said.

She gave him a look that said no one told her what to wear. But on this occasion it wasn't about her. This was for Grace. She still felt a bit mulish—if only because Kruz was the type of man she guessed liked his women served up fancy, with all the trimmings. Elusive as he was, she'd seen a couple of shots of him with society beauties, and though he had looked bored on each occasion the girls had been immaculately groomed. But, in fairness to the women, the only time she'd seen Kruz animated was in the throes of passion.

'Something funny?' he said.

'I'll wear my best party dress,' she promised him with a straight face.

'Saturday,' he said, straightening up to his full imposing height. 'I'll pick you up your place at eight.'

Her eyes widened. She had thought he'd meet her at the hotel. Was she Kruz's *date?*

No, stupid. He's just making sure you don't change your mind and let The Family down.

'That's fine by me,' she confirmed. 'Before you go I'll jot my address down for you.'

He almost cracked a smile. 'Have you forgotten what business I'm in?'

Okay, Señor Control-Freak-Security-Supremo. Point taken.

Her address was no secret anyway, Romy reasoned, telling herself to calm down. 'Eight o' clock,' she said, holding Kruz's mocking stare in a steady beam.

'Until Saturday, Romy.'

'Kruz.'

She only realised when she'd closed the door behind him and her legs almost gave way that she was shaking. Leaning back against the peeling paintwork, she waited until Kruz's footsteps had died away and there was nothing to disrupt the silence apart from the hum of the fluorescent light.

This was ridiculous, she told herself some time later. She was being everything she had sworn never to be. She had allowed herself to become a victim of her own overstretched heart.

There was only one cure for this, Romy decided, and she

would find it when she worked out her frustrations in the ring at the gym tonight. Meanwhile she would lose herself in work. Maybe tonight she would be better giving the punch-bag a workout rather than taking on a sparring partner. She didn't trust herself with a living, breathing opponent in her present mood. And she needed the gym. She needed to rebalance her confidence levels before Saturday. She wanted to feel her strength and rejoice in it—her strength of will, in particular. She had to remember that she was strong and successful and independent and safe—and she planned to keep it that way. She especially had to remember that on Saturday.

Saturday!

What the hell was she going to wear?

CHAPTER SIX

'LOOKING HOT,' ONE of the guys said in passing, throwing a wry smile her way as Romy finished her final set of blows on the punch-bag.

The bag must have taken worse in its time, but it had surely never taken a longer or more fearsomely sustained attack from a small angry woman with more frustration to burn off than she could handle. Romy nodded her head in acknowledgement of the praise. This gym wasn't a place for designer-clad bunnies to scope each other out. This was a serious working gym, where many of the individuals went on to have successful careers in their chosen sport.

'What's eating you, Romy?' demanded the grizzled old coach who ran the place, showing more insight into Romy's bruised and battered psyche than her fellow athlete as Romy rested, panting, with her still gloved hands braced on her knees. 'Man trouble?'

You know me too well, she thought, though she denied it. 'You know me, Charlie,' she said, straightening up. 'Have camera, will travel. No man gets in the way of that.'

'I bet that camera's cosy to snuggle up to on a cold night,' Charlie murmured in an undertone as he moved on to oversee the action in another part of his kingdom.

What did Charlie know? What did *anyone* know? Romy scowled as she caught sight of herself in one of the gym's full-length mirrors. What man in his right mind would want a sweating firebrand with more energy than sense? *Kruz wouldn't.* With her bandaged hands, bitten nails, boy's shorts and clinging, unflattering vest, she looked about as appealing as a wet Sunday. She probably smelled great too. Taking a step back, she nodded her thanks as another athlete offered to help her with the gloves.

'Looking fierce,' he said.

'Ain't that the truth?' Romy murmured. She was a proper princess, complete with grubby sweatband holding her electro-static hair off her surly, sweaty face.

He saw her the moment he walked into the gym. Or rather something drew his stare to her. She felt him too. Even with her back turned he saw a quiver of awareness ripple down her spine. And now she was swinging slowly round, as if she had to confirm her hunch was correct.

We have to stop meeting like this, he thought as they stared at each other. He nodded curtly. Romy nodded back. Yet again rather than looking at him, like other women, Romy Winner was staring at him as if she was trying to psych him out before they entered the ring.

That could be arranged too, he reflected.

They were still giving each other the hard stare when the elderly owner of the gym came up to him. 'Hey, Charlie.' He turned, throwing his towel round his neck so he could extend a hand to greet an old friend warmly.

'You've spotted our lady champion, I see,' Charlie commented.

Kruz turned back to stare at Romy. 'I've seen her.'

Romy had finished her routine. He was about to start his. She looked terrific. It would be rude not to speak to her.

Oh... Argh! What the...?

Romy blenched. For goodness' sake, how could anyone look *that* good? Kruz was ridiculously handsome. And what the hell was he doing in *her* gym? Wasn't there somewhere billionaire health freaks could hang out together and leave lesser mortals alone to feel good about themselves a few times a week?

Even with the unforgiving lights of the workmanlike sports hall blazing down on him Kruz looked hot. Tall, tanned and broader than the other men sharing his space, he drew attention like nothing else. And he was coming over—oh, *good*. Even a warrior woman needed to shower occasionally, and Kruz was as fresh as a daisy.

Gym kit suited him, she decided as he advanced. With his confident stroll and those scars and tattoos showing beneath his skimpy top he was a fine sight. She wanted him all over again. If she'd never met him before she'd want him. And, inconveniently, she wanted him twice as much as she ever had. A quick glance around reassured Romy that she wasn't the only one staring. She couldn't blame the gym members for that. Muscles bunched beneath his ripped and faded top, and the casual training pants hung off his hips. Silently, she whimpered.

And Kruz didn't walk, he prowled, Romy reflected, holding her ground as he closed the distance between them. His pace was unhurried but remorseless and, brave as she was, she felt her throat dry—it was about the only part of her that was.

'We meet again,' he said with some amusement, stopping tantalisingly within touching distance.

'I didn't expect it to be so soon,' she said off-handedly, reaching for a towel just as someone else picked it up.

'Here—have this. I can always grab another.'

'I couldn't possibly—'

Kruz tossed his towel around her neck. Taking the edges, she wrapped it round her shoulders like a cloak. It still held his warmth.

'So you're really serious about the gym?' he said.

'I like to break sweat,' she agreed, shooting him a level

stare as if daring him to find fault with that. 'Why haven't I seen you here before?' she said as an afterthought. 'You slumming it?'

'Please,' Kruz murmured. 'My office is only round the corner.'

'And you don't have a gym?' she said, opening her eyes wide with mock surprise.

'It's under construction,' he said, giving her the cynical look he was so good at.

'I'm impressed,' she said.

'You should be.'

If only that crease in his cheek wasn't so attractive. 'Maybe I'll come and take a look at it when it's finished.'

'I might hold you to that.'

Please. 'I'm very busy,' she said dryly, still holding the dark, compelling stare. 'I have a very demanding private client.'

Kruz's eyes narrowed as he held her gaze. 'I hope I know him.'

'I think you do. So, how do you know Charlie?' she said, seizing on the first thing that came to mind to break the stare-off between them.

'Charlie's an old friend,' Kruz explained, pulling back.

'Were you both in the army?' she asked on a hunch.

'Same regiment,' Kruz confirmed, but then he went quiet and the smile died in his eyes. 'I'd better get started,' he said.

'And I'd better go take my shower,' she agreed as they parted.

'Don't miss the fun,' Charlie called after her.

'What fun?'

'Don't miss Kruz in the ring.'

She turned to look at him.

'Why don't you come in the ring with me?' Kruz suggested. 'You could be my second.'

'Sorry. I don't do second.'

He laughed. 'Or you could fight me,' he suggested.

'Do I look stupid? Don't answer that,' she said quickly, holding up her hands as Kruz shot her a look.

This was actually turning out better than she had thought when she'd first seen Kruz walk into the gym. They were sparring in good way—verbally teasing each other—and she liked that. It made her feel warm inside.

Charlie caught up with her on the way to the changing rooms. 'Don't be too hard on him, Romy.'

'Who are we talking about? Kruz?'

'You know who we're talking about,' the old pro said, glancing around to make sure they weren't being overheard. 'Believe me, Romy, you have no idea what that man's been through.'

'No, I don't,' she agreed. 'I don't know anything about him. Why would I?'

Did Charlie know anything? Had Kruz said something? Her antennae were twitching on full alert.

'You should know what he's done for his friends,' Charlie went on, speaking out of the corner of his mouth. 'The lives he's saved—the things he's seen.'

The guarded expression left her face. This was the longest speech she had ever heard Charlie make. There was no doubt in her mind Charlie was sincere, and she felt reassured that Kruz hadn't said anything about their encounter to him. 'I don't think Kruz wants anyone to go easy on him,' she said thoughtfully, 'but I'll certainly bear in mind what you've said.'

Charlie shook his head in mock disapproval. 'You're a hard woman, Romy Winner. You two deserve each other.'

'Now, that's something I have to disagree with,' Romy said, lightening up. 'You just don't know your clientele, Charlie. Shame on you.' She smiled as she gave Charlie a wink.

'I know them better than you think,' Charlie muttered beneath his breath as Romy shouldered her way into the women's changing room. 'Go take that shower, then join me ringside,' he called after her.

Romy rushed through her shower, emptying a whole bottle of shower gel over her glowing body before lathering her hair with a half a bottle of shampoo. The white tiled floor in the utilitarian shower block was like a skating rink by the time she had finished. Thank goodness her hair was short, she reflected, frantically towelling down. She didn't want to miss a second of this bout. She stared at herself in the mirror. Make-up? Her eyes were bright enough with excitement and her cheeks were flushed. Tugging on her leggings, her flat boots and grey hoodie, she swung her gym bag on to her shoulder and went to join the crowd assembling around the ring at the far end of the gym.

The scent of clean sweat mingled with anticipation came to greet her. This was her sort of party.

'Quite a crowd,' she remarked to Charlie, feeling her heart lurch as Kruz vaulted the ropes into the ring. When he turned to look at her, her heart went crazy. Naked to the waist, Kruz was so hot her body couldn't wait to remind her about getting up close and personal with him. She pressed her thighs together, willing the feeling to subside. No such luck. As Kruz turned his back and she saw his muscles flex the pulse only grew stronger.

'It's not often we get two champions in the ring—even here at my gym,' Charlie said, his scratchy voice tense with anticipation.

The other kick-boxer was a visitor from the north of England called Heath Stamp. He'd been a bad boy too, according to rumour, and Romy knew him by reputation as a formidable fighter. But Heath was nothing compared to Kruz in her eyes. Kruz's hard, bronzed body gleamed with energy beneath the lights. He was a man in the peak of health, just approaching his prime.

A man with the potential to happily service a harem of women.

'Stop,' she said out loud, in the hope of silencing her inner voice.

'Did you say something, Romy?' Charlie enquired politely, cupping his ear.

'No—just a reminder to myself,' she said dryly.

'There's no one else the champ can spar with,' Charlie confided, without allowing his attention to be deflected for a second from the ring.

'Lucky Kruz came along, then.'

'I'm talking about Kruz,' Charlie rebuked her. 'Kruz is the champ. I should know. I trained him in the army.'

She turned to stare at the rapt face of the elderly man standing next to her. He knew more about Kruz than she did. And he would be reluctant to part with a single shred of information unless it was general info like Kruz's exploits in the gym. What *was* it with Charlie today? She'd never seen him so animated. She'd never seen such fierce loyalty in his eyes or heard it in his voice. It made her want to know all those things Kruz kept secret—for he did keep secrets. Of that much she was certain.

So some men were as complex as women, Romy reasoned, telling herself not to make a big deal out of it as the referee brought the two combatants together in the centre of the ring. Kruz was entitled to his privacy as much as she was, and he was lucky to have a loyal friend like Charlie.

As the bout got under way and the onlookers started cheering Romy only had eyes for one man. The skill level was intense, but there was something about Kruz that transcended skill and made him a master. Being a fighter herself, she suspected that he was holding back. She wondered about this, knowing Kruz could have ended the match in Round One if he had wanted to. Instead he chose to see it through until his opponent began to flag, when Kruz called a halt. Proclaiming the match a draw, he bumped the glove of his opponent, raising Heath Stamp's arm high in the air before the referee could say a word about it.

'That's one of the benefits of having a special attachment to this gym,' Kruz explained, laughing when she pulled him up on it as he vaulted the ropes to land at her side.

'A special attachment?' she probed.

'I used to own it,' he revealed casually, his voice muffled as he rubbed his face on a towel.

'You used to own this gym?'

'That's right,' Kruz confirmed, pulling the towel down.

She glanced round, frowning. Charlie was busy consoling the other fighter. She'd known Charlie for a number of years and had always assumed *he* owned the gym. 'I had no idea you were in the leisure industry,' she said, turning back to Kruz.

'Amongst other things.' Grabbing a water bottle from his second, Kruz drank deeply before pouring the rest over his head. 'I own a lot of gyms, Romy.'

'News to me.'

'My apologies,' he said with a wry look. 'I'll make sure my PA puts you on my "needs to know" list right away.'

'See that you do,' she said, with a mock-fierce stare. Were they getting on? Were they *really* getting on?

'So, what are you doing next?' Kruz asked her.

'Going home.'

'What about food?'

'What about it? I'm not hungry.'

'Surely you're over your sickness now?'

'Yes, of course I am.' Actually, she *had* felt queasy again earlier on.

'Hang on while I take a shower,' he said. 'I'll see you in Reception in ten.'

'But—'

That was all she had time for before Kruz headed off. Raking her short hair with frustration, she was left to watch him run the gauntlet of admirers on his way to the men's changing room. Why did he want to eat with her? Or was food not on the menu? Her heart lurched alarmingly at the thought that it might not be. She wasn't about to fall into ever-ready mode. Just because she enjoyed sex with a certain man it did *not* mean Kruz had a supply on tap.

In all probability he just wanted to talk about the charity project, her sensible self reassured her.

And if he didn't want to chat...?

They'd be in a café somewhere. What was the worst that could happen?

They'd leave the food and run?

Clearly the bout had put Kruz in a good mood, Romy concluded as he came through the inner doors into the reception area.

'Ready to go?' he said, holding the door for her.

So far so good. Brownie points for good manners duly awarded.

'There's a place just around the corner,' he said, 'where we can get something to eat.'

'I know it.' He was referring to the café they all called the Greasy Spoon—though nothing could be further from the truth. True enough, it was a no-nonsense feeding station, with bright lights, Formica tables, hard chairs, but there was a really good cook on the grill who served up high-quality ingredients for impatient athletes with colossal appetites.

They found a table in the window. There wasn't much of a view as it was all steamed up. The air-conditioning was an open door at the back of the kitchen.

'Okay here?' Kruz said when they were settled.

'Fine. Thank you.' She refused to be overawed by him— but that wasn't easy when her mind insisted on undressing him.

She was working for the Acosta family now, Romy reminded herself, and she had to concentrate on that. It was just a bit odd, having had the most amazing sex with this man and having to pretend they had not. Kruz seemed to have forgotten all about it—or maybe it was just one more appetite to slake, she reflected as the waitress came to take their order.

'Do you mind if I take a photo of you?' she said, pulling out her phone.

'Why?' Kruz said suspiciously.

'Why the phone? I don't have my camera.'

'Why the photograph?'

'Because you look half human—because this is a great setting—because everyone thinks of the Acostas as rarefied beings who live on a different planet to them. I just want to show people that you do normal things too.'

'Steak and chips?' Kruz suggested wryly, tugging off his heavy jacket.

'Steak and chips,' she agreed, returning his smile. Oh, boy, how that smile of his heated her up. 'You'd better not be laughing at me,' she warned, running off a series of shots.

'Let me see,' he said, holding out his hand for her phone.

'Me first,' she argued. *Wow.* She blew out a slow, controlled breath as she studied the shot. Kruz's thick, slightly too long hair waved and gleamed like mahogany beneath the lights. The way it caught on his sideburns and stubble was...

'Romy?' he said

'Not yet,' she teased. 'You'll have to wait for the newsletter.' *To see those powerful shoulders clad in the softest airforce blue cashmere and those well-packed worn and faded jeans...*

'Romy?' Kruz said, sounding concerned when she went off into her own little dreamworld.

Snap! Snap!

'There. That should do it,' she said, passing the phone across the table.

'Not bad,' Kruz admitted grudgingly. 'You've reminded me I need to shave.'

'Glad to be of service,' she said, blushing furiously half a beat later. Being that type of service was not what she meant, she assured herself sternly as Kruz pushed the phone back to her side of the table.

Fortunately their food arrived, letting her off the hook. She had ordered a Caesar salad with prawn, while Kruz had ordered steak and fries. Both meals were huge. And every bit as delicious as expected.

'This is a great place,' she said, tucking in. As Kruz murmured agreement she made the mistake of glancing at his mouth. Fork suspended, she stared until she realised he was looking at her mouth too. 'Yours good?' she murmured distractedly. Kruz had a really sexy mouth. And an Olympian appetite, she registered as he called for a side of mushrooms, onion rings and a salad to add to his order.

'Something wrong with your meal, Romy?'

'No. It's delicious.' She stared intently at her salad, determined not to be distracted by him again.

Food was a great ice-breaker. It oiled the wheels of conversation better than anything she knew. 'So, tell me more about Charlie's gym. I've been going there for years and I had no idea you used to own it.'

Kruz frowned. 'What do you want to know?'

'I always thought Charlie owned it. Not that it matters,' she said.

'He does own it.' And, when she continued to urge him on with a look of interest, Kruz offered cryptically, 'Things change over time, Romy.'

'Right.' The conversation seemed to have gone the same way as their empty plates. 'Charlie never stopped talking about you,' she said to open it up again. 'He admires you so much, Kruz.'

Personal comments were definitely a no-no, she concluded

as Kruz gave her a flat black look. 'Do you want coffee?' He was already reaching for his wallet. This down-time was over.

'No. I'm fine. Let me get this.'

For once in her life she managed not to fumble and got out a couple of twenties to hand to the waitress before Kruz had a chance to disagree.

He did not look pleased. 'You should not have done that,' he said.

'Why not? Because you're rich and I'm not?'

'Don't be so touchy, Romy.'

She was touchy? 'I'm not touchy,' she protested, standing up. 'Aren't you the guy who's taking me to some swish event on Saturday?' She shrugged. 'The least I can do is buy you dinner.'

'You will be a guest of the family on Saturday,' he said.

Heaven forfend she should mistake it for a date.

'And where Charlie's concerned I'd prefer you don't say anything about the gym to him,' Kruz added. 'That man is not and never has been in my debt. If anything, I'm in his.'

She hadn't anticipated such a speech, and wondered what lay behind it—especially in light of Charlie's words about Kruz. *The plot thickens,* she thought. But as it showed no sign of being solved any time soon she followed Kruz to the door.

'Until Saturday,' he said, barely turning to look at her as he spoke.

Someone was touchy when it came to questions about his past. 'I'll meet you at the hotel,' she said briskly, deciding she really did not want him at her place. She was surprised when he didn't argue.

She watched Kruz thread his way through the congested traffic with easy grace—talking of which, for Grace's sake she would find something other than sweats or leggings to wear on Saturday night. She wanted to do the family proud. She didn't want to stand out for all the wrong reasons. Khalifa's department store was on her way home, so she had no excuse.

In the sale she picked out an understated column of deep blue silk that came somewhere just above her knees. It was quite flattering. The rich blue made her hair seem shinier and brought out the colour of her eyes. No gel or red tips on Saturday, she thought, viewing herself in the mirror. She normally dressed to please herself, but she didn't want to let Grace down. And, okay, maybe she *did* want strut her stuff just a little bit in front of Kruz. This was one occasion when being 'wiry', as Charlie frequently and so unflatteringly referred to her, was actually an advantage. The sale stuff was all in tiny sizes. She even tried on a pair of killer heels—samples, the salesgirl told her.

'That's why they're in the sale,' the girl explained. 'You're the first person who can get her feet into them. They're size Tinkerbell.'

Romy slanted her a smile. 'Tinkerbell suits me fine. I always did like to create a bit of mayhem.'

They both laughed as they took Romy's haul to the till.

'You'll have men flocking,' the girl told her as she rang up Romy's purchases.

'Yeah, right.' And the one man she would like to come flocking would be totally unmoved. 'Thanks for all your help,' Romy said, flashing a goodbye smile as she picked up the bag.

CHAPTER SEVEN

SOMETHING PROPELLED HIM to his feet. Romy had just entered the sumptuously dressed ballroom. He might have known. Animal instinct had driven him to his feet, he acknowledged wryly as that same instinct transferred to his groin. Romy had taken his hint to dress for the occasion, expanding his thoughts as to what she might wear beyond his wildest dreams. Hunger pounded in his eyes as her slanting navy blue gaze found his. Nothing could have prepared him for this level of transformation, or for the way she made him feel. He acted nonchalant as she began to weave her way through the other guests, heading for their table, but with that short blue-black hair, elfin face and the understated silk dress she was easily the most desirable woman in the room.

'Kruz...'

'Romy,' he murmured as she drew to a halt in front of him.

'Allow me introduce you around,' he said, eventually remembering his manners.

His family smiled at Romy and then glanced at him. He was careful to remain stonily impassive. His PA had arranged the place cards so that Romy was seated on the opposite side of the table to him, where he could observe her without the need to engage her in conversation. He had thought he would prefer it that way, but when he saw the way his hot-blooded brothers reacted to her he wasn't so sure.

It was only when it came to the pudding course and Grace

suggested they should all change places that he could breathe easily again.

'So,' he said, settling down in the chair next to Romy, 'what did you and Grace decide about the charity?' The two women hadn't stopped talking all evening and had made an arresting sight, Grace with her refined blond beauty and Romy the cute little gamine at her side.

'We discussed the possibility of a regular newsletter, with lots of photographs to show what we do.'

'We?' he queried.

'Do you want me to own this or not?' Romy parried with a shrewd stare.

'Of course I do. It's important to me that everyone involved feels fully committed to the project.' Surprisingly, he found Romy's business persona incredibly sexy. 'That's how I've found employees like it in the past.'

'I'm not your employee. I work for myself, Kruz.'

'Of course you do,' he said, holding her gaze until her cheeks pinked up.

She was all business now—talking about anything but personal matters. That was what he expected of Romy in this new guise, but it didn't mean he had to like it.

'We also talked about a range of greetings cards to complement the calendar—Kruz, are you listening to me?'

'It sounds as if you and Grace have made a good start,' he said, leaning back in his chair.

The urge to sit with Romy and monopolise her conversation wasn't so much a case of being polite as a hunting imperative. His brothers were still sitting annoyingly close to her, though in fairness she didn't seem to notice them.

She was so aroused she was finding it embarrassing. Her cheeks were flushed and she didn't even dare to look down to see if her ever-ready nipples were trying to thrust their way through the flimsy silk. She couldn't breathe properly while she was sitting this close to Kruz—she couldn't think.

She could only feel. And there was a lot of feeling going on. Her lips felt full, her eyes felt sultry. Her breasts felt heavy. And her nipples were outrageously erect. *There*. She knew she shouldn't have looked. Her breathing was super-fast, and she felt swollen and needy and—

'More wine, madam?'

'No, thank you,' she managed to squeak out. She'd hardly touched the first glass. Who needed stimulus when Kruz Acosta was sitting next to her?

'Would you like to dance?'

She gaped at the question and Kruz raised a brow.

'It's quite a simple question,' he pointed out, 'and all you have to say is yes or no.'

For once in her life she couldn't say anything at all. The table was emptying around them. Everyone was on their feet, dirty-dancing to a heady South American beat. The dance floor was packed. Kruz was only being polite, she reasoned. And she could hardly refuse him without appearing rude.

'Okay,' she said, trying for off-hand as she left the table.

There was only one problem here—her legs felt like jelly and sensation had gathered where it shouldn't, rivalling the music with a compelling pulse. Worse, Kruz was staring knowingly into her eyes. He didn't need to say a word. She was already remembering a grassy bank beneath a night sky in Argentina and a press coach rocking. His touch on her back was all the more frustrating for being light. They had around six inches of dance floor to play in and Kruz seemed determined they would use only half those inches. Pressed up hard against him, she was left wondering if she could lose control right here, right now. The way sensation was mounting inside her made that seem not only possible but extremely probable.

'Are you all right, Romy?' Kruz asked.

She heard the strand of amusement in his voice. He knew, damn him! 'Depends what you mean by all right?' she said.

Somehow she managed to get through the rest of the dance

without incident, and neither of them spoke a word on their way back to the table. The palm of Kruz's hand felt warm on her back, and maybe that soothed her into a dream state, for the next thing she knew he had led her on past the table, through the exit and on towards the elevators.

They stood without explanation, movement or speech as the small, luxuriously upholstered cabin rose swiftly towards one of the higher floors. She didn't mean to stare at it, but there was a cosy-looking banquette built into one side of the restricted space. She guessed it was a thoughtful gesture by the hotel for some of its older guests. Generously padded and upholstered in crimson velvet, the banquette was exerting a strangely hypnotic effect on her—that and the mirror on the opposite side.

She sucked in a swift, shocked breath as Kruz stopped the elevator between floors.

'No…' she breathed.

'Too much of a cliché?' he suggested, with that wicked grin she loved curving his mouth.

They came together like a force of nature. It took all he'd got to hold Romy off long enough for him to protect them both. Remembering the last time, when she had wrenched the shirt from his pants, he kept her hands pinned above her head as he kissed her, pressing her hard against the wall. She tasted fresh and clean and young and perfect—all the things he was not. His stubble scraped her as he buried his face in her neck and her lips were already bruised. Inhaling deeply, he kissed her below the ear for the sheer pleasure of feeling tremors course through her body. His hands moved quickly to cup the sweet remembered swell of her buttocks.

This was everything he remembered, only better. Her skin was silky-smooth. His rough hands were full of her. In spite of being so tiny she had curves in all the right places and she fitted him perfectly. Lodging one thigh between her legs, he moved her dress up to her waist and brought her lacy underwear down. 'Wrap your legs around me, Romy,' he ordered, positioning her on the very edge of the banquette.

Pressing her knees back, he stared down as he tested that she was ready. This was the first time he had seen her—really seen her—and she was more than ready. Those tremors had travelled due south and were gripping her insistently now.

'Oh, please,' she gasped, holding her thighs wide for him.

She alternated her pleas to him with glances in the mirror, where he knew the sight of him ready and more than willing to do what both of them needed so badly really turned her on. He obliged by running the tip of his straining erection against her. She panted and mewled as she tried to thrust her hips towards him to capture more. He had her in a firm grasp, and though he was equally hungry it pleased him to make her wait.

'What do you want?' he murmured against her mouth, teasing her with his tongue.

He should have known Romy Winner would tell him, in no uncertain language. With a laugh he sank deep, and rested a moment while she uttered a series of panting cries.

'Good?' he enquired softly.

Her answer was to groan as she threw her head back. Withdrawing slowly, he sank again—slowly and to the hilt on this occasion. Some time during that steady assault she turned again to look into the mirror. He did too.

'More,' she whispered, her stare fixed on their reflection.

A couple of firm thrusts and she was there, shrieking as the spasms gripped her, almost bouncing her off the banquette. The mirror was great for some things, but when it came to this only staring into Romy's eyes did it for him. But even that wasn't enough for them. It wasn't nearly enough, he concluded as Romy clung to him, her inner muscles clenching violently around him. Picking her up, he maintained a steady rhythm as he pressed her back against the wall.

'More,' he agreed, thrusting into her to a steady beat.

'Again,' she demanded, falling almost immediately.

'You're very greedy,' he observed with satisfaction, taking care to sustain her enjoyment for as long as she could take it.

'Your turn now,' she managed fiercely.

'If you insist,' he murmured, determined to bring her with him.

Romy was a challenge no man could resist and he had not the slightest intention of trying. She was hypersensitive and ultra-needy. She was a willing mate and when he was badly in need of someone who could halfway keep up. Romy could more than keep up.

This was special. This was amazing. Kruz was so considerate, so caring. And she had thought the worst of him. She had badly misjudged him, Romy decided as Kruz steadied her on her feet when they had taken their fill of each other. For now.

'Okay?' he murmured.

Pulling her dress down, she nodded. Feeling increasingly self-conscious, she rescued her briefs and pulled them on.

'I'll take you upstairs to freshen up,' Kruz reassured her as she glanced at her hair in the mirror and grimaced.

Kruz was misunderstood, she decided, leaning on him. Yes, he was hard, but only because he'd had to be. But he could be caring too—under the right circumstances.

'Thanks,' she said, feeling the blush of approval spreading to her ears. 'I'd appreciate a bit of tidy-up before I return to the ballroom.'

She had a reputation for being a hard nut too, but not with Kruz...never with Kruz, she mused, staring up at him through the soft filter of afterglow. Maybe after all this time her heart was alive again. Maybe she was actually learning to trust someone...

They exited the elevator and she quickly realised that the Acostas had taken over the whole floor. There were security guards standing ready to open doors for them, but what she presumed must be Kruz's suite turned out to be an office.

'The bathroom's over there,' he said briskly, pointing in the direction as his attention was claimed by a pretty blond woman who was keen to show him something on her screen.

This wasn't embarrassing, Romy thought as people shot covert glances as her as she made her way between the line of desks.

And if she would insist on playing with fire...

Locking herself in the bathroom, she took a deep, steadying breath. When would she ever learn that this was nothing more than sex for Kruz, and that she was nothing more than a feeding station for him? And it was too late to worry about what anyone thought.

Running the shower, she stripped off. Stepping under the steaming water felt like soothing balm. She would wash every trace of Kruz Acosta away and harden her resolve towards him as she did so. But nothing helped to ease the ache inside her. It wasn't sexual frustration eating away at her now. It was something far worse. It was as if a seed had been planted the first time they met, and that seed had not only survived but had grown into love.

Love?

Love. What else would you call this certain feeling? And no wonder she had fallen so hard, Romy reasoned, cutting herself some slack as she stepped out of the shower. Kruz was a force of nature. She'd never met anyone like him before.

She was a grown woman who should have known better than to fall for the charms of a man like Kruz—a man who was in no way going to fall at her feet just because she willed it so.

And maybe this grown woman should have checked that there was a towel in the bathroom before she took a shower?

Romy stared around the smart bathroom in disbelief. There was a hand-dryer and that was it. Of course... The hotel had let this as an office, not a bedroom with *en-suite* bathroom. Wasn't that great? How much better could things get?

'Are you ready to go yet?' Kruz bellowed as he hammered on the door.

Fantastic. So now she was the centre of attention of everyone in the office as they waited for her to come out of the bathroom.

'Almost,' she called out brightly, in her most business-like voice.

Almost? She was standing naked, shivering and dripping all over the floor.

'Couple of minutes,' she added optimistically.

Angling her body beneath a grudging stream of barely warm air wasn't going so well. But there was a grunt from the other side of the door, and retreating footsteps, which she took for a reprieve. Giving up, she called it a day. Slipping on her dress, she ran tense fingers through her mercifully short hair and realised that would have to do. Now all that was left was the walk of shame. Drawing a deep breath, she tilted her chin and opened the door.

Everyone in the office made a point of looking away. *Oh...* She swayed as a wave of faintness washed over her. This was ridiculous. She had never fainted in her life.

'Are you all right, Romy?' Kruz was at her side in an instant with a supporting arm around her shoulders. 'Sit here,' he said, guiding her to a chair when all she longed for was to leave the curious glances far behind. 'I'll get you a glass of water.'

It was a relief when the buzz in the office started up again. She tried to reason away her moment of frailty. She'd hardly drunk anything at the dinner. Had she eaten something earlier that had disagreed with her?

'I'm fine, honestly,' she insisted as Kruz handed her a plastic cup.

'You're clearly not fine,' he argued firmly, 'and I'm going to call you a cab to take you home.'

'But—'

'In fact, I'm going to take you home,' he amended. 'I can't risk you fainting on the doorstep.'

He was going to take her to the tiny terrace she shared with three other girls in a rundown part of town?

Things really couldn't get any better, could they?

She didn't want Kruz to see where she lived. Her aim was one day to live in a tranquil, picturesque area of London by the canal, but for now it was enough to have a roof over her head. She didn't want to start explaining all this to Kruz, or to reveal where her money went. Her mother's privacy was sacrosanct.

She expected Kruz to frown when he saw where she lived. He had just turned his big off-roader into the 'no-go zone', as some of the cabbies called the area surrounding Romy's lodgings. She sometimes had to let them drop her off a couple of streets away, where it was safer for them, and she'd walk the rest of the way home. She wasn't worried about it. She could look after herself. This might look bad to Kruz, but it was home for her as it was for a lot of people.

'What are you doing living here, Romy?'

Here we go. 'Something wrong with it?' she challenged.

Kruz didn't answer. He didn't need to. His face said it all—which was too bad for him. She didn't have to explain herself. She didn't want Kruz Acosta—or anyone else, for that matter—feeling sorry for her. This was something she had chosen to do—*had* to do—took pride in doing. If she couldn't look after her family, what was left?

Stopping the car, Kruz prepared to get out.

'No,' she said. 'I'm fine from here. We're right outside the front door.'

'I'm seeing you in,' he said, and before she could argue with this he was out of the car and slamming the door behind him. Opening her door, he stood waiting. 'This isn't up for discussion,' he growled when she hesitated.

Was anything where Kruz was concerned?

CHAPTER EIGHT

ROMY HAD GOT to him when no one else could.

So why Romy Winner?

Good question, Kruz reflected as he turned the wheel to leave the street where Romy lived. As he joined the wide, brilliantly lit road that led back to the glitter of Park Lane, one of London's classiest addresses, he thought about his office back at the hotel and wondered why he hadn't asked one of his staff to drive her home.

Because Romy was his responsibility. Why make any more of it?

Because seeing her safely through her front door had been vital for him.

Finding out where she lived had been quite a shock. He might have expected her to live in a bohemian area, or even an area on the up, but in the backstreets of a nowhere riddled with crime…?

He was more worried than ever about her now. In spite of Romy's protestations she had still looked pale and faint to him. The kick-ass girl had seemed vulnerable suddenly. The pint-sized warrior wasn't as tough as she thought she was. Which made him feel like a klutz for seducing her in the elevator—even if, to be fair, he had been as much seduced as seducer.

Forgetting sex—*if he could for a moment*—why did Romy live on the wrong side of the tracks when she must make plenty of money? She was one of the most successful photo-journalists of her generation. So what was she doing with all the money she earned?

And now, in spite of all his good intentions, as he drew the off-roader to a halt outside the hotel's grandiose pillared entrance, all he could think about was Romy, and how she had left him hungry for more.

She was a free spirit, like him, so why not?

Handing over his keys to the hotel valet, he reasoned that neither of them was interested in emotional ties, but seeing Romy on a more regular basis, as Grace had suggested, would certainly add a little spice to his time in London. His senses went on the rampage at this thought. If Romy hadn't been under par this evening he wouldn't be coming back here on his own now.

She was sick on Monday morning. Violently, sickeningly sick. Crawling back into bed, she pulled the covers over her head and closed her eyes, willing the nausea to go away. She had cleaned her teeth and swilled with mouthwash, but she could still taste bile in her throat.

Thank goodness her housemates had both had early starts that morning, Romy reflected, crawling out of bed some time later. She couldn't make it into work. Not yet, at least. Curling up on the battered sofa in front of the radiator, still in her dressing gown, she groaned as she nursed a cup of mint tea, which was all she could stomach after the latest in a series of hectic trips to the bathroom.

She couldn't be... She absolutely couldn't be—

She wouldn't even think the word. She refused to voice it. She could not be pregnant. Kruz had always used protection.

She had obviously eaten something that disagreed with her. She must have. She had that same light-headed, bilious feeling that came after eating dodgy food.

Dodgy food at one of London's leading hotels? How likely

was that? The Greasy Spoon was famously beyond reproach, and she was Mrs Disinfectant in the kitchen...

Well, *something* had made her feel this way, Romy argued stubbornly as she crunched without enthusiasm on a piece of dry toast.

A glance at the clock reminded her that she didn't have time to sit around feeling sorry for herself; she had a photoshoot with the young star of a reality show this morning, and the greedy maw of *ROCK!* magazine's picture section, infamously steered by Ronald the Remorseless, wouldn't wait.

Neither would the latest invoice for her mother's nursing care, Romy reflected with concern as she left the house. She had already planned her day around a visit to the nursing home, where she checked regularly on all those things her mother was no longer able to sort out for herself. She had no time to fret. She just had to get on and stop worrying about the improbability of two people who had undergone the same emotional bypass coming together to form a new life.

But...

Okay, so there was a chemist just shy of the *ROCK!* office block.

Dragging in the scent of clean and bright air, Romy assured herself that her visit to the chemist was essential to life, as she needed to stock up on cold and flu remedies. There was quite a lot of that about at the moment. Grabbing a basket, she absentmindedly popped in a pack of handwipes, a box of tissues, some hairgrips—which she never used—and a torch.

Well, you never know.

Making her way to the counter, she hovered in front of the *'Do you Think you Could be Pregnant?'* section, hoping someone else might push in front of her. Finally palming a pregnancy test, with a look on her face which she hoped suggested that she was very kindly doing it for a friend, she glanced around to make sure there was no one she knew in the shop before approaching the counter. As she reached for her purse the pharmacist came over to help.

'Do you have a quick-fire cure for a stomach upset?' Romy enquired brightly, pushing her purchases towards the woman, with the telltale blue and white box well hidden beneath the other packages.

'Nausea?' the pharmacist asked pleasantly. 'You're not pregnant, are you?' she added, filleting the pile to extract the box containing the pregnancy test with all the sleight of hand of a Pick-up-Sticks champion.

'Of course not.' Romy laughed a little too loudly.

'Are you sure?' The woman's gaze was kind and steady, but her glance did keep slipping to the blue and white packet, which had somehow slithered its way to centre stage. 'I have to know before I can give you any medication...'

'Oh, that's just for a friend,' Romy said, feeling her cheeks blaze.

Meanwhile the queue behind her was growing, and several people were coughing loudly, or tutting.

'I think we'd better err on the side of caution,' the helpful young pharmacist said, reaching behind her to pick up some more packages. 'There are several brands of pregnancy test—'

'I'll take all of them,' Romy blurted.

'And will you come back for the nausea remedy?' the woman called after her. 'There are some that pregnant women can take—'

Then let those pregnant women take them, Romy thought, gasping with relief as she shut the door of the shop behind her. How ridiculous was this? She didn't even have the courage to buy what she wanted from a chemist now.

'Someone's waiting for you in your office,' the receptionist told her as she walked back into the building.

Not Kruz. Not now. 'Who?' she said warily.

'Kruz Acosta,' the girl said brightly. 'He was here a couple of days ago, wasn't he? Aren't you the lucky one?'

'I certainly am,' Romy agreed darkly. Girding her loins, she headed for the basement.

'Weren't you with him the other night?' someone else chipped in when she stepped into the crowded elevator. 'Great shot of you on the front page of the *West End Chronicle*, Romy,' someone else chirruped. 'In fact, both you and Kruz look amazing...'

General giggling greeted this.

'Can I see?' She leaned over the shoulder of the first girl to look at the newspaper she was holding.

OMG!

'Oh, that was just a charity thing I attended,' she explained off-handedly, feeling sicker than ever now she'd seen the shot of her and Kruz, slipping not as discreetly as they had thought into the elevator. Kruz's hand on her back and the expression on her face as she stared up at him both told a very eloquent story. And now there was the type of tension in the lift that suggested the slightest comment from anyone and all the girls would burst out laughing. The banner headline hardly helped: *'Are You Ready for Your Close-Up, Ms Winner?'*

Was that libellous? Romy wondered.

Better not to make a fuss, she concluded, reading on.

'Who doesn't envy Romy Winner her close encounter with elusive billionaire bad-boy Kruz Acosta? Kruz, the only unmarried brother of the four notorious polo-playing Acostas brothers—'

Groaning, she leaned her head against the back of the lift. She didn't need to read any more to know this was almost certainly the reason Kruz was here to see her now. He must hold her wholly responsible for the press coverage. He probably thought she'd set it up. But it took two to tango, Romy reminded herself as she got out of the elevator and strode purposefully towards her cubbyhole.

Breath left her lungs in a rush when she opened the door. Would she *ever* get used to the sight of this man? 'Kruz, I'm—'

'Fantastic!' he exclaimed vigorously. 'How are you this morning, Señorita Winner? Better, I hope?'

'Er…' *Maybe pregnant…maybe not.* 'Good. Thank you,' she said firmly, as if she had to convince herself.

Slipping off her coat, she hung it on the back of the office door. Careful not to touch Kruz, she sidled round the desk. Dumping her bag on the floor at her side, she sat in her swivel chair, relieved to have a tangible barrier between them. Kruz was in jeans, a heavy jacket with the collar pulled up and workmanlike boots—a truly pleasing sight. Especially first thing in the morning…

And last thing at night.

And every other time of day.

Waving to the only other chair in the room—a hard-backed rickety number—she invited him to sit down too. And almost passed out when he was forced to swoop down and move her bag. It was one of those tote things that didn't fasten at the top, and all her purchases were bulging out—including a certain blue and white packet.

'I didn't want to knock your bag over,' he explained, frowning when he saw her expression. 'Still not feeling great?'

Clearly blue and white packets held no significance for a man. 'No…I'm fine,' she said.

'Good,' Kruz said, seeming unconvinced. 'I'm very pleased to hear it.'

So why were his lips still pressed in a frown?

And why was she staring at his mouth?

Suddenly super-conscious of her own lips, and how it felt to be kissed by Kruz, she dragged her gaze away. And then remembered the scratch of his stubble on her skin. The marks probably still showed—and she had been too distracted by hormonal stuff this morning to remember to cover them. So everyone had seen them. Double great.

'What can I do for you?' she said.

'You haven't read the article yet?' Kruz queried with surprise.

He made it impossible for her to ignore the scandal sheet as he laid it out on her desk. 'I like the way you went after publicity,' he said.

Was that a glint in his wicked black eyes? She put on a serious act. 'Good,' she said smoothly. 'That's good...'

'The article starts with the usual nonsense about you and me,' he reported, leaning over her desk to point to the relevant passage, 'but then it goes on to devote valuable column inches to the charity.' He looked up, his amused dark eyes plumbing deep. 'I'd like to compliment you on having a colleague standing by.'

'You think I *staged* this?' she exclaimed, mortified that Kruz should imagine she would go to such lengths.

'Well, didn't you?' he said.

There was a touch of hardness in his expression now, and she was acutely conscious of the pregnancy test peeping out of her bag, mocking her desire to finish this embarrassing interview and find out whether she was pregnant or not. There was also a chance that if Kruz caught sight of the test he might think she had set *him* up too. Sick of all the deception, she decided to come clean.

'I'm not sure how that photograph happened,' she admitted, 'other than to say there are always photojournalists on the look-out for a story—especially at big hotels when there's an important event on. I'm afraid I can't claim any credit for it...' She held Kruz's long, considering stare.

'Well, however it happened,' he said, 'it's done the charity no harm at all. So, well done. Hits on our website have rocketed and donations are flooding in.'

'That *is* great news,' she agreed.

'And funny?' he said.

Perhaps it was hormones making want to giggle. She'd heard it said that Romy Winner would stop at nothing to get a story. She had certainly put her back into it this time.

'So you're not offended by the headline?' she said, reverting to business again.

'It amused me,' Kruz confessed.

Well, that wasn't quite what she'd been hoping for. 'Me too,' she said, as if fun in a lift were all part of the job. 'It's all part of the job,' she said out loud, as if to convince herself it were true.

'Great job,' Kruz murmured, cocking his head with the hint of a smile on his mouth.

'Yes,' she said.

'On the strength of the publicity you've generated so far, I'm going to take you to lunch to discuss further strategy.'

Ah. 'Further strategy?' She frowned. 'Lunch at nine-thirty in the morning?'

She was going to visit her mother later. It was the highlight of her day and one she wouldn't miss for the world. It was also something she couldn't share with Kruz.

'We'll meet at one,' he said, turning for the door.

'No. I can't—'

'You have to eat and so do I,' he said.

'I've got a photoshoot,' she remembered with relief. 'And then—' And then she had finished for the day.

'And then you eat,' Kruz said firmly.

'And then I've got personal business.'

'We'll make it supper, then,' he conceded.

By which time she would know. Vivid images of losing control in the elevator flashed into her head—a telling reminder that she had enjoyed sex with Kruz not once, but many times. And it only took one time for a condom to fail.

They exchanged a few more thoughts and comments about

the way forward for the charity, and then Kruz left her to plunge into a day where nothing went smoothly other than Romy's visit to her mother. That was like soothing balm after dealing with a spoiled brat who had screamed for ten types of soda and sweets with all the green ones taken out before she would even consider posing for the camera.

What a day of contrasts it had been, she reflected later. When she held her mother's soft, limp hand everything fell into place, and she gained a sense of perspective, but then it was all quickly lost when she thought about Kruz and the possibility of being pregnant.

He studied the report on Romy with interest. She was certainly good at keeping secrets. But then so was he. At least this explained why Romy lived where she did, and why she worked all hours—often forgetting to eat, according to his sources. Romy was an only child whose father had died in jail after the man had left her mother a living corpse after his final violent attack. Romy was her mother's sole provider, and had been lucky to come out of that house alive.

No wonder she was a loner. The violence she had witnessed as a child should have put her off men for life, but it certainly went some way to explaining why Romy snatched at physical relief whilst shunning anything deeper. There had been brief relationships, but nothing significant. He guessed her ability to trust hovered around zero. Which made *him* the last partner on earth for her—not that he was thinking of making his relationship with Romy anything more than it already was. His capacity for offering a woman more than physical relief was also zero.

They made a good pair, he reflected, flinging the document aside, but it wasn't a good pairing in the way Romy wanted it to be. He'd seen how she looked at him, and for the first time in his life he wished he had something to offer. But he had learned long ago it was only possible to survive, to achieve and to develop, to do any of those things, if emotion was put aside. It was far better, in his opinion, to feel nothing and move forward than look back, remember and break.

CHAPTER NINE

WHAT A CRAZY day. Up. Down. And all points in between.
And it wasn't over yet. The blue and white packet was still
sitting where she had left it on the bathroom shelf, and after
that she had supper with Kruz to look forward to—and no
way of knowing how it would go.

But her meeting with Kruz would be on neutral territory,
Romy reminded herself as she soaped down in the tiny shower
stall back at the house she shared with the other girls. She
would be in public with him. What was the worst that could
happen?

*The reporter from the scandal sheet might track them down
again?*

Kruz had seemed to find that amusing. So why hadn't she?

The thought that Kruz meant so much to her and she didn't
mean a thing to him hurt. She'd never been in this position
before. She'd always been able to control her feelings. She
certainly didn't waste them. She cared for her mother, and
for her friends, but where men were concerned—there were
no men. And now of all the men in the world she'd had to fall
for Kruz Acosta, who had never pretended to be anything
more than an entertaining companion with special skills—a
man who treated sex like food. He needed it. He enjoyed it.
But that didn't mean he remembered it beyond the last meal.

While *she* remembered every detail of what he'd said and
how he'd said it, how he'd looked at her, how he'd touched

her, and how he'd made her feel. It wasn't just sex for the sake of a quick fix for her. It was meaningful. And it had left her defences in tatters.

More fool her.

She was not going slinky tonight, Romy decided in the bedroom. She was going to wear her off-duty uniform of blue jeans, warm sweater and a floppy scarf draped around her neck.

Glancing at her reflection in the mirror, she was satisfied there was nothing provocative about her appearance that Kruz could possibly misinterpret. She looked as if she was going for supper with a friend, which in some ways she was, but first she had something to do—and the sooner she got it over and done with the sooner she would know.

She already knew.

He stood up and felt a thrill as Romy walked into the steak bar. She looked amazing. She always did to him.

'Romy,' he said curtly, hiding those thoughts. 'Good to see you. Please sit down. We've got a lot I'd like to get through tonight, as I'm going to be away for a while. Before I go I need to be sure we're both singing from the same hymn sheet. Red wine or white?'

She looked at him blankly.

'It's a simple question. Red or white?'

'Er—orange juice, please.'

'Whatever you like.' He let it go. Whatever was eating Romy, it couldn't be allowed to get in the way of their discussion tonight. There was a lot he wanted to set straight—like the budgets that she had to work to.

The waiter handed Romy a menu and she began to study it, while he studied her. After reading the report on Romy he understood a lot more about her. He saw the gentleness she hid so well behind the steel, and the capacity for caring above and beyond anything he could ever have imagined. He jerked his gaze away abruptly. He needed this upcoming trip. He needed space from this woman. No one distracted him like Romy, and he had a busy life—polo, the Acosta family interests, *his* business interests. He had no time to spare for a woman.

To make the break he had arranged a tour of his offices worldwide, with a grudge match with Nero Caracas at the end of it to ease any remaining frustration. A battle between his own Band of Brothers polo team and Nero's Assassins would be more than enough to put his life back in focus, he concluded as Romy laid down the menu and stared at him.

'You're going away?' she said.

'Yes,' he confirmed briskly. 'So, if you're ready to order, let's get back to the agenda. We've got a lot to get through tonight.'

The food was good. He ate well.

Romy picked at her meal and seemed preoccupied.

'Do I?' she said when he asked her about it.

She gave a thin smile to the waiter as she accepted a dessert menu. She'd hardly eaten anything.

'Coffee and ice cream?' he suggested when the waiter returned to take their order. 'They make the best of both here. The ice cream's home-made on the premises—fresh cream and raw eggs.'

She blinked. 'Neither, thank you. I think I've got everything I need here,' she said, collecting up her things as if she couldn't wait to go.

'I'll call for the bill.' This was not the ending to the night he had envisaged. Yes, he needed space from Romy—but on his own terms, and to a timetable that suited him.

Business and pleasure don't mix, he reflected wryly as she left the table, heading for the door. When would he ever learn? But, however many miles he put between them, something told him he would never be far enough away from Romy to put her out of his head.

* * *

She guessed shock had made her sick this time. It must be shock. It was only ten o'clock in the evening and she had just brought up every scrap of her picked-over meal. Shock at Kruz going away—just like that, without a word of warning. No explanation at all.

And why would he tell her?

She was nothing to him, Romy realised, shivering as she pulled the patchwork throw off her bed to wrap around her shaking shoulders. She was simply a photographer the Acostas had tasked with providing images for their charitable activities—a photographer who had lost her moral compass on a grassy bank, a press coach and in an elevator. *Classy.* So why hadn't she spoken out tonight? Why hadn't she said something to Kruz? There had been more than one opportunity for her to be straight with him.

About this most important of topics she had to be brutally honest with herself first. This wasn't a business matter she could lightly discuss with Kruz, or even a concern she had about working for the charity. This was a child—a life. This was a new life depending on her to make the right call.

Swivelling her laptop round, she studied the shots she'd taken of Kruz. Not one of them showed a flicker of tenderness or humour. He was a hard, driven man. How would he take the news? She couldn't just blurt out, *You're going to be a daddy,* and expect him to cheer. She wouldn't do that, anyway. The fact that she was having Kruz's baby was so big, so life-changing for both of them, so precious and tender to her, she would choose her moment. She only wished things could be different between them—but wishing didn't make things happen. Actions made things happen, and right now she needed to make money more than she ever had.

As she flicked through the saleable images she hadn't yet offered on the open market, she realised there were plenty— which was a relief. And there were also several elevator shots on the net to hold interest. Thank goodness no one had been around for the grassy bank...

She studied the close-ups of her and Kruz as they had been about to get into the elevator and smiled wryly. They made a cool couple.

And now the cool couple were going to have a baby.

He ground his jaw with impatience as his sister-in-law gave him a hard time. He'd stopped over at the *estancia* in Argentina and appreciated the space. He was no closer to sorting out his feelings for Romy and would have liked more time to do so. The irony of having so many forceful women in one family had not escaped him. Glancing at his wristwatch, he toyed with the idea of inventing a meeting so he had an excuse to end the call.

'Are you still there, Kruz?'

'I'm still here, Grace,' he confirmed. 'But I have pressing engagements.'

'Well, make sure you fit Romy into them,' Grace insisted, in no way deterred.

'I might have to go away again. Can't you liaise with her?'

'And choose which photographs we want to use?'

He swore beneath his breath. 'Forgive me, Grace, but you're in London and I'm not right now.'

'I'll liaise with Romy on one condition,' his wily sister-in-law agreed.

'And that is?' he demanded.

'You see her again and sort things out between you.'

'Can't do that, Grace. Thousands of miles between us,' he pointed out.

'So send for her,' Grace said, as if this were normal practise rather than dramatic in the extreme. 'I've heard the way your voice changes when you talk about Romy. What are you afraid of, Kruz?'

'Me? Afraid?' he scoffed.

'Even men like Nacho have hang-ups—before he met me, that is,' his sister-in-law amended with warmth and humour in her voice. 'Don't let your hang-ups spoil things for you, Kruz. At least speak to her. Promise me?'

He hummed and hawed, and then agreed. What was all the rush about? Romy could just as easily have got in touch with *him*.

Maybe there were reasons?

What reasons?

Maybe her mother was ill. If that were the case he would be concerned for her. Romy's care of her mother was exemplary, according to his investigations. He hadn't thought to ask about her. Grace was right. The least he could do was call Romy and find out.

'Kruz?'

She had to stop hugging the phone as if it were a lifeline. She had to stop analysing every micro-second of his all too impersonal greeting. She had to accept the fact that Kruz was calling her because he wanted to meet for an update on the progress she was making with the banners, posters and fly-ers for the upcoming charity polo match. She had to get real so she could do the job she was being paid to do. This might all be extra to her work for *ROCK!*, but she had no intention of short-changing either the magazine or the Acosta family. She believed in the Acosta charity and she was going to give it everything she'd got.

'Of course we can meet—no, there's no reason why not.' Except her heart was acting up. It was one thing being on the other end of a phone to Kruz, but being in the same room as him, which was what he seemed to be suggesting...

'Can you pack and come tomorrow?'

'Come where?'

'To the *estancia*, of course.'

Shock coursed through her. 'You're calling me from Argentina? When you said you were going away I had no idea you were going to Argentina.'

'Does that make a difference?' Kruz demanded. 'I'll send the jet—what's your problem, Romy?'

You. 'Kruz, I work—'

'You gave me to understand you were almost self-employed now and could please yourself.'

'Sort of...'

'Sort of?' he queried. 'Are you or aren't you? If your boss at *ROCK!* acts up, check to see if you've got some holiday owing. Just take time off and get out here.'

So speaks the wealthy man, Romy thought, flicking quickly through the diary in her mind.

'Romy?' Kruz prompted impatiently. 'Is there a reason why you can't come here tomorrow?'

Pregnant women were allowed to travel, weren't they? 'No,' she said bluntly. 'There's no reason why I can't travel.'

'See you tomorrow.'

She stared at the dead receiver in her hand. To be in Argentina tomorrow might sound perfectly normal to a jet-setting polo player, but even to a newshound like Romy it sounded reckless. And it gave her no chance to prepare her story, she realised, staring at an e-mail from Kruz containing her travel details that had already flashed up on her screen. Not that she needed a story, Romy reassured herself as she scanned the arrangements he had made for her to board his private jet. She would just tell him the truth. Yes, they had used protection, but a condom must have failed.

Sitting back, she tried to regret what had happened—was happening—and couldn't. How could she regret the tiny life inside her? Mapping her stomach with her hands, she realised that all she regretted was wasting her feelings on Kruz—a man who walked in and out of her life at will, leaving her as isolated as she had ever been.

*Like countless other women who had to make do and mend
with what life had dealt them.*

She would just have to make do and mend *this,* Romy
concluded.

Having lost patience with her maudlin meanderings, she
tapped out a brief and businesslike reply to Kruz's e-mail.
She didn't have to sleep with him. She could resist him. It
was just a matter of being sensible. The main thing was to do
a good job for the charity and leave Argentina with her pride
intact. She would find the right moment to tell Kruz about the
baby. They were two civilised human beings and would work
it out. She would be on that flight tomorrow, she would finish
the job Grace had given her, and then she would decide the
way ahead as she always had. Just as she had protected her
mother for as long as she could, she would now protect her
unborn child. And if that meant facing up to Kruz and telling him how things were going to be from here on in, then
that was exactly what she was going to do.

The flight was uneventful. In fact it was soothing compared
to what awaited her, Romy suspected, resting back. She tried
to soothe herself further by reflecting on all the good things
that had happened. She had worked hard to establish herself
as a freelance alongside her magazine work, and her photographs had featured in some of the glossies as the product of
someone who was more than just a member of the paparazzi.
One of her staunchest supporters had turned out to be Ronald,
who had made her cry—baby-head, she realised—when he'd
said that he believed in her talent and expected her to go far.

Well, she was going far now, Romy reflected, blowing out
a long, thoughtful breath as she considered the journey ahead
of her. And as to what lay on the other side of that flight…
She could only guess that this pampering on a private jet,
with freshly squeezed orange juice on tap, designer food and

cream kidskin seats large enough to curl up and snooze on, would be the calm before the storm.

Tracing the curve of her stomach protectively as the jet circled before swooping down to land on the Acostas' private landing strip, Romy felt her heart bump when she spotted the *hacienda*, surrounded by endless miles of green with the mountains beyond. The scenery in this part of Argentina was ravishingly beautiful, and the *hacienda* nestled in its grassy frame in such a favoured spot. Bathed in sunlight, the old stone had turned a glinting shade of molten bronze. The pampas was only a wilderness to those who couldn't see the beauty in miles of fertile grass, or to those with no appreciation of the varied wildlife and birdlife that called this place home.

She craned her neck to catch a glimpse of thundering waterfalls crashing down from the Andes and lazy rivers moving like glittering ribbons towards the sea. It made her smile to see how many horses were grazing on the pampas, and her heart thrilled at the sight of the *gauchos* working amongst the herds of Criolla ponies. They were no more than tiny dots as the jet came in to land, and the ponies soon scattered when they heard the engines. She wondered if Kruz was among the riders chasing them...

She was pleased to be back.

The realisation surprised her. She must be mad, knowing what lay ahead of her, Romy concluded as the seatbelt sign flashed on, but against all that was logical this felt like coming home.

After flying overnight, she stepped out of the plane into dry heat on a beautifully sunny day. The sky was bright blue and decorated with clouds that looked like cotton wool balls. The scent of grass and blossom was strong, though it was spoiled a little by the tang of aviation fuel. Slipping on her sunglasses, Romy determined that nothing was going to spoil her enjoyment of this visit. This was a fabulous country, with fabulous people, and she couldn't wait to start taking pictures.

There was a *gaucho* standing next to a powerful-looking truck, which he had parked on the grass verge to one side of the airstrip, but there was no sign of Kruz. She should be relieved about that. It would give her time to settle in, Romy reasoned as the weather-beaten *gaucho* came to greet her. He introduced himself as Alessandro, explaining that Kruz was away from the *estancia*.

Would Kruz be away for a long time? Romy wondered, not liking to ask. Anyway, it was good to know that he wasn't crowding her. *But she missed him.*

Hard luck, she thought wryly as the elderly ranch-hand pointed away across the vast sea of grass. Ah, so Kruz wasn't *staying* away—he was out riding on the pampas. Her heart lifted, but then she reasoned that he must have seen the jet coming into land, yet wouldn't put himself out to come and meet her.

That was good, she told herself firmly. No pressure.

No caring, either.

She stood back as Alessandro took charge of her luggage. 'You mustn't lift anything in your condition,' he said.

She blushed furiously. Was her pregnancy so obvious? She was wearing jeans with a broad elastic panel at the front, and over the top of them a baggy T-shirt *and* a fashionable waterfall cardigan, which the salesgirl had assured Romy was guaranteed to hide her small bump. *Wrong,* Romy concluded. If Alessandro could tell she was pregnant, there would be no hiding the fact from Kruz.

Perhaps people were just super tuned-in to nature out here on the pampas, she reflected as Alessandro opened the door of the cab for her and stood back. Climbing in, she sat down. Breathing a sigh of relief as the elderly *gaucho* closed the door, she took a moment to compose herself. The interlude was short-lived. As she turned to smile at Alessandro when he climbed into the driver's seat at her side her heart lurched at the sight of Kruz, riding flat out across the pampas towards them.

It struck her as odd that she had never seen such a renowned horseman riding before, but then they actually knew very little about what made each other tick. At this distance Kruz was little more than a dark shadow, moving like an arrow towards her, but it was as if her heart had told her eyes to look for him and here he was. Her spirits rose as she watched him draw closer. Surely a man who was so at one with nature would be thrilled at the prospect of bringing new life into the world?

So why did she feel so apprehensive?

She should be apprehensive, Romy concluded, nursing her bump. This baby meant everything to her, and she would fight for the right to keep her child with her whatever a powerful man like Kruz Acosta had to say about it, but she couldn't imagine he would make things easy for her.

'And now we wait,' Alessandro said, settling back as he turned off the engine.

He had promised himself he would stay out of Romy's way until the evening, giving her a chance to settle in. He wanted her know she wasn't at the top of his list of priorities for the day. Which clearly explained why he was riding across the pampas now, with his sexual radar on red alert. No one excited him like Romy. No one intrigued him as she did. Life was boring without her, he had discovered. Other women were pallid and far too eager to please him. He had missed Romy's fiery temperament—amongst other things—and the way she never shirked from taking him on.

Reining in, he allowed his stallion to approach the truck at a high-stepping trot. Halting, he dismounted. His senses were already inflamed at the sight of her, sitting in the truck. The moment the jet had appeared in the sky, circling overhead, he had turned for home, knowing an end to his physical ache was at last in sight.

Striding over to the truck, he forgot all his good intentions about remaining cool and threw open the passenger door. 'Romy—'

'Kruz,' she said, seeming to shrink back in her seat.

This was not the reception he had anticipated. And why was she hugging herself like that? 'I'll see you at the house,' he said, speaking to Alessandro. Slamming the passenger door, he slapped the side of the truck and went back to his horse.

He could wait, he told himself as he cantered back to the *hacienda*. The house was empty. He had given the housekeepers the day off. He wanted the space to do with as he liked—to do with Romy as he liked.

He stabled the horse before returning to the house. He found Romy in the kitchen, where Alessandro was pouring her a cold drink. The old man was fussing over her like a mother hen. He had never seen that before.

'Romy is perfectly capable of looking after herself,' he said, tugging off his bandana to wipe the dust of riding from his face.

As Alessandro grunted he took another look at Romy, who was seated at the kitchen table, side on to him. She seemed small—smaller than he remembered—but her jaw was set as if for battle. So be it. After his shower he would be more than happy to accommodate her.

'Journey uncomfortable?' he guessed, knowing how restless *he* became if he was caged in for too enough.

'Not at all,' she said coolly, still without turning to face him.

'I'm going to take a shower,' he said, thinking her rude, 'and then I'll brief you on the photographs Grace wants you to take.'

'Romy needs to rest first.'

He stared at Alessandro. The old man had never spoken to him like that before—had never danced attendance on a woman in all the years he'd known him.

'I'd love a shower too,' Romy said, springing up.

'Fine. See you later at supper,' he snapped, mouthing, *What?* as Alessandro gave him a sharp look. And then, to his amazement, his elderly second-in-command took hold of Romy's bags and led the way out of the kitchen and up the stairs. 'Maria has prepared the front room overlooking the corral,' he yelled after them.

Neither one of them replied.

'What the hell is going on?' he demanded, the moment Alessandro returned.

'You had better ask Señorita Winner that question,' his old *compadre* told him, heading for the door.

'You know—*you* tell me.'

The old *gaucho* answered this with a shrug as he went out through the door.

She shouldn't have left the door to her bedroom open, Romy realised, stirring sleepily. It wasn't wide open, but it was open enough to appear inviting. She had meant to close it, but had fallen asleep on the bed after her shower. Jet-lag and baby-body, she supposed. She needed a siesta these days.

She needed more than that. Holly Acosta had warned her about this phase of pregnancy…hormones running riot…the 'sex-mad phase', Holly had dubbed it, Romy remembered, clutching her pillow as she tried to forget.

Maybe she had left the door open on purpose, Romy concluded as Kruz, still damp from his shower and clad only in a towel, strolled into the room. Maybe she had deluded herself that they could have one last hurrah and then she would tell him. But she had not expected this surge of feeling as her body warmed in greeting. She had not expected Kruz simply to walk into the room expecting sex, or that she would feel quite so ready to oblige him. What had happened to all those bold resolutions about remaining chaste until she had told him about the baby?

She didn't speak. She didn't need to. She just made room for him on the bed. She was well covered in a sheet—which was more than could be said for Kruz. Her throat felt as if it was tied in knots when the towel he had tucked around his waist dropped to the floor.

Settling down on the bed, he kept some tantalising, teasing space between them, while she covered the evidence of her pregnancy with the bedding. Resting on one elbow, he stared into her eyes, and at that moment she would have done anything for him.

Anything.

He toyed with her hair, teasing her with the delay, while she turned her face to brush her lips along his hand. Remembered pleasure was a strong driver—the strongest. She wanted him. She couldn't hide it. She didn't want to. Her body had more needs now than ever before.

'You've put on weight, Romy,' he murmured, suckling on her breasts. 'Don't,' he complained when she tried to stop him, nervous that Kruz might take his interest lower. 'The added weight suits you. I meant it as a compliment.'

Kruz was in a hurry—which was good. She wasn't even sure he noticed the distinct swell of her belly on his way to his destination. She was all sensation…all want and need… with only one goal in mind. She wasn't even sure whether Kruz pressed her legs apart or whether she opened them for him. She only knew that she was resting back on a soft bank of pillows while he held her thighs apart. And when he bent to his task he was so good… Lacing her fingers through his hair, she decided he was a master of seduction—not that she needed much persuasion. He was so skilled. His tongue… His hands… His understanding of her needs and responses was so acute, so knowing, so—

He paused to protect them both. She thought about telling him then, but it would have been ridiculous, and anyway the hunger was raging inside her now. She wanted him. He wanted her. It was a need so deep, so primal, that nothing could stop them now. She groaned as he sank deep. This was so good—it felt so right. Kruz set up a rhythm, which she followed immediately, mirroring his moves, but with more fire, more need, more urgency.

'That's right—come for me, baby.'

She didn't need any encouragement and fell blindly, violently, triumphantly, with screaming, keening, groaning relief. And Kruz kissed her all the while, his strong arms holding her safe as she tumbled fast and hard. His firm mouth softened to whisper of encouragement as he made sure she enjoyed every second of it before he even thought of taking his own pleasure. When he did it raised her erotic temperature again. Just seeing him enjoying her was enough to do that. The pleasure was never-ending, and as wave after wave after wave of almost unbearable sensation washed over her it was Kruz who kept her safe to abandon herself to this unbelievable union of body and soul.

Sensation and emotion combined had to be the most powerful force any human being could tap into, she thought, still groaning with pleasure as she slowly came down. Clinging to Kruz, nestling against his powerful body, left her experiencing feelings so strong, so beautiful, she could hardly believe they were real. She smiled as she kissed him, moving to his shoulders, to his chest, to his neck. After such brutally enjoyable pleasure this was a rare tender moment to treasure. A life-changing moment, she thought as Kruz continued to tend to her needs.

'Romy?'

She sensed the change in him immediately.

'What?' she murmured. But she already knew, and felt a chill run through her when Kruz lifted his head. The look in his eyes told her everything she needed to know. They were black with fury.

'When were you planning to tell me?' he said.

CHAPTER TEN

SHE HAD EVERY reason to hate the condemnation in Kruz's black stare. She loved her child already. Yes, cool, hard, emotionless Romy Winner had turned into a soft, blobby cocoon overnight. But still with warrior tendencies, she realised as she wriggled up the bed. If he wanted a fight she was ready.

Two of them had made this baby, and their child was a precious life she was prepared to defend with her own life. She surprised herself with how immediately her priorities could change. She wasn't alone any more. It would never be just about her again. She was a mother. In hindsight, she had been mad to think Kruz wouldn't notice she was pregnant. The swell of her belly was small, but growing bigger every day, as if the child they'd made together was as proud and strong as its parents.

She was happy to admit her guilt. She *was* guilty of backing away at the first hurdle and not telling Kruz right away. Allowing him to find out like this way was a terrible thing to do. It had been seeing him and forgetting everything in the moment…

'Are you ashamed of the baby?' he said. Springing into a sitting position, he loomed over her, a terrifying powerhouse of suppressed outrage.

Before her mouth had a chance to form words he detached himself from her arms and swung off the bed. Striding across the room, he closed the door on the bathroom and she heard

him run the shower. He was shocked and she was frantic.
Her mind refused to cooperate and tell her what to do next.
She'd really messed up, and now she would be caught in the
whirlwind.

He'd been away, she reasoned as she listened to Kruz in
the bathroom.

*There was the telephone. There was the internet. There
was always a way of getting hold of someone. She just hadn't
tried.*

They didn't have that kind of relationship.

What *did* they have?

She hadn't been prepared for pregnancy because she'd had
no reason to suppose she was in line to make a baby.

You had sex, didn't you?

The brutal truth. They'd had sex vigorously and often. Two
casual acquaintances coming together for no other purpose
than mindless pleasure until the charity gave them a common aim. They had enjoyed each other greedily and thought-
lessly, with only a mind to that pleasure. Maybe Kruz thought
she was going to hit him with a paternity suit. Holly had explained to her once that the Acostas were so close and kept
the world at bay because massive wealth brought massive
risk. They found it hard to trust anyone, because most people had an agenda.

'Kruz—'

She flinched as the door opened and quickly wrapped the
sheet around her. Yet again she was wasting time thinking
when she should be doing. She should have got dressed and
then she could face him as an equal, rather than having to
try and tug the sheet from the bottom of the bed so she could
retain what little dignity was left to her.

'No— Wait—' Kruz had pulled on his jeans and top and
was heading for the door. Somehow she managed to yank the
sheet free and stumble towards him. 'Please—I realise this
must be a terrible shock for you, but we really have to talk.'

'A *shock*?' he said icily, staring down at her hand on his arm.

She recoiled from him. Suddenly Kruz's arm felt like the arm of a stranger, while she felt like a hysterical woman accosting someone she didn't know.

She tried again—calmly this time. 'Please... We must talk.'

'*Now* we need to talk?' he said mildly.

She had hurt him. But it was so much more than that. Kruz was shocked—felled by the enormity of what she'd been keeping from him. His brain was scrambled. She could tell he needed space. 'Please...' she said gently, trying to appeal to a softer side of him.

'No,' he rapped, pulling away. 'No,' he said again, shaking her off. 'You can't just hit me with this and expect me to produce a ready-made plan.'

She didn't expect anything from him, but she couldn't just let him turn his back and walk away. Moving in front of him, she leaned against the door. 'Well, that's up to you. I can't stop you leaving.'

Kruz's icy expression assured her this was the case.

'I don't want anything from you,' she said, trying to subdue the tremor in her voice. 'I know a baby isn't a good enough reason for us to stay together in some sort of mismatched hook-up—'

'I wasn't aware we were *planning* to hook up,' he cut in with a quiet intensity that really scared her.

She moved away from the door. What else could she do? She felt dead inside. She should have told him long before now, but Kruz's reaction to finding out had completely thrown her. They were both responsible for a new life, but he seemed determined to shut that fact out. She would have to speak to him through lawyers when she got back to England, and somehow she would have to complete her work for the charity while she was here in Argentina—with or without Kruz Acosta's co-operation.

Needing isolation and time to think, she hurried to the bathroom and shut the door—just in time to hear Kruz close the outer door behind him.

No! No! No! This could not be happening. He micro-managed every aspect of his life to make sure something unexpected could never blindside him. So how? Why now?

Why ever?

With no answers that made sense he stalked in the direction of the stables.

A child? *His* child? His baby?

His mind was filled with wonder. But having a child was unthinkable for him. It was a gift he could never accept. He couldn't share his nightmares—not with Romy and much less with an innocent child. Who knew what he was capable of?

In the army they'd said there were three kinds of soldiers: those who were trained to kill and couldn't bring themselves to do it; those who were trained to kill and enjoyed it; and those who were trained to kill and did so because it was their duty. They did that duty on auto-pilot, without allowing themselves to think. He had always thought that last type of soldier was the most dangerous and the most damned, because they had only one choice. That was to live their lives after the army refusing to remember, refusing to feel, refusing to face what they'd done. He was that soldier.

There was only one option open to him. He would allow Romy to complete her work here and then he would send her back. He would provide for the child and for Romy. He would write a detailed list of everything she must have and then he would hand that list over to his PA.

From the first night he had woken screaming he had vowed never to inflict his nightmares on anyone. The things he'd witnessed—the things he'd done—none of that was remotely acceptable to him in the clear light of peace. He was damned for all time. He had been claimed by the dark side, which was the best reason he knew to keep himself aloof from decent people. He could not allow himself to feel anything for Romy, or for their child—not unless he wanted to damage them both. The best, the *only* thing he could do to protect them was to step out of Romy's life.

The mechanical function of tacking up his stallion soothed him and set his decision in stone. The great beast and he would share the wild danger of a gallop across the pampas. They both needed to break free, to run, to seize life without thought or plan for what might lay ahead.

He rode as far as the river and then kicked his booted feet out of the stirrups. Throwing the reins over the stallion's head, he dismounted. All he could see wherever he looked was Romy, and all he could hear was her voice. The apprehension and concern in her eyes was as clear now as if she were standing in front of him. She was frightened she wasn't ready for a baby. *He* would never be ready. His family, who tolerated him, knew more than most people did about him, was enough.

Tipping his face to the sun, he realised this was the first time he had ever backed away from any challenge. He normally met each one head-on. But this tiny unborn child had stopped him dead in his tracks without a road map or a solution. He didn't question the fact that the child was his. The little he knew about Romy gave him absolute trust in what she told him. Whistling up his stallion, he sprang into the saddle and turned for home.

She packed her case and then left the *hacienda* to take the shots she needed for Grace. She knelt and waited silently on the riverbank for what felt like hours for the flocks of birds feeding close by to wheel and soar like ribbons in the sky. She could only marvel at their beauty. It gave her a sort of peace which she hoped would transmit to the baby.

There was no perfect world, Romy concluded. There were

only perfect moments like this, populated by imperfect human beings like herself and Kruz, who were just trying to make the best of their journey through life. It was no use wishing she could share this majestic beauty with their child. She would never be invited to Argentina. She might never see the snow-capped Andes and smell the lush green grass again, but her photographs would remind her of the wild land the father of her child inhabited.

Hoisting her kitbag onto her shoulder, she started back to the *hacienda*. She had barely reached the courtyard when she saw Kruz riding towards her. She loved him. It was that simple. Turning in the opposite direction, she kept her head down and walked rapidly away. She wasn't ready for this.

Would she ever be ready for this?

She stopped and changed direction, following him round to the stables, where she found him dismounting. Without acknowledging her presence, he led the stallion past her.

He had been calm, Kruz realised. The ride had calmed him. But seeing Romy again had shaken him to the core. He wanted her—and more than in just a sexual way. He wanted to put his arm around her and share her worries and excitement, to see where the road took them. But Romy's life wasn't an experiment he could dip into. He might not be able to shake the feeling that they belonged together, but the only safe thing for Romy was to put her out of his life.

'Kruz…'

He lifted the saddle onto the fence and started taking his horse's bridle off.

'How could I go to bed with you, knowing I was pregnant,' she said, 'and yet say nothing?'

Her voice, soft and shaking slightly, touched him somewhere deep. He turned to find her frowning. 'Don't beat yourself up about it,' he said without expression. 'What's done is done.'

'And cannot be undone,' she whispered as the stallion turned a reproachful gaze on him. 'Not that I…'

As her voice faded his gaze slipped to her stomach, where the swell of pregnancy was quite evident on her slender frame. In his rutting madness he had chosen not to see it. He felt guilty now.

The stallion whickered and nuzzled him imperatively, searching for a mint. He found one and the stallion took it delicately from his hand. Clicking his tongue, he tried to move the great beast on, but his horse wasn't going anywhere. As of this moment, one small girl with her chin jutting out had half a ton of horseflesh bending to her will.

'He needs feeding,' he said without emotion as he waited for Romy to move aside.

'I have needs too,' she said, but her soft heart put the horse first, and so she moved, allowing him to lead the stallion to his stable.

'Are you going to make me wait as I made you wait?' she said as she watched him settle the horse.

He was checking its hooves, but lifted his head to look at her.

'Okay, I get it—you're not so petty,' she said. 'But we do have to talk some time, Kruz.'

He returned to what he'd been doing without a word.

She waited by the stable door, watching Kruz looking after his big Criolla. What she wouldn't do for a moment of that studied care…

So what are you standing around for?

'Can I—'

'Can you what?' he said, still keenly aware of her, apparently, even though he had his back turned to her.

'Can I come in and give him a mint?' she asked.

The few seconds' pause felt like an hour.

'Hold your hand out flat,' he said at last.

She took the mint, careful not to touch Kruz more than

she had to. Her heart thundered as he stood back. There was nothing between her and the enormous horse that just stood motionless, staring at her unblinking. Her throat felt dry, and her heart was thundering, but then, as if a decision had been made, the stallion's head dropped and its velvet lips tickled her palm. Surprised by its gentleness, she stroked its muzzle. The prickle of whiskers made her smile, and she went on to stroke its sleek, shiny neck. The warmth was soothing, and the contact between them made her relax.

'You're a beauty, aren't you?' she whispered.

Conscious that Kruz was watching her, she stood back and let him take over. He made the horse quiver with pleasure as he groomed it with long, rhythmical strokes. She envied the connection between them.

She waited until Kruz straightened up before saying, 'Can we talk?'

'You're *asking* me?' he said, brushing past her to put the tack away.

His voice was still cold, and she felt as if she had blinked and opened her eyes to find the last few minutes had been a dream and now it was back to harsh reality. But her pregnancy wasn't something she could put to one side. Now it was out in the open she had to see this through, and so she followed Kruz to the tackroom and closed the door behind them. He swung around and, leaning back against the wall, with a face that was set and unfriendly, waited for her to speak.

'I would have told you sooner, if—'

'If you hadn't been climbing all over me?' he suggested in a chilly tone.

She lifted her chin. 'I didn't notice you taking a back seat at the time.'

'So when were you going to tell me that you're pregnant?'

'You seem more concerned about my faults than our child. There were so many times when I wanted to tell you—'

'But your needs were just too great?' he said, regarding

her with a face she didn't recognize—a face that was closed off to any possibility of understanding between them.

'I remember my need being as great as yours,' she said. 'Anyway, I don't want to argue with you about this, Kruz. I want to discuss what has happened while we've got the chance. For God's sake, Kruz—what's wrong with you? Anyone would think you were trying to drive me away—taking *your* child with me.'

'You'll stay here until I tell you to go,' he said, snatching hold of her arm.

'Let me go,' she cried furiously.

'There's nowhere for you to go—there's just thousands of miles of nothing out there .'

'I'm leaving Argentina.'

'And then what?' he demanded.

'And then I'll make a life for me and our baby—the baby you don't care to acknowledge.'

Was that a flicker of something human in his eyes? Had she got through to him at last? His grip had relaxed on her arm.

It was a feint of which any fighter would be proud. Kruz was still hot from his ride, still unshaven and dusty, and when his mouth crashed down on hers she knew she should fight him off, but instead she battled to keep him close.

'It's that easy, isn't it?' he snarled, thrusting her away. '*You're* that easy.'

She confronted him angrily. 'You shouldn't have kissed me. You shouldn't have doubted me.' She paused a beat and shook her head. 'And I should have told you sooner than I did.'

'You kissed me back,' he said, turning for the door.

Yes, she had. And she would kiss him again, Romy realised as heat, hope and longing surged inside her. What did that make her? Deluded?

'Where are you going?' she demanded as Kruz opened the door. 'We have to talk this through.'

'I'm done talking, Romy.'

Moving ahead of him, she pressed herself against the door like a barricade. 'I'm just as scared as you are,' she admitted.

'You? Scared?' he said.

'We didn't plan this, Kruz, but however unready we are to become parents, we're no different than thousands of other couples. Whether we're ready or not, in less than a year our lives will be turned upside down by a baby.'

'*Your* life, maybe,' he snapped.

His eyes were so cold…his face was so closed off to her. 'Kruz—'

'I need time to think,' he said sharply.

'No,' she fired back. 'We need to talk about this now.'

Pressing against the door, she refused to move. She was going to say what she had to say and then she would leave Argentina for good.

'There's nothing for you to think about,' she said firmly. 'The baby and I don't need you—and we certainly don't want your money. When I get back to England I'll speak to my lawyers and make sure you have fair access to our child. But that's it. Don't think for one moment that I can't provide everything a baby needs and more.'

The blood drained from his face. He was furious, but Kruz contained his feelings, which made him seem all the more threatening. Her hands flew to cradle her stomach. She was right to feel apprehensive. She had no lawyers, while Kruz probably had a whole team waiting on him. And she had to find somewhere decent to live. For all her brave talk she was in no way ready to welcome a baby into the world yet.

'Do you mind?' he said coldly, staring behind her at the door.

Standing aside, she let him go. What else could she do? She had no more cards to play. If Kruz didn't want any part in the life of his child then she wasn't going to beg. She couldn't pretend it didn't hurt to think he could just brush her off like this. She understood that he guarded his privacy fiercely, but the birth of a baby was a life-changing event for both of them.

But this was day one of her life as a single mother, so she had to get over it. With the lease about to run out on her rented house, she couldn't afford to be downhearted. Her priority was to find somewhere to live. So what if she couldn't afford the area she loved? She maybe never would be able to afford it. She could still find somewhere safe and respectable. She would work all hours to make that happen.

She waited in the shadowy warmth of the tackroom, breathing in the pleasant aroma of saddle soap and horse until she was sure Kruz was long gone, and then she walked out into the brilliant sunlight of the yard to find the big stallion still watching her, with his head resting over the stable door.

'I've made a mess of everything, haven't I?' she said, tugging gently on his forelock. She smoothed the palm of her hand along his pricked ears until he tossed his head and trumpeted. She imagined he was part of the herd who were still out there somewhere on the pampas.

Biting back tears, she glanced towards the *hacienda*. Kruz would be showering down after his ride, she guessed. He would be washing away the dust of the day and, judging by his reaction to her news, he would be washing away all thoughts of Romy and their baby along with it.

CHAPTER ELEVEN

HE'D SLEPT ON it, and now he knew what he was going to do. Towelling down after his shower the next morning, he could see things clearly. Romy's news had stunned him. How could it not, considering his care where contraception was concerned? It shouldn't have happened, but now it *had* happened he would take control.

Tugging on a fresh pair of jeans and a clean top, he raked his thick dark hair into some semblance of order. The future of this baby was non-negotiable. He would not be a part-time parent. He knew the effect it had had on him when his parents had been killed. It wasn't Nacho's fault that Kruz had run wild, but he did believe that a child needed both its parents. Romy could have her freedom, and they would live independent lives, but she must move here to Argentina.

The internet was amazing, Romy concluded as she settled into her narrow seat on the commercial jet. She'd used it to sell the images she didn't need to keep back for the Acosta charity, or for Grace, and had then used the proceeds to book her flight home. Alessandro had insisted on driving her to the airport and carrying her luggage as far as the check-in desk. He was a lovely man, sensitive enough not to ply her with questions. She didn't care that she wasn't flying home in style in a private jet. The staff in the cabin were polite and helpful, and before long she would be back in London on the brink of a new life.

As soon as she had taken the last shot she needed and made plans to leave Argentina she had known there would be no going back. This was the right decision—for her and for her child. She didn't need a man to help her raise her baby. She was strong and self-sufficient, she had her health, and she could earn enough money for both their needs. One thing was certain—she didn't need Kruz Acosta.

Really?

She had panicked to begin with, Romy reasoned as the big, wide jet soared high into the air. But making the break from Kruz was just what she needed. It was a major kick-start to the rest of her life. He was the one losing out if he didn't want to be part of this. She was fine with it. She could live man-free, as she had before.

Reaching for the headphones, she scrolled through the channels until she found a film she could lose herself in—or at least attempt to tune out the voice of her inner critic, who said that by turning her back on Kruz and leaving Argentina without telling him Romy had done the wrong thing yet again.

'Señorita Romily has gone,' Alessandro told him.

'What the hell do you mean, she's gone?' he demanded as Alessandro got out of the pick-up truck.

'She flew back to England this morning,' his elderly friend informed him, stretching his limbs. 'I just got back from taking her to the airport.' Alessandro levelled a challenging look at Kruz that said, *And what are you going to do about it?*

They didn't make men tame and accepting on the pampas, Kruz reflected as he met Alessandro's unflinching stare. 'She went back to England to *that* house?' he snarled, beside himself with fury.

Alessandro's shoulders lifted in a shrug. 'I don't know where she was going, exactly. "Back home" is all she told me. She talked of a lovely area by a canal in London while we were driving to the airport. She said I would love it, and that even so close to a city like London it was possible to find quiet places that are both picturesque and safe. She told me about the waterside cafés and the English pubs, and said there are plenty of places to push a pram.'

'She was stringing you along,' Kruz snapped impatiently. 'She guessed you wouldn't take her to the airport if you knew the truth about where she lived.' And when Alessandro flinched with concern at the thought that he might have led Romy into danger, Kruz lashed out with words as an injured wolf might howl in the night as the only way to express its agony. 'She lives in a terrible place, Alessandro. Even with all the operatives in my employ I cannot guarantee her safety there.'

'Then follow her,' his wise old friend advised.

Kruz shook his head, stubborn pride still ruling him. Romy was having his baby and she had left Argentina without telling him. Twisting the knife in the wound, his old friend Alessandro had helped Romy on her way. 'Why?' he demanded tensely, turning a blazing stare on his old friend's face. 'Why have you chosen to help her?

'I think you know why,' Alessandro said mildly.

'You think I'd hurt her?' he exclaimed with affront. 'You think because of everything that happened in the army I'm a danger to her?'

Alessandro looked sad. 'No,' he said quietly. 'You are the only one who thinks that. I helped Señorita Winner to go home because she's pregnant and because she needs peace now—not the anger you feel for yourself. Until you can accept that you have every right to a future, you have nothing to offer her. You have hurt her,' Alessandro said bluntly, 'and now it's up to you to make the first approach.'

'She didn't tell me she was pregnant.'

'Did you give her a chance?'

'I didn't know—'

'You didn't want to know. *I* knew,' Alessandro said quietly.

Kruz stood rigid for a moment, and then followed Alessandro to the stable, where he found the old *gaucho* preparing to groom his favourite horse.

'You drove her to the airport,' he said, still tight with indignation. '*Dios*, Alessandro, what were you thinking?'

When Alessandro didn't speak he was forced to master himself, and when he had done so he had to admit Alessandro was right. His old friend had done nothing wrong. This entire mess was of Kruz and Romy's making—mostly his.

'So she didn't tell you she was leaving?' Alessandro commented, still sweeping the grooming brush down his horse's side in rhythmical strokes.

'No, she didn't tell me,' he admitted. And why would she? He hadn't listened. He hadn't seen this coming. So the mother of his child had just upped and left the country without a word.

What now?

She wasn't *all* to blame for this, but one thing was certain. Romy might have pleased herself in the past, but now she was expecting his baby she would listen to *him*.

'No,' Romy said flatly, preparing to cut the line having refused Kruz's offer of financial help. 'And please don't call me at the office again.'

'Where the hell else am I supposed to call you?' he thundered. 'You never pick up. You can't keep on avoiding me, Romy.'

The irony of it, she thought. She knew they should meet to discuss the baby, but things had happened since she'd come back to England—big things—and now she was sick with loss and just didn't think she could take any more. Her mother had died. There—it was said…thought…so it must be true. It *was* true. She had arrived at the nursing home too late to see her mother alive. Somehow she had always imagined she would be there when the time came. The fact that her mother had slipped away peacefully in her sleep had done nothing to help ease her sense of guilt.

And none of it was Kruz's fault.

'Okay, let's meet,' she agreed, choosing an anonymous café on an anonymous road in the heart of the bustling metropolis. The café was close by both their offices, and with Kruz back in London the last thing she wanted was for them to bump into each other on the street.

'I could meet you at the house,' he said, 'if that's easier for you.'

There *was* no house. The lease was up. The house had gone. She was sleeping on a girlfriend's sofa until she found somewhere permanent.

'This can't be rushed, Romy,' Kruz remarked as she was thinking things through. 'Five minutes of your time in a crowded café won't be enough.'

He was right. In a few months' time they would be parents. It still seemed incredible. It made her heart ache to be talking to him about such a monumental event that should affect them both equally while knowing they would never be closer than this. 'I'll make it a long lunch,' she offered.

She guessed she must have sounded patronising as Kruz repeated the address and cut the line.

Without him asking her to do so she had taken a DNA test to prove that the baby was his. She had had to do it before a solicitor would represent her. Putting everything in the hands of a stranger had felt like the final nail in the coffin containing their non-existent relationship. This meeting in the café with Kruz to sort out some of the practical aspects of parental custody was not much more.

Not much more? Did she really believe that? Just catching sight of Kruz through the steamed-up windows of the chic city centre café was enough to make her heart lurch.

He'd already got a table, and was sipping coffee as he read the financial papers. He'd moved on with his life and so had she, Romy persuaded herself. She had suffered the loss of her mother while he'd been away—a fact she'd shared with no one. Kruz, of all people, would probably understand, but she wouldn't burden him with it. They weren't part of each other's lives in that way.

'Hey,' she murmured, dropping her bag on the seat by his side. 'Watch that for me, will you, while I get something to drink?'

Putting the newspaper down, he stood up. He stared at her without speaking for a moment. 'Let me,' he said at last, brushing past.

'No caffeine,' she called. 'And just an almond croissant, please.'

Just an almond croissant? Was that a craving or lack of funds?

He should have prepared himself for seeing Romy so obviously pregnant. He knew how far on she was, after all. He should have realised that the swell of her stomach would be more pronounced because she was so slender. If he had been prepared he might be able to control this feeling of being a frustrated protector who had effectively robbed himself of the chance to do his job.

Taking Romy's sparse lunch back to the table, he sat down. She played with the food and toyed with mint tea. *I hope you're eating properly,* he thought, watching her. There were dark circles beneath her eyes. She looked as if she wasn't sleeping. That made two of them.

'Let's get this over with,' he said, when she seemed lost in thought.

She glanced up and the focus of her navy blue eyes sharpened. 'Yes, let's get it over with,' she agreed. 'I've appointed a lawyer. I thought you'd find that easier than dealing with me directly—I know I will. I'm busy,' she said, as if that explained it.

'Business is good?' he asked carefully.

'You should know it is.' She glanced up, but her gaze quickly flickered away. 'Grace keeps me busy with the charity, and my work for that has led me on to all sorts of things.'

'That's good, isn't it?'

She smiled thinly.

'Are you still living at the same place?'

'Why do you ask?' she said defensively.

He should have remembered how combative Romy could be. He should have taken into account the fact that pregnancy hormones would accentuate this trait. But Romy's wellbeing and that of his child was his only concern now. He didn't want to fight with her. 'Just interested,' he said with a shrug.

'I don't need your money,' she said quickly. 'With money comes control, and I'm a free agent, Kruz.'

'Whoah…' He held his hands up. She was bristling to the point where he knew he had to pull her back somehow.

'I'd do anything for my child,' she went on, flashing him a warning look, 'but I won't be governed by your money and your influence. I don't need you, Kruz. I am completely capable of taking care of this.'

And completely hormonal, he supplied silently as Romy's raised voice travelled, causing people to turn and stare.

'I'm not challenging your rights,' he said gently. 'This child has changed everything for both of us. Neither of us can remain isolated in own private world any longer, Romy.'

She had expected this meeting with Kruz to be difficult, but she hadn't expected to feel quite so emotional. This was torture. If only she could reach out instead of pushing him away.

The past was a merciless taskmaster, Romy concluded, for each time she thought about the possibility of a family unit, however loosely structured, she was catapulted back into that house where her mother had been little more than a slave to her father's much stronger will.

'You don't know anything about this,' she said distractedly, not even realising she was nursing her baby bump.

'I know quite a lot about it,' Kruz argued, which only made the ache of need inside her grow. 'I grew up on an *estancia* the size of a small city. I saw birth and death as part of the natural cycle of life. I saw the effect of pregnancy on women. So I do understand what you're going through now. And I know about your mother, Romy, and I'm very sorry for your loss.'

Kruz knew everything about everything. Of course he did. It was his business to know. 'Well, thank you for your insight,' she snapped, like a frightened little girl instead of the woman she had become.

Not all men were as principled as Kruz, but he would leave her to pick up the pieces eventually. Better she pushed him away now. It wasn't much of a plan, but it was all she'd got. She just hadn't expected it to be so hard to pull off.

'When the baby's born,' she said, straightening her back as she took refuge in practical matters, 'you will have full visiting rights.'

'That's very good of you,' Kruz remarked coldly.

She was being ridiculous. Kruz had the means to fight her through the courts until the end of time, while *her* resources were strictly limited. She might like to think she was in control, but that was a fantasy he was just humouring. 'Independence is important to me—'

'And to me too,' he assured her. 'But not at the expense of everyone around me.'

She was glad when he fell silent, because it stopped her retaliating and driving another wedge between them. 'I hope we can remain friends.'

'I'd say that's up to you,' he said, reaching for his jacket.

She wanted to say something—to reach out and touch

him—but it had all gone wrong. 'I'll get the bill,' she offered,
feeling she must do something.

Ignoring her, Kruz called the waitress over.

She wanted him in her life, but she couldn't live with the
control that came with that. She felt like crying and banging
her fists on the table with frustration. Only very reluctantly
she accepted that those feelings were due to hormones. Her
emotions were all over the place. She ached to share her hopes
and fears about the baby with Kruz, and yet she was doing
everything she could to drive him away.

'Ready to go?' he said, standing. 'My lawyers will be in
touch with yours.'

'Great.'

This was it. This was the end. Everything was being
brought to a close with a brusque statement that twisted in
her heart like a knife. She got up too, and started to leave the
table. But her belly got stuck. Kruz had to move the table for
her. She felt so vulnerable. She couldn't pretend she didn't
want to confide in him, share her fears with him. He stood
back as she walked to the door. Somehow she managed to
bang into someone's tray on one of the tables, and then she
nearly sent a child flying when she turned around to see
what she'd done.

'It's okay, I've got it,' Kruz said calmly, making sure everything was set to rights in his deft way, with his charisma
and his smile.

'Sorry,' she said, feeling her cheeks fire up as she made
her apologies to the people involved. They hardly seemed to
notice her. They were so taken with Kruz. 'Sorry,' she said
again when he joined her at the door. 'I'm so clumsy these
days. When the baby's born we'll have another chat.'

He raised a brow at this and made no reply. Now he'd seen
her he must think her ungainly and clumsy.

'I'll be in touch,' he said.

This was all happening too fast. The words wouldn't come out of her mouth quickly enough to stop him.

Pulling up the collar on his heavy jacket, he scanned the traffic and when he saw a gap dodged across the road.

Her heart was in shreds as her gaze followed him. She stayed where she was in the doorway of the café, sheltering in blasts of warm, coffee-scented air as customers arrived and left. When the door was opened and the chatter washed over her she began to wonder if a heart could break in public, while people were calling for their coffee or more ketchup on their chips.

Grace had taken her in, insisting Romy couldn't expect to keep healthy and look after her unborn child while she was sleeping on a friend's sofa. There was plenty of room in the penthouse, Grace had explained. Romy hadn't wanted to impose, but when Grace insisted that she'd welcome the company while Nacho was away on a polo tour Romy had given in. They could work together on the charity features while Romy waited for the birth of her child, Grace pointed out.

Romy had worked out that if she budgeted carefully she would have enough money to buy most of the things she needed for the baby in advance. She searched online to find bargains, and hunted tirelessly through thrift shops for the bigger items, but even with her spirit of make do and mend she couldn't resist a visit to Khalifa's department store when she noticed there was a sale on. She bought one adorable little suit at half-price but would have loved a dozen more, along with a soft blanket and a mobile to hang above the cot. But those, like the cuddly toys, were luxuries she had to pass up. The midwife at the hospital had given her a long list of essentials to buy before she gave birth.

Get over it, Romy told herself impatiently as her hormones got to work on her tear glands as she walked around the baby department. This baby was going to be born to a mother who adored it already and who would do anything for it.

A baby who would never know its grandmother and rarely see its father.

'Thanks a lot for that helpful comment,' she muttered out loud.

She could do without her inner pessimist. Emotional incontinence at this stage of pregnancy needed no encouragement. Leaning on the nearest cot, she foraged in her cluttered bag for a tissue to stem the flow of tears and ended up looking like a panda. Why did department stores have to have quite so many mirrors? So much for the cool, hard-edged photographer—she was a mess.

It had not been long since her mother's funeral, Romy reasoned as she took some steadying breaths. It had been a quiet affair, with just a few people from the care home. There was nothing sadder than an empty church, and she had felt bad because there had been no one else to invite. She felt bad now—*about everything*. Her ankles were swollen, her feet hurt, and her belly was weighing her down.

But she had a career she loved and prospects going forward, Romy told herself firmly as an assistant, noticing the state she was in, came over with a box of tissues.

'We see a lot of this in here,' the girl explained kindly. 'Don't worry about it.'

Romy took comfort from the fact that she wasn't the only pregnant woman falling to pieces during pregnancy—right up to the moment when the assistant added, 'Does the daddy know you're here? Shall I call him for you?' Only then did she notice Romy's ring-free hands. 'Oh, I'm sorry!' she exclaimed, slapping her hand over her mouth. 'I really didn't mean to make things worse for you.'

'You haven't,' Romy reassured her as a fresh flood of tears followed the first. She just wanted to be on her own so she could howl freely.

'Here—have some more tissues,' the girl insisted, thrusting a wad into Romy's hands. 'Would you like me to call you a cab?'

'Would you?' Romy managed to choke out.

'Of course. And I'll take you through the staff entrance,' the girl offered, leading the way.

Thank goodness Kruz couldn't see her like this—all bloated and blotchy, tear-stained and swollen, with her hair hanging in lank straggles round her face. Gone were the super-gelled spikes and kick-ass attitude, and in their place was…a baby.

He'd kept away from Romy, respecting her insistence that she was capable of handling things her way and that she would let him know when the baby was born. They lived in different countries, she had told him, and she didn't need his help. He was in London most of the time now, getting the new office up to speed, but he had learned not to argue with a pregnant woman. Thank goodness for Grace, who was still in London while Nacho was on a polo tour. At least she could reassure him that Romy was okay—though Grace had recently become unusually cagey about the details.

The irony of their situation wasn't lost on him, he accepted as he reversed into a space outside Khalifa's department store. He had pushed Romy away and now she was refusing to see him. She was about to give birth and he missed her. It was as simple as that.

But even though she refused his help there was nothing to say he couldn't buy a few things for their baby. Grace had said this was the best place to come—that Khalifa's carried a great range of baby goods.

The store also boasted the most enthusiastic assistants in London town, Kruz reflected wryly as they flocked around him. How the hell did he know what he wanted? He stood, thumbing his stubble, in the midst of a bewildering assortment of luxury goods for the child who must have everything.

'Just wrap it all up,' he said, eager to be gone from a place seemingly awash with happy couples.

'Everything, sir?' an assistant asked him.

'You know what a baby needs better than I do,' he pointed out. 'I'll take it all. Just charge it to my account.'

'And send it where, sir?'

He thought about the Acosta family's fabulous penthouse, and then his heart sank when he remembered Romy's tiny terrace on the wrong side of the tracks. He would respect her wish to say there for now, but after the birth…

The store manager, hurrying up at the sight of an important customer, distracted him briefly—but not enough to stop Kruz remembering that the only births he had attended so far were of the foals he owned, all of which had been born in the fabulous custom-built facility on the *estancia*.

No one owned Romy, he reflected as the manager continued to reassure him that Khalifa's could supply anything he might need. Romy was her own woman, and he had Grace's word for the fact that she would have the best of care during the birth of their baby at a renowned teaching hospital in the centre of London. But after the birth he suspected Romy would want to make her nest in that tiny terraced house.

Another idea occurred to him. 'Gift-wrap everything you think a newborn baby might need,' he instructed the manager, 'and have it made ready for collection.'

'Collection by van, sir?' The manager glanced around the vast, well-stocked floor.

'Yes,' Kruz confirmed. 'How long will that take?'

'At least two hours, plus loading time—'

He shrugged. 'Then I will return in two hours.'

Brilliant. Women loved surprises. He'd hire a van, load it up and deliver it himself.

The thought of seeing Romy again made him smile for the

first time in too long. It would be good to see her shock when he rolled up with a van full of baby supplies. She would definitely unwind. Maybe they could even make a fresh start—as friends this time. Whatever the future held for them, he suspected they could both do with some down-time before the birth of their baby threw up a whole new raft of problems.

CHAPTER TWELVE

THAT WAS NOT a phantom pain.

Bent over double in the small guest cloakroom in the penthouse while Grace was at the shops buying something for their supper was not a good place to be…

Romy sighed with relief as the pain subsided. There was no cause for panic. If it got any worse she'd call an ambulance.

For once he didn't even mind the traffic because he was in such a good mood, and by the time he pulled the hired van outside the terraced house he was feeling better than positive. They would work something out. They both had issues and they both had to get over them. They had a baby to consider now.

Springing down from the van, he stowed the keys. Relying on Grace for snippets of information about Romy wasn't nearly good enough, but he was half to blame for allowing the situation to get this bad. Both he and Romy were always on the defensive, always expecting to be let down. Raising his fist, he hammered on the door. Now he just had to hope she was in.

Oh, oh, oh… She had managed to crawl into the bathroom. *Emergency!*

They'd mentioned pressure at the antenatal classes, so she was hoping this was just a bit of pressure—

Pressure everywhere.

And no sign of Grace.

'Grace…' she called out weakly, only to have the silence of an empty apartment mock her. 'Grace, I need you,' she whimpered, knowing there was no one to hear her. 'Grace, I don't know what to do.'

Oh, for goodness' sake, pull yourself together! Of course you know what to do.

Now the pain had faded enough for her to think straight, maybe she did. Scrabbling about in her pockets, she hunted for her phone. All she had to do was dial the emergency number and tell them she was having a baby. What was so hard about that?

'Grace!' she exclaimed with relief, hearing the front door open. 'Grace? Is that you?'

'Romy?' Grace sounded as panicked as Romy felt. 'Romy, where are you?'

'On the floor in the bathroom.'

'On the floor—? Goodness—'

She heard Grace shutting her big old guide dog, Buddy, in the kitchen before moving cautiously down the hall with her stick. 'Grace, I'm in here.' There were several bathrooms in the penthouse, and Grace would find her more easily if she followed the sound of Romy's voice.

'Are you okay?' Grace called out anxiously, trying to get her bearings.

That was a matter of opinion. 'I'm fine,' Romy managed, and then the door opened and Grace was standing there. Just having someone to share this with was a help.

Grace felt around with her stick. 'What on earth are you doing under the sink?'

'I had a little accident,' Romy admitted, chucking the towel she'd been using in the bath. 'Can't move,' she managed to grind out as another contraction hit her out of nowhere. 'Stay where you are, Grace. I don't want you slipping, or tripping over me—I'll be fine in a minute.'

'I'm calling for an ambulance,' Grace said decisively, pulling out her phone.

'Tell them my waters have broken and the baby's coming—and this baby isn't waiting for anything.'

'Okay, keep calm!' Grace exclaimed, sounding more panicked than Romy had ever heard her.

He had thoughts of reconciliation and an armful of Romy firmly fixed in his head as he hammered a second time on the door of the small terraced house. Like before, the sound echoed and fell away. Shading his eyes, he peered through the window. It was hard to see anything through the voile the girls had hung to give them some privacy from the street. His spirits sank. His best guess…? The tenants of this house were long gone.

How could he not have known? He should have kept up surveillance—but if Romy had found out he was having her followed he would have lost her for good.

There was nothing more pitiful than a man standing outside an empty house with a heart full of hope and a van full of baby equipment. But he had to be sure. Glancing over his shoulder to check the street was deserted, he delved into the pocket of his jeans to pull out the everyday items that allowed him entry into most places. This, at least, was one thing he was good at.

The house was empty. Romy and her friends had packed up and gone for good. There were a few dead flowers in a milk bottle, as if the last person to turn out the lights hadn't been able to bear to throw them away and had given them one last drink of water.

That would be Romy. So where the hell was she?

Grace would know.

* * *

Grace had called the emergency services, and Romy was reassured to hear her friend's succinct instructions on how to access the penthouse with the code at the door so she wouldn't have to leave Romy's side. But the ambulance would have to negotiate the rush hour traffic, Romy realised, starting to worry again as her baby grew ever more insistent to enter the world. Even with sirens blaring the driver would face gridlock in this part of town.

She jumped as Grace's telephone rang. The sight of Grace's face was enough to tell her that the news was not good. 'Grace, what is it?'

'Nothing…'

But Grace's nervous laugh was less than reassuring. 'It must be something,' Romy insisted. 'What's happened, Grace?' She really hoped it wasn't bad news. She wasn't at her most comfortable with her head lodged beneath the sink.

'Seems the first ambulance can't get here for some reason,' Grace admitted. 'But they've told me not to worry as they're sending another—'

'Don't worry?' Romy exclaimed, then felt immediately guilty. Grace was doing everything she could. 'Can you ring them back and tell them I need someone right away? This baby won't wait.'

'I'll do that now,' Grace agreed, but the instant she started to dial her phone rang. 'Kruz?'

'No!' Romy exclaimed in dismay. 'I don't want to speak to him—there's no time to speak to him—' A contraction cut her off, leaving her panting for breath. By the time it had subsided Grace was off the phone. 'You'd better not have told him!' Romy exclaimed. 'Please tell me you didn't tell him. I couldn't bear for him to see me like this.'

'Too late. He's on his way.'

Romy groaned, and then wailed, 'I need to push!'

'Hold on—not yet,' Grace pleaded.

'I can't hold on!' She added a few colourful expletives. 'Sorry, Grace—didn't mean to shout at you—'

Kruz had heard some of this before Grace cut the line. He had called an ambulance too, but the streets were all blocked. It was rush hour, they'd told him—as if he didn't know that. Even using bus lanes and sirens the ambulance driver could only do the best he could.

'Well, for God's sake, *do* your best!' he yelled in desperation. And he never yelled. He had never lost his cool with anyone. *Other than where Romy and his child were concerned.*

The traffic was backed up half a mile away from where he needed to be. Pulling the van onto the pavement, he climbed out and began to run. Bursting into the penthouse, he followed the sound of Grace's voice to the guest cloakroom, where he found Romy wedged at an awkward angle between the sink and the door.

'Get off me,' she sobbed as he came to pick her up. 'I'm going to have a baby—'

As if he didn't know that! 'You're as weak as a kitten and you need to be strong for me, Romy,' he said firmly as he drew her limp, exhausted body into his arms. 'Grace, can you bring me all the clean towels you've got, some warm water and a cover for the baby. Do we have a cradle? Something to sponge Romy down? Ice if you've got it. Soft cloths and some water for her to sip.'

By this time he had shouldered his way into a bedroom, stripped the duvet away and laid Romy down across the width of the bed. He found a chair to support her legs. This was no time for niceties. He'd seen plenty of mares in labour and he knew the final stages. Romy's waters had broken in the cloakroom and now she was well past getting to the hospital in time.

'What are you doing?' she moaned as he started stripping off her clothes.

'You're planning to have a baby with your underwear on?'

'Stop it... Not you... I don't want you undressing me.'

'Well, Grace is busy collecting the stuff we're going to need,' he said reasonably. 'So if not me, who else do you suggest?'

'I don't want you seeing me like this—'

'Hard luck,' he said as she whimpered, carrying on with his job. 'Strong, Romy. I need strong, Romy. Don't go all floppy on me. I need you in fighting mode,' he said firmly, in a tone she couldn't ignore. 'This baby is ready to enter the world and it needs you to fight for it. This isn't about you and me any longer, Romy.'

As he was speaking he was making Romy as comfortable as he could.

'Are you listening to me, Romy?' Tenderly taking her tear-stained face between his hands, he watched with relief as her eyes cleared and the latest contraction subsided. 'That's better,' he whispered. And then, because he could, he brushed a kiss across her lips. 'We're going to do this together, Romy. You and me together,' he said, staring into her eyes. 'We're going to have a baby.'

'Mostly me,' she pointed out belligerently, and with a certain degree of sense.

'Yes, mostly you,' he confirmed. Then, seeing her eyes fill with apprehension again, he knelt on the floor at the side of the bed. 'But remember this,' he added, bringing her into his arms so he could will his strength into her, 'the harder you work, the sooner you'll be holding that baby in your arms. You've got to help him, Romy.'

'Him?'

'Or her,' he said, feeling a stab of guilt at the fact that he hadn't attended any of the scans or check-ups Romy had been to.

Yes, she'd asked him not to—but since when had he ever done anything he was told? Had she tamed the rebel? If she had, her timing was appalling. He should have been with her from the start. But this was not the best time to be analysing where their stubbornness had led them.

'Whether this baby is a boy or a girl,' he said, talking to Romy in the same calm voice he used with the horses, 'this is your first job as a mother. It's the first time your baby has asked you for help, so you have to get on it, Romy. You have to believe in your strength. And remember I'm going to be with you every step of the way.'

She pulled a funny face at that, and then she was lost to the next contraction. They were coming thick and fast now.

'How long in between?' he asked. 'Have you been keeping a check on things, Grace?' he asked Grace as she entered the room.

'Not really,' Grace admitted.

'Don't worry—you've brought everything I asked for. Could you put a cool cloth on Romy's head for me?'

'Of course,' Grace said, sounding relieved to be doing something useful as she felt her way around the situation in a hurry to do as he asked. 'I didn't realise it would all happen so quickly.'

'Neither did I,' Romy confessed ruefully, her voice muffled as she pressed her face into his chest.

'This is going really well,' he said, hoping he was right. 'It's not always this fast,' he guessed, 'but this is better for the baby.'

At least Romy seemed reassured as she braced herself against him, which was all that mattered. The speed of this baby's arrival had surprised everyone—not least him.

'Grace, could you stay here with Romy while I scrub up?'

'No, don't leave me,' Romy moaned, clinging to him.

'You're going to be all right,' he said, gently detaching himself. 'Here, Grace—I'll pull up a chair for you.' Having made Romy comfortable on the bed, he steered Grace to the chair. 'Just talk to her,' he instructed quietly. 'Hold her hand until I get back.'

'Don't go,' Romy begged him again.

'Thirty seconds,' he promised.

'Too long,' she managed, before losing herself in panting again.

'My sentiments entirely,' he called back wryly from the bathroom door.

He was back in half that time. 'I'm going to take a look now.'

'You can't look!' Romy protested, sounding shocked.

Bearing in mind the intimacy they had shared, he found her protest endearing. 'I need to,' he explained. 'So please stop arguing with me and let's all concentrate on getting this baby safely into the world.'

'How many births have you attended?' Romy ground out as he got on with the job.

'More than you can imagine—and this one is going to be a piece of cake.'

'How can you know that?' she howled.

'Just two legs, and one hell of a lot smaller than my usual deliveries? Easy,' he promised, pulling back.

'How many human births?' she ground out.

'You'll be the first to benefit from my extensive experience,' he admitted, 'so you have the additional reassurance of knowing I'm fresh to the task.'

She wailed again at this.

'Just lie back and enjoy it,' he suggested. 'There's nowhere else we have to be. And with the next contraction I need you to push. Grace, this is where you come in. Let Romy grip your hands.'

'Right,' Grace said, sounding ready for action.

'I can see the head!' he confirmed, unable keep the excitement from his voice. 'Keep pushing, Romy. Push like you've never pushed before. Give me a slow count to ten, Grace. And, Romy? You push all the time Grace is counting. I'm going to deliver the shoulders now, so I need you to pant while I'm turning the baby slightly. That's it,' he said. 'One more push and you've got a baby.'

'*We've* got a baby,' Romy argued, puce with effort as she went for broke.

Romy's baby burst into the world with the same enthusiasm with which her parents embraced life. The infant girl didn't care if her parents were cool, or independent, or stubborn. All she asked for was life and food and love.

The paramedics walked in just as she was born. A scene of joy greeted them. Grace was standing back, clasping her hands in awe as the baby gave the first of many lusty screams, while Kruz was kneeling at the side of the bed, holding his daughter safely wrapped in a blanket as he passed her over to Romy. Grace had the presence of mind to ask one of the paramedics to record the moment on Romy's phone, and from then on it was all bustle and action as the medical professionals took over.

He could hardly believe it. They had a perfect little girl. A daughter. *His* daughter. His and Romy's daughter. He didn't need to wonder if he had ever felt like this before, because he knew he never had. Nothing he had experienced came close to the first sight of his baby daughter in Romy's arms, or the look on Romy's face as she stared into the pink screwed-up face of their infant child. The baby had a real pair of lungs on her, and could make as much noise as her mother and father combined. She would probably be just as stubborn and argumentative, he concluded, feeling elated. All thoughts of him and Romy not being ready for parenthood had vanished. Of course they were ready. He would defend this child with his life—as he would defend Romy.

Once the paramedics were sure that both mother and baby were in good health, they offered him a pair of scissors to cut the cord. It was another indescribable moment, and he was deeply conscious of introducing another treasured life into the world.

'You've done well, sir,' one of the health professionals told him. 'You handled the birth beautifully.'

'Romy did that,' he said, unable to drag his gaze away from her face.

Reaching for his hand, she squeezed it tightly. 'I couldn't have done any of this without you,' she murmured.

'The first part, maybe,' he agreed wryly. 'But after that I think you should get most of the praise.'

'Don't leave me!' she exclaimed, her stare fearful and anxious on his face as they brought in a stretcher to take Romy and their baby to hospital.

As soon as the paramedics had her settled he put the baby in her arms. 'You don't get rid of me that easily,' he whispered.

And for the first time in a long time she smiled.

CHAPTER THIRTEEN

SHE WOKE TO a new day, a new life. A life with her daughter in it, and—

'Kruz?'

She felt her anxiety mount as she stared around. *Where was he?* He must have slipped out for a moment. He must have been here all night while she'd been sleeping. She'd only fallen asleep on the understanding that Kruz stayed by her side.

Expecting to feel instantly recovered, she was alarmed to find her emotions were in a worse state than ever. She couldn't bear to lose him now. She couldn't bear to be parted from him for a moment. Especially now, after all he'd done for her. He'd been incredible, and she wanted to tell him so. She wanted to hold his hand and stare into his eyes and tell him with a look, with her heart, how much he meant to her. Kruz had delivered their baby. What closer bond could they have?

Hearing their daughter making suckling sounds in her sleep, she swung cautiously out of bed. Just picking up the warm little bundle was an incredible experience. The bump was now a real person. Staring down, she scrutinised every millimetre of the baby's adorable face. She had her father's olive skin, and right now dark blue eyes, though they might change to a compelling sepia like his in time. The tiny scrap even had a frosting of jet-black hair, with some adorable kiss curls softening her tiny face. The baby hair felt downy soft against her lips, and the scent of new baby was delicious—

fresh and clean and powdered after the sponge-down she had been given in the hospital.

'And you have amazing eyelashes,' Romy murmured, 'exactly like your father.'

She looked up as a nurse entered the room. 'Have you seen Señor Acosta?' she asked.

'Mr Acosta left before dawn with the instruction that you were to have everything you wanted,' the nurse explained, with the type of dreamy look in her eyes Romy was used to where Kruz was concerned.

'He left?' she said, trying and failing to hide her unease. 'Did he say when he would be back?'

'All I've been told is that Mr Acosta's sister-in-law, Grace Acosta, will be along shortly to pick you up,' the nurse informed her.

Romy frowned. 'Are you *sure* he said that?'

'I believe your sister-in-law will be driven here.'

'Ah…' Romy breathed a sigh of relief, knowing Grace would laugh if she knew Romy's churning emotions had envisaged Grace trying to walk home with Romy at her side, carrying a newly delivered baby, and with a guide dog in tow.

A chauffeur-driven car!

This was another world, one Romy had tried so hard not to become caught up in—though she could hardly blame Grace for travelling in style. She should have thought this through properly long before now. She should have realised that having Kruz's baby would have repercussions far beyond the outline for going it alone she had sketched in her mind.

'The car will soon be here to take you and the baby back to the penthouse,' the nurse was explaining to her.

'Of course,' Romy said, acting as if she were reassured. She would have felt better if Kruz had been coming to pick them up, but that wouldn't happen because she had drawn up the rules to exclude him, so she could prove her independence and go it alone with her baby.

But he couldn't just walk away.

Could he?

She shook herself as the nurse walked back in.

'It was a wonderful birth—thanks to your partner. I bet you can't wait to start your new life together as a family.' The nurse stopped and looked at her, and then passed her some tissues without a word.

Like the assistant in the department store, the nurse must have seen a lot of this, Romy guessed, scrubbing impatiently at her eyes. She was still trying to tell herself that Kruz had only gone to take a shower and grab a change of clothes when the nurse added some more information to her pot of woe.

'Mr Acosta said he had to fly as he had some urgent business to complete.'

'Fly?' Romy repeated. 'He actually said that? He said he had to *fly*?'

'Yes, that's exactly what he said,' the nurse confirmed gently. 'Get back into bed,' she added firmly as Romy started hunting for her clothes. 'You should be taking it easy. You've just given birth and the doctor hasn't discharged you yet.'

'I need my phone,' Romy insisted, padding barefoot round the room, collecting up her things.

So Kruz was just going to fly back to Argentina after delivering their baby? He was going to fly *somewhere*, anyway; the nurse had just said so. And she'd thought Kruz might have changed. The overload to her hormones could only be described as nuclear force meeting solar storm. She might just catch him before he took off, Romy concluded, trying to calm down when she found her phone.

'Mr Acosta did say you might want to take some pictures, so he had your camera couriered over.'

Of course he did, Romy thought, refusing to be placated.

The nurse gave her a shrewd and slightly amused look as a frowning Romy began to stab numbers into her phone. 'I'll leave you to it,' she mouthed.

'Kruz?' Romy was speaking in a dangerously soft voice as the call connected. 'Is that you?'

'Of course it's me. Is something wrong?'

'Where are you? If you're still on the ground get back here right away—we need to talk.'

'Romy?'

She'd cut the line. He rang back. She'd turned her phone off.

With a vicious curse he slammed his fist down on the wheel. Starting the engine, he thrust the gears into Reverse and swung the Jeep round, heading back to the hospital at speed, with his world splintering into little pieces at the thought that something might have happened to Romy or their child.

'You were going to leave us!' Romy exclaimed the moment he walked back into the room.

'Don't you *ever* do that to me again,' he said. Ignoring her protests, he took Romy in his arms and hugged her tight.

'Do what?' she said in a muffled voice.

'Don't ever frighten me like that. I thought something had happened to you or the baby. Do you have any idea how much you mean to me?'

She stared into his eyes, disbelieving, until the force of his stare convinced her.

'If they hadn't told me at Reception that you were both well I don't know what I would have done.'

'Flown to Argentina?' she suggested.

'You can't seriously think I'd do that now?'

'The nurse said you had to fly.' Romy's mouth set in a stubborn line.

'I did have to fly—I had an appointment.'

'What were you doing? I know,' she said, stopping herself. 'Sorry—none of my business.'

'It's a long story,' Kruz agreed. 'Why don't I ring Grace and give her some warning before I take you back?'

'Good idea.' It was hard to be angry with Kruz when he looked like this, as he stared down at their child, but nothing had changed. This man was still Kruz Acosta—elusive, hard and driven. A man who did what he liked, when he liked. While she was still Romy Winner—self-proclaimed battle-axe and single mother.

'Well, that's settled,' Kruz said as he cut the line. 'Grace is going back to Argentina. Nacho is coming to collect her now, so you'll have the penthouse to yourself.'

She should be grateful for the short-term loan of such a beautiful home. 'Okay,' she said brightly, worrying about how she and the baby would rattle round the vast space.

'There's plenty of staff to help you,' Kruz pointed out.

'Great,' she agreed. The company of strangers was just what she needed in her present mood. 'I'll get my things together.'

'Grace has organised everything for you, so there's nothing to worry about,' Kruz remarked as he leaned over the cradle.

She loved the way he cared about their baby, but she felt the first stirring of unease. Now the drama was over, would Kruz claim their daughter? He could provide so much more than she could for their child. Would it be selfish of her to cling on?

Of course not. There was no conflict. She kicked the rogue thought into touch. No one would part her from her baby. But would she be in constant conflict with Kruz for ever?

'You can't buy her,' she whispered, thinking out loud.

'*Buy* her?' Kruz queried with surprise. 'She's already mine.'

'Ours.'

'Romy, are you guilty of overreacting to every little comment I make, by any chance?' Before she could answer, Kruz pointed out that she *had* just given birth. 'Give yourself a break, Romy. I know how much your independence means to you, and I respect that. No one's going to take your baby away from you—least of all me.'

Biting her lip, she forced the tears back. Why did everything seem like a mountain to climb? 'I don't know what to think,' she admitted.

'Is this what I've been missing over the past few months?' Kruz asked wryly.

'I'm glad you think it's funny,' she said, knowing she *was* overreacting, but somehow unable to stop herself. 'Do you think you can house me in your glamorous penthouse and pull my strings from a distance?'

'Romy,' Kruz said with a patient sigh, 'I could never think of you as a puppet. Your strings would be permanently tangled. And if we're going to sort out arrangements for the future I don't want to be doing it in a hospital. Do you?'

She flashed a look at him. Kruz's gaze was steady, but those arrangements for the future he was talking about meant they would part.

Count to ten, she counselled herself. *Right now you're viewing everything through a baby-lens.*

She slowly calmed down—enough to pick up her camera. 'Just one shot of you and the baby,' she said.

'Why don't we ask the nurse if she'll take one of all three of us together?' Kruz suggested. 'There will never be another moment like this as we celebrate the birth of our beautiful daughter.'

'You're right,' Romy agreed quietly. 'I feel like such a fool.'

'No,' Kruz argued. 'You feel like every new mother—full of hope and fear and excitement and doubt. You're exhausted and wondering if you can cope. And I'm telling you as a close observer of Romy Winner that you can. And what's more you look pretty good to me,' he added, sending her a look that made her breath hitch.

She hesitated, not knowing whether to believe him as the

nurse came in to take the shot. 'Do I look okay?' she asked, suddenly filled with horror at the thought of ruining the photo of gorgeous Kruz and his beautiful daughter—and her.

'Take the baby,' he said, putting their little girl in her arms. 'You look great. I like your hair silky and floppy,' he insisted, 'and I like your unmade-up face. But if you want gel spikes and red tips, along with tattoos in unusual places and big, black Goth eyes, that's fine by me too.'

'You're being unusually understanding,' Romy commented, trying to make a joke of it. Once a judgement was made regarding their daughter's future they would be parents, not partners, and she should never get the two mixed up.

'I'm undergoing something of an emotional upheaval myself,' Kruz confessed, putting his arm loosely around her shoulders for the happy family shot. 'I guess having a child changes you…' His voice trailed off, but his tender look spoke volumes as he glanced down at their daughter, sleeping soundly in Romy's arms.

'I've never seen you like this before,' Romy commented as Kruz straightened up.

Kruz said nothing.

'So, will you be going back to Argentina as soon as everything's settled here?' she pressed as the nurse took the baby from her and handed her to Kruz.

'I'm in no hurry,' Kruz murmured, staring intently at his daughter.

This was a *very* different side of Kruz, Romy realised, deeply conscious of his depth of feeling as she checked she had packed everything ready for leaving. He was oblivious to everything but his daughter, and that frightened her. *Would* he try to take her baby from her?

His overriding concern was that his child should grow up as part of a strong family unit as he had—thanks to Nacho. But Romy must make her own decisions and he would give her time.

'Are we ready?' he said briskly, once Romy was seated in the wheelchair in which hospital policy insisted she must be taken outside.

'Yes, I'm ready,' Romy confirmed, her gaze instantly locking onto their baby as he placed their daughter in her arms.

'Then let's go.' He was surprised by his eagerness to leave the hospital so he could begin his new life as a father. He couldn't wait to leave this sterile environment where no expressions of intimacy or emotion were possible. He longed to relax, so he could express his feelings openly.

'Kruz—'

'What?' he said, wondering if there was any more affecting sight than a woman holding her newborn child.

Romy shook her head and dropped her gaze. 'Nothing,' she said.

'It must be something.' She was exhausted, he realised, coming to kneel by her side. 'What is it?' he prompted as the nurse discreetly left the room.

'I'm just…' She shook her head, as new to the expression of emotion as he was, he guessed. And then she firmed her jaw and looked straight at him. 'I'm just worrying about the effect of you walking in and out of our baby's life.'

'Don't look for trouble, Romy.'

Why not? her look seemed to say. He blamed the past for Romy's concerns. He blamed the past for his inability to form close relationships outside his immediate family. He guessed that the birth of this child had been a revelation for both of them. It wasn't a case of daring to love, but trying not to— if you dared. Hostage for life, he thought, staring into his daughter's eyes, and a willing one. This wealth of feeling was something both he and Romy would have to get used to and it would take time.

'Don't push me away just yet,' he said, sounding light whilst inwardly he was painfully aware of how much they both stood to lose if they handled this badly. 'I've done as you asked so far, Romy. I've kept my distance for the whole of your pregnancy, so grant me a little credit. But please don't ask me to keep my distance from my child, because that's one thing I can't do.'

'I thought you didn't want commitment,' she said.

He wanted to say, *That was then and this is now,* but he wasn't going to say anything before he was ready. He wouldn't mislead Romy in any way. He had to be sure. From a life of self-imposed isolation to this was quite a leap, and the feelings were all new to him. He wanted them to settle, so he could be cool and detached like in the old days, when he'd been able to think clearly and had always known the right thing to do.

'Grace said you've never shared your life with anyone,' she went on, still fretting.

'People change, Romy. Life changes them.'

He sprang up as the nurse returned. This wasn't the time for deep discussions. Romy had just had a baby. Her hormones were raging and her feelings were all over the place.

'Time to go,' the nurse announced with practised cheerfulness, taking charge of Romy's chair.

While the nurse was wrapping a blanket around Romy's knees and making sure the baby was warmly covered, Romy turned to him. Grabbing hold of his wrist, she made him look at her. 'So what do you want?' she asked him.

'I want to forget,' he said, so quietly it was almost a thought spoken out loud.

CHAPTER FOURTEEN

ROMY REMAINED SILENT during the journey to the penthouse. She was thinking about Kruz's words.

What did he want to forget? His time in the Special Forces, obviously. Charlie had given her the clue there. Charlie had said Kruz was a hero, but Kruz clearly didn't believe his actions could be validated by the opinion of his peers. Medals were probably just pieces of metal to him, while painful memories were all too vivid and real. She couldn't imagine there was much Kruz couldn't handle—but then she hadn't been there, hadn't seen what he'd seen or been compelled to do what he had done. She only knew him as a source of solid strength, as his men must have known him, and her heart ached to think of him in torment.

'Are you okay?' he said, glancing at her through the mirror.

'Yes,' she said softly. *But I'm worried about you...so worried about you.*

Everything had been centred around her and the baby, and that was understandable given the circumstances, but who was caring for Kruz? She wanted to...so badly; if only he'd let her. There were times for being a warrior woman and times when just staring into the face of their baby daughter and knowing Kruz was close by, like a sentinel protecting them, was enough. Knowing they were both safe because of him had given her the sort of freedom she had never had before—odd when she had always imagined close relationships must be confining. He'd given her that freedom. He'd given her so much and now she wanted to help him.

He wasn't hers to help, she realised as Kruz glanced at her again through the driving mirror. She mustn't be greedy. But that was easier said than done when his eyes were so warm and so full of concern for her.

'My driving okay for you?'

As he asked the question she laughed. Kruz was driving like a chauffeur—smoothly and avoiding all the bumps. The impatient, fiery polo-player was nowhere to be seen.

'You're doing just fine,' she said, teasing him in a mock-serious tone. 'I'll let you know if anything changes.'

'You do that,' he said, his eyes crinkling in the mirror. 'You must be tired,' he added.

'And elated.' And worried about the future…and most worried of all about Kruz. They had no future together—none they'd talked about, anyway—and what would happen to him in the future? Would he spend his whole life denying himself the chance of happiness because of what had happened in the past?

She pulled herself together, knowing she couldn't let anything spoil this homecoming when Grace and Kruz had gone to so much trouble for her.

'I'm looking forward so much to seeing Grace,' she said, 'and being on familiar ground instead of in the hospital. It makes everything seem…' She really was lost for words.

'Exciting,' Kruz supplied.

Her eyes cleared as she stared into his through the mirror. 'Yes, exciting,' she agreed softly.

'I can understand that. Grace has been rushing around like crazy to get things ready in time. She's as excited as we are.'

We? He made them sound like a couple…

It was just a figure of speech, Romy reminded herself, though Kruz was right about life changing people. They had both been cold and afraid to show their feelings until the baby arrived, but now it was hard to hide their feelings. She'd been utterly determined to go it alone after the birth of their child. The baby had changed her. The baby had changed them both. She couldn't be more thrilled that Kruz would be sharing this homecoming with her.

She gazed at the back of his head, loving every inch of him—his thick dark hair, waving in disorder, and those shoulders broad enough to hoist an ox. She loved this man. She loved him with every fibre in her being and only wanted him to be happy. But first Kruz had to relearn how to enjoy life without feeling guilty because so many of his comrades were dead. She understood that now.

She had so much to be grateful for, Romy reflected as Kruz drove smoothly on. As well as meeting Kruz, and the birth of their beautiful daughter, these past few months had brought her some incredible friendships. Charlie and Alessandro—and Grace, who was more of a sister than a friend.

And Kruz.

Always Kruz.

Her heart ached with longing for him.

'Grace has been working flat out with the housekeeper to get the nursery ready,' he revealed, bringing her back to full attention.

'But I won't be staying long,' she blurted, suddenly frightened of falling into this seductive way of life when it wasn't truly hers. And Kruz wasn't her man—not really.

'We both wanted to do this for you,' Kruz insisted. 'The penthouse is your home for as long as you want it to be, Romy. You do know that, don't you?'

'Yes.' Like a lodger.

She couldn't say anything more. Her feelings were so mixed up. She was grateful—of course she was grateful—but she was still clinging to the illusion that somehow, some day, they could be a proper family. And that was just foolish. Now tears were stabbing the backs of her eyes again. Pressing her lips together, she willed herself to stop the flow. Kruz had enough on his plate without her blubbing all the time.

'I really appreciate everything you've done,' she said when she was calmer. 'It's just—'

'You don't want to feel caged,' he supplied. 'You're proud and you want to do things your way. I think I get that, Romy.'

There was an edge to his voice that told her he felt shut out. Maybe there was no solution to this—maybe she just had to accept that and move on. She could see she was pushing him away, but it was only because she didn't know what else to do without appearing to take too much for granted.

'You're very kind to let me stay at the penthouse,' she said, realising even as she spoke that she had made herself sound more like a grateful lodger thanking her landlord than ever.

Kruz didn't appear to notice, thank goodness, and as he pulled the limousine into the driveway of the Acosta family's Palladian mansion he said, 'And now you can get some well-earned rest. I'm determined you're going to be spoiled a little, so enjoy it while you can. Stay there—I'm coming round to help you out.'

She gazed out of the window as she waited for Kruz to open the door. The Acosta family owned the whole of this stately building, which was to be her home for the next few weeks. Divided into gracious apartments, it was the sort of house she would never quite get used to entering by the front door, she realised with amusement.

'This isn't a time for independence, Romy,' Kruz said, seeing her looking as he opened the door. 'You'll be happy here—and safe. And I want you to promise me that you'll let Grace look after you while she's here. It might only be for a few more days, but it's important for Grace too. She's proving something to herself—I think you know that.'

That her blind friend could have children and care for them as well as any other mother? Yes, she knew that. The fact that Kruz knew too proved how much they'd both changed.

'Grace has been longing for this moment,' he went on. 'Everyone has been longing for this moment,' he added, taking their tiny daughter out of her arms with the utmost care.

She would have to get used to this, Romy told herself wryly as Kruz closed her door and moved round to the back of the vehicle. But not too much, she thought, gazing up at the grand old white building in front of them. This sort of life—this sort of house—was the polar opposite of what she could afford.

Every doubt she had was swept away the moment she walked inside the penthouse and saw Grace and the staff waiting to welcome her, and when she saw what they'd done, all the trouble Grace had gone to, she was instantly overwhelmed and tearful. They had transformed one of the larger bedroom suites into the most beautiful nursery, with a bathroom off.

'Thank you,' she said softly, walking back to Grace, who was standing in the doorway with her guide dog, Buddy. Touching Grace's arm, Romy whispered, 'I can't believe you've done all this for me.'

'It's for Kruz as well as for you,' Grace said gently. 'And for your baby,' she added, reaching out to find Romy and give her a hug. 'I wanted you to come home to something special for you and your new family, Romy.'

If only, Romy thought, glancing at Kruz. They weren't a proper family—not really. Kruz was doing this because he felt he should—because he was a highly principled man of duty and always had been.

Kruz caught her looking at him and stared back, so she nodded her head, smiling in a way she hoped would show him how much she appreciated everything he and Grace had done for her, whilst at the same time reassuring him that she didn't expect him to devote the rest of his life to looking out for her.

She felt even more emotional when she put their tiny daughter into the beautifully carved wooden crib. Grace had dressed it with the finest Swiss lace, and the lace was so delicate she could imagine Grace selecting this particular fabric by touch. The thought moved her immeasurably. She wanted to hug Grace so hard neither of them could breathe. She wanted to tell Grace that having friends like her made her glad to be alive. She wanted to tell her that, having been so determined to go it alone, she was happy to be wrong. She wanted to be able to express her true feelings for Kruz, to let him know how much he meant to her. But she had to remind herself that they had agreed to do this as individuals, each of them taking a full part in their daughter's life, but separately, and she couldn't go back on her word.

Damn those pregnancy hormones!

The tears were back.

How could anyone who had been such a fearless reporter, a fearless woman, be reduced to this snivelling mess? When it came to being a woman in love, she was lost, Romy realised as Grace explained that the housekeeper had helped her to put everything in place. Romy was only too glad to be called back from the brink by practical matters as Grace went on to explain that she had also hired a night nurse, so that Romy could get some rest.

'I hope you don't mind me interfering?'

'Of course not,' Romy said quickly. 'It isn't interfering. It's kindness. I can't thank you enough for all you've done.'

'You're crying?' Grace asked her with surprise when she broke off.

Grace could hear everything in a voice, Romy remembered, knowing how Grace's other senses had leapt in to compensate for her sight loss. 'Everything makes me cry right now,' she admitted. 'Hormones,' she added ruefully, conscious that Kruz was listening. 'I've been an emotional train wreck since the birth.'

She seemed to have got away with it, Romy thought as Grace and the nurse took over. Or maybe Grace was just too savvy to probe deeper into her words, and the nurse was too polite. Kruz seemed unconcerned—though he did suggest she take a break. Remembering his words about Grace wanting to help, she was quick to agree.

'Champagne?' he suggested, leading the way into the kitchen. Her heart felt too big for her chest just watching him finding glasses, opening bottles, squeezing oranges.

'What you've done for me—' Knowing if she went on she'd start crying again, she steeled herself, because there were some things that had to be said. 'What you've done for our baby—the way you helped me during the birth—'

'It was a privilege,' Kruz said quietly.

Her cheeks fired red as he stared at her. She didn't know what he expected of her. There was so much she wanted to say to him, but he had turned away.

'Drink your vitamins,' he said, handing her the perfect Buck's Fizz.

'Thanks...' She didn't look at him. Was she supposed to act as if they were just friends? How was she supposed to act like a rational human being where Kruz was involved? How could she close her heart to this man? Having Kruz deliver their baby had brought them closer than ever.

'You're very thoughtful,' he said as he topped up her glass with the freshly squeezed juice.

'I was just thinking we almost had something...' Her face took on a look of horror as she realised what she'd said. Her wistful thoughts had poured out in words.

'And now it's over?' he said.

'And now it can never be the same,' she said, making a dismissive gesture with her hand, as if all those feelings inside her had been nothing more than a passing whim.

Kruz made no comment on this. Instead he said, 'Shall we raise a glass to our daughter?'

Yes, that was something they could both do safely. And they *should* rejoice. This was a special day. 'Our daughter, who really should have a name,' she said.

'Well, you've had a few months to think about it,' Kruz pointed out. 'What ideas have you had?'

'I didn't want to decide without—' She stopped, and then settled for the truth. 'I didn't want to decide without consulting you, but I thought Elizabeth...after my mother.'

Kruz's lips pressed down with approval. 'Good idea. I've always liked the name Beth. But what about you, Romy?' he said, coming to sit beside her.

'What about me?'

She stared into her glass as if the secret of life was locked in there. There was only one place she wanted to be, and that was right here with this man. There was only one person she wanted to be, and that was Romy Winner—mother, photographer and one half of this team.

'Come on,' Kruz prompted her. 'What do you want for the future? Or is it too early to ask?'

A horrible feeling swept over her—a suspicion, really, that Kruz was about to offer to fund whatever business venture she had in mind. 'I can't see further than now.'

'That's understandable,' he agreed. 'I just wondered if you had any ideas?'

She looked at him in bewilderment as he moved to take the glass out of her hand, and only then realised that she'd been twisting it and twisting it. She gave it up to him, and asked, 'What about you? What do *you* want, Kruz?'

'Me?' He paused and gave a long sigh, rounded off with one of those careless half-smiles he was so good at when he wanted to hide his true feelings. 'I have things to work through, Romy,' he said, his eyes turning cold.

Was this Kruz's way of saying goodbye? A chill ran through her at the thought that it might be.

For what seemed like an eternity neither of them spoke. She clung to the silence like a friend, because when he wasn't speaking and they were still sitting together like this she could pretend that nothing would change and they would always be close.

'I've seen a lot of things, Romy.'

She jerked alert as he spoke, wondering if maybe, just maybe, Kruz was going to give her the chance to help him break out of his self-imposed prison of silence. 'When you were in the army?' she guessed, prompting him.

'Let's just say I'm not the best of sleeping partners.'

He was already closing off. 'Do you have nightmares?' she pressed, feeling it was now or never if she was going to get through to him.

'I have nightmares,' Kruz confirmed.

They hadn't done a lot of sleeping together, so she wouldn't know about them, Romy realised, cursing her lust for him. She should have spent more time getting to know him. It was easy to be wise after the event, she thought as Kruz started to tell her something else—something that surprised her.

'I'm going to move in downstairs,' he said. 'There's an apartment going begging and I want to see my daughter every day.'

Part of her rejoiced at this, while another part of her felt cut out—cut off. To have Kruz living so close by—to see him every day and yet know they would never be together...

'It's better this way,' he said, drawing her full attention again. 'I'm hard to live with, Romy, and impossible to sleep with. And you need your rest, so this is the perfect solution.'

'Yes,' she said, struggling to convince herself. If Kruz was suffering she had to help him. 'Maybe if you could confide in someone—'

'You?'

She realised how ridiculous that must sound to him and her face flamed red. Romy Winner, hard-nosed photojournalist, reduced not just to a sappy, hormonal mess but to a woman who couldn't even step up to the plate and say: *Yes, me. I'm going to do it.* 'I'll try, if you'll give me the chance,' she said instead.

Pressing his lips together, Kruz shook his head. 'It's not that easy, Romy.'

'I didn't expect it would be. I just think that when you've saved so many lives—'

'Someone should save *me*?' He gave a laugh without much humour in it. 'It doesn't work that way.'

'Why not?' she asked fiercely.

'Because I've done things I'll never be able to forget,' he said quietly, and when he looked at her this time there was an expression in his eyes that said: *Just drop it*.

But she never could take good advice. 'Healing is a long process.'

'A lifetime?'

Kruz's face had turned hard, but it changed just as suddenly and gentled, as if he was remembering that she had recently given birth. 'You shouldn't be thinking about any of this, Romy. Today is a happy day and I don't want to spoil it for you.'

'Nothing you could say would spoil it,' she protested, wanting to add that she could never be truly happy until Kruz was too. But that would put unfair pressure on him. She sipped her drink to keep her mouth busy, wondering how two such prickly, complicated people had ever found each other.

'Believe me, you should be glad I'm keeping my distance,' Kruz said as he freshened their drinks. 'But if you need me I'm only downstairs.'

And that was a fact rather than an invitation, she thought—a thought borne out as Kruz stood up and moved towards the door. 'I have to go now.'

'Go?' The shock in her voice was all too obvious.

'I have business to attend to,' he explained.

'Of course.' And Kruz's business wasn't her business. What had she imagined? That he was going to pull her into his arms and tell her that everything would be all right—that the past could be brushed aside, just like that?

He stopped with his hand on the door. 'You believe in the absolution of time, Romy, but I'm still looking for answers.'

She couldn't stop him leaving, and she knew that Kruz could only replace his nightmares when something that made him truly happy had taken their place.

'It's good that you'll be living close by so you can see Beth,' she said. Perhaps that would be the answer. She really hoped so.

Kruz didn't answer. He didn't turn to look at her. He didn't say another word. He just opened the door and walked through it, shutting it quietly behind him, leaving her alone in the kitchen, wondering where life went from here. One step at a time, she thought, one step at a time.

She couldn't fault him as a devoted father. Kruz spent every spare moment he had with Beth. But where Romy was concerned he was distant and enigmatic. This had been going on for weeks now, and she missed him. She missed his company. She missed his warm gaze on her face. She missed his solid presence and his little kindnesses that gave her an opening to reach in to his world and pay him back with some small, silly thing of her own.

Grace had returned to Argentina with Nacho—though they were expected back in London any day soon. This was a concern for Romy, as she knew Grace had hoped a relationship might develop between Romy and Kruz. It was going to be a little bit awkward, explaining why Romy's new routine involved Beth, mother and baby groups, and learning to live life as a single mother, while the father of her baby lived downstairs.

Kruz had issues to work through, and she understood that, but she wished he'd let her help him. She had broached the subject on a few occasions, but he'd brushed her off and she'd drawn back, knowing there was nothing she could say if he wouldn't open up.

The day after Nacho and Grace arrived back in London, Kruz dropped by with some flowers he'd picked up from the market. 'I got up early and I felt like buying all you girls some flowers,' he said, before breezing out again.

This was nice—this was good, Romy told herself firmly as she arranged the colourful spray in a glittering crystal vase. She felt good about herself, and about her life here in Acosta heaven. She was already taking photographs with thoughts of compiling a book. She treasured every moment she spent with her baby. And watching Kruz with Beth was the best.

Crossing to the window, she smiled as she watched him pace up and down the garden, apparently deep in conversation with their daughter. She longed to be part of it—part of them—part of a family that was three instead of two. But she had to stick to the unofficial rules she'd drawn up—rules that allowed Romy to get on with her life independently of Kruz. They both knew that at some point she would leave and move into rented accommodation, and when she did that Kruz had promised to set up an allowance for Beth, knowing very well that Romy would never take money for herself.

As if the money mattered. Her eyes welled up at the thought of parting from Kruz. What if she moved to the other side of London and never saw him again except when he came to collect Beth? When had such independence held any allure? She couldn't remember when, or what that fierce determination to go it alone had felt like. Independence at all costs was no freedom at all.

This wasn't nice—this wasn't good. Sitting down, she buried her face in her hands, wishing her mother were still alive so they could talk things through as they'd used to before her father had damaged her mother's mind beyond repair. Angry with herself, she sprang up again. She was a mother, and this was no time for self-indulgence. It was all about Beth now.

She was used to getting out there and looking after herself. No wonder she was frustrated, Romy reasoned. In fairness, Kruz had suggested that a babysitter should come in now and then, so Romy could gradually return to doing more of the work she loved. She had resigned from *ROCK!*, of course, but even Ronald, her picture editor, had said she shouldn't waste her talent.

She started as the phone rang and went to answer it.

'I'm bringing Beth up.'

'Oh, okay.' She sounded casual, but in her present mood she might just cling to him like an idiot when he arrived, and burst into tears.

No. She would reassure him by pulling herself together and carrying on alone with Beth as she had always planned to do; anything less than that would be an insult to her love for Kruz.

He bumped into Nacho and Grace on his way back into the house. They were staying in the garden apartment on the ground floor, to ensure they had some privacy. It was a good arrangement, this house in London. Big enough for the whole Acosta family, it had been designed so each of them had their own space.

Nacho asked him in for a drink. Grace declined to join them, saying she would rather play with Beth while she had the chance, but he got the feeling, as Grace took charge of the stroller, that his brother's wife was giving them some time alone.

'You've made a great marriage,' he observed as Grace, her guide dog, Buddy, and baby Beth made their way along the hallway to the master suite.

'Don't I know it?' his brother murmured, gazing after his bride.

As he followed Nacho's stare he realised that for the first time in a long time he felt like a full member of the family again, rather than a ghost at the feast. It was great to see

Nacho and to be able to share all his news about Romy and their daughter, and how being present at the birth of Beth had made him feel.

'Like there's hope for me,' he said, when Nacho pressed him for more.

'You've always been too hard on yourself,' Nacho observed, leading the way into the drawing room. 'And a lifetime of self-denial changes nothing, my brother.'

Coming from someone whose thoughts he respected, those straight-talking words from his brother hit home. It made him want to draw Romy and Beth together into a family— *his* family.

'Have you told Romy how you feel about her?' Nacho said.

'How I...?' Years of denying his feelings prompted him to deny it, but Nacho knew him too well, so he shrugged instead, admitting, 'I bought her some flowers today.'

'Instead of talking to her?'

'I talk.'

Nacho looked up from the newspaper he'd been scanning on the table.

'You talk?' he said. 'Hello? Goodbye?'

They exchanged a look.

'I'm going to find my wife,' Nacho told him, and on his way across the room he added, 'Babies change quickly, Kruz.'

'In five minutes, brother?'

'You know what I mean. Romy will move out soon. We both know it. She's not the type of woman to wait and see what's going to happen next. She'll make the move.'

'She won't take Beth away from me.'

'You have to make sure of that.'

'We live cheek by jowl already.'

'What?' Nacho scoffed, pausing by the door. 'You live downstairs—she lives upstairs with the baby. Is that what you want out of life?'

'It seems to be what Romy wants.'

'Then if you love her change her mind. Or I'll tell you what will happen in the future. You'll pass Beth between you like a ping-pong ball because both of you stood on your pride. You're not in the army now, Kruz. You're not part of that tight world. *You* make the rules.'

Kruz was still reeling when Nacho left the room. His brother had made him face the truth. He had returned to civilian life afraid to love in case he jinxed that person. He had discarded his feelings in order to protect others as he had tried to protect his men. By the time Romy turned his world on its head he hadn't even been in recovery. But she had started the process, he realised now, and there was no turning back.

The birth of Beth had accelerated everything. The nightmares had stopped. He looked forward to every day. Every moment of every day was precious and worthwhile now Romy and Beth were part of his life. That was what Romy had given him. She had given him love to a degree where not allowing himself to love her back was a bigger risk to his sanity than remembering everything in the past that had brought him to this point.

Nacho was right. He should tell Romy what she'd done for him and how he felt about her. Better still, he should show her.

CHAPTER FIFTEEN

WHEN KRUZ CALLED to explain to Romy that he and Beth were down with Grace and Nacho, so she didn't worry about Beth, he added that he wanted to take her somewhere and show her something.

She fell apart. Not crying. She was over that. Her hormones seemed to have settled at last. It was at Kruz's suggestion that Nacho and Grace should look after Beth while he took Romy out. Take her out without Beth as a buffer between them? She wasn't ready for that.

She would never be ready for that.

Her heart started racing as she heard the strand of tension in his voice that said Kruz was fired up about something. Whatever this something was, it had to be big. There was only one thing she could think of that fired the Acosta boys outside the bedroom. And the bedroom was definitely off the agenda today. In fact the bedroom hadn't been on the agenda for quite some time.

And whose fault was that?

Okay, so she'd been confused—and sore for a while after Beth's birth.

And now?

Not so sore. But still confused.

'Is it a new polo pony you want me to see?' she asked, her heart flapping wildly in her chest at the thought of being one to one with him.

'No,' Kruz said impatiently, as if that was the furthest thing from his mind. 'I just need your opinion on something. Why all the questions, Romy? Do you want to come or not?'

'Wellies, jeans and mac?' she said patiently. 'Or smart office wear?'

'You have some?'

'Stop laughing at me,' she warned.

'Those leggings and flat boots you used wear around *ROCK!* will do just fine. Ten minutes?'

'Do you want a coffee before we go—?' Kruz was in a rush, she concluded as the line was disconnected.

Ten minutes and counting and she had discarded as many outfits before reverting reluctantly to Kruz's suggestion. It was the best idea, but that didn't mean that following anyone's suggestions but her own came easily to her. Her hair had grown much longer, so she tied it back. She didn't want to look as if she was trying too hard.

What would they talk about…?

Beth, of course, Romy concluded, adding some lips gloss to her stubborn mouth. And a touch of grey eyeshadow… And just a flick of mascara… Oh, and a spritz of scent. That really was it now. She'd make coffee to take her mind off his arrival—and when he did arrive she would sip demurely, as if she didn't have a care in the world.

While she was waiting for the coffee to brew she studied some pictures that had been taken of Kruz at a recent polo match. *She* would have done better. She would have taken him in warrior mode—restless, energetic and frustratingly sexy.

While she was restless, energetic and *frustrated*, Romy concluded wryly, leaning back in her chair.

She leapt to her feet when the doorbell rang, feeling flushed and guilty, with her head full of erotic thoughts. Kruz had his own key, but while she was staying at the penthouse he always rang first. It was a little gesture that said Kruz respected her privacy. She liked that. Why pretend? She liked everything about him.

She had to force herself to take tiny little steps on her way to the door.

Would she ever get used to the sight of this man?

As Kruz walked past her into the room he filled the space with an explosion of light. It was like having an energy source standing in front of her. Even dressed in heavy London clothes—jeans, boots, jacket with the collar pulled up—he was all muscle and tan: an incredible sight. *You look amazing,* she thought as he swept her into his arms for a disappointingly chaste kiss. Was it possible to die of frustration? If so, she was well on her way.

'I've missed you,' he said, pulling her by the hand into the kitchen. 'Do I smell coffee? Are you free for the rest of the day?'

'So many questions,' she teased him, exhaling with shock as he swung her in front of him. 'I have *some* free time,' she admitted cautiously, suddenly feeling unaccountably shy. 'Why?'

'Because I'm excited,' Kruz admitted. 'Can't you tell?'

Pressing her lips down, she pretended she couldn't.

He laughed.

Her heart was going crazy. Were they teasing each other now?

'There's something I really want to show you,' he said, turning serious.

'Okay…' She kept her expression neutral as Kruz dropped his hands from her arms. She still didn't know what to think. He was giving her no clues. 'Did you tell Nacho and Grace where we're going?' She dropped this in casually, but Kruz wasn't fooled.

'You don't get it out of me that way,' he said. 'Don't look so worried. We'll only be a few minutes away.'

All out of excuses, she poured the coffee.

'Smells good.'

Not half as good as Kruz, she thought, sipping demurely as wild, erotic thoughts raged through her head. Kruz smelled amazing—warm, clean and musky man—and he was just so damn sexy in those snug-fitting jeans, with a day's worth of stubble and that bone-melting look in his eyes.

'I could go away again if you prefer,' he said, slanting her a dangerous grin to remind her just how risky it was to let her mind wander while Kruz was around. 'Come on,' he said, easing away from the counter. 'I'm an impatient man.' Dumping the rest of his coffee down the sink, he grabbed her hand.

'Shall I bring my camera?' she said, rattling her brain cells into line.

'No,' he said. 'If you can't live without recording every moment, I'll take some shots for you.'

He said this good-humouredly, but she realised Kruz had a point. She would relax more without her camera and take more in. Whatever Kruz wanted to show her was clearly important to him, and focusing a camera lens was in itself selective. She didn't want to miss a thing.

If she could concentrate on anything but Kruz, that was, Romy concluded as he helped her into her coat. It wasn't easy to shrug off the seductive warmth as his hands brushed her neck, her shoulders and her back. Kruz was one powerful opiate—and one she mustn't succumb to until she knew what this was about.

'So what now?' she said briskly as she locked up the penthouse.

'Now you have to be patient,' he warned, holding the door.

'I have to be *patient*?' she said.

Kruz was already heading for the stairs.

'Remember the benefits of delay.'

She stopped at the top of the stairs, telling herself that it was just a careless remark. It wasn't enough to stop fireworks going off inside her, but that was only because she hadn't thought about sex in a long time.

Today it occupied all her thoughts.

She was thrilled when Kruz drove them to the area of London she loved. 'You remembered,' she said.

He had drawn to a halt outside a gorgeous little mews house in a quaint cobbled square. It was just a short walk from the picturesque canal she had told him about.

'You haven't made any secret of your preferred area,' he said, 'so I thought you might like to take a look at this.'

'Do you own it?' she asked, staring up at the perfectly proportioned red brick house.

'I've been looking it over for a friend and I'd value your opinion.'

'I'd be more than happy to give it,' she said, smiling with anticipation.

And happy to dream a little, Romy thought as Kruz opened the car door for her. There was nothing better than snooping around gorgeous houses—though she usually did it between the covers of a glossy magazine or on the internet. This was so much better. This was a dream come true. She paused for a moment to take in the cute wrought-iron Juliet balconies, with their pots of pink and white geraniums spilling over the smart brickwork. The property was south-facing, and definitely enjoyed the best position on the square.

She hadn't seen anything yet, Romy realised when Kruz opened the front door and she walked inside. 'This is gorgeous!' she gasped, struck immediately by the understated décor and abundance of light.

'The bedrooms are all on the ground floor,' he explained, 'so the upper floor can take advantage of a double aspect view over the cobbled square, and over the gardens behind the building. You don't think having bedrooms downstairs is a problem?'

'Not at all,' she said, gazing round. The floor was pale oak strip, and the bedrooms opened off a central hallway.

'There are four bedrooms and four bathrooms on this level,' Kruz explained, 'and the property opens onto a large private garden. Plus there's a garage, and off-street parking—which is a real bonus in the centre of London.'

'Your friend must be very wealthy,' Romy observed, increasingly impressed as she looked around. 'It's been beautifully furnished. I love the Scandinavian style.'

'My friend can afford it. Why don't we take a look upstairs? It's a large, open-plan space, with a kitchen and an office as well as a studio.'

'The studio must be fabulous,' she said. 'There's so much light in the house—and it feels like a happy house,' she added, following Kruz upstairs.

She gave a great sigh of pleasure when they reached the top of the stairs and the open-plan living room opened out in front of them. There were white-painted shutters on either side of the floor-to-ceiling windows, and the windows overlooked the cobbled square at one end of the room and the gardens at the other. Everywhere was decorated in clean Scandinavian shades: white, ivory and taupe, with highlights of ice-blue and a pop of colour played out in the raspberry-pink cushions on the plump, inviting sofa. Even the ornaments had been carefully chosen—a sparkling crystal clock and a cherry-red horse, even a loving couple entwined in an embrace.

'And there's a rocking horse!' she exclaimed with pleasure, catching sight of the beautifully carved dapple grey. 'Your friends are very lucky. The people who own this house have thought of everything for a family home.'

'And even if someone wanted to work from home here, they could,' Kruz pointed out, showing her the studio. 'Well?' he said. 'What do you think? Shall I tell my friend to go ahead and buy it?'

'He'd be mad not to.'

'Do you think we had better check the nursery before I tell him to close the deal?'

'Yes, perhaps we better had,' Romy agreed. 'At least I have some idea of what's needed in a nursery now.' She laughed. 'So I can offer my opinion with confidence.'

'Goodness,' she said as Kruz opened the door on a wonderland. 'Your friend must have bought out Khalifa's!' she exclaimed. Then, quite suddenly, her expression changed.

'Romy?'

Mutely, she shook her head.

'What is it?' Kruz pressed. 'What's wrong?'

'What's wrong,' she said quietly, 'is that it took me so long to work this out. But I got there eventually.'

'Got where? What do you mean?' Kruz said, frowning.

She lifted her chin. 'I mean, you got *me* wrong,' she said coldly. 'So wrong.'

'What are you talking about, Romy?'

'You bring me to a fabulous mews house in my favourite area of London because you think I can be bought—'

'No,' Kruz protested fiercely.

'No?' she said. 'You're the friend in question, aren't you? Why couldn't you just be honest with me from the start?'

'Because I knew what you'd say,' Kruz admitted tersely. '*Dios*, Romy! I already know how pig-headed you are.'

'*I'm* pig-headed?' she said. 'You'll stop at nothing to get your own way.'

All he could offer was a shrug. 'I wanted this to be a surprise for you,' he admitted. 'I've never done this sort of thing before, so I just went ahead and did what felt right to me. I'm sorry if I got it wrong—got *you* wrong,' he amended curtly.

'Tell me you haven't bought it,' she said.

'I bought it some time ago. I bought it on the day I brought you home from hospital—which is why I had to leave you. I bought it so you and Beth would always have somewhere nice to live—whatever you decide about the future. This is your independence, Romy. This is my gift to you and to our daughter. If you feel you can't take it, I'll put it in Beth's name. It really is that simple.'

For you, she thought. 'But I still don't understand. What are you saying, Kruz?'

'What I'm saying is that I'm still not sure what you want, but I know what *I* want. I've known for a long time.'

'But you don't say anything to me—'

'Because you're never listening,' he said. 'Because you haven't been ready to hear me. And because big emotional statements aren't my style.'

'Then change your style,' she said heatedly.

'We've both got a lot to learn, Romy—about loving and giving and expressing emotion, and about each other. We must start somewhere. For Beth's sake.'

'And that somewhere's here?' she demanded, opening her arms wide as she swung around to encompass the beautiful room.

'If you want it to be.'

'It's too much,' she protested.

'It isn't nearly enough,' Kruz argued quietly. Putting his big warm hands on her shoulders, he kept her still. 'Listen to me, Romy. For God's sake, listen to me. You have no idea what you and Beth have done for me. My nightmares have gone—'

'They've gone?' She stopped, knowing that nothing meant more than this. This meant they had a chance—Kruz had a chance to start living again.

'Baby-meds,' he said. 'Who'd have thought it?'

'So you can sleep at last?' she exclaimed.

'Through the night,' he confirmed.

It was a miracle. If she had nothing more in all her life this was enough. She could have kicked herself. She'd had baby-brain while Kruz had been nothing but considerate for her. The way he'd removed himself to give her space—the way he was always considerate with the keys, with Beth, with every-thing—the way he never hassled her in any way, or pushed her to make a decision. And had she listened to him? Had she noticed what was going on in his world?

'I'm so sorry—'

'Don't be,' he said. 'You should be glad—*we* should be glad. All I want is for us to be a proper family. I want it for Beth and I want it for you and me. I want us to have a proper home where we can live together and make a happy mess—not a showpiece to rattle round in like the penthouse. I don't think you want that either, Romy. I think, like me, you want to carry on what we started. I think you want us to go on healing each other. And I know I want you. I love you, and I hope you love me. I want us to give our baby the type of home you and I have always dreamed of.'

'And how will we make it work?' she asked, afraid of so much joy.

'I have no idea,' Kruz admitted honestly. 'I just know that if we give it everything we've got we'll make it work. And if you love me as much as I love you—'

'Hang on,' she said, her face softening as she dared to be-lieve. 'What's all this talk of love?'

'I love you,' Kruz said, frowning. 'Surely you've worked that out for yourself by now?'

'It's nice to be told. I agree you're not the best when it comes to big emotional declarations, but you should have worked that out. Try telling me again,' she said, biting back a smile.

'Okay…' Pretending concentration, Kruz held her close so he stared into her eyes.

'I've loved you since that first encounter on the grassy bank—I just didn't know it then. I've loved you since you went all cold on me and had to be heated up again. I loved you very much by then.'

'Sex-fiend.'

'You bet,' he agreed, but then he turned serious again. 'And now I love you to the point where I can't imagine life without you. And whatever you want to call these feelings—' he touched his heart '—they don't go away. They get stronger each day. You're a vital part of my life now—the *most* vital part, since you're the part I can't live without.'

'And Beth?' she whispered.

'She's part of you,' Kruz said simply. 'And she's part of me too. I want you both for life, Señorita Winner. And I want you to be happy. Which is why I bought you the house—walking distance to the shops—great transport links...'

'You'd make an excellent sales agent,' she said over the thunder of her happy heart hammering.

'I must remember to add that to my CV,' Kruz teased with a curving grin. 'Plus there's an excellent nursery for Beth across the road.'

'Where you've already put her name down?' Romy guessed with amusement.

Kruz shrugged. 'I thought we'd live part of the year here and part on the pampas in Argentina. Whatever you decide the house is yours—or Beth's. But I won't let you make a final decision yet.'

'Oh?' Romy queried with concern.

'Not until you test the beds.'

'All of them?' She started to smile.

'I think we'd better,' Kruz commented as he swung her into his arms.

'Ah, well.' Romy sighed. 'I guess I'll just have to do whatever it takes...'

'I'm depending on it,' Kruz assured her as he shouldered open the door into the first bedroom.

'Let the bed trials begin,' she suggested when he joined her on the massive bed. 'But be gentle with me.'

'Do you think I've forgotten you've just had a baby?'

Taking her into his arms, Kruz made her feel so safe.

'What?' she said, when he continued to stare at her.

'I was just thinking,' he said, stretching out his powerful limbs. 'We kicked off on a mossy bank on the pampas beside a gravel path, and we've ended up on a firm mattress in your favourite part of London town. That's not so bad, is it?'

Trying to put off the warm honey flowing through her veins for a few moments was a pointless exercise, Romy concluded, exhaling shakily with anticipation. 'Are you suggesting we work our way back to the start?'

'If none of the beds here suit, I'm sure we can find a grassy bank somewhere in the heart of London...'

'So what are you saying?' she whispered, shuddering with acute sexual excitement as Kruz ran his fingertips in a very leisurely and provocative way over her breasts and down over her belly, where they showed no sign of stopping...

'I'm saying that if you can put up with me,' he murmured as she exclaimed with delight and relief when his hand finally reached its destination, 'I can put up with you. I'm suggesting we get to know each other really, really well all over again—starting at the very beginning.'

'Now?' she said hopefully, surreptitiously easing her thighs apart.

'Maybe we should start dating first,' Kruz said, pausing just to provoke her.

'Later,' she agreed, shivering uncontrollably with lust.

'Yes, maybe we should try the beds out first, as we agreed...' Covering her hand with his, he held her off for a moment. 'I'm being serious about us living together,' he said. 'But I don't want to rush you, Romy. I don't want to make you into something you're not. I don't want to spoil you.'

'This house isn't spoiling me?' she said.

'Pocket change,' Kruz whispered, slanting her a bad-boy smile. 'But, seriously, I don't want to change anything about you, Romy Winner.'

'No. You just want to kill me with frustration,' she said. 'I can't believe you're suggesting we go out on dates.'

'Amongst other things,' he said.

'Then I'll consider your proposition,' she agreed, smiling against his mouth as Kruz moved on top of her.

'You'll do better than that,' he promised, in his most deliciously commanding voice.

'Just one thing,' she warned, holding him off briefly.

'Tell me…'

She frowned. 'I need time.'

'Does for ever suit you?' Kruz murmured, touching her in the way she liked.

'For ever doesn't really sound long enough to me,' she whispered against the mouth of the man she had been born to love.

EPILOGUE

IT WAS THE wedding of the year. Eventually.

It took five years for Kruz to persuade Romy that their daughter was longing to be a bridesmaid and that she shouldn't deny Beth that chance.

'So, for your sake,' she told her adorable quirky daughter, who was never happier than when she had straw in her hair and was wearing shredded jeans with a ripped top covered in hoof oil and horse hair, 'we're going to have that wedding you keep nagging me about, and you are going to be our chief bridesmaid.'

'Great,' Beth said, too busy taking in the intricacies of the latest bridle her father had bought her to pay much attention.

Kruz had finally managed to convince Romy that a wedding would be a wonderful chance to affirm their love, when to Romy's way of thinking she and Kruz already shared everything—with or without that piece of paper.

'But no frills,' Beth insisted, glancing up.

So she *was* listening, Romy thought with amusement. 'No frills,' she agreed—not if she wanted Beth for her bridesmaid.

And a slinky column wedding dress was out of the question for the bride as Romy was heavily pregnant for the third time. Kruz was insatiable, and so was she—more than ever now she was pregnant again. The sex-mad phase again. How lovely.

She felt that same mad rush of heat and lust when he

strode into the bedroom now. Pumped from riding, in a pair of banged-up jeans and a top that had seen better times, he looked amazing—rugged and dangerous, just the way she liked him.

Who knew how many children they would have? Romy mused happily as Kruz swung Beth into the air. A polo team, at least, she decided as Kruz reminded their daughter that she was supposed to be going swimming with friends, and had better get a move on if she wasn't going to be late.

Leaving them to plan the wedding…or not, Romy concluded when he finally looked her way.

'The baby?'

She flashed a glance at the door of the nursery where their baby son was sleeping. 'With his nanny.'

She turned as Beth came by for a hug, before racing out of the room, slamming the door behind her. A glance at Kruz confirmed that he thought this was working out just fine. She did too, Romy concluded, taking in the power in his muscular forearms as Kruz propped a hip against her desk.

'Is this the guest list?' he asked, picking up the sheaf of papers Romy had been working on. 'You *do* know we only need two people and a couple of witnesses?'

'You have a big family—'

'And getting bigger all the time,' Kruz observed, hunkering down at her side.

'Who would have thought it?' Romy mused out loud.

'I would,' Kruz murmured wickedly. 'With your appeal and my super-sperm, what else did you expect?' He caressed the swell of her belly and then buried his head a little deeper still.

'I think you should lock the door,' she said, feeling the familiar heat rising.

'I think I should,' Kruz agreed, springing up.

He smiled as he looked down at her. 'I'm glad you lost those red-tipped gel spikes.'

'She frowned. 'What makes you bring those up?'

'Just saying,' Kruz commented with amusement, drawing her into the familiar shelter of his arms.

She had almost forgotten the red-tipped gel spikes. She didn't feel the need to present that hard, *stay-away-from-me* person to the world any more. And now she came to think about it losing the spikes hadn't been a conscious decision; it had been more a case of have baby, have man I love and have *so* much less time for me. And she wouldn't have it any other way.

'So, you like my natural look?' she teased as Kruz undressed her.

'I love you any way,' he said as she tugged off his top and started on his belt. 'Though the closer to nature you get, the more I like it…'

'Back to nature is best,' Romy agreed, reaching for her big, naked man as he tipped her back on the bed.

'Will I ever get enough of you?' Kruz murmured against her mouth as he trespassed at leisure on familiar territory.

'I sincerely hope not,' Romy whispered, groaning with pleasure as her nerve-endings tightened and prepared for the oh, so inevitable outcome.

'Spoon?' he suggested, moving behind her. 'So I can touch you…?'

Her favourite position—especially now she was so heavily pregnant. Arching her back, she offered herself for pleasure.

'Tell me again,' she told him much, much later, when they were lying replete on the bed.

'Tell you what again?' Kruz queried lazily, reaching for her.

'Do you *never* get enough?'

'Of you?' He laughed softly against her back. 'Never. So what do you want me to tell you?'

'Tell me that you love me.'

Shifting position, he moved so that he could see her face, and, holding her against the warmth of his body, he stared into her eyes. 'I love you, Romy Winner. I will always love you. This is for ever. You and me—we're for ever.'

'And I love you,' she said, holding Kruz's dark, compelling gaze. 'I love you more than I thought it possible to love anyone.'

'I especially love making babies with you.'

'You're bad,' she said gratefully as Kruz settled back into position behind her. 'You don't think…?'

'I don't think what?' he murmured, touching her in the way she loved.

'I'm expecting twins this time. Do you think it will be triplets next?'

'Does that worry you?'

She shrugged. 'We both love babies—just thinking we might need a bigger house.'

'Maybe…' he agreed. 'If we practise enough.'

She was going to say something, but Kruz had a sure-fire way of stopping her talking. And—*oh*… He was doing it now.

'No more questions?' he queried.

'No more questions,' she confirmed shakily as Kruz set up a steady beat.

'Then just enjoy me, use me. Have pleasure, baby,' he suggested as he gradually upped the tempo. 'And love me as I love you,' he added as she fell.

'That's easy,' she murmured when she was calmer, and could watch Kruz in the grip of pleasure as he found his own violent release. 'For ever,' she whispered as he held her close.

* * * * *

MILLS & BOON®

Mills & Boon have been at the heart of romance since 1908… and while the fashions may have changed, one thing remains the same: from pulse-pounding passion to the gentlest caress, we're always known how to bring romance alive.

Now, we're delighted to present you with these irresistible illustrations, inspired by the vintage glamour of our covers. So indulge your wildest dreams and unleash your imagination as we present the most iconic Mills & Boon moments of the last century.

Visit **www.millsandboon.co.uk/ArtofRomance** to order yours!